A Kind Of Wrath

Sandra E. Drake

Plain View Press
P. O. 42255
Austin, TX 78704

plainviewpress.net
sb@plainviewpress.net
512-441-2452

Cover art "Deep Valley" by Somdev Bhattacharji

Acknowledgments

To all the people who encouraged and assisted me in my writing, and specifically in writing this novel, I am grateful. Every one of these gave me something unique that I think made the novel better. Errors and infelicities are my own. Among them I especially thank:

- My parents, St. Clair and Elizabeth Drake. My father died before I began seeking readers for this form of the manuscript; he read and carefully commented on the work leading up to it. My mother read early versions of the first chapters, and would have read more had her health permitted and had she lived to see the novel's completion. For their unfailing support and encouragement of my writing throughout my life, I thank them.
- My brother, Karl J. Drake, who is expert in what are to me the arcanities of much computer work and of piloting aircraft, assisted me in preparing the manuscript and advised me on matters related to flying.
- Barbara Charlesworth Gelpi read an early version. Her comments about the character Paula were especially useful.
- Kim B. Gillespie went through an early draft chapter by chapter and made extensive and very valuable written comments.
- Roger L. Harm made me the offer, as he had done with everything I wrote for over twenty years: "I'll read it." His evaluations were always generous and provided useful guidance on my way.
- My husband, Ray Meyer, listened to sections I read aloud, went over written drafts, and gave detailed critiques from which the manuscript has greatly benefited.
- My cousin, Somdev Bhattacharji, offered me a selection of paintings from the body of work he produced while in Hawai'i pursuing his career as a geologist. I chose "Deep Valley" for the cover of this book.
- My publisher at Plain View Press, Susan Bright, and my layout artist, Pam Knight, worked with me throughout the production of this book with great patience and skill.

For my brother Karl

and

for our parents
St. Clair Drake and Elizabeth Johns Drake
1911–1990 and 1915–1996

Contents

1

First Flight

"You're Miss Kajiyama?"

He startled her. She turned fast from the window of the tiny airport lounge and its view of the long gradual slope of Mauna Loa. She tried to speak confidently, to hide thoughts as troubled as the clouds gathering over the mountain.

"I'm Ms. Kajiyama. Paula Kajiyama."

She corrected him because she wanted distance between them, boundaries. They were alone in the room. From the first moment she sensed the violence in him. Violence ritualized, and, deeper still, chaotic violence. The military? Vietnam? He was of her generation. All the violences inflicted upon her rose to menace her again.

"Miz Kajiyama," he acknowledged, expressionless. He touched his hand to his temple. "Then I reckon I'm your pilot. Will Cawdry's the name."

Weather had beaten his face to a bronze almost as dark as her complexion, contrasting unnervingly with the ice-blue eyes. Thick straight hair, once deep blonde and now sun-damaged to the color and texture of straw, fell to his shoulders, and sheltered a place on his neck where the skin showed, surprisingly, white and almost fragile.

He stood six and a half feet at least, weighed two hundred and fifty pounds, over a foot taller than she was, well over a hundred pounds heavier, all of it bone and muscle. His face was a powerful badlands: rock-hard cheekbones, jutting nose, a thin-lipped ravine of a mouth slashed beneath.

She squinted at the identification card slung on a cord around his neck, but could not make out the words. The photograph was blurred and sinister. Quickly, before he could notice her scrutiny, she averted her eyes.

Her life had taught her to fear eyes like his: pale and difficult for her to read. Held slitted, as if in incessant defensive battle against a tropical sun, they fixed her now; something in the sight of her struck him suddenly still. Then he shook himself hard, once, dispelling the trance.

She wondered who or what he had seen. Before she had learned to be careful of White men who made her an exotic, a lover had called her eyes "classically North Asian." A would-be poet, he had written, "Austerely sculpted lids describe a dramatic downward line," and the words stayed, an ironic recollection. His appreciation had been balm, for eyes like hers had made her a target, and the country had been at war with Asia since long before she was born. The lover had left when he found she possessed neither the submissiveness nor the innate sophisticated eroticism he expected — only the downward line of eye.

Motionless, she evaluated contradictory information.

Since the Mississippi summer of her nineteenth year, 1964, half her life ago, accents like his, from south of Mason-Dixon, had set her on visceral alert.

That summer meant Patchagoula 1964, Freedom School, Voter Registration, and the bomb the Night Riders threw that blew up the house around her as she slept.

She was familiar with Black Southern cadences, in their variety. Long before she crossed Mason-Dixon, her block on the South Side of Chicago began to bloom with an aural mosaic of those who had migrated from Down Home: regions of Mississippi, Alabama, Louisiana, occasionally the sharp divergence of Gullah, from those isolated islands off the Carolina Coast. She had failed to recognize it as English at first. For a long time she could not understand these many Englishes, and even after she could, she retained synesthetic first impressions, aural and visual: pitch of voice, rapidities and rhythms, elongated sliding sounds, and colors evoked by sound: deep chocolates, auburns, crimson, gold.

Later, the twang of White Appalachia joined them on her block.

In this man's voice she could hear familiar elements. Appalachia, and something she knew less well and from later in his life, Texas somewhere. Though it seemed improbable, she would have said Black New Orleans too. Yet the ensemble she did not recognize. Now that she was a translator and interpreter, and had recovered her ear for Japanese, so different from any version of the English tongue, Will's speech further disconcerted her. She could not immediately justify the impression, but in both individual sound-shape and something deeper backing it, she detected influences from Japanese, and from other tongues as far removed as Japanese from any form of English.

Japanese? Maybe. He had accorded her name the respect of a crisp Japanese pronunciation as good as her own.

After a moment she extended her hand, setting the terms of association as formal and socially equal. He didn't anticipate the gesture; she filed that information too. His hand engulfed hers; her awareness of his strength was heightened by its conscious restraint. She ended their physical contact quickly.

He hesitated, then gave a mock-salute. "Whenever you're ready, Ms. Kajiyama, Volcano Flights is at your service."

"I'm ready," she said briefly, and went with him out to the tarmac.

"A Caravan." Love and pride softened his twang. He laid his big hand reverently against the airplane's silvery skin.

"Transportation of choice for drug runners, I've heard," she commented dryly, and he laughed.

"For folks running other contraband too. Don't worry, Miz Kajiyama, I'm reformed. Part-time, anyway. And this flight's on the up-and-up, you can tell because your fellow passengers are all certified legal." He cracked open the cargo door, and indicated the official labels pasted on the sides of two animal crates.

"Well, that's good to know. Who are these mysterious fellow passengers? It looks as if they're going incognito."

"They're nēnēs — Hawaiian geese. There was supposed to be more, but for some reason they only sent a pair. It's the State Bird. Endangered, like most things Hawaiian, especially those as gets too close to the State." He grinned. "These especially need a little help. Some calls them lōlō —'lōlō' means foolish, slow on the uptake. They don't avoid people quick enough to keep from getting killed, so they get called stupid. They ain't really — just ain't quite assimilated all the evil facing them when they face humankind. This pair's moving to upland Maui. You do know you're hitching on a milk run?"

"Yes, your dispatcher told me I'm getting the special 'since he's going anyway' rate, but I'd still see the overflight-of-the-Big-Island-and-Maui highlights. Except you won't fly over Halem'aum'au, you never do, he said."

"It's true." He spoke a shade belligerently, as if he expected her to object. "From ancient Hawaiian times there has been footfalls at the volcano. I don't mind them, as long as they fall lightly. But I don't fly over, nor do I go to the volcano for amusement. Just ain't respectful, to my mind."

She shrugged. "That's fine with me. Seems at least we could leave Pele in peace in her own home. And I'm honored to travel with the nēnēs. I've done wildlife work. Why are they being moved?"

"Because there's fears the military may set up a bombing range near the Park here. The bombing won't do the nēnēs much good. Don't reckon it does nothing much good, do you?"

And he gave a smile, so blank, so disconnected, that it chilled her through and set her nape hairs on end, telling her that nothing could touch this man. He had gone to some inconceivable place, deep as outer space, beyond all boundaries.

Then he splayed his fingers through his coarse clean hair, and the smile vanished as if it had never been.

A year and a half ago in San Francisco, at the Legal Co-op, a profound verbal failure, springing from a deep fault in her of silence, had stopped her speaking the words her client José Sánchez had needed to save his life. When she saw where his life had ended, saw him swinging from a hook in his shabby Tenderloin room, her own life had fallen apart, she had been robbed of confidence hard-won over long years; so that now she wondered if she had imagined Will Cawdry's smile.

But she knew that she had not; knew that she had glimpsed in this man a profound abyss of soul, a threat of something she knew too well in too many forms: schism and collapse.

"Well now," he exclaimed, as if returning from a distance. "Let's get this show on the road." With sure hands he checked the tie-downs fastening the crates to the floor of the plane.

"Will they be safe back there?"

He paused, hands resting on the crates. A small plane trundled down the runway beside them. The draft from its passage lifted the ends of the red kerchief tied around his neck, that lent a jaunty air to his outfit of jeans and red-checked shirt. He drawled with unmistakable exaggeration, "Ah reckon. They got everything but leg shackles. Took me a while, being I'm country slow. First few flights I just trussed 'em and tossed 'em in, but the mess when I —"

"All right," she conceded, hands raised in mock surrender. "Sorry. I shouldn't be telling you your job."

And she had reason to accept his professional competence; she had made inquiries.

Will Cawdry laughed. "Miz Kajiyama, I'll make you a deal. What kind of work do you do?"

"I was trained as a lawyer," she said stiffly, wondering why she identified herself that way as she heard her words, "but I'm a translator now."

"Trained as a lawyer? Funny, you don't put me in mind of my tax lawyer."

"I was in public interest law, not tax law."

"Don't rightly know what that is."

"Civil rights. Immigration. Environmental law."

"For true? Well, if you sit back and place a little confidence in me while I'm ferrying you and these Sunday dinners around, I'll give you a chance to try a new line of lawyering if you ever take it up again. I'll let you have first crack at my tax returns. Now, how's that? Myself, I think it's more than fair. If the choice is headwinds or the Wrath of Sam, I'll take my chances with headwinds any day. You know who Sam is?"

"I do indeed."

"Thought you might," he said cryptically. "With your kind of lawyering, I'll bet you know about Charlie too. Now, I'm a right good pilot, but you don't want to push me too far. I'm subject to fits under pressure. All us Cawdrys is. You probably heard of the Snopeses and Ty-Ty and the Jukeses or was it the Kallikaks, all them folks? Well, they ain't got nothing on Cawdrys. Cawdrys take fits. And if you want to know how come they let me fly, it's because even some Cawdrys got sense enough not to take 'em around clients and safety inspectors. Though I almost think I feel one coming on, what with ferrying a Ms. and two Sunday dinners around."

He had understood her correction of his form of addressing her.

"So you make sure your belt's fastened good and tight, you hear?" he continued. He paused, and when he spoke again his tone had not changed but she knew he was deadly serious. "And if you can't trust me, you'd best find another pilot."

"You come very well recommended. I think I'll take my chances."

To her surprise, she saw by the protected place below his ears that he had blushed at her words. But he only allowed,

"There's folks hereabouts knows my work."

He shut the cargo door and checked that it was locked, then with a mock-courtliness gave her a hand into the seat next to the pilot's.

"Ever been up in a small plane?"

"Once. Not here in Hawai'i."

"And not with me." She caught the glint in his eyes, like sun striking metal in high grass; humor, she was almost sure. "I reckon it's your first flight then."

Switching on the radio, he entered into arcane conversation with the control tower, and the immediate change in his manner struck Paula. Everything but the flight and its requirements had become peripheral.

And his speech: gone was "Yeh" for "yes," "naw" for "no," "mebbe" for "maybe." When talking to the control tower, he came out with Standard Mainstream American.

The engine whined louder and louder, and the plane began to roll.

Will darted his hand down and up again, between the door and his seat, on the side away from her, where she could not see.

They soared into the wide morning.

He banked the plane, and nodded at the window.

"Mauna Kea. Snow Sleeper lives at the summit — the Lady's little sister."

"The Lady?"

"Pele. Tūtū Pele – the Lady of the Volcano. Snow Sleeper's kind of her opposite. You always know what the Lady's feeling what with volcanic eruptions, earthquakes and all. Her and her boar boyfriend with many eyes, who you've got to watch out for in the deep 'ōhi'a forest, you know they're around. But Snow Sleeper's — remote."

She glanced at him sharply. Once again, she did not know how to interpret him. His remarks might be a poetic extension of their shared views about respecting Halem'aum'au. But his tone suggested not poetry but a statement of fact.

His meanings, then, were as enigmatic as his accents.

Will continued,

"This mountain, it's almost fourteen thousand feet to the naked view, and counting from its true base at sea bottom, the tallest mountain in the world. You can't see all of it, but all of its power is in this place, hid from view or not." He stared, absorbed. "She's wearing blue and lavender today. You can tell the weather from her dress. Great mountains make their own weather."

They were flying over vast forbidding expanses of black and gray.

"And there below us now — that's the Lava Wastes."

"Power and desolation," she remarked.

"There's both of those for sure." He hesitated, then glanced at her curiously. "They does draw you too?"

She nodded.

"I thought as much. We're alike in that, I reckon."

She felt herself recoil from the suggestion of similarity.

The Lava Wastes stretched on and on, a landscape like the moon, until the plane turned and they flew over cultivated land and pastureland, over foothills sloping to the coast. She glimpsed a river shining at intervals through dense jungle-forest, then breaking into visibility among low buildings and plunging into a bay.

"That's the Wailuku, the river that runs right through our town. Hilo. Have you had a chance to look it over yet?"

"No. I got in from Honolulu this morning and drove straight up to Volcano."

"That mountain just yonder, the one that makes a pair with Mauna Kea, that's Mauna Loa. Almost as tall as Mauna Kea, and made of iron. It's the densest mass between the sun and Mars."

They soared out over the water, hypnotic in its expanse, so that she was startled when his voice broke into her reverie.

"Miz Kajiyama, we're setting down."

"So soon?"

He smiled, reaching for the radio. "It's called rock-hopping, crossing the Eight Seas, as the Hawaiians name these channels between the islands. Look right here, just beneath us. We're over Maui now. That's Haleakala."

A huge, scooped-out mountainside dropped away to a windswept caldera floor, a barren eerie expanse of rust and black.

"Some say Haleakala was Pele's last home before she came to the Big Island, to Halem'aum'au."

Then he was talking to the tower, getting them cleared for landing.

Growing larger, spreading out and away, green and brown against the blue surrounding sea, gourd-waisted Maui rose swiftly to meet them.

When he went to open the plane's cargo section, Paula glanced into the cockpit on the pilot's side. The object he had touched when starting take-off was fastened to a worn leather thong, its end twisted around the seat-bracing. It was a St. Christopher medal.

"You can help me here, Miz Kajiyama, seeing as you've done wildlife rescue work. Let's check that these Sunday dinners are okay after the flight."

He watched her carefully as she withdrew the bird, vetting her as she vetted untried volunteers at the wildlife group she worked with.

"You've got a right nice touch with that critter."

His hands almost swallowed up the other nēnē, alarming her obscurely. But the bird nestled trustingly into his palms, its black bright eyes peering out at the world.

A stocky man about fifty approached, pushing a dolly. He was of Asian ancestry but a mix unfamiliar to Paula; that had been happening a lot to her here in Hawai'i. He called out something to Will in Hawaiian English, too fast for Paula to understand, and Will replied in kind.

The translator in Paula noted to herself that he had yet another tongue in his repertoire.

Will switched to his form of mainly-Southern speech, saying, for Paula's benefit,

"Hey, Tim. It's the Range Rustler, making half a delivery. Sold the others to the illegal exotic animal trade."

Tim included Paula in the banter with a glance. Mainstream U.S. English, with a Hawaiian accent. "Well, Cawdry, we got you under surveillance." Then, to her, "Actually, you know, he flies them free. He don't like to admit it, though."

And she could see that indeed Will was discomfited. "No skin off my nose getting them out of shooting range. Most generally, I'm making the run anyway."

Paula watched Will Cawdry, unable to find in this genial, easy-going man, obviously well-liked and well-respected, any trace of the killing chill she had seen so recently in his smile.

"Tim, do me a favor, would you? Grab that camera I keep in the plane, you know where, and let's get this event recorded for posterity, Miz Kajiyama and the nēnēs and all."

While Tim retrieved the camera, Will positioned Paula with the bird and then stationed himself beside her, holding the second nēnē.

"Okay, Miz Kajiyama, smile, now! Smile, birds! We all is being immortalized on film."

The photograph was taken. The birds were returned to their crates. Tim and Will signed some papers, then Tim loaded the crates on the dolly and wheeled it away.

"Well, I guess we done our good turn for the day. Here's to upcountry Maui and many generations of happy nēnē birds. Now, Miz Kajiyama, I got a little business yet I need to see to. Would you care to wait for me in the lounge? I won't be long."

2

Kamikaze Gambler, Poolhall Dancer

A counterman brought her a can of guava juice, on the house he said, since she was with Will. Then he excused himself to return to the kitchen.

Again, as at the Kilauea airport, she was the only person in the lounge. A worn-looking pool table stood in a corner, and she took her drink over to it.

Once she had been a gambler — in the courtroom, and by loving in ways that crossed forbidden lines, and in the street at political barricades, and poised, cue in hand, at the brink of irrevocable decisions.

Her glance at the table was hungry. But she was also afraid. She had not chanced a game since the sight of José Sánchez's body dangling in the shadows of his shabby room had damaged her balance in life. She had learned that balance, that inner way of moving with life's lines and angles and forces, by learning the lines and angles and forces at a rectangular felt table. Now the table was as fraught with menace as with a lifetime's delight.

Her earliest memories were of living isolated and endangered on an East European battlefield on the South Side of Chicago; and of her parents' silence.

They were silent about where they had come from and how they had ended up in that dangerous wilderness; silent about why other tenuous contacts with other people who looked like them, where Paula felt safe, had ended almost before she could remember. There had, once, been Sundays at a Congregational church whose membership was mostly Japanese-American. Her father had worked as a CPA then while he studied law at night; and elderly Japanese people, often escorted by sons and daughters, came to see her father on weekends for help with legal and financial matters. From his study the sound of voices speaking staccato Japanese would come to her, her father's voice among them. Yet not until years later did she put the sounds and her father together and realize that he had been fluent in the language, for Japanese speech was not a part of his life that he had brought to her.

Why had those associations ceased? She did not know, but suspected it was because her parents realized that as she grew older such contacts risked breaching the silence at the heart of the family, the compact that held it together.

She had understood very early that the *Kamikaze* pilots of Saturday afternoon movies were not her enemy. She needed their pride and energy to survive the murderous blue-eyed streets of her childhood.

She had been willing to die in those streets; she almost did. The knowledge of her willingness had chilled her when she became conscious of it years later. But, American child, she had adapted *Kamikaze* willingness without insistence on suicide.

"Slant! Gook!" Sometimes they got her antecedents right, but the nation's perennial war with Asia was flaring in Korea: some of the young men who tormented her had fought there. They reviled her for being "Korean" as well as for being "Japanese." They knew nothing of the complex history, the ancient bitterness, between Korean and Japanese. The Asian enemy was all the same to them.

"*Kamikaze!*" she had shrieked as she fought back as best she could, digging chunks of sharp-edged asphalt from rotting streets with bleeding nails. She rejoiced in every thud against flesh that she scored.

"*Kamikaze!*" She learned early that the word paralyzed her parents, and though she did not understand why, she sensed it was connected with the mandatory silence. In uttering it she was less vulnerable than they because she could speak, and the power over them that speech conferred both frightened her and filled her with glee. For among feelings of respect and much love for them, she knew openly then, and recovered with deep disturbance in later years, that she also despised them. Her tormentors smashed her with bottles and stones. She had almost lost an eye. "I fell," she told her parents. How could they have believed her? They did not believe her, she had intuited, they knew what had happened. They loved her and yet they let her almost die. The silence possessed them, but not until her father died did she concede its power.

Once she was a gambler . . .

Abruptly, now, in the airport on Maui, she tested the cues, made her selection and chalked it, and racked the balls. They nestled with their multicolored plumage against the emerald felt glowing with life beneath the soft intense light hung overhead.

Here was a great mystery. Mathematics made tangible. Triangle cradling spheres. Potential: lines and angles, forces and contacts, certainty and unknowability. The game gathered her. Its beauty, like life's, was a kind of wrath; like love, a kind of knowledge.

She raised the rack with sacramental ceremoniousness, defensively ironic but at bottom not. Her playing was a great gift, for her father had taught her. As Cruz had taught him, here in Hawai'i, long ago.

Cue balanced, body aligned. The preparation was all one's own; and the decision about the moment of release, of giving over, of admitting loss and limitation, that was one's own also. After that it was not one's own.

She leaned over with a lover's gesture.

"*Kamikaze!*" she whispered.

Wood clapped flatly against wood, a call to commitment: the great gamble, the great giving over.

Balls scattered, profoundly and incomprehensibly ordered as a flock of birds hurtling away into the sky. Their bright breathtaking flight became, mystically, her father's brightly colored laugh, alive in the world again.

José Sánchez: a bad business. So much of her work involved bad business. It had gotten to her after all these years, she knew. Her work forced the re-evocation of her clients' terrors, and she had gone down in a profound and ever-deepening sadness, a slowly-consuming dread of the world that produced such terrors and that she had dedicated herself to battling. And now it was the Reagan era, the rollback of so much of the legal advance of the '60's, a hardening of attitudes, of climate. She felt it as a physical assault, held her body tenser in these times. And battling was dangerous to her, psychologically: she had always known that, for her clients' terrors echoed the submerged but unsubdued terrors she herself had known.

In her waking and her sleeping, sometimes dominating her thought, sometimes driven to an unquiet continuous undercurrent, the last words she and José Sánchez had exchanged repeated again and again.

"I need to confirm these details. I'm sorry," she had said.

"Again?"

"Again. I hope this will be the last time."

He had submitted. What else could he do? Hating it all, she droned to distance the meaning of words. The identification: José Luis Sánchez, 46, of the town of Santa Clara los dos Rivieras. Then, the name of his country, and his occupation: farmer, but they knew he'd been a political organizer too. And he was making application for political asylum.

The statement: They came in the night. They were the paramilitary . . . my wife Ana and the children . . . Rosita, she was ten, Manuel, four,

Miguel, three . . . then they took my wife, and . . . and Rosita . . . in front of us all of us yes, that is what I mean, they raped them. . .then they shot them, then the boys, then me . . . near the eye . . . but somehow I lived. Only I lived. Why me? It was because of me that those men came . . .

For the purposes of the documentation, of course, she omitted the last two sentences. Omitting reference to those words on the document was all right. Still, inside she knew, that day, that omitting reference between them was not.

But she could not speak with him. The childhood habit of silence was too deeply ingrained. She determined that day to find him a counselor at the People's Clinic. But she herself could not speak. The question echoed off deep questions distorting her own life, about her own life, that she did not know how to face. There was no answer anyway, she told herself.

There was no answer but the answer wasn't the point. The point was to stay with someone while the question was asked. To find words, somehow, that weren't an answer but that were a help. And she had not stayed with José Sánchez that day, nor found those words. Breaking silence was too difficult for her.

Instead she'd folded the papers together, wished him good-night, and gone home, promising herself to take him to lunch, to talk the next day with Peter, her friend at the Clinic, about José's deepening depression.

Policemen like the ones who had fractured her skull in Oakland, during the war at home against the war abroad, pounded at her door, driving her from sleep. They took her to see where José's body swung in the shadows.

On a scrap of paper from the Legal Aid office, left on his rickety bedside table, José had scribbled the words in Spanish, Why me?

"What's that mean?" a cop had asked. She shook her head, and thought, It means that I could not find the right words and so he died.

But she had said nothing, then or since.

"Where'd a lady learn a game like yours? You move around that table like a dancer moves."

Paula froze. Her personal radar was sharp, honed on those dangerous childhood streets and in dangerous situations later. Yet Will Cawdry had been able to approach very close and watch her without her knowledge.

"'Lady'? Jumping to conclusions, aren't you? I'm a 'Miz,' remember."

"I always try to give folks the benefit of the doubt. Even Mizzes."

"I answer to 'woman' but not to lady."

"I reckon that's an important distinction?"

"To me it is. 'Woman' is a statement of fact. 'Lady' is a set of directives about how to live my life. And my father taught me to play."

"He taught you well. 'Tis easy to see you love the game."

"He did teach me well. Want a game? Put some money on it?"

"Not on that game, not with you. I'm pretty good with a cue myself. Good enough to know I'll wind up without enough for the next drink if I take on a player fine as you."

She grinned. "You're wise. I've been earning pocket money and then a nice side income I was eight."

He picked up a cue. "Don't surprise me at all. I don't mind knocking some balls around, though, friendly-like."

She nodded.

Paula seldom played congenially with people; she was a competitor with a cue. And, of all people, she would never have predicted that she and Will Cawdry would be natural partners, in that indefinable way that sometimes happened when rhythms of play harmonized. She was disturbed as well as surprised; for her, that kind of harmony was akin to the harmonies of desire and of love. She rebelled against the idea in connection with this man in whom she had intuited such terrifying violence, such deep discontinuity of soul; a man capable of that appalling smile.

3

Flying Through the Sun

Later, they sat at the counter and ate sandwiches and drank guava juice.

"Miz Kajiyama," he began.

"Please, call me Paula."

The game had raised Paula's confidence, emboldening her to move against the fear this man evoked in her and remove her foreign, self-erected barrier of formality.

"I'd be right honored to move from 'Miz Kajiyama' to 'Miz Paula.' And folks call me Will. I just know you like my 'Miz,' you being a woman and not a lady. 'Miz' is easy enough for me to say. We did always say it so, down to Hibbits, Texas. Advanced place, Hibbits. Well, Miz Paula, have you been in these parts long?"

"What makes you think I'm not from here?"

"Oh, I dunno, maybe because you move so fast, even for Honolulu. We're always losing Mainlanders out to sea. These are islands, you know."

Paula laughed. "You win. Sort of. This is my first time on the Big Island or Maui. But I came to Hawai'i six months ago from San Francisco, where I've lived since I was fourteen. Well, there and Berkeley, where I went to college. I mostly grew up in Chicago, but —"

His odd expression halted her, a tightening of the skin across the bone, as if all his face were under structural stress. Then the expression was gone. She waited a moment, giving him space to speak, but he didn't, so she went on, "But now I live in Honolulu, and I'm here to stay."

"That so? I know a lot of hippie-folks came to your San Francisco, sight unseen, and came here too. And folks come from the Mainland for some other reason first. The Service. A vacation, mebbe. The place do suit them. They come back, stay on, almost without realizing it. Things do happen. Time do pass." He looked at her shrewdly. "You've got a feel of anti-Establishment about you, as they used to say, but you ain't a hippie. I'd guess you're one of those political folks, what with your kind of lawyering and all. Me, I ain't a political person. So what drew you here? You got people in the islands?"

"Not any more. My father's family was from Kahuku, on O'ahu. He was born and grew up there. My mother's from a little coastal town South of San

Francisco where her family had had a nursery for two generations. Roses. They met when they were at school at Berkeley together — for awhile."

A fogginess webbed her thoughts, momentarily stopped her speech. A year and a half ago in San Francisco when José Sánchez died, policemen had taken her away, as others like them had taken her parents in that city in 1942, ripping them from work, from school, shipping them to the camp, shattering their lives.

"I'm sorry to hear you got no people here."

"Why should you be?"

He grinned. "You gonna get mad at me, but I reckon I'll risk it now we've talked pleasant awhile. I'm sorry because this world's a wilderness. It ain't no kind of place for a nice little girl like you to be wandering. I know, 'tis for you to say if you're a lady, and you already told me you ain't, you're a woman. I ain't speaking to that. I've just been wondering where your daddy is and why he ain't seen to getting you placed in life. He took all that trouble to teach you to handle a pool cue, he must surely treasure you."

She was scathing. "I've been seeing to my own place in life for awhile now. My father's been dead a long time. I'm neither little nor a girl, and no one has ever accused me of being 'nice.' You see, I'm older than I look — to you. Maybe you can't tell."

"Sit easy, Miz Paula. Next to me you're little — though 'tis true most folks are. And 'girl's' a manner of speaking, no offense meant. I got a pretty good idea how old you are. I been in Asia and the islands a long time now, and I've learned to see what I'm looking at."

"What's that supposed to mean?"

"Just what you meant, I reckon. I can see you when I look at you Asian folks. You don't all look young to me, nor do you all look the same, nor do you look inscrutable. Seems to me ideas like inscrutability and they-all-look-alike are a luxury, for those as run things. If you have to deal with people kind of on an even level, you can't afford not to see them. Can be downright dangerous. Yeah, I make you pretty close to my age."

She was thrown off balance. Few people even acknowledged hearing references to racial stereotypes, much less pulled them straight into the open, as he had done.

"If you're so close to my age, why hasn't your mother seen to placing you in life?"

"Oh," said Will, off-hand, "she's been dead a long time too. Besides, the world's a different place for a man." He drained his juice can and crushed it in his fist.

"I've seen it bash up a man or two," said Paula curtly.

A beat of silence followed. Then, "Have you now," said Will. "Well, it's true the world ain't much of a place for woman nor man either to wander."

When she glanced at him, his eyes were no longer uncompromisingly blue, but flecked with gray, like the complex interior of flawed ice.

"Well. Let's see," he resumed, playful now. "Poolhall dancer, wildlife rescuer. A lady — 'scuse me, a woman — of many parts." He grinned. "Sounds kind of obscene put like that, don't it? No offense, I'm sure. Just where did your daddy teach you your game?"

"At the local pool hall. When I was little our neighborhood was mostly East European. Later, it changed — got pretty mixed — Black people up from the South, some students and even a few faculty members at the University, White people from Appalachia, later Puerto Ricans. And then there was my family. My father got to be good friends with a Black graduate student next door — Jim Jordan — and they started going to the Black Star Club at the corner, to have a few beers, shoot a little pool, talk politics. See, they'd really gotten friendly when they were both accused of being Communists and ordered down to Springfield to testify at the hearings in 1952. The man who ran the Black Star was from Jamaica. His name was Thomas Graves. He'd been a follower of Marcus Garvey, who led the big Back-to-Africa movement among Blacks in the '20's and '30's. The place was named for the shipping line Garvey started. And it was a neighborhood club, and a place for political meetings and arguments, and he ran a little bookstore in one corner, with Garvey's writings and other books called *The Truth About the Black Man Founder of Civilization* and things like that."

She stopped. So many years had passed — decades — since she had spoken of all this, and with startling power her words conjured up again the dust and sweat and peanut and beer smell of the Black Star, the eager voices of her father and his friends, vivid in intense debate, erupting into loud laughter at intervals, sometimes jovial, sometimes ironic, sometimes knifed through with scalding bitterness. Thomas Graves: "Garvey taught us to emulate the Japanese. They are a colored people strong in their own land, who've taken on the White man at his own game twice in this century. They won in 1905 and they damn near did it again in '45. We all know that, who were fighting then." And her father and Jim Jordan: "The problem of the twentieth century is the problem of the color line, just like Du Bois says, but it's because of class with race used as a dividing tactic." Thomas Graves rebutting: "The problem is with the White man's racism."

And her father and Jim Jordan: "Well, no argument about that." Laughter. "It's just a question of whether there's any hope for him." Thomas Graves: "None, man. And the only hope for us is to go home and build up our own land."

It was at the Black Star that she had first heard her father talk story, first heard that bright clear laugh. Though her parents loved each other there had been little laughter in their isolated family. She knew why her father had liked his time at the Black Star; she had liked it too. Her mother had not wanted him to go there and wanted even less for him to take Paula. She would not go herself, though other women came to the Black Star. She felt it was undignified, or maybe she simply felt more alien there than Paula's father did. She had grown up on the cold gray Northern California coast, not in the tumbled ethnic mix of plantation Hawai'i, like Paula's father. Like Thomas Graves in his plantation Caribbean. There were many ties between her father and the Black men at the Black Star. At first, her father had been welcomed as Jim Jordan's friend, and because Garvey had respected the Japanese. Then, he and Thomas Graves found out about their similar childhoods, down low in tropical plantation society. Then, she thought, her father had become welcome for himself, for his conversation, vivid and trenchant but never hostile, for his bright laugh like a flight of birds.

She had lost track of her surroundings. She could tell that Will Cawdry was repeating himself when he said,

"You did say you're a lawyer?"

"I was trained as a lawyer. I used to be a trial lawyer." And a damned good one, too, she thought, for all that the stress sent me home shaking at night.

Good in court, with arguments, with juries. Not with people up close.

"That's when you aren't tending to critters in distress or ruining poor unsuspecting passersby with a cue?"

"Right." The image of José Sánchez's body rose before her eyes and blurred her vision. She shook it away.

"Now this — what'd you call it? — 'public interest law'. Do it pay well?"

"Not often. A lot of the clients that come can't pay."

"Clients that can't pay. That do sound a mite thin, financially speaking. Not like my lawyer-tax-man. And you're a translator now? That means you know languages?"

"Some." She didn't want to talk about her work life any more.

He looked at her a moment, recognizing her barrier she thought, and gave a good-humored nod.

"Well, if you need extra money you can always do like me, flying Sunday dinners from one coop to another. Raiding the crates if times get tough." He shook his head. "Didn't know a body could stop being a lawyer. Sounds like down home to Hibbits, where a man can start and stop being a preacher, as my Uncle Bert did, depending on whether he was backslid or in a state of grace that week. I thought being a lawyer was more like with them Catholic folks, where once you're a priest you're one for keeps. Unless you do something truly dreadful, of course, then they — what do you say? — disrobe you? No, defrock I reckon. Is it like that with lawyers too?"

"Nothing so exciting." She looked at him narrowly, not absolutely sure that he was putting her on. "It's a staid calling. We merely get disbarred."

Will shook his head, and she caught the gleam in his eyes. Was he joking then? And at whose expense?

"Mighty complicated. Too much for a country boy like me. Is that what happened to you?"

"No." She realized she cared that he know that, and was disturbed that she cared what he thought. "I — just stopped. That's all."

He was silent a moment. "Well, I didn't really think you'd been disbarred. And I'm sorry to hear you stopped lawyering, Miz Paula. Seems like being a lawyer meant something to you, and I'd take odds you was a good one. It's always a shame when a body stops work they're good at and proud of. I ain't surprised your lawyering weren't about money, nor your leaving it neither. And then, it ain't hard to get money, anyhow. You just got to be willing to do whatever it is that people with money will pay for."

She cast him a sharp look, but the sudden bleakness threading his voice did not show in his face.

"That's one philosophy of life, I guess."

The bleakness was gone when he replied.

"Well, I don't know as I'd put it that fancy. It's just something I've come to know, in my travels."

"And have they been varied then, your travels?"

"I been here and there."

"Doin' this and that," she ventured teasing. She recognized that now he was the one erecting a barrier, with his words, and with hers she explored his tolerance of her pressure on it.

He was very still for a moment, and she went tautly alert. Then,

"I got to remember me that. 'I been here and there, doin' this and that.' Well, Miz Paula, I been in Hong Kong and I been in Singapore. I been in Indonesia and I been in the Philippines, and a few other places, besides."

I bet you've been in a few other places she thought. Vietnam, for instance, when you were fighting Charlie, when you were working for Sam.

In a gesture become a habit that she had long tried to break, she found herself pressing her fingertips against her left temple, against the raised white scar beneath her hair. Her skull had shattered there. The scar was a souvenir of those times, when she stood in front of an induction center as she sought to dissuade young men her age — his age — from taking that one forward step, fateful, perhaps fatal. Where had Will Cawdry been on that afternoon?

"Got a headache?"

"What? Oh — no." She dropped her hand to her knee. Not at the moment, she refrained from saying. At intervals ever since that afternoon they disabled her, sometimes for days at a time.

Will went on, "I seen something of most all the islands in these seas, and I been fifteen years on this island. That's the here and there. As for the this and that, some of it bears the telling and some don't, so for now I reckon I'll leave it."

He smiled, and this time she accepted his barrier, and the smile he offered to ease the sting. It was more than she had offered, a moment ago.

He pushed away his empty bowl and said,

"If you're ready we can start back."

They rose. He called toward the kitchen,

"We're off, Ned. Thanks."

"How much do I owe?"

"For what we had? Not a red cent. I reckon Ned can spare a couple of cans of guava juice and a bowl of chili or two. Hasn't bankrupted him yet."

Still she hesitated, anxious not to be beholden.

"Miz Paula, Ned'll get it back next time he comes over to see me. Or when I get back here, I'll buy him two cans of guava juice that he don't want, on your account." She was sure this time that the gleam in his eyes was humor.

"It's barter, like, Miz Paula. Must seem like the back of beyond to a big-city Mainland girl like you."

"Oh, come on. Hibbits, Texas, isn't the Mainland?"

"I reckon it is at that. But for sure it ain't the big city — and I've been a long time gone."

The conversation had stirred troubled memories for Paula, of José Sánchez, of earlier wars at home and abroad that had never ended, and she felt her limbs slowed by emotion unresolved. She moved as if the air had the consistency of molasses, hardly noticing either their takeoff or the view, until Will had finished talking to control, and addressed her.

"Fastened tight? Because I'm going to take you somewhere worth seeing that's not part of the regular tour. Ready?"

"Ready." She forced a jauntiness into her voice.

"Hold on to your petticoats then, Miz Paula."

The plane shot straight up. Paula slammed breathless back against her seat, as they blazed towards the black sun looming before her eyes, beating at the back of her lids. They flung through its heart and her throat closed with terror that shattered abruptly like glass, spinning her into jubilation as they emerged at the other side, wheeling in some unheard-of dimension, without worry or weight, grounding or goal.

Back on the tarmac at the airport near Volcano, Will handed her out the door.

"That was straight-out magical."

"Well, Miz Paula, I'm right glad to have pleased you. Walking to the plane you looked like the weight of all time were on your shoulders. Recollections, I expect. A long-standing weariness do have a certain look. I have felt so myself. And when I do, ain't nothing to shake it off that I've ever found to beat flying through the sun."

"Flying through the sun? It seemed like that to you too?"

"'Tis what it was."

He walked her to her rental car. As she shut the door he leaned his hand on the window frame, at first glance casually, but she was startled to see his grip was so tight his knuckles showed white.

"Miz Paula." Under stress his accent grew stronger. "Miz Paula, might I invite you for dinner tonight, should you happen to be free? 'Tis a respectable place, you can ask folks about it if you like, Euph's and the Pine Tar, there'll be other ladies there. And I can promise you a dinner as good as any you'll ever eat."

She heard herself saying, "Yes. Thank you."

"Around six?"

"Six is fine."

She told him the name of her hotel. He walked to an impeccably kept cherry-red Jeep parked nearby.

Before he even reached it Paula drove rapidly away.

4

The Place On the Water

A giant banyan towered in a tangled thicket of twisted limbs before Paula's hotel. Now, emerging like some spirit of darkness at its heart, Will Cawdry stepped forth from its shadow. His saunter seemed to say he'd been walking awhile. Yet Paula spied the cherry-red Jeep parked down the block behind him.

She had been watching for him from the lobby, yet had not seen him coming; that frightened her. She wondered if she had suffered another of the momentary black-outs attributed by her doctor to stress and depression after José Sánchez died. Or perhaps she was still half-drowned in her afternoon's nap. She fought an oppressive conviction that Will had been near while she slept that afternoon, that some unremembered dream had been instinct with him, that his roots were sunk deep in her psychic past.

He was upon her.

"Evening, Miz Paula."

His eyes seemed a deeper blue than she remembered. She sensed that his emotional balance had shifted radically. For the first time she thought of him as capable of happiness.

Struggling for emotional balance of her own, she managed to reply, "Evening to you."

"So you keep a dragon guardian."

She had no idea what he meant. Then she followed the direction of his gaze to her left wrist and the coiled brass bracelet with the dragon's head.

"Oh this. I found it at a garage sale. I liked it right away." His tone disturbed her; it was too charged with meaning.

The bracelet, her plain blue shift, and sandals were the only clothes besides hiking gear she had brought, a concession to her custom when traveling alone of taking herself out for a nice dinner on the last night of her trip. The simplicity of her outfit heightened the extravagance of his: long-sleeved shirt tucked into narrow pants, pants and shirt both of some bright turquoise stuff, satin and shimmering, lavishly and complexly embroidered in silver thread. He had exchanged his work shoes for high black leather boots polished to a mirror gleam, with heels that gave him another two inches' height advantage over her.

As they stepped through the door, a flock of shrieking mynah birds sailed low overhead, returning for the night to their roost in the banyan. Paula watched them settle into its branches.

"There's a tree like that in the courtyard outside my door in Honolulu," she said. "And a flock of mynah birds."

"The banyan? It's most common hereabouts, and it's the mynah birds' favorite. It's majestic, the banyan, and terrible too, the way it takes a death-embrace on other trees. 'Tis for that it's called the strangler fig."

He took her to a place on the water, vivid with red and yellow hibiscus. Groves of coconut palms, banana plants, and other foliage she could not identify hid the town across the Bay from view, and half-obscured two buildings, clapboarded in dark wood.

"My place," Will announced. "That's Euph's over there." He nodded to the smaller of two structures. "It's a gathering place. And this here's the Pine Tar restaurant. Looks like a full house tonight." He pulled into one of the last available spaces in the parking lot. "WILL" showed out across the asphalt in large white letters.

The Pine Tar was L-shaped. The short length rested on lava stilts built out over a brimming lagoon, one of those inlets of the sea trembling with a fragile surface tension, just level with the shore. Now and then, under the influence of a distant swell, a sudden overlap gave chill warning of how little kept this land from inundation. Paula knew from her father's reminiscences that at times in these islands, inconceivable winds roared from beyond the horizon, whipping the ocean to towering destructiveness. The precarious perch of Euph's and the Pine Tar touched her irrationally.

As if giving voice to her thought, Will said,

"It's been struck by storm and tide, but so far ain't been neither blown nor washed away."

She intuited that he was describing himself as well as his fortunes.

"Now," he said, "let's go round back so you and Ben can meet."

Their passage along the left side of the restaurant sent a flock of hens into a clacking flustered scatter; he settled them easily with a murmured word.

At the screen door he hesitated, then pushed through, saying loudly,

"Ben, I want you to meet the lawyer-lady I told you about earlier, Miz Paula, Paula Kajiyama. That's spelled "M-S" and she's big into Public Interest issues and such, liable to have an in with the Health people. So just knock the roaches out of sight, kind of mash them down into the red sauce, okay?"

He drew Paula into a large kitchen, meticulously clean. Steam and a confounding delicious brew of rich odors filled her senses. Shards of light glinted off the blades of racked cutting implements, and off the shiny chrome of huge refrigerators and freezers along the walls. The room's centerpiece was an enormous wooden working table.

Incongruous among the modern appliances, two old black iron gas ranges stood side by side. The man tending them was about fifty, compactly built, with a square pockmarked copper-colored face and the dark frizzy hair of the Pacific islands, but he was small-boned and short compared to the Hawaiians Paula knew. A voluminous white apron, neatly belted, protected his immaculate white shirt and pants. He glided on sandaled feet between black cauldrons that bubbled on the black stoves, wielding a large wooden spoon in each hand like a conductor before an orchestra. He did not pause in his choreography to acknowledge their entrance or Will's words.

"Miz Paula, this is Ben."

She offered her hand. "Pleased to meet you."

The man stopped, and fixed her momentarily with tiny black eyes bright beneath thick black brows. To her, their expression was inscrutable. His gesture was not as he very deliberately turned his back to make microscopic adjustments of the flames beneath the cauldrons.

Angry and embarrassed, she clenched her hands at her sides. The skin in the sheltered places behind Will's ears turned rosy.

"Ben ain't used to shaking hands with wimmen no more'n I am, so I hope you'll excuse him, though I do wish you'd make an exception for Miz Paula, Ben. Also, he maybe thinks you really are from the Health people, or maybe he ain't in a mood to appreciate my humor, which I can't claim is the understated kind. Lastly he don't like people in the kitchen when he's cooking no more'n I do, so I hope you'll excuse me, Ben. Like I told you earlier, Miz Paula and me'll be dining in the Alcove Room, and we're going to Euph's now, so if you could let me know when dinner's ready I'd most appreciate it."

He ushered Paula out the door, then went back and exchanged several sentences with Ben, anxious on his side, curt on Ben's. The low voice wasn't necessary; they spoke a language unlike any she had ever heard.

She was still annoyed and shaken, and thinking that Will had offered two excuses more for Ben's behavior than necessary, sidestepping the real and obvious one: for some reason, surprising Will, the man had disliked her on sight.

"I did know Ben took a bit funny when I mentioned I'd be bringing you by," said Will ingenuously, frowning. "He's most likely had a trying day, and I ain't been here to help."

In just the few moments they had spent in the kitchen, the evening had descended suddenly. In the narrow space between near-tropical night and day the altered light imparted to the dark shingles of both buildings a meditative reddish tone. Through the coconut grove and past squat banana plants with broad leaves black in the approaching night, Paula followed Will down a path sketched out in lava flagstones that led to Euph's.

Swinging open the door, he flipped switches and stood aside for her to enter. A flood of soft yellow light bathed them, and overhead the wooden blades of a ceiling fan began to turn lazily.

"This is Euph's."

A large rectangular room extended lengthwise. A huge mirror along the left wall, behind a bar of scarred solid dark wood, doubled its size by reflection. From shelves on each side of the mirror, cut facets of liquor bottles flashed rich ruby, amber and emerald light. A pool table and a hanging blackboard for scoring stood to the right of the door. Sturdy cane tables and canebottom chairs defined a spacious central area. Diamond-patterned pandanas-reed matting covered the walls, inset from the floor to the height of her waist with bamboo canes, varied slightly in height like panpipes. Their smooth surfaces gleamed a soft gray-yellow. On three sides the upper walls were given over to half-open wooden-louvered windows. She could feel the heavy languid water dark beneath them, and moist air drenched in the fragrance of plumeria wafted in with the night. Behind the bar a door opened into a small kitchen; through an open door in the wall facing the entrance, she glimpsed a corridor. To the right of that door, angled against the wall, stood a grand piano, its burnished black surface gleaming like a living skin.

Perhaps it was the jeweled light from the bottles, the lavish textures of cane and grass and cloth that she explored with tingling fingertips as she moved around the room, but from the moment of stepping across the threshold Paula felt herself transported into a realm of powerfully conjured fantasy or dream.

As she touched the finely maintained felt of the pool table, Will joked, "Might be you'll find your fortune at Euph's."

Self-conscious, she left the table. "What's through there?" she nodded at a door in the back of the room.

"I'll show you. It's just my bunking place. 'Tis where Ben and I slept the first year, till he started courting Emma and moved into town."

The door gave onto a corridor. Will swung open another door directly opposite, and they stepped into a long narrow room that ran the length of the building.

The wooden louvers of the room's two windows opened directly above the dark lagoon, and water-freshened air filled the space. A far door, slightly ajar, led to a bathroom. The room's furnishings had all seen better days.

A huge old-fashioned dresser of dark wood, with wide drawers and an attached oval mirror, struck Paula not as out of place but reminiscent of another place and time. Following her gaze, Will said,

"I found that at an estate sale."

"It might have come from an old farmhouse."

"It did, from a big place near Waimea."

Besides the dresser, the room held an iron double bed tightly made up with a brown wool blanket, and a small battered wooden bedside table. A green armchair big enough for Will, a wide ottoman that didn't match it, and a standing lamp set near the chair, angled for reading, completed the furnishings.

Along the right wall ran a dowel for his clothes. Somehow she had expected this man to live in chaos. But the garments were neatly ranged, and the heels of boots and shoes beneath were aligned as if along an invisible chalk mark. The orderliness of the entire room conveyed a profoundly willed and painful constraint.

They moved back into Euph's. Paula stopped beside the piano.

In an embrasure cut into the wall behind it stood a small photograph in an ornately figured gold-colored frame.

"That's Euph." Will pressed a switch, illuminating the piano and the picture: an old Black man, seated on an upturned crate before a simple one-story wooden building, box-like and ramshackle.

The man's fraying straw hat could have been woven from the same pandanas fronds as the plaited matting on the walls around her. Between overall-clad legs, planted strongly apart, his gnarled hands hung relaxed.

"Is he still alive? Euph?"

"Aw no. Euph crossed a long time ago now."

The snapshot was in black and white, out of focus and poorly developed, taken with a cheap camera in some distant time. Yet the man's personality

— his very presence — seemed to emerge three-dimensionally from the two-dimensional representation of the past. He radiated an essential balance, despite his weary countryman's pose; and, despite the snapshot's blurriness and what she felt was his deliberate veiling of his eyes, they gleamed with sharp but ambiguous amusement, an expression that inexplicably struck her as familiar.

"I have always wished I had a better snapshot. Euph, he were kind of shy of cameras, and none too pleased when he found Bertha'd took this picture, but I did ask for it and in the end he let me keep it. Put away, like, till after I left Hibbits."

"Who was Bertha? Euph's wife?"

"Wife? Bertha? Uh — no. Not Bertha. She, uh, she worked at the Blue Box. That's the Blue Box, that building there behind him in the photograph. 'Twas what Euph called a jook joint. The man who owned it, he lived down the road in Andrewsville. He let Euph have a little room in the rear, and garden rights in the back plot, in exchange for playing the piano and pouring the drinks and generally seeing to the place. If Euph had a wife, 'twere before he came to Hibbits, and I don't know nothing about that."

"And this place is named for him?"

"It is."

"What's the Pine Tar named for?"

"It's short for pine tar likker. Brewed from a bitter stunted tree grows everywhere in those parts." He grinned, and the quick gleam in his eyes she had noticed that morning told her suddenly why Euph's expression was familiar. Yet she could not possibly deduce a biological kinship between these two.

"You see," Will continued, the humor still in his eyes, "my drink of choice these days is Johnny Black, but 'tweren't always so. Pine tar likker were Euph's drink, and my first drink, only after all this time away from the Starvesoil I prob'ly ain't still man enough to handle it. Yessir, pine tar likker were Euph's drink. Don't know whether that snapshot's so blurry because Bertha was shaking, or Euph. Both, most likely. Bertha drank bourbon, which next to tar likker's about like mango juice, but they both did like their libation."

The gleam died. "He used to say the tar likker were what helped him get through, and I reckon that's so. And like a lot of what helps people get through — wimmen and religion and patriotism and such-like — it helped to kill him too. But this place is named for him, and the restaurant for his likker."

"And you knew him in Hibbits? Hibbits, Texas? That's where you're from?"

"Yes'm, there's only one Hibbits I know of, and that's one too many. And as for my being from there, not rightly. Out behind the town is the Thornbrake Starvesoil. The thornbrake, it's this plant, grows high as a man's shoulders, in thickets no one can get through, carrying spines long as my finger. That's where I come from, not the town, but there's no way to locate it for folks when you're away, except to call it Hibbits."

"And what's the 'Starvesoil'?"

"It's a wilderness, just like in the Bible where the Israelites wandered forty years. At least I didn't have to put in that much time there, though it seemed like forty times forty again. And again . . . the good folks of Hibbits, two hundred or so of them, they had a church and a school and even a doctor, everything a real community needs, including Black folks — of course they had other names for them. I have heard that elsewhere in Texas the good folks has Mexicans instead of Black folks. Life's a fight between the Starvesoil and the Thornbrake, on the one side, and the crops, on the other. Some say, 'You weaken, and the Thornbrake wins,' but 'tisn't true. The Thornbrake always wins. Because the bitterness is that the Starvesoil is thin and dry, and breaks up between your fingers, and what you got to do to it just to raise a crop and live, breaks it up more and gives it to the Thornbrake in the end. Everyone knows it, but there's nothing else to do. 'Tain't no place, really . . . "

"It sounds like very much of a place to me," contradicted Paula quietly, thinking that if it had produced him, it might be fearsome, but it could not be negligible.

He shrugged.

"A wilderness," he repeated. "And may be you're right, 'tis a place, but no place to be . . . and in the Thornbrake there's razorbacks. Wild hogs, they are, and powerful fierce, like those you'll find here in the deep 'ōhi'a forest, brought by the haoles long ago." He shook himself, the way she had seen him do that morning, as if breaking a spell. "But this ain't no way to entertain a lady. Or pardon me, a woman. Or anyone, for that matter."

He shook himself again. "Don't know what come over me, I ain't talked about all of that for the longest time. Ain't thought of it, even."

"Not at all," said Paula. "I'm glad to hear about it. Had Euph's family lived in Hibbits a long time?"

"Euph? His family? Aw no. Euph was a city man, sure as you're a city lady. He come from New Orleans." He pronounced it "Nawlins."

"Euph," he went on, "weren't just quite what he seemed. And I figure he had a powerful reason for not liking no fool messing around him with a camera, because it would've taken a powerful reason to drive Euph from New Orleans at all, let alone keep him buried in a godforsaken place like the Thornbrake Starvesoil. 'Tis sure that life takes folks strange places. And it has brought me here to Euph's and the Pine Tar. Euph's and the Pine Tar, it's my place."

He paused. "My place," he said again. "Here, I don't have to pay." His manner oddly formal, he added, "you're most welcome in my place, Miz Paula."

"Thank you." She felt herself speaking stiffly in the face of his odd ceremoniousness. "Do you — do you play the piano?"

"I do, for my pleasure. Next to Euph, I wouldn't hardly say I play. I keep his picture just there to help keep me honest and honorable in my music. Blues, jazz, ragtime, anything he took a mind to — he played. He did say, if I kept on honestly, I'd be good as him someday, and maybe better. But I don't put too much stock in that, 'cause he were fond of me spite all. Though 'tis true as well, I won't never know, 'cause I ain't been honest and honorable, in other ways than music, anyway. But I acknowledge him in every note I play."

Paula contemplated Euph's enigmatic face and reflected that he looked like a strong man and a complex one, and someone whose honesty as well as his honor would have been of his own defining.

"He were a man with a powerful teaching," said Will. "I learned most of my music from him, and how to read and write and how to think about what I read, and I learned other things as well."

He sighed. "Ain't nothing no man can do to Euph no more. Recollecting how he did hate having his picture taken, 'tis clear to me now and I think I kind of understood even as a boy, that he were laying low. I reckon that powerful teaching of his had set him afoul of the Klan and other forces too, in his day. Well, well." The words were a sigh in themselves. "They do say death's a release from fear and flight. A great blessing — for those as ain't got hellfire to face certain sure."

Rebellious against the melancholy chord his mood struck too easily in her, Paula retorted,

"But life has some things to recommend it too. Even without the fear of hellfire as the alternative."

Will pulled his gaze away from the past and inwardness, back to the present and to her. She had a sudden odd experience of being outside herself, of looking at the two of them standing there in a dark clapboarded shack on the edge of a lagoon, set in a banyan and banana grove. Coconut fronds rattled above them at night, and Euph looked out on them with hooded eyes.

"Well," Will said, "I reckon it does at that. Since it has brought me a day like today, which has brought me you." He broke the heavy mood by adding, "and two nēnēbirds as well, setting out on a new life together. Yes'm, quite a day."

But his drollery did not quite suffice to dispel the somberness that had stood around him like a forcefield, and mostly to divert them both from it, Paula said,

"Play the piano for me."

"Aw now, I know you're a well-brought-up lady, but no need to carry politeness so far."

"It isn't just politeness." This was true; she was curious to know what music this man might make.

He hesitated, then said, "All right, I'll be your Tambourine Man. A fine song, that one."

His raw-boned huge hands were as unexpectedly sensitive and sure on the keys as they had been on the controls of his plane and against the nēnē's wing; and in an extraordinary moment his music spun Paula once again into a solar heart, as when he had taken them flying through the sun, sent her soaring with that same thrust beyond all boundaries to plunge deep into some secret fundamental joyousness. Become, herself, elusive and quicksilver as sun on the sea here, she found herself borne along on the ancient beat of Hawaiian traditional chant, joined but not eclipsed by riffs of jazz, by the curl of European melody, all mingled to a harmony with the feel of movement of nearby living water, of vivid air, of the rich glint of ruby and amber and emerald light.

The sound dissolved into the attentive night. His fingers still lay on the keys as if in some lingering benediction.

"That was — remarkable." Off-balance, Paula resorted to expressions of high praise conventional in her milieu by asking, "Do you play professionally?"

The question struck her at once as wide of any mark. Of all the things this man might be, a professional in the sense meant in her world was not one of them. "Here?" she added, to make the word seem less inappropriate, glancing around the room, and then wondered if she seemed incredulous, insulting.

"No Ma'am, not here nor nowhere. And Euph's ain't about professions or making money. Kind of like your lawyering that way, I reckon. But I thank you kindly for your words."

"It's your composition, isn't it?" She was sure he had been improvising; she had been present at a creation.

"Yeh, it is."

"Not done yet."

"Not done yet."

"It's about structure. Living structure."

"I don't take your meaning."

"It reminds me of trying to find just the right words and form of words to make a translation." She was embarrassed at the comparison, about what she was saying. She loved listening to music and possessed a certain knowledge, but she did not think that she was truly musical, and though translation could be an art, she did not think that hers was.

"It sounded like light and air and water and feeling moving together." Her face grew hot at the increasing clumsiness of her verbal attempts, and she told herself to be quiet.

But Will's face took on a look of pleasure and comprehension.

"Well, that's right interesting, because it was looking at the sea when I was flying that put the first of the music in my head. The Hawaiian people know the sea like no others. And I have never sailed the sea as they do. But I sail the air, and I sail over these Eight Seas, and the sea and the air are joined movement. 'Tis a most special air here, too, with the live winds almost always blowing, touching the skin and its hairs, bringing news. So maybe I do take something of your meaning after all. Might be I'm telling of the structure of the sea, which is a living thing for true like the air and the land and so is always changing."

He nodded, as if well satisfied; and Paula found that she felt herself understood.

"I liked it," she ventured suddenly, and immediately was shy as she heard the strength of the feeling that charged her bare words.

Will lowered the fallboard, gently.

"Did you now. I'm right glad."

And the skin behind his ears went rosy.

From across the banana and banyan grove a wooden gong reverberated against metal.

Will stood.

"That's Ben calling us now, to tell us the Alcove Room is ready."

He straightened the piano bench, switched off the lamp that illuminated the embrasure, and led the way through the rear door into the corridor that ran the length of the building. He quenched the overhead fixture.

As they passed through the narrow door from Euph's into the corridor, their bodies brushed. A sexual shock struck her like a blow, made more powerful by the powerful simultaneous shock she felt in him.

Light blazed. She blinked, momentarily blinded.

Ben stood in the doorway at the far left end of the corridor, in a way that cast his face into shadow.

"The Alcove Room is ready." He spoke in an eloquently expressionless, guttural voice and with an accent she had never heard. Again, as a while before in the presence of Euph's photograph, she had the sensation of being out of her body. She saw herself, standing, her palms pressed against the rough board wall of the corridor, her heart pounding with arousal and profound obscure fear. Again, she was watching some strange configuration of people, of personalities:

Will immobile, his big hands clenched at his sides.

Ben, stationed before them, an indecipherable silhouette.

Through the open door to Euph's, an old man's knowing eyes watched Will, watched her, from long ago, from wherever he had got to now, she thought absurdly. And equally absurdly, she wondered what he thought of her.

Only to be filled suddenly with the conviction that he had given her his blessing.

Will said easily,

"We're just coming along now, Ben. Thanks."

Ben turned without answering him. Suddenly, she knew that Will had completely submerged any awareness he might have had of the electric moment between them; but that Ben knew.

To Paula Will said, "We'll come back here after our meal, when folks set the place alive with music and with their pleasure in company, and then you'll see what Euph's is about."

He followed Ben out the door, Paula close behind.

"Watch your step now," Will said to her. "This is a patch of rough ground here. Rougher than it looks, unless your feet know the place."

5

A Loved Space Long Abandoned

They followed Ben's stern back through the restaurant's main entrance. He continued across the room and vanished through swinging doors at the rear.

This was a completely different space from Euph's. Magnificent hardwood floors glowed richly, smooth and soft as brown-gold honey. Eight tables were skillfully angled, then sheltered by vine-covered latticework, to create intimate dining areas. Vases of carved 'ōhi'a wood, centered on each table, supported gracefully arcing sprays of white island orchids. The lower half of the walls was papered in flocked crimson, the upper in a pattern of pink and crimson trellises. Old-fashioned gas sconces set near the ceiling disguised electric fixtures and softened their light, which gleamed off the silver cutlery, enriching the texture of thick crimson linen tablecloths and orchid-lavender linen napkins. Sensually lovely, just barely over the edge of elegance into opulence, the place evoked descriptions Paula had read of New Orleans brothels. Yet gentility was so clearly the intended effect, the unawareness of the other associations so evident, that the result struck her as innocent, almost naïve, creating a bizarre seductiveness, compelling and disturbing, that mingled unconsciousness with decadence.

"The Pine Tar," Will announced. "The way it's fixed up, it's all my arranging." He grinned. "This is the high-class part of the establishment. I don't spend much time here myself, not out front. The kitchen or over to Euph's is more my kind of setting-down place. I leave the Pine Tar to classier folks like Jeremy here." He nodded to a blonde man, in his early twenties, tending bar. "Miz Paula, meet Jeremy Harker. Jeremy, this here's my guest, Miz Kajiyama. She's visiting from Honolulu. I were just telling her you're one of those that keeps the Pine Tar running despite me and my ways."

"Wouldn't be a place except for you, Will. Glad to meet you, Miss Kajiyama."

"Wouldn't be a me without the place, that's more the truth. Jeremy, would you be so kind when you get a moment as to bring a couple of the very best of the Chardonnays, and a good supply of the usual? We'll be in the Alcove Room."

"Ben told me. Sure, right away."

Paula smiled goodbye to the young man and Will escorted her across the floor, greeting diners as they went. Some regarded her with open curiosity. At the rear of the room, he stopped at a magnificent floor-to-ceiling curtain of forest-green beads and dark brown kukui nuts that rattled as he parted it. Behind the curtain stood a pair of Japanese doors in light-colored wood, finely polished. He slid them open with a flourish.

"The Alcove Room."

On a raised dais, a table was set for two. The louvers of the window, of the same wood as the doors, were angled above the lagoon, so freshness and the plumeria fragrance entered, but no one could see in. She heard the sound of lapping waves, and of a gentle unremitting rain that stirred the surface of the water.

A row of covered silver dishes was carefully ranged on a sideboard below the windows. Candle-warmers cherished their contents.

Paula seated herself, self-conscious and awkward because of Will's unaccustomed assistance with her chair, and picked up a fine gray rice-paper menu laid beside her plate, lettered in sumi ink, and apparently composed especially for this meal. The arresting angled calligraphy reminded her of the line the Koolau Mountain Range etched against the sky behind Honolulu.

A knock sounded at the door, and at Will's "Come on in," Jeremy appeared. He set out ice buckets and bottles of pale wine, and placed a bottle of Johnny Black beside the orchids in the 'ōhi'a-wood vase on the sideboard. Evidently, thought Paula, the drink of choice was chosen often enough that it was also known as "the usual."

"Thanks kindly, Jeremy. I'll use the buzzer if I need anything else."

"Sure, Will." The young man withdrew.

Will served her, his gestures almost courtly. Two meats: succulent cubes of pork, neither greasy nor dry, cooked as tender as a loving touch and embraced in mint leaves; and chicken coated with a sauce fragrant with ginger. Fluffy mashed breadfruit brushed with butter. Tiny crisp lettuces with a mango dressing. Then, a pastry that melted like snowflakes on her tongue, bathed in a vanilla and kiwi sauce, and cups of coffee as rich as the Kona lava soil that had nourished it.

He handled the food with reverence, in startling contrast to the way he ate: very quietly, very neatly, and very fast, snapping up large mouthsful as if they might be snatched from him. He had told her he came from the Starvesoil, and the sudden painful insight struck her that scars from the wound of hunger distorted his motions in the world.

"You were right," she told him, speaking honestly. "I've never eaten a better meal. Ben knows his work." If not his manners, she added to herself.

His eyes shone with pleasure. "He surely does, Miz Paula, but this meal's my doing, first to last."

"Yours?"

"First to last," he repeated.

"I am truly impressed. My compliments to the chef."

"I thank you kindly. Ben, he's the seafood man, and none better anywhere. Me, I got no touch for sea fruits. But such dishes as these, the meats and vegetables particularly, they're my specialty. I got to admit, pastry's a mite chancier, but today seems the ingredients did know 'twas for you. That's how I passed my afternoon, and I'm mighty glad you find 'twas time well spent. I left it all to Ben to tend while I was with you. Wouldn't trust it to no one else."

She noted his confidence — well-justified — that Ben would honor this meal and this occasion, despite his disapproval of her.

"Miz Paula," said Will in a rush, "I were thinking, since you find my cooking edible and my piano playing don't pain your ears, on top of which I didn't crash the plane, I'd be most honored to show you round the island tomorrow. We can pay our respects to the Lady, see something of her realm."

"That sounds good to me."

"Well, then, that's settled. So — tell me about yourself."

He had been alert to any drop in the level of wine in her glass. Distracted by her conflicting reactions to the man, her puzzlement about Ben, the strong impression made on her by the place on the water, she had given up keeping track of the amount she had drunk. Her febrile responsiveness to these many modalities of feeling told her it must have been more than was her habit. She found herself telling him of matters that remained unspoken for years, things much on her mind since she had made the decision, deep-rooted in her family and past, to come to Hawai'i. She talked about her father, about the Association, about her father's death and her reserved mother's retreat into deeper silence and an early death of her own.

"What's this Association you're speaking of?"

"The Forsythe-Windermere Neighborhood Association. Our neighborhood wasn't rich, but it wasn't impoverished either. When I was small it was East European, but about 1953 the realtors began to blockbust it, you know, sell a house to a Black family, panic the East European Whites, so they sold out cheap to the realtors and moved away to the suburbs. Then the buildings were subdivided and the rents went way up because Blacks were prevented from living in other neighborhoods. But in 1955 it was still transitional and actually quite integrated, with a lot of Black and Puerto Rican and Appalachian and Southern White families. Some very poor, most just not well off, you know, but holding it together. The kids had fights, but not like before, when the East European and Black gangs were going at it."

She stopped, shivering suddenly. "*Kamikaze!*" Her voice when she was a little girl rang startlingly clear in her memory. She drank and went on,

"Because in 1955 the situation hadn't hardened, you see. Things were in flux, it was a mixed community where all those people were getting along fairly well. If the city, and the University, had been interested in supporting it, the area could have become a kind of model for an integrated ordinary neighborhood."

She drank again, deeply, and went on. "But the powers that be had other plans. The University entered on a military operation. We got urban-removed. The University decided to clear everyone out and establish a perimeter at the Park that it could hold against the lesser breeds without the law, because when they'd gotten rid of them they could build upscale faculty housing and other expensive rental property for profit. So my father and his friend Jim Jordan — you remember, I mentioned him this afternoon, the Black graduate student at the University — they founded the Association to fight the urban removal. The FBI was always at our door. Well, the Association became one of the best-known organizations like it in the country. There've been books written about it, and training for organizers based on it, and in other places people have won following that model of organization. But the Association was the first, and we didn't win. It didn't work out."

"Life's a powerful hard thing to make work out, right enough. And sounds like this were a case Sam weren't going to let folks win if he could help it. First one sets a precedent. Ain't that what you lawyers say? What were your Daddy's place in all this, besides founding it?"

"He was a CPA, studying at night to be a lawyer. When the crunch came he'd just gotten his law degree. The Association didn't have any money. He took the case pro bono. It was his first one. He lost it and — other people — in the Association — blamed him. But what was worse was he blamed himself. When I was in law school I looked into the case. We lost on a minor technicality, that the judge could have taken either way. But we had no margin, you see. The fix was in. The University and the City weren't giving any quarter. And my father died."

The air shivered with the words. Will said quietly, "And you're your daddy's girl. You became a lawyer works with all kinds of folks in trouble, like he did. A lawyer for the people, you political folks say. People who can't pay. He were a lawyer before you; you're a lawyer after him."

"He's dead. He was hardly ever a lawyer at all. And I'm not a lawyer any more."

"And that's a right shame. All of it. But your folks left a lot behind with you."

"They didn't leave much. They didn't have much. My father left me a calabash. It's come down for several generations. It's old and beautiful, but it — it got broken. And my mother left me a teapot and a scroll and a photograph that I don't understand."

"Well, 'tis clear they left you passion and protest too. Your daddy, anyway. And someone left you a powerful gift in your fingers. I reckon that's from your mama?"

"What?"

Will nodded downward. Following his gaze, she saw that while she talked, her fingers had gone on with a life of their own, radically altering the design of the bouquet on the table. Petals and leaves were stripped and laid neatly aside on a saucer, so only two stems and one blossom remained, etched boldly against space. Four dark branches angled away from them, stark and eloquent.

Paula pulled her hands back as if they had walked into flame against her will.

"She taught me flower arranging," she allowed austerely. "I gave it up, though, a long time ago." The night her father died.

"Did you now. I reckon word didn't get through to your hands. Was that your mother's passion and protest?" He nodded again at the betraying arrangement, and further jarred Paula with this additional insight. But her surprise sufficed to deflect her annoyance and the underlying fear.

"Yes," she said slowly. "I think it was."

"A question of style then. And the irony of such a style, in that place and situation."

"Yes," she said again, and thought that this was an astonishing man in many ways.

She continued. "Anyway, the Association lost the case, the landlord evicted us and everyone else in the building so they could sell it to the University, and my mother and I went to live in San Francisco with her older sister and her husband. My mother had always wanted to go back there . . . my father absolutely refused. I was fourteen. Uncle Hiro was Japanese and — quite traditional. He and I butted heads for three years until I started college and moved into the dorm at Berkeley. My mother kept the books for his import-export firm in Japantown and except for going there she hardly left that house again until she died of the flu two months after I went to college."

Unlike most people, Will just nodded gravely, didn't express astonishment at such a mundane illness taking her. Now Paula knew that thousands of people a year died of it; but at the time she had been astonished, stunned. On Friday when she called her from the dorm, her mother complained of a headache, a cold. The following Thursday Aunt Florence had called to tell Paula her mother was dead of a raging pneumonia that had turned to a pericardial infection.

Still, Paula had always suspected that her mother succumbed because she didn't really want to live; that she had agreed to life just long enough to see her child out of childhood and on her way.

"So Chicago got your folks," said Will meditatively. "Sam in Chicago's a most powerful foe. I know that for myself."

"You lived in Chicago? When? Where?"

"I did. Not far from where you lived. From when I was six to when I was nine. Let's see, that would make it 1951 to 1954. Reckon your Daddy and that Association would've been fighting for me and my Little Mama too, had we been there still. You know the Windermere Gardens?"

"Of course."

His smile was sour.

"I can see you do, from your face. Well, 'twas rotten as your expression do tell, and worse."

"All I know is that the building caught on fire every year." She was untruthful in her defensiveness, embarrassed by the recoil he'd noticed at the thought of living there. She had heard all about the Windermere Gardens from her father. The huge apartment block had been the worst building in the Association's area, a notorious festering slum, and the Association had battled the City for years, trying to force the landlord to bring it up to code.

"Burned down like clockwork," agreed Will. "I were at home for the conflagration only once, though." He emptied his glass of Johnny Black at a swallow and refilled it to the brim. "Chicago's powerful cold. For some, war abroad in the harsh tropics is the worst of trials. But for me, ain't no crueller killing ground, body, heart and soul, than some folks' lives in a Chicago winter. 'Tis the war at home for true." He drank and poured to the brim again.

Paula gave this assessment all the weight it was due, coming as it did from a man she was certain had done hard time in Vietnam.

"So what brings you here now," he asked, " for the first time, just at this time in your life?"

"I lost a client."

"Well, now, pardon me, Miz Paula, but that don't seem like something to throw over your work about — one client not having the sense to appreciate you."

"I didn't lose him that way. He killed himself — because I — asked him hard things one time too many, and didn't say the right thing at all. His whole family had been tortured and murdered in front of him, and he'd been tortured — but survived. I had to get details. Everything had to be documented — with details. It isn't easy to win political asylum now, not for a Socialist labor organizer from Central America."

"Ah," said Will. "He had to remember so you could get him a future, and the past got him instead. That's different than I thought, right enough. And I can see 'twould be a hard blow for true, for someone conscientious-like, the way you are. Still, I got to say, though such a thing is terrible enough, yet to my way of thinking there's neither shame nor blame in it, for him or for you. You ain't to blame if a grown man decides he's had enough. And that decision's each man's own."

"Maybe." She emptied her glass, refilled it herself. "But I pushed him to speak."

"I think you're taking more on yourself than's rightly yours. Maybe even being a bit egotistical, Miz Paula."

"Maybe," she said again, and drained half her glass. "I — I'm not good with speaking and silence. My parents were big on silence, then my father broke it at the end, then he died, and my mother was — triumphant about it. It proved her right — that breaking silence brings disaster. Maybe she was right. She went into silence until she died."

Her glass, mysteriously, was full again, and again she drank, hurriedly. Pale jeweled drops spilled on the crimson linen. Her own voice, brittle and scattered like shards of broken glass, scared her as she said,

"So those are your views on suicide. Are you tolerant of *hara-kiri*, too?"

Hatred and challenge and hope struggled in her tone. She wondered what she was doing, and whether Will heard the dangerous complex edge.

"'Twere that for real, your daddy's dying? *Harakiri?*"

"Some said it was *harakiri*. I think he was a *kamikaze* pilot."

"Well, the both of them's rooted deep in a deep culture that's most different from the American. I wouldn't've thought American folks of Japanese blood would necessarily have looked at the world so. Still I reckon it could come down taught through the generations."

"Many credits to you." She squinted. Objects were growing blurry. "You don't automatically think Japanese-American is the same as Japanese." Classically North Asian, she thought, and pushed away the memory. "I bet you could even tell me what a No-No Boy was."

"You'd win your bet. Your Daddy was a No-No Boy?"

Paula nodded, proud, and said, "You know a lot about matters Japanese, and Japanese-American."

"Well, as I told you, I seen a good deal of the islands in these seas, and I have also spent some time in Japan. Elsewhere, I have had business dealings with folks born in Japan and with other folks of Japanese blood born other places. Fact is, near half of all the folks on this island are of Japanese blood. As for *harakiri* and *kamikaze*, though, I'm no expert. Some would've said it was a form of *kamikaze* to be in business with me at all; and the only attempted deaths involved in those dealings, I'm sorry to say, was with knives pointed at me. And, I'm also sorry to say, not without provocation. But 'tweren't *kamikaze* nor *hara-kiri* on their minds, I don't reckon, just revenge. And telling you this is right honorable of me, since it sure don't put me in a good light as a businessman not to get along with my partners no better'n that. So," he said reflectively, "your daddy grew up in the islands."

"Yes." She paused, stared straight ahead, and suddenly recited something in Japanese. Will laughed.

"To see your face now, Miz Paula! What surprises you so?"

"I don't know where that came from, after all these years."

"I reckon it comes from your daddy, like your flower arranging do from your mama. And I reckon it came to him from his time on the plantation." He translated her words:

We came to this place seeking a better life
But life here is sho-nuff hard
The canefields are hell
And the luna is the devil.

'Luna' is Hawaiian for overseer, you know, or paterroller, as Euph might've called such folks for the resemblance to the drivers on plantations back in slavery times. My version's got a touch of Starvesoil Black folks' talk to it, but it catches the spirit right enough."

"You know Japanese?" She was surprised, then recalled how well he had pronounced her name when they met.

"Passably. And you do? Your translating work's with Japanese?"

"Most of it, yes."

"So your daddy was a plantation boy."

"It was a hard life," she said, subdued with alarm at the sudden escape of her fingers and her tongue. "But my father was proud of the union movement his relatives were involved in. And he had friends, and solidarity. I think he felt at home, even happy there, hard as life was, and I don't think he ever felt that way again except for the time the Association was working — before it all collapsed. So I came here when things — collapsed — for me."

Will raised his glass. "May you be happy here too, then, like your daddy before you. And now that we've finished this meal, do you come with me to Euph's, where the people will be gathering now. Perhaps you'll find good days again, like those at the Black Star."

He picked up the vase with her flower arrangement and ushered her through the folding doors and the rustling kukui-nut curtain.

6

A Certain Smile

The rain had stopped, though clouds moved skittishly across the moon. Lights glowed from the louvered windows of Euph's, and the gravel parking area was two-thirds full of vehicles, mostly battered pickups.

A boy in his late teens appeared under the front light and called something in Hawaiian English too rapid for Paula to understand.

"They need a hand inside with the equipment," Will told her.

"You go on. If you're setting up, you don't need an audience. I'll walk around out here." She could use a few minutes to collect herself.

As Will disappeared through the main door of Euph's, Paula heard intermittently from somewhere near, dictated by the shifting breeze, the sound of Hawaiian drums.

The breeze shifted again and she heard a man's formal chanting. Rhythmic dancing sticks honored by imitation the sound of bamboo stalks clacking against each other. She had first heard the sound hiking high in the Koolaus above Honolulu. There the bamboos grew wider than her doubled handspan, and when the Trade Winds rushed through the upper peaks the whole forest sang in concert with them.

She walked around to the back of Euph's, pulled by the rhythm of the drums and dancing sticks, and saw between the rear wall of the building and the edge of the water a lānai, surrounded by bananas and coconut palms and sheltered overhead by a wooden frame bower loaded with bougainvillea. The space was dramatically illuminated by the flare of two Hawaiian torches fixed in the ground at each end of the lānai.

Several shadowy figures sat in a semi-circle around their spherical gourd instruments. A girl stood before them, a silhouette figure in flaring raffia skirt and bushy lei. As Paula watched, a luminous guitar sang out suddenly like a fall of silver from the moon overhead, supporting the soar of the girl's mele, and her fluid dancing.

Paula stepped back into the darkness out of sight, to avoid distracting them.

A boy's voice muttered something roughly, and the mele's aching falsetto skidded out of balance, tangling in a ripping guitar twang. Music disintegrated into a clash of young male and female voices. Again, she was unable to follow the Hawaiian English; but the slashing emotional discord was unmistakable.

The seated figures jumped up, facing each other confrontationally. One peeled away and stamped around the far side of the building. The others argued a moment longer, then followed, all but the girl and one boy. The girl stood, her lips pressed tight, fighting tears Paula thought, while the boy extinguished the torches. Then they went away together in the dark.

Paula remained where she was, desolated out of all proportion to her involvement with the scene, knowing that the incident had stirred memories of similar episodes in her life that she did not wish to recover.

A figure materialized beside her in the darkness, and she jumped.

"You're from Honolulu," said Ben.

"I live there, yes." She felt herself disorganized by his appearance, by the rancorous collapse she had just witnessed, of a little circle seeking to create concert.

"Will don't like Honolulu. He don't like cities. Oh, he's been in enough," Ben added quickly, as if Paula had accused Will of being countrified. "Bigger ones than Honolulu. He don't like them."

"Well," she replied warily, "there are good reasons for not liking cities."

He gave her a sharp look, as if not sure whether the remark were as neutral as it seemed.

"It ain't just that he don't like them. They're no good for him. They give him a soul-sickness. A self-losing sickness. Cities ain't no good at all for Will."

His hostility towards her was palpable. He might as well have added aloud, "And neither are you." Yet oddly she also had the impression that he was pleading with her.

Deeply uncomfortable, she said, recognizing the awkward inanity of her words, "I hope he gets over it soon," then, "excuse me, please."

She stepped around him and went quickly through the back door into the rear corridor of Euph's.

She could hear a muffled hubbub from beyond the closed door down the hall that led into the main room of Euph's. Immediately to her right, she saw now, was a public restroom. She went in and rinsed her face and the back of her neck with cold water, trying to restore her sense of control.

A woman entered behind her. She was in her forties, of middle height, hefty, with hair assisted in being relentlessly auburn, and features that were hard but, like her shrewd dull-greenish eyes, not unkind. Paula thought she was White until she moved forward and the shift in light pointed up an unusual brown-yellow tone to her skin.

"Hello," said the woman. "I'm Cora Dugan. I work with Emma Miller, Ben's wife. You're Paula Kajiyama. From Honolulu." It was a statement, not a question; she didn't need the affirmative nod Paula gave her. She spoke with a slight island accent, like others Paula had heard.

Cora Dugan took up a position beside her at the mirror and snapped open a cosmetics case.

"Have you known Will long?" she inquired.

"About ten hours," replied Paula dryly, fishing a comb from her purse.

"Mmm." Cora was working on her lipstick. "Will travels a lot on business. I know he goes to Honolulu sometimes. I thought maybe you knew him from there."

"No."

"Well, you're the first lady he's ever brought around, from on or off-island. Lots of people come to Euph's and the Pine Tar — well, Will's friends come to Euph's, mostly. But you're the first lady he's ever invited as a guest. Can't blame us for being curious." She laughed with such frank good humor that Paula laughed too.

"I can understand being curious."

"Anyway, looks like you passed. Emma approves."

Paula wondered on what basis Emma approved of her. Certainly not on her husband's view, she reflected, and her sense of unreality, of being off balance, increased.

"Will's an institution here, you know," Cora went on. "Euph's is a place for all kinds of people to come, and have a good time, but no rough stuff. A place where ladies can go without being bothered. He's most particular about that, and he's a man I'd guess has spent his share of time in the other kind of place. He's good for the young people too. They're always welcome at Euph's, to practice music, dance, or just hang around like young people need to do, shoot some pool or something. No harm in it. And he lets their bands perform for customers. One group even went on to make records. My son played guitar here with a band when he was in high school. Have you heard Will play piano?" Paula nodded. "He's really good, isn't he?"

"He certainly is." A genius of some kind.

"Do you have children?"

"No."

"I've got three. Two daughters and my boy. He's in college on the Mainland now," she said proudly. "At Washington State. Will's like — a host

— for everyone who comes to Euph's. No one here knows much about Will's past, not even Emma, I don't think." Paula felt confirmed in her suspicion that Cora's curiosity extended not only to Paula but to anything she might be privy to about Will. "Nor about Ben's past, for that matter," Cora went on. "Ben's steady, a real family man. Emma's made a good match there. Now, Ben knows about Will, he came with him, but Ben's not talking. If you watch a man for fifteen years, though, you know whether you want him in your community or not. And I'm glad Will's here. Still," she said, narrowing the green eyes and confirming Paula's impression that she was shrewd, "it's a fact, he doesn't let much slip or show. And when Will gets a certain smile, a person understands right away why there's no trouble at Euph's. I wouldn't want that smile turned on me."

Night had come and Euph's was alive. Unexpectedly, Paula felt as if she had been transported back through the years to the Black Star. The sense of homecoming was swiftly followed by the brush of cold fingers warning of paralyzing grief lying in wait for her in memories of her childhood. She pushed all these emotions down and stepped into the ambiance she knew so well, a night place, a neighborhood place, welcoming its people, and drawing life from them as it sustained them. Jeremy was pouring drinks. Ben glided back and forth between the bar and the small rear kitchen, supplying the tables with baskets of crisp taro chips and little dishes of spicy dip. The dim smoky atmosphere was kept from offensiveness by the constant breeze that removed most of the odor but somehow left a softening haze.

In front of the piano, lights and stands had been set up for two guitars and a drum. Will knelt beside one of the lights, giving a final adjustment to a wire and a plug, greeting people by name as they entered, calling out, joking, laughing. Unlike the Pine Tar's patrons, this crowd was only sprinkled with a few haoles, and consisted mostly of casually-clad men and women clearly of various mixed Asian and Pacific Island ancestries. But as with Ben, Paula was unsure of peoples' origins. The overlap of racial and ethnic backgrounds had shifted slightly but definitely from the mix she was familiar with in California.

Will looked up and caught sight of her, and she braced herself against the pleasure that sprang into his eyes; still more against the way she was drawn by it despite her deep misgivings.

He came to her and led her to a table towards the rear. Discomfort gripped her under the eyes of people watching because Will was escorting her.

"I recognize a proprietor's table," she said with forced lightness, "from my days at the Black Star."

A woman sat there, placidly pouring beer from a bottle of Budweiser into a glass. She was about fifty, heavy-set, with the squared face and wide lower cheeks that Paula had come to recognize as characteristically Hawaiian. Black gray-streaked hair foamed down her back, caught at the nape by a green plastic barrette. She wore a green-and-turquoise print dress and sandals, and she regarded Paula now from enormous luminous brown eyes that were nevertheless almost expressionless, by design Paula was sure.

"Emma," said Will, "please to meet Paula, who I told you about earlier today. Paula, Emma's Ben's wife, Emma Miller."

"How do you do," said Paula. She did not extend her hand this time. Despite Cora's assurance, she did not propose to risk the rebuff this woman's husband had visited upon her. Paula had the sudden idea that Emma had stationed herself at the table expressly to meet her and look her over.

The woman remained a moment longer, not looking directly at Paula, but Paula was nevertheless certain that her attention was on her. Then she gave an almost imperceptible nod, rising as she did so and gathering her bottle and glass into large square hands with blunt scarlet nails. Emma approves of you, Cora Dugan had told her. Was this what the nod signified? To whom? To her? To Will? Or did it indicate some internal confirmation?

"I got to go help Ben in the back," she said, gestured at the table, and concluded, "sit down, the show's gonna begin soon," and went away.

Paula sat, unnerved by the succession of strange encounters the past half hour had brought her. She was beginning to register that she had been the main topic of conversation in this community for the entire afternoon.

By unspoken agreement, it seemed, the clientele had cut a magical space of privacy around the proprietor's table. Will poured her a flute of champagne and himself a glass of Johnny Black.

Three boys of about seventeen began to play "Eleanor Rigby" with a soft syncopation.

"They're experimenting with the Beatles and local rhythm," said Will. "Don't know how far it'll take them, but it might take them somewhere else after that. Hard to say."

"Who was the group practicing behind the building earlier?"

"Oh, that would be the Princess's dance troupe. Our Pearlie's, I'm meaning — Pearlie Forrest, she's Emma's niece, lives with Ben and Emma, and she's writing and choreographing the piece. She calls it "A Chant for All the Islands." She's mighty talented, that little girl."

Paula noted the warmth and pride with which he spoke of her, and also that he spoke as if she were a child, although from what she had seen Pearlie must be at least in her mid-teens.

Will drank.

"Paula Y.," he mused. "That's how you gave your name to my dispatcher when you arranged the flight. Might I take a guess on what the 'Y' stands for?"

"Go ahead."

"Well, I never yet did know a person of Japanese blood from the Mainland who didn't have a Japanese middle name. I'm not saying it couldn't be," he assured her with mock earnestness, "I just ain't never come across it in my travels." And seeing as you're a lady — anyway, not a gentleman —" he grinned "— it's not gonna be 'Yukio' or 'Yunichiro.' So taking all that into account, which means putting aside 'Yolanda' and 'Yvonne,' I reckon 'Yumi's' a right good bet. Specially since even more'n those good reasons, you just do seem like a 'Yumi' to me. Beautiful and gentle."

His guess was not so surprising, certainly not enough to account for the jolt she felt, as if once again she had been viewed without her knowing, or viewed better than she knew. She had felt this, crazily, gazing at Euph's portrait, and with Emma and Cora, with Ben too somehow, and also with the way Will had approached her at the pool table in the Maui airport without her hearing him. She wrapped herself in light sarcasm.

"Flatterer. Actually, you're right that it's 'Yumi.'"

"No flattery. Oh, I ain't saying I'd want to come up against you in court, no more'n at the pool table. I reckon when you're working or when you're riled, you kind of put the gentleness aside. But it's there right enough, alongside the beauty." He made a mock bow, complicating any rejection of the compliment. "And may I call you that? Yumi? Paula's a good name, but Yumi do suit you something special."

She wanted to refuse. No one but her father had ever called her Yumi, and when Will spoke, the sound of her name sang out like the ring she had just struck accidentally against the fine crystal wine glass, and seemed to fill a loved space long abandoned.

"Looks like you're about where I was a while ago, talking about Euph and Hibbits. As if you're back someplace that mattered so-much and yet you've put aside-like, not spoke or thought of directly in so-long."

"A loved space long abandoned," whispered Paula to herself, and knew that the wine and the sound of her long-lost name singing in her ears, these beautiful islands that were still strange to her, where her father had been born and that he had loved, this enigmatic and disturbing man and the place he had built and the people around him, were conspiring with the upset of the last six months to shake her from her usual reserve. A sense of danger shivered along her spine, yet all these things seduced her too.

"Yes," she said. "Call me Yumi."

"I'm honored," said Will simply.

They sat, mostly silent, absorbed in the music; the band turned out to be surprisingly good.

They took a break after an hour, and suddenly a voice, angry and loud, cut through the convivial laughter and conversation. At the other end of the room, Jeremy stumbled back and banged against the bar.

The man who had shoved him was big with longish dirty-blond hair. He wore a sleeveless red T-shirt. Blue tattoos moved on his muscled biceps as he traveled in towards the younger man, now struggling to stand upright.

Paula didn't see Will move, but then he was in front of the man, who halted at the big unexpected presence.

She couldn't make out Will's words, but his tone was easy, genial. His hands were loose at his sides.

The man's angry voice rose again, and he leaned forward.

Will looked straight at him and smiled.

It was kin to the smile Paula had seen that morning at the airfield at Volcano. The smile Cora had spoken of: the smile that assured there was no trouble at Euph's.

The man averted his eyes. He seemed palpably to shrivel. He backed up to his table and sat down, subsiding over his drink. After a moment the people in the room resumed conversation. Laughter rose. Will drifted back toward Paula and their table.

When she glanced towards the place where the troublemaker had been sitting, he was no longer there.

Will loomed over her.

Suddenly she had had enough of this man and this bizarre lovely place, of the shuttered and flaring passions she sensed among the people here but did not understand, and of the ones he stirred in her and which she did not understand either.

"I'm very tired," she said. "I'd like to go back to the hotel now."

He assessed her with a glance.

"It's been a right long day," he agreed. "And you'll be my guest for it all? The flight, dinner of course."

She hesitated, then said, "Yes. Thank you. And the dinner was all you said it would be."

"I'm most pleased it pleased you."

As she rose, she caught sight of the embrasure behind the piano that contained the photograph of Euph, and saw, with another surge of disproportionate disturbance, that he had set before it the vase containing her unconsciously created flower arrangement.

Outside they sat in the Jeep a moment.

"Would seven be too early to start tomorrow?" he asked. "It's good to get moving in the fresh of the day. I could pick you up then."

"Seven's fine, but I'll walk over. I'd enjoy that."

"If you're sure."

"I am. I'll be at Euph's at seven."

Will sat on. This was the moment where conventionally she might expect an attempted embrace. But she sensed that that was not where he was involved just then with regard to the two of them.

He looked around, his big arm loose across the steering wheel, surveying his domain.

The moonlight silvered the water. The Pine Tar was dark. Bars of yellow light glowed in bars through the louvers at Euph's, nestled among the palms, bananas and banyans. The clink of glasses and the weave of voices and laughter and music floated to them through the soft black night.

"Yeah," Will said suddenly, and repeated his words spoken earlier, that afternoon in Euph's. "This is my place. My place. Here, I don't have to pay."

7

Trouble In Paradise

The next morning Paula walked through clear light to the place on the water. By the time she arrived, the dull ache in her head from the wine the previous evening had almost disappeared.

She paused a moment, looking at the buildings, watching the lapping of gentle waves and the tossing hibiscus and palm fronds. The scenery and her mood were both open, uncomplicated, and light, very different from the scenery and the mood of the night before.

The front door to Euph's stood ajar. Stepping inside, she saw that the place had undergone another of its metamorphoses. It was neither the shadowed, almost mystical space she had first seen, nor the place alive and magical with community a few hours later. Now the big room was empty, but in the dappled light entering through the open louvers evidence was everywhere of recent group activity different from last night's preoccupations. Chairs and tables had been pushed back along the wall. Squares of posterboard lay angled across the floor, some already boldly lettered with slogans in green and orange, yellow and black. Claim and protect the Hawaiian Homeland . . . the forest. Kanaka maoli . . . 'Ohana . . . Aloha 'ohana . . . Aloha 'aina . . . Hawai'i for the Hawaiians . . . We Remember Our Beloved Queen Lili'uokalani . . .

In the still heat of the room, odors of paint mingled with the smell of fresh water from the lagoon, and with hints of plumeria drifting and then disappearing like an olfactory mirage. In a corner a pile of laths lay ready to be stapled to the signs.

A wave of complex emotions — a rush of adrenalin, urgency, dread, anticipation, grief, exultation and exaltation — surged over Paula, as if she were stepping back into a central scene of her life. She was seized by the excitement and intensity of positions argued at white heat among comrades when danger threatened everyone, by the fear of physical and emotional damage they risked incurring in imminent confrontation. And she was seized by the contradictory grip of pride in courage and solidarity in the face of those dangers, and the corrosive suspicion of hidden betrayal; by pride in loyalty that so often didn't break when it might well have, and the desolation, unlike any other, of betrayal, when, sometimes, stunningly, loyalty did break. All this overwhelmed her and she beat the feelings back. Right now she couldn't afford the bonds of that lifelong involvement. Yet it was her life lived. To deny it in the past was self-obliteration; to deny it in the present was to be only half alive.

The breeze shifted slightly and brought to her with sudden clarity the sound of clucking chickens in the run between Euph's and the Pine Tar.

And then it brought her, not loudly but so unmistakably that she wondered at not having heard it before, the sound of a girl singing a Hawaiian melody.

Strangely compelled and touched, she picked her way across the signs on the floor. Through the louvers, she saw the girl of the rear lānai the night before — Will's "our Pearlie." She too had undergone a metamorphosis; raffia skirt and lei were replaced by a yellow short-sleeved cotton blouse and blue jeans, though a cluster of yellow plumeria in her hair provided a touch of continuity. She was seated on the floor of the side lānai, like the larger rear lānai also overhung by salmon bougainvillea, stitching up the hem of a large banner cut from thick white cloth. It bore words painted in red and green but it fell in folds across Pearlie's lap and Paula could not make them out.

Pearlie was having a little difficulty with both the sewing and the song. At intervals, for one reason or another, both singing and stitching would stop while she shifted her head, the yellow blossom brushing her cheek, as she worked her way out of a hitch with one or the other.

Paula had heard the melody before. Her first introduction to Hawaiian music had been to the saccharine and commercial. Time had been required before she came to appreciate its complexity and subtlety. Now, listening to Pearlie singing, it reminded her again, in Will's words, of the structure of the sea, at once repetitious in its movements and vastly and minutely varied, charged by oblique running lines of light and melody like oceanic crosscurrents. Listening to the girl, she was struck, however, for the first time by the resources the consonants of Hawaiian constituted. Its prominent 'p's' and 'k's' caught the vowel-flow of song to redirect and weave it into a garment of sound and light. She wondered if the language fell that way on the ears of those who understood it well.

Alone, absorbed in work and song, Pearlie was completely unself-conscious, and suddenly that made her seem vulnerable and made Paula feel stealthy and deceptive. She went outside and cleared her throat as she approached, saying too heartily,

"Hello. I'm Paula Kajiyama. Is Will Cawdry around? He's expecting me."

The girl jumped and she added, "I'm sorry, I didn't mean to startle you."

Standing, Pearlie brushed hair out of her eyes, setting the yellow plumeria nodding. She was not heavy but stockily built, with a cloud of frizzy hair, walnut skin, and startling light-green eyes, and the distinctive Hawaiian legs Paula found so esthetically appealing: short, full-calved, the rear line cut sharp and clean as a canoe's prow, radiating rootedness and strength.

"Oh, hello, Will said to tell you he's gone to put gas in the Jeep. He'll be back in a few minutes." She paused, and said a little shyly,

"I'm Pearlie Forrest. Will said you're a lawyer for your people."

Paula had said 'lawyer for the people', and Will had understood that, but Pearlie's understanding was true if not exhaustive — Paula had fought for Japantown housing, for Ethnic Studies — so she answered,

"Yes. For other people too I hope. But I did a lot of work around Japanese-American issues."

"Maybe I'd like to be a lawyer."

"It can be a useful occupation. So is what you're doing. Will says you're working on a performance piece." She wondered if the question were tactless, given the dissension she had overheard the night before.

"Yes. It's a chant for all the islands. I'm dedicating it to Will, because he encouraged me and helped me with the musical ideas. That's what I'd really like my work and my whole life to be — a chant for all the islands."

She spoke with the same unself-consciousness and unpretentiousness that she had displayed unobserved, of a kind found only, and only sometimes, among children. She was truly, thought Paula, in the very middle of adolescence.

The beautiful phrase, the beautiful idea, struck Paula powerfully. She smiled. "If you can be that, I wouldn't give it up for the law. Will said you lived near San Francisco for awhile?"

"In Fremont. With my Auntie Edith. Before I came here to Auntie Emma. I wanted to come back. It's kind of exciting there. But scary too. Too big and fast, dangerous. And people kept thinking I was Chicana or Black, and I'm not, you know, I'm Hawaiian. The place didn't mean anything to me inside, it wasn't here — Hawai'i nei."

Paula found the girl very attractive, with her lively intelligence, her open, seemingly unprotected, personality, that reached out so readily even upon first meeting. This vulnerability made Paula fear for her, too. Yet she also sensed, at odds with her other impression, a deep place in Pearlie where she curled protectively over anger and hurt.

"Morning to you both."

Will was beside them. Unnervingly, he had crossed without a sound the crunchy 'a'ā or volcanic rubble that made up the parking area.

He dropped a hand on Pearlie's shoulder, and Pearlie's went up to meet it. Their fingers interlaced. Paula felt a complex pang at this unguarded intimacy: fear for their vulnerability, surprise at this chink in Will's armor, and a wave of longing and inexplicable nostalgia. "Well, Princess, how're the poster signs coming along? Miz Kajiyama giving you any pointers from her vast experience fomenting riot and civil disorder?"

Paula laughed. "I don't think the people who made those signs in there need pointers."

"Well, you two have other points of mutual interest, too. Princess, did Miz Kajiyama tell you about her calabash? Sounds like a right fine one, that's come down in her family, plugged more than once, and needing repair again."

Interest sparked in the girl's eyes.

"Really? Maybe I could help you, if you like," she said shyly. "I know a little. If Auntie Lydia agrees."

"The Princess here is an expert. She's learning all the old crafts. Auntie Lydia accepted her as a student, and she only takes the most promising," Will announced proudly.

Pearlie contradicted, with an odd childlike dignity,

"I'm not an expert. Auntie Lydia's an expert, and it's true she thinks I have ability. And I have learned a little."

"It's very generous of you to offer." Paula wondered why they spoke as if the occasion would certainly arise, as if when she left that evening she would certainly return.

"Now, Miz Kajiayama and me'd best be going, we have a lot of ground to cover today."

"Goodbye, Miz Kajiyama."

"Please, call me Paula."

"Okay — Paula. I hope you and Will have a good time."

They took the way back to town, heading for the Volcano Road.

"I heard some of the rehearsal Pearlie's dance troupe was doing last night on the back lānai while you were setting up inside."

"Did you now? The girl's dedicating it to me, did you know?" Will's pleasure was palpable.

"Yes, she told me. She said you had encouraged her and helped her a lot with the music. The performance was very impressive. On the lānai last night, though, it sounded like the group was having a major disagreement."

He sobered. "I wouldn't be surprised. There's pilikia — trouble — here in Paradise, for true. Hawaiian folks has heavy matters to decide. Some in Pearlie's group of friends, in her troupe too, want only instruments and forms of performance as was here before the haoles. Some wants only folks in the land as was here before the haoles. Others are willing to expand both boundaries a little."

Paula's stomach lurched with memories of old struggles, of schism and collapse.

"I kin see," Will said briefly, "Hawaiians got no cause to love haoles. Now, we turn just here to get to the place I want to show you first. 'Twas me named her 'Princess', you know," he reverted unsequentially to his previous topic. "Let's see, she's sixteen now, that must have been one, two months after she come to Ben and Emma — she were nine then. It didn't work out for her on the Mainland with her Auntie Edith, she's sister to Pearlie's mother and to Emma. Auntie Edith pushed for her to come, to get better schooling she said. But like a sensible person Pearlie wanted to be back in the islands. When she came, 'twere summertime, no school, Emma at work all day, and Pearlie were moping around blue about all the sadness and change in her life. She started tagging along to the Pine Tar with Ben, and I put her to work with the kitchen crew carrying out trash and sweeping up." He laughed. "'Twere flat-out exploitation of child labor, I reckon, but she had the time of her life, pleased as punch to be helping run the restaurant. She were the most reliable member of the crew, too, as I told her, the others being teenagers and having other things on their minds. Anyhow, I promoted her to Chief Waiter in Charge of Breadbaskets at Lunch.

"So one day she takes this Mainlander-woman and her husband a basket and the woman asks her what her name is, all fake-sweet like, then says to her husband, 'Isn't it amazing what these people will call their children?' I happened to overhear, and Pearlie and me were so incensed that I gave her a lesson in how to discourage low-class guests like those folks, which is as important in running a first-rate restaurant as figuring out how to get ree-fined people to come back.

"Well, you know Cawdrys is subject to fits. 'Twere plumb bad luck one come on me so's I spilled a pitcher of icewater all over their laps.

"Pearlie and me had a good laugh in the kitchen." He laughed again, remembering. "I told her that down to Hibbits, 'Pearlie' was a name for princesses, just like pearls was for princesses, and both name and pearl suited her, that she was a princess for true. That's the only time I recollect ever voluntarily identifying myself with my place of birth, but 'twas an emergency situation. She asked me was Hibbits on this island, or on some other island, and I told her 'tweren't on an island at all, excepting as all lands are islands if you look at maps in a certain way. We pulled out an atlas to find Hibbits — well, somewhere kinda near, Hibbits ain't on no map nowhere — and see how all lands are islands. Then she says, 'Don't you miss your 'ohana?' 'Ohana means family, y'know. 'Don't have no 'ohana there to miss,' I told her, not tellin' her, 'cause it's not the sort of thing you tell a child, that I wouldn't miss my Uncle Bert if I did, even were he still aboveground. 'Well,' she says, all serious, 'you have this place, and you have us. We're you're 'ohana now.' And I told her I sure got the better part of that deal. And now," he turned the conversation and the Jeep simultaneously, "let me show you something of Pele's realms, here at the Sacred Mountain."

Deep in the forest on the slopes of Mauna Loa, the visible world was only a few feet wide. Nourished by gloom, crowding the interlocking branches of the 'ōhi'a trees, gigantic rust-colored ferns erected monstrous fiddleheads like cobras. Their tiny offspring clawed at ankles, their dead loomed all around, like cast insect skeletons, supported by the massed undergrowth. Untouched, they poised indefinitely on the brink of disintegration. Paula brushed against one: exquisitely fragile, it crumbled to gray-brown dust.

She and Will climbed with the intent silence of those in a place where the pacing of a step can mean the difference between living and falling to disaster.

"Are there animals to watch out for? Snakes?"

"Naw, nothing, not in the daytime, not here. Higher up, there's wild boars. No snakes anywhere." He grinned. "One of the many things these islands have going for them."

"I'll stay out of their way, but I'm not phobic about them. Spiders bother me more."

"Not too many spiders here either. One kind we got's found no place else. Now snakes — reckon might could be I am phobic about snakes, at that. But then," he said cryptically, "I don't suppose you've had quite the relationship with them I have had. Watch your step, now, just along here. 'Tis falling to be feared, not critters."

Gradually the path leveled out. Paula paused by a deep crevice in the moist soil, half-hidden by undergrowth, from which smoke seemed to be rising into the air. She reached towards it. The air around the opening was very warm. Will caught her wrist, then dropped it at once, as if shying from the contact.

The wind that played perpetually, low around the ground, made one of its unpredictable turns, and a blast of vapor scalded her. She jerked away, coughing as sulphur fumes tangled in her throat.

"'Tis the Lady's breath," said Will. "And the way into her body."

8

The Lava Wastes

"The Lava Wastes," said Will.

They had wandered to a far fantastic place, built to a mighty scale and over a vast epochal span, without any sign of life. Massive schismed blocks of upturned black-brown rock rose higher than Will's head, stretching for miles.

The lava had poured down as molten metal and mineral, shot with rust and gray, gold and green, then hardened in huge intricate loops and whorls. The blocks of rock were riven with chasms almost invisible in shadow, ready to catch and snap an ankle, to betray seeming solidity and to collapse at a touch. Pāhoehoe, the whorls of hardened lava, that had looked so smooth at a distance, proved to be covered with a skin of 'a'ā rubble that skidded dangerously underfoot.

She had never seen anything similar. This seemed to her the most ancient landscape imaginable, the landscape of the planet's birth. Yet she realized that paradoxically here on this living fiery earth it was also its youngest landscape, as if the process of continuous birthing collapsed time in on itself so that it became a black hole dense with space and matter.

"I was born on the lava wastes. But they aren't like these."

"For true? Where would that be?"

"Northeastern California. Near where the Modoc people took their last stand against the U.S. Cavalry. They held out in those lava fortresses for a year and a half." She paused, then added, "I was born in an internment camp. Tule Lake."

"'Twas a shameful thing, those camps."

He spoke composedly, yet she believed the intensity in his words.

"Yes. I went back once. The land there didn't seem like this. It seemed — sterile. Even though more grows there than here. It's potato country."

"This don't seem sterile to you?"

"No. Not sterile. Not barren." She thought a moment. "It's just — not productive yet. It feels — latent. Full of potential."

"'Tis a difference, all right. And look just here."

For a moment she thought her own reflections on the lava waste's potential had conjured up a mirage. But at her toes, apparently rooted in solid rock, a tiny fern danced in the wind, the same kind as the giants that she had encountered so recently in the forest.

"'Tis most wonderful. See out there, those green patches, not the shiny ones, but the ones almost like scales? That's lichen growth. Turns the rock to soil. This whole landscape, 'tis a future of ferns and lichens."

They mounted a ridge. Low-growing bushes carrying small red berries began to dot the forbidding rock, dipping in the breeze and the movement of the fumes from the solfataras.

"Oheleberries. By tradition, they are sacred to the Lady. I do never touch them out here — I leave them for the nēnēbirds, who she is willing to share them with. But other places I eat them and I have some planted at the house I am building in the forest. They are sweet and tart at once. Take heed!"

At his cry, she pulled back the hand she had spread to gain a grip.

"'Tis the Lady's hair."

"This?" It could have been a puff of blown black plant down.

"Yes. Pele's Hair, it's called. Looks like your hair, matter of fact; this whole realm of the Lady's does speak to me of you, one way and another, sweet-tart oheleberries, flame, and all." He grinned. "But if you touched it, it'd cut you like razorgrass, like boar tusk. 'Tis volcanic glass, my drinking buddy Mike at the Observatory tells me. And these here — " he pointed to two tiny pear-shaped pebbles. "Pele's Tears. Which do resemble your eyes."

She stared at the strange forms of bonded earth and fire. "Pele's Hair": a tangle that lacerated flesh. "Pele's Tears": grief made manifest in lava gems like onyx.

Carefully, Will gathered Pele's Hair and Pele's Tears into a leather pouch he drew from his waistpack, and tucked them away.

"'Tisn't common to see them in this kind of terrain. 'Tis a sign, I think. From the Lady. Because you have come here today, with me."

Paula could not decide if he was joking.

"And here we are, the place we were aiming for. Halem'aum'au. Where the Lady lives now."

They stood at the brink of a crater, in the center of the caldera floor.

Far away, marring the vast emptiness, she saw the thin dry scar of a road. A lone automobile, tiny in the somber expanse, was just disappearing down it.

Will removed a pineapple and a papaya from his pack and handed her the pineapple.

She remembered the flowers she had left amongst the barbed wire at the ruins of the camp at Tule Lake. For her parents and for herself, for all the ones who had come out of that place. For her great-grandfather, her father's grandfather, who had died there, and all the others who had never come out. For the living and the dead: descendants and ancestors.

They set the fruit at the smoking rim, near but not among the other offerings, and went away.

They hiked out across the flats and began the climb back up the caldera wall.

A volcanic eruption had shaken loose a huge block of mountain, scraping and scouring the vegetation for a quarter mile along the sides, hurling a mass of shattered rock to the cliff base below the wound made by its passage.

"The Lady's doing," said Will. "She gets riled. Sometimes those that feels it aren't the ones did the riling. A lot like life in general, that way. We'd best be getting back to the rim. The fog'll be coming faster than before. We don't want to try to climb out of here through that."

Paula saw that where ten minutes earlier the sky had been clear, wisps of gray were descending. Learning the ebb and flow of the fog here would be like learning the pattern of the tide along a specific shore.

They retraced their steps, Will never for a moment inattentive to the changing, silent weather high above them, dropping massively from the caldera rim.

The Lodge was perched at the edge of Halem'aum'au Crater. Paula stared through the window at a ghostly scene. Fog shrouded a forbidding landscape only half-visible now. It seemed inconceivable that not half an hour before she and Will had wandered there. No one would suspect the existence of the colossal sheer drop from the rim into Kilauea, only a few feet beyond the glass. A stumble, a fall. What lay beyond the window did not seem to her, now, for human exploration. She shivered.

When he saw Will the bartender slid a Johnny Black across the counter. Paula ordered a Courvoisier, and the bartender winked at Will and passed both bottles across to him. Will carried them to an almost empty lounge and they settled into chairs near the hearth.

"I drank too much last night and it showed in my behavior here and there," she said. "Sorry."

"Don't worry a second. We got to talking and it slipped your notice how many times I refilled your glass. I'm a natural host, that's what it is. But I'm also a sight bigger than you and have been pouring alcohol down my throat steady-like a good bit longer than you too I reckon." He hoisted his glass. "Speaking of racial traits, as we were yesterday, inscrutability, *hara-kiri*, *kamikaze*, and so on, serious drinking's a racial trait we got down to Hibbits." He grinned. "An odd one. Both the White and the cullud have it, as Euph and I stood witness."

"How did you meet Euph?"

"'Tweren't a question of meeting Euph. I did always know him. Euph had seen some rough times by the period I come along, but he were an educated man with a library of books in his head, which were the only safe place for a Black man to keep them in Hibbits. A head full of books and a heart full of their passion, and a powerful teaching."

"What was his teaching?"

"Euph were a believer in education for the Black man; like your Thomas Graves, he had once been involved in the Garvey movement, and other movements of the type folks have called "nationalist." He called himself a "Race Man." Euph ran a school, in a manner of speaking, in the yard back of the Blue Box, or in his room when 'twere raining. The hours were a mite irregular, 'cause they depended on whether the tar likker had let go enough for him to concentrate. But I learned a lot, in the time I came back down from Chicago, mebbe most specially about how to learn. He taught me how to read, and he taught me to read all I can but not necessarily to believe the most of it, and to be right careful what I write and sign. He taught me not to never trust Sam who has a myriad nefarious ways. The time in my life I failed to heed that teaching brought most dreadful consequences. I ended up working for Sam." He smiled mirthlessly. "'Tweren't no regular school for 'the cullud' in Hibbits, you see. The respectable colored folks wouldn't let their kids near the Blue Box — on account of drinking, you know, and — well — other things. I reckon those scruffy little Black kids whose parents didn't care where they were, and a few whose parents knew Euph was something special, got an education worth having. And so did I. I were the only White one there."

He finished his drink at a gulp and refilled his glass. "Euph had some money, he didn't say from where. Originally 'twere meant for his funeral, and in case he ended up some place he couldn't brew his own likker and had to buy. But he said the time came he didn't care no more about his funeral, and whatever else it ran out of the Starvesoil weren't likely to run out of tar pines, so better to give the money to folks so they could run out of the Starvesoil. So he staked them. One year he staked a Black family to go to St. Louis, where they did powerful well. But they had two people full-grown who could work, and another boy 'bout old enough to start, and kinfolks in St. Louis as well. When he staked us the next year there was just my Little Mama could work, 'cause I weren't but six."

"Your father didn't go?" Paula sought to tread carefully, acutely aware that Will had never mentioned him.

"My father were a boy from Andrewsville down the road who died in World War II. Leastways that's what my Little Mama told me." He downed his drink, poured again, and continued his narration.

"My Little Mama had set her heart on a big city and a lake, and Chicago met her specifications. We didn't have no lakes down to Hibbits. Rivers didn't appeal — not even the big ole one in New Orleans Euph told her about. And not the lake there neither that he tried to talk her into. Different things appeal to different folks, as he said. Still, though he admitted the lake weren't so big, he argued New Orleans were a sight warmer and closer and cheaper and generally less mighty and terrible than Chicago. But she could be stubborn, my Little Mama, and so we went on up North."

"She sounds brave and imaginative," protested Paula. "Wanting to go see a big city and a lake, taking her chance and doing it."

"You truly think so, Yumi? I confess it has always seemed so to me, but others, such as her brother, my Uncle Bert, has said 'twere plumb dumb. She didn't have no skills. She weren't like you, a city person through and through and an educated lady. She couldn't make it in the city. She couldn't hardly read or write. It didn't work out, you know, same as the Association for your father. When that happens 'tis harder to argue that 'twere more a brave thing to do than dumb."

"I don't agree with that at all. Just because things don't work out doesn't mean they weren't worth trying — personal or political."

"Well, it warms me to hear you say so. 'Twere also partly for me that she went — that she left Hibbits, anyway. She'd learned from Euph that education was a precious thing to have, and I think she wanted me out of Hibbits before I started school. And I did well in school, too. Euph give me a good start, with the reading and writing and thinking. Up in Chicago she would sit with me every night and make sure I'd done what the teacher told me to for school next day — though right soon she didn't know enough to follow what it was. Still she made sure I did it — till she took sick. She got a job waitressing, see, but then winter came. We weren't used to it, she slipped on the ice and hurt her back, and couldn't be on her feet no more."

He poured again.

"Will," said Paula circumspectly, noting that the dining room had opened and thinking of the long road to Hilo and the dropping level of the whiskey in the bottle, "Let's eat, okay? I'm hungry."

"Okay, but I can tell you, the food here just ain't up to par."

"Well, that's what comes of cooking like you do. You're spoiled for normal human fare." She rose, and he followed her, grasping the bottle by the neck. "What kind of work did your mother do after the fall?"

"Oh — she made arrangements, this and that, here and there. She'd done so in Hibbits but I reckon she'd hoped to — move on, leave all that behind. We ran out of Euph's money, see, and frightening fast. My Little Mama were most particular then that I write him and not let on that we were in trouble, to tell him every penny he gave her she had used as well as she could. And I believe 'twere true she did. But the money just didn't go very far. Which was what Euph had tried to tell her it wouldn't in a city like Chicago."

"What did you do when the money was gone?"

"We went to try and find the only person Euph knew there, a man from the Nationalist days. He ran a bookstore on Cottage Grove Avenue. That's the heart of Black folks' Chicago South Side, as most likely I don't have to tell you. We were the only White folks to see for blocks around. But the store were all boarded up. The neighbors said he'd died the year before. Euph had given us a letter for the man, which I read then to see were there a mention of other folks might help us. But there weren't." Will laughed. "In the letter Euph asked the man to do right by us though we was White, and I reckon he would've. I remember when Euph gave us the letter he said the man had always been more than he professed — that the best men always were."

He pulled out Paula's chair and sat himself, then turned to consult with the waiter. "I'll take your lasagna, and the soup. I recommend the same, Yumi." When the man had left he said, "It's the best they can do here. Don't touch the salad, that's my recommendation.

"Anyway," he went on, "after my Little Mama passed and my Uncle Bert came to fetch me and ride the body back down home, I made a point to tell Euph, how my Little Mama used his money well.

"He said he'd expected no less of her. Though in truth, had she had her — illness — and his money at the same time, she might have — disappointed him, in the end. But Euph would probably have understood, and not held it against her. He had a tolerance of human frailty, he did."

"What was wrong with your mother — besides her back? You said she — took sick?"

The phrase was strange on her tongue.

Will gave the mirthless smile again.

"Life, I reckon. She had bad painings, from her back, and even worse I reckon 'twas strain on the heart, like your Daddy. And she turned to a medicine which made things worse. One of those things I spoke of yesterday, that gets you through and kills you in the end."

Back in the lounge, he crossed the room as if drawn strongly to the huge hearth where a fire leaped.

"As I mentioned yesterday, to use your phrasing, I been here and there, doing this and that. I been in all kinds of tropics, of which the one here — 't'ain't the tropics properly speaking — is mild. There's plenty of men find the harsh tropics a killing place. But like I said, for me there ain't nothing as killing as winter. We went up to Chicago in the summer, but summer were soon gone and then we knew what Euph meant when he said Chicago were powerful cold."

After all the years, Will shivered uncontrollably, and held his hands out to Pele's fire that snapped like breaking bones.

Then he pointed to a set of painted portraits all along one wall.

"The eight leaders of the nation of Hawai'i, and Ka'iulani Victoria, who should have been the ninth, but for the U.S. Marines overthrowing her Auntie." He spoke easily, but respectfully, "Kamehameha the Great; Kamehameha II. Liholiho; Kamehameha III. Keaukaouli; Kamehameha IV. Liholiho Alexander; Kamehameha V. Lot; Lunalilo, Prince Bill; Kalākaua, David; and Kamakaeha, Lydia, Queen Lili'uokalani, the last of them — the last so far, as the Princess would remind us most sharply."

He had recited the names unself-consciously but almost ceremoniously. Paula recognized that this was something he knew and cared about deeply.

"Lili'uokalani and Lot I most specially admire," he said. "Good rulers, their own man — and woman — and understood what the haoles had in mind and took decisive steps to try and stop it. Lili'uokalani and Lot — sometimes I think if they could have gotten together, things might have turned out different for Hawai'i nei. But I also admire Lot most specially for the funeral he gave his sister, Kamamalu Victoria, who he cared for mightily. She followed the old ways and wanted a traditional funeral. And despite all the thundering the missionaries could do, and all the mocking the rich respectable haoles could do, he saw that she got it, on the Palace grounds. When drunken haoles came to jeer, the dancers formed up in a kind of phalanx and danced them right out of the place."

As they turned to leave, Will pointed to the upper part of of the fireplace mantel giving onto the chimney. A carving there had escaped her notice earlier, for though it was cut strongly from dark wood, the chimney shadows half-concealed it.

The carving depicted a powerfully-built, somber-faced old woman with heavy bare breasts and flowing bushy hair.

"The Lady. Madame Pele — Tūtū Pele. Tūtū means Grandmother."

"I thought Pele was a beautiful young woman."

"She is that too," said Will.

9

At the Sacred Forest: Here In Hawai'i Nei

They were tired, and spoke little driving down the Volcano Road toward Hilo. Once, Will nodded at the forest wall to their left.

"I'm building my house down there." Paula craned to see, but he stepped on the accelerator, so she could catch only a glimpse of a narrow overhung lane disappearing into the trees. "No name to the street. That's what the path's called. I stuck up a sign, by the road there, kind of a joke, it read 'Noname Lane.' Then I heard some tourists speaking of 'No-nah-may Lane,' wondering what it meant in Hawaiian." He laughed. "Well, give 'em credit for trying. So now I live in 'No-nah-may' Glade, down 'No-nah-may' Lane. I moved the sign farther in, though. I don't need tourists making it a scheduled visit on a bus trip."

Fifteen miles beyond, as they neared the edge of town, he turned the Jeep suddenly so they bumped down another narrow track through the forest. Then he stopped. They got out. The sound of the car doors closing was loud in the silence.

They were standing in a broad glade, among long jumbled lines of heaped lava rock, none higher than her knee. Then, like a trick picture, the lines metamorphosed and took on meaning; Paula saw she was looking at the foundations of a ruined structure.

"A heiau," said Will. "A Hawaiian temple. I don't know how much you know about Hawaiian history and ways?"

"I know some," said Paula, who had been reading, talking and listening since moving to the islands. "But compared to you, or what there is to know, very little, I imagine. Please talk."

"Well, this heiau's not so large or fancy as some which has been restored for the tourist trade. Seems like a lot of those were dedicated to Ku, the god of war, you know. There's those say the old-time Hawaiians did some human sacrificing to him. Others say it never happened. Me, I don't care, one way or the other. As I see it, every people I ever heard of made human sacrifices to the god of war. Some calls them raw recruits. The old-time Hawaiians, though, they did have ways most folks would call strange I reckon. 'Mongst the highest ali'i, that's the rulers, brother and sister could marry."

"I've read about that. Brother-sister royal incest? I think the ancient Egyptians, and some other people, had that custom too. Here, wasn't the idea that the rulers, the ali'i, had the most power — mana, right? — so it could be most powerfully concentrated by joining the ones who had the most of it, for the benefit of the people as a whole?"

"Yeh, that's how I make it out. You take it right calmly."

"It makes logical sense in the system," said Paula a little defensively, thinking she heard censoriousness in Will's tone. "It's a long way from the worst custom I've heard of in human societies. And a long way from the worst you can do with incest. With the Hawaiians, it seems like it wasn't abuse. With us it's about abuse of power, betraying trust. So's sex generally, for that matter, often enough."

"With us! You ain't saying such a thing as relations carrying-on so hardly ever happens with us!"

She felt ignobly pleased at shocking him, after his qualification of her the previous day as a nice little girl; the more so because she had not intended to shock.

"Oh, I don't know about that. No one knows how often incest happens because usually no one tells. It's beginning to come out, now, especially in women's groups. I've been in a few. Though I know two men who were raped. One by a father, one by an uncle."

"Lord, I guess Berkeley and San Francisco are as strange as folks say!"

She laughed, and leaned down to examine the lava wall more closely, impressed by the exquisite work, at how snugly the blocks fit together without benefit of mortar. "They just talk more openly about things there. In the Bay Area no one ever shuts up about anything."

"But 'tisn't possible, to have such people amongst you and not know."

"Why not? From what I've seen of them and of people who've been messed with, child molesters are major-league sickos, and they do a lot of damage. But they're just people."

"Surely you could tell!"

What she read as an obtuse moralism increased her obstinacy.

"How? They don't run around with horns, and no one's learned their psychological characteristics because no one's really looked. Probably they've got some and probably there's a syndrome after sexual abuse, some characteristic kind of difficulties people have the same as for any other kind of trauma, but no one knows what they are for either the molesters or the molested because no one's studied it because no one talks about it because no one wants to think about it. Anyone you pass in the street could be a molester or abused or the product of an incestuous relationship for that matter. How'd you know, a Mark of Cain?"

"I take it you don't put much stock in sin or the Mark of Cain."

"I certainly don't. Do you?"

He grinned, but without humor.

"I reckon I must, because I put stock in the existence of evil. Might could be I'm just a good Southern Baptist boy at heart."

"And redemption? I guess that's the religious equivalent of successful therapy, for 'sinners' and 'sinned against'. Sometimes redemption seems to get short shrift, compared to punishment, in the religious framework."

"Amazing grace on earth? Well, about that I don't know. It makes logical sense in the system, like you'd say, and many folks do live by its promise. But I never seen sign of it myself. Now evil — that, I've seen."

"I'm with you there. I have, too."

She was becoming aware that the conversation was disturbing her, in a way both profound and distanced. As she spoke the last words, the air around her changed, the earth shifted beneath her feet, physical objects grew thin. She recognized what was happening: the dread of a dream that had tormented her intermittently since adolescence was stirring: and back of the dream a deeper dread: something from before.

If it was a dream it was like no other dream: whatever it meant it was about her nemesis.

Doubly jarred, by the visitation and because she was seldom attacked in the day, she squeezed her eyes shut a brief moment. She opened them to find Will watching her. That made her feel exposed and in danger.

"I do believe you have seen evil, at that," he said soberly.

She turned away from him, forcing the dread back into its lair. "Tell me about this particular heiau."

"Well, it's dedicated to Lono, the god of harvest. Some say he's the favorite of ordinary folks. 'Twas the priests and the warriors liked Ku."

"How long has it been abandoned?"

"Oh, I don't reckon folks has worshiped here more recently than last night." His eyes gleamed, he was teasing. "Watch where you set your foot, now. Someone raised that pineapple most careful, and likely got their fingers pricked picking and placing it just so."

"It's an offering?"

"It is. A lot of Hawaiians have died, since the haoles came, and a lot of Hawaiian ways has gone too. But others has survived, still others has changed but are Hawaiian in heart still I think. I saw a most interesting thing once on the beach. Someone had raised an altar, I saw Hawaiian folks leaving fruit offerings and such. And among the offerings they were leaving was one of those cheap plastic baby-doll hula dancers, made for tourists, a scandal really, got nothing to do with real hula. And seeing that, I thought about how the missionaries came, drove hula underground, called the Hawaiians sinners and savages on account of it. Next the missionaries' grandsons steal the Hawaiians' land, then get the Marines to come and help them overthrow the Hawaiian government. And the Hawaiian people has fallen on hard times for sure. Yet here on that beach someone, without even thinking it out so maybe, took the cheap image and turned it to become the center of an altar, right in view of a sacred beach the haole tourists were desecrating by sunbathing on it. Seemed to me like whoever put the doll there got their mana back, undid all that heartbreak and loss by that action of turning haole images of Hawaiians, meant to mock, to a Hawaiian way of showing respect for Hawaiian ways."

Long ago Paula's lover Rick Kawabata, instructing her in Japanese-Way, had said, in his interpretation of the teaching of the time, "Use the language of the enemy, the images the enemy has made of you, the way you use the energy of martial art, and turn it back on the source." By the time she walked out his door she had understood that she had known that for herself, when, facing down alone the boys in gangs, the conquistador-tormentors, on the violent South Side streets of her Chicago childhood, she had shouted, "*Kamikaze!*"

Now Will with his conquistador eyes had understood this gesture too, on his own; and now he misunderstood her silence.

"But I'm talking fanciful. I do get turns like that, at times. Don't pay me no heed."

"Why not? You've got an interesting mind."

The delicate skin behind his ears flamed.

"Well, that's right kind of you." He gave a mocking bow. "There's those as has wondered if I had a mind at all. Well," he turned back to the Jeep, "you'll be seeing a whole passel of Christian churches and Buddhist temples, in these islands. I just thought you might like to see the oldest religious building hereabouts."

"This here's a fine view of our big little town, and out there over the Hamakua Coast as well, where so much of the cane was grown. But this whole coast has fallen on lean days. Sugar ain't what it was, and nothing's been found yet to take its place."

She stared out across Hilo Bay and the lush forested slopes to the Northwest, sheltered by the great mountain, wreathed in cloud from two thirds of its height to its peak.

"The sea in front. And behind, the volcano."

"It's a pretty, peaceful little place," Will agreed, answering her idea rather than her words, "and its littleness is deceiving, its peacefulness too. There's creation down below, and that ain't never peaceful."

They turned and strolled through the downtown area, with its streets of long low-roofed one and two-story buildings, vertically fronted and overhung by sharp half-triangles of metal awning, shelter against sun and rain. The architecture put Paula in mind of the ordered architecture of a pool table. They were simply constructed, almost humble; she intuited in them a profound and elusive element of harmony.

She could not ground the intuition and that embarrassed her lawyerly logicality. She said lightly,

"A town of lines and angles."

They had come to the end of the downtown street that paralleled Hilo Bay.

"The Wailuku River," Will announced. "It flows from the island's heart."

Paula glanced at the sky, thinking of the view she had had of this spot from the air the day before, then leaned on the edge of a bridge parapet. Through a tangle of giant banyans on the riverside she could discern downstream a double waterfall. On the boulders jutting up mid-river halfway to the falls stood a man, a still silhouette, body arced backwards, motionless. "See there?" Will pointed at him. "How you can't see his line?"

She saw, and was puzzled for a moment about what he was doing, then sun caught the thin silver of his fishing cord almost spanning the stream; a trick of light still made the rod invisible. The man might have been a tiny spider dependent on his body-spun glistening filament, cast to the mercy of the Trades.

The river ran swiftly here, opaque and deep green, swirling with a complex current that seemed at odds with itself, as if fighting to go upstream at the same time as it struggled toward the sea.

"Shall we cross?"

He touched her elbow, barely, in symbolic gallant assist, apparently indifferent otherwise to the physical contact.

A shock went through her. Sexual? A contrast with the enormous reserve, the restraint or inhibition she sensed in him — and his unawareness.

Seen from the other end of the bridge, the water changed to deep rich blue, barely touched with green and deceptively calm.

Back in the Jeep, they wandered South along the Puna Coast, where coconut groves sentineled low rocky lava shores. The winding road was so narrow that when vehicles met, one driver pulled over and the other raised a hand in thanks. Dirt paths ran back through groves of hibiscus and banana to half-hidden houses with corrugated iron roofs, perched on stilts amidst vegetable gardens and orchards of breadfruit.

"This region do put me in mind of my Little Mama's garden in Chicago. She found a patch in the park, and put in all manner of things. Potatoes, cabbages, carrots, tomatoes, even tried her hand at corn. My Little Mama, she sure did have a green thumb, and there's good soil in Chicago, you know, under all that concrete and asphalt. But one day while we were weeding — I can't think how she got as far with it as she did without being caught — the poh-lees came. My Little Mama!" He shook his head and laughed. "She asked weren't there some way to share — that's share-crop — in the city! They just tore out our plants and threw 'em in the garbage. Pure meanness. Speakin' of the Devil —"

He pointed ahead to two squad cars, angled across the edge of the road, back wheels partially blocking their lane.

Will pulled the Jeep to a stop.

In front of a handcuff of cyclone fencing and barbed wire cutting into the dense forest, a crowd of about seventy people bobbed and surged. Signs rose and fell above their heads like sails. Paula recognized some of the slogans she had seen on the posters spread out that morning on the floor at Euph's.

"Isn't that the Hawaiian state motto?" She pointed.

Will grinned. "Yeh, and truth to tell I reckon this demonstrator means it closer to the original than what the usual politicians make of it. Specially if you consider the context in which it were first uttered, which was right after the Hawaiians succeeded in getting the country back from the British, who had seized it most unceremonious-like. Myself, I'd translate it something-so: 'Things are going to be better, now that matters of governing are back to the ancestral Hawaiian way they're supposed to be — and were, before the late unpleasantness.' Last part understood." He nodded at the crowd. "There's the Princess. With Kenny, her beau. That'd be the helmeted warrior."

Paula glimpsed Pearlie's curly dark head between two larger figures, a tall skinny boy with a blond ponytail, and a pair of broad male Pacific Islander shoulders clad in a black T-shirt. The shirt depicted a mightily-muscled Hawaiian paddling a war canoe, and wearing full military regalia, including the feather-crested gourd helmet that covered the head. Beneath the figure the words were printed in bright red: Hawaiian Pride: Hawai'i for the Hawaiians. The boy turned and she recognized the person who had helped Pearlie extinguish the torches on the back lānai after the quarrel among the members of the dance troupe, and then gone off with her.

"What's the demonstration about?" she asked.

"This is a most sacred place in the forest. Sacred to the Lady. And there's a plan afoot, with government and big business interests in cahoots, to dig down and tap the steam from the Lady's realms underground for geothermal energy, to send to estate developers here and by cable to Maui and O'ahu for the hotels and casinos."

Memories assaulted Paula; her ears roared, faintly at first, then louder. Her throat constricted as she watched two officers moving towards the crowd, not very fast, lightly slapping their palms with their nightsticks, not very threateningly yet. She was aware of how hollow she became now at any threat of physical force, how fragile she had grown. She looked away.

"If the Princess gets herself in trouble she'll catch it from Emma and Ben." Will frowned, and made to open the door. "And she's liable to get herself hurt. I better —"

"Don't." She surprised herself. She surprised him too: he looked at her, brows raised.

"She's old enough to understand what she's doing. It's her right to be there." For an instant Paula saw her younger self, fifteen, head banging as the police dragged her down the steps of San Francisco City Hall: HUAC hearings, 1960. Like a tree that's standing by the water, she and her comrades had sung, We shall not be moved. Thinking all the time of her father at the Springfield hearings ten years before.

"Well, I'll defer to you on this, Miz Yumi. I don't care for it, don't care for it at all. Tangling with Sam's right dangerous — as you know."

"This geothermal project sounds like a terrible idea. Do the people around here want it?"

"Not so's you could tell from polls or normal conversation with folks. Mike, my drinking buddy up at Jaggar Observatory who I've mentioned, thinks the idea's most unwise scientifically speaking — which is what his job is, to speak scientifically. That's on account of instability of this terrain, which is known."

"What do you think?"

"I think it's no way to treat a lady. Most specially not this Lady."

"Can it be be stopped?"

Will stared straight ahead at the ebbing and flowing human tumult, his face expressionless.

"If the Princess and her friends have their way."

"Are you involved in the protests?"

He shook his head. "Like I told you, I ain't a political person."

Without warning he floored the accelerator and with a shriek the Jeep tore back onto the blacktop amid a spurt of 'a'ā pebbles, past the squad cars, and sped away.

Late that afternoon, Paula stood, stiff with the tension of imminent departure, prepared to board the shuttle flight to Honolulu.

"I do thank you for two fine days, Miz Yumi."

"I've had a good time too. I thank you for your hospitality."

"Miz Yumi." His hands were clenched together the way they had been on the door of the Jeep the night before when he invited her to dinner at Euph's and the Pine Tar. The whitened skin on his knuckles looked ready to tear. "Miz Yumi, I have your telephone number from the reservation you made with Volcano Flights. Might I call you at your home in Honolulu?"

"Yes. Please. Do."

Awkwardly, she darted out across the tarmac.

10

Honolulu City Lights: Lilith

They could be found in every city. Places on the border, like the Black Star and Euph's. Night-places, drinking places, where a woman could swing free but wouldn't have to fight men every instant for her survival space. Places where green felt tables glowed richly beneath light that enabled precise and magical gestures, the flight of brightly colored spheres.

In the week following her return from Hilo Paula searched out, and found, the Tip-Top, in Honolulu. As she had on such forays in San Francisco, she wore a self-designed, custom-tailored, one-piece garment of black satin, pant leg tightly cupping the round of muscular calf, bodice cut square and low where the dip of her breasts began. Her shoes were jet-black, their comfort and sure grip cleverly concealed by a glamorous line, and adorned with a dazzle of faux emeralds, matched by squared faux-emerald earrings.

The habitués of the Tip-Top did not know what to make of her, this woman no one had been able either to bed or to best at the table. She was masterful with the cue, and masterful at keeping them off-balance. So they called her 'Emerald'. But unlike most naming, this one did not attempt possession, but acknowledged her self-remove.

In Honolulu, as in San Francisco, there were other times when she went by night to elegant hotel lounges. The men there thought they knew what to make of her; and she let them think it. She went effectively disguised, a figure of fantasy: dramatically dressed and made up, variously coiffed, and with a different name for each man, here, as in San Francisco, almost always tourist-men. She selected carefully, knowing herself potential prey; slept with each man once, and left them behind to vanish like smoke with the name she had given.

In her own mind, at pool table and in hotel lounge, she called herself 'Lilith.'

Once, in San Francisco, she had gone with a man she had met in her other, lawyer-life. But he had not recognized her.

She dealt with witnesses in court. She knew how strongly context and expectation shaped perception.

Still, she wondered sometimes whether her invisibility sprang not from perceptual illusion but from a true absence, whether the division was not of persona only, but of self.

At such times she would whisper to her alienated face in the mirror, "You must be crazy," as she whispered when remembering her lonely childhood as a *kamikaze* battler on bloody streets; and she shivered.

But the whisper vanished with the men and the names, and she returned to days filled with arduous and conventional work. She was always a degree removed from both lives, and in the days Lilith turned with the planet to become as remote as the moon.

Paula flung herself upright in bed, fighting the enshrouding sheets, skin streaming with blood that stank of death, her hands desperate at her slashed throat. This was the dream that, if it was a dream, was like no other dream.

Spawned in adolescence, receding as she grew into adulthood, assaulting her more violently in times of distress and disaster, creeping from its lair again since the night José Sánchez had died.

She struck out for the lamp switch in the gloom of the shaded room, and in the sudden saving light sat shaking and hugging her knees.

"I'm not in Patchagoula." She recited the mantra she had cobbled together over the years to exorcise the dread-filled ungraspable images. "This is Honolulu. This is 1983, not 1964. This is not Chicago. This is not San Francisco. . ."

Her fingers moved across the deep ridge on her scalp beneath her hair, souvenir of that fractured skull. Pressed against the scar on her temple, that she tried to cover with a wing of hair, from the bottle that had missed her eye by an eighth of an inch, on the Chicago streets she had barely survived.

They massaged her fractured shoulder, never right since the night in Patchagoula.

There was no scar at her throat; yet her fingers lingered there, obsessively.

No scar at her throat: in the alley behind her yard, beneath a groaning treasure of lilacs (it must have been summer; was she eight, or ten?) a board fence, a knife at her throat, a young man's arm, conquistador arm, one of the veterans of that war abroad come back to fight it at home on South Side Chicago streets. And around him the thugs, who had never left the domestic battleground. Her breath choked, first by the arm, then by her own stillness against the blade: pouring over her like scalding oil the words they hurled at her, in the streets, the contempt in their voice as painful as the words. Terrified enraged and humiliated, she suffered the hard hurting hand between her legs.

Deus ex machina: life imitating art? Two women stepping into the alley laughing, at the end of the block; her attackers running away. So life prevailed, for once. Survivor's guilt: After the Nightriders blew up South Regional Headquarters, she had spent long weeks in a limbo of half-consciousness. When she returned to sojourn on earth, people had said to her, "You are so lucky to be alive!" Surely it had to be true. As a survivor, she felt guilt thinking of those who were not alive. So she found it impossible to tell those well-meaning people that she scarcely felt lucky to be alive. The violences she had lived through merged in her dream-drenched mind, and back of all those she could name lay that early, lilac-shrouded violence, a death-grip that impelled her out into anonymous venues with anonymous men who did not know her name and whose grip she could escape like a wraith, a wreath of smoke.

To survive those violences that mocked voice and voided meaning meant recreating voice and meaning both; and she lived, fragilely, in the knowledge that after South Regional Headquarters, that regeneration had been almost beyond her capacity.

She had not been able, either, to tell people that their premise was not quite true. Sometime, even before the explosion, the force-fields of destruction had sucked her protoplasm to a place where for at least a moment she belonged more to death than life. Paradoxically, the trespass that indelibly marked her was the one that had left no physical mark, the one that drew her fingers to her throat. Because of this trespass, walking along on any ordinary day, she knew how the world at any moment might schism and collapse. Her foot, brought down to touch the earth in that elemental gesture of trust essential to life's movement, might fail to find solidity, might keep on plunging, pulling her body after in a fall through fire and space, forever.

In the week after her return from Hilo, the time with Will Cawdry, the demonstration at the Sacred Forest, she began to understand why she had settled in Waikīkī.

In this appalling place, amidst the ruins of an almost-destroyed community, ground zero of urban exploitation and depredation in the islands, increasingly squeezed between the tourist buses and the developers, Paula felt both insane and oddly, even perversely, grounded. She knew that she was in the belly of the beast. Now she understood that her family had been there in Chicago, when her father tangled with Sam; the beast had shattered her family and their community. As a child, she had been at its mercy. But now she felt her location to be perfect for attack. Knowing where she was, and what was happening, she knew what she needed to do. She thought with satisfaction of the two O'ahu legal suits already won, based largely on her donated legal research. One limited tour buses in Waikīkī, the other affirmed Native Hawaiian fishing rights along the coast North of Honolulu.

Now, standing on the roof of her house, she was involved in organizing a political action again for the first time since coming to the islands. She stretched her arms high to fasten a banner. Pearlie hemming her banner had brought back an earlier Paula. The words rippled, then stood out clearly as the cloth bellied in the trade winds: *Waikīkī Neighborhood Committee. Come Fight . . .* She cocked her head, and ascertained that the time and place of the meeting were readable. A sudden gust caught the cloth like a sail and snapped it so hard she staggered, sending exultation through her in shock waves: joy at life, at being in struggle again. This building, where she rented a large studio apartment, was one of a bucolic group of wooden dwellings, made gracious by wide rooms and verandahs, subdivided now but well-kept, in a tiny lane off Tusitala Street. Against all odds they still stood, driven down to the basement of the world by the concrete hotel towers all around them that shot screaming away into the sky.

Traffic streamed down Kuhio Avenue, down Kalākaua Avenue, down Ala Wai Boulevard where it intersected Kap'iolani. She could see the downtown skyscrapers. In their midst, she knew, stood the statue of Kamehameha the Great, across from 'Iolani Palace. She had heard how in that Royal Palace, each morning at dawn, a royal retainer had awakened King Kalākaua by chanting his genealogy back a thousand years. On the Palace grounds, Kamehameha V. Lot had seen that his sister Victoria Kamamalu got the traditional funeral she wanted, missionaries be damned. Paula paused, remembering how vividly Will had recounted the event, how immediate and vital his recounting had made it. She wondered why it was so fraught with significance for him. In the grip of that contagious immediacy of historical memory, staring out across Honolulu on a contemporary, automobile-dominated day, Paula suddenly saw torches flaring, drums conferring order on space, bare feet raising heartbeats from the earth, all creating the ceremony for the dead princess. The powerful grace of dancers brought forth a place of proud, beleaguered privacy and respect, as they maneuvered feather and foliage anklets and wristlets to choreograph protection from the damaging haole gaze, manoeuvred their bodies to remove the interlopers from the honored space.

She thought of Pearlie's dance troupe, struggling for definition and continuity. She thought of the demonstration at the Sacred Forest. A true succession. What is, won't last forever. This was what Paula read in the expression of the Queen's face in photographs she had seen. Bad times will not last forever for kanaka maoli. What comes will be different, but a true succession.

High on her roof, Paula turned slowly, following the jagged line of green dark-gullied hills rising steeply behind the city to become the sharp-ribbed flanks of the Koolaus, the mountains that made O'ahu's spine. Their irregular peaks were unexpectedly back-tilted, their sculpted violence rock-recorded memory, fire frozen ages ago, wreathed every afternoon in angry cloud. One hundred eighty degrees behind her she faced the scarred leonine flanks of Lē'ahi that the haoles had called Diamond Head, rising majestically against the sky.

"The banner's beautiful, Paula," called Ginnie from where she wrestled with the other end. "It'll show all the way down Ala Wai."

She had met Ginnie in the neighborhood group; she was a librarian at the University.

"We lucked out on the angle, all right."

She scrambled to the pavement through the upstretched limbs of a breadfruit tree. She let herself drop, and as her running shoes bounced on cement her body shook to a tremendous boom and crash. The beautiful old house at the corner of her lane and Tusitala Street doubled over under the blow of a wrecking ball, then exploded in a tremendous cloud of dust. Paula choked as it sifted down over the rubble.

An elderly man, brown-skinned, with mournful oblique eyes, halted in his painful way down the street. His wracking coughs seemed to threaten the life in his frail body. When he lifted his head Paula saw that tears ran down his cheeks, from mourning, not dust.

"Why can't they find something to do with good houses besides tear them down for hotels? Such a lovely house. People could live there."

"They won't find something better to do. But we will."

"It's good to see the banner anyway. God bless you." And he continued on his painful way, shrouded eerily in gray ash.

"Come to our meeting," called Paula.

"Thanks for the update on the list of O'ahu internees," said Kaz Nakamura on the telephone from San Francisco, later that day. Paula leaned back against her futon cushions, sipping Chardonnay, abruptly aroused by the memory of brief and few sexual encounters they had had, Kaz's arrogant high-bridged nose and powerful thighs. Boalt Hall like her, a year ahead: both had stood third in their class. Theirs had been an impossible relationship. They were constantly at odds, not politically but personally and professionally, and gave up the sexual relationship for a bristly friendship in the context of the group of lawyers working on reparations for internment. "When are you moving back?"

"I'm not. I told you that months ago."

He gave an exaggerated sigh that whistled over the wires and for the first time told of the distance between them.

"Okay, so you need a longer vacation in lotus land than I thought. Just don't forget that we need you here."

"Kaz, I'm touched, I really am." Her tone was ironic. "And I love flattery as much as anyone, but I'm not indispensable anywhere. The group's made it fine for eighteen months without me. And this isn't lotus land," she said tartly. "Things need doing here, too."

"I know, I mean this info you're getting to us is very useful. But —"

"I don't mean only that. Other things. Our U.S. issues, yes, and — others. Our issues are different here than there. Other configurations of people, our people and other peoples, other — issues," she repeated. Paused. "It's a different place. It has a different history."

"I'll bet. What do you do for cultural stimulation out there after a long day at the beach?"

"Watch that Bay-Area Chauvinism, Kaz." She was surprised at how strongly his attitude annoyed her. "What kind of left politics is that?"

"Okay, okay, mea culpa. But seriously, don't melt away in the sun. Keep checking in, will you?"

"You know I will."

She hung up and watched the light dance off the honey-colored wine in her glass and regarded the low brick and board shelf along the opposite wall. There, she had arranged most of the items that she had selected as keepsakes from the little her parents had possessed. The fewness of the keepsakes and the deep significance they held for her seemed suddenly to speak of the spareness and intensity of the relationship that had obtained among the three of them, for so short a time.

Her mother had been deeply reserved. She cared for Paula physically with meticulous attention, but when Paula as a child felt the familiar touch as her mother combed her hair, cleaned her body, straightened her garments, she also felt how her mother was withdrawn, not rejecting her but as if, in some way natural to her, she was according both of them the respect of physical autonomy and privacy. In a different register, Paula had something of her mother's intense self-containment, and a kind of composure accompanying it. Though reserved, even inhibited, socially, she possessed a deep sensual authority. Her awareness of her body's potential for pleasure was acute, and she assumed responsibility for her satisfaction and her protection in attaining it. She burned and vibrated under the world's assault, that overstimulated her senses, offended and threatened her with other demanding presences. She had never wanted children, animal companions, roommates, lovers who lived with her. Their invasiveness seared her like the flame in her throat when South Regional Headquarters blew up, left her yearning for the soothing cool of space and solitude, of a place where she could stretch and soar, feel the uninterrupted reach of her sinews and her mind towards a clear spare end: a line of thought, a sexual arc, the austere moment of solitude at the end of a two-day hike alone, after attaining a mountaintop.

Now she drank wine and reflected that certainly she was temperamentally more like her mother than her father. Perhaps that was why he, and the world of the Black Star where he had thrived, had seemed so magical to her.

At the rear of a wide brick and board shelf stood two matching square boxes made of ebony; they contained her parents' ashes. The shelf also supported a tiny framed black and white photograph, with the serrated edges of thirty years ago. It portrayed her father holding her when she was about five. She moved through the world at all times strengthened by the feel of his heart beating against her chest, of his strong forearms beneath her knees.

Next to the photograph stood a heavy cast-iron teapot that had come down through generations on her mother's side, along with a small brown wooden box that stood beside it. The box contained an ancient scroll with characters in black ink faded almost beyond distinguishing. This was a family blessing, or something like that: the recollection was hazy. And alongside the box, from within an intricately figured oval silver-colored frame, two women, one old and one young, in a black and white photograph now turned sepia, looked out into Paula's Honolulu room. They were Paula's mother and her mother, Paula's mother had told her.

Paula had no idea where the photograph had been taken, or when. Her mother turned back questions. It was long ago, it was a long way away, your grandmother has been dead a long time. Paula could never find her mother in the kimono-garbed girl kneeling on the tatami matting beside the kimono-garbed matriarch; she had never seen her mother in a kimono. She was quite sure her mother had never owned one, not during Paula's lifetime, favoring slacks and print blouses around the house. When she went outside, she dressed formally: a good-quality linen or wool suit, depending on the season (she possessed two of each, the linen light green, the wool dark green) and long-sleeved cotton blouses that buttoned to the neck. Nylons, and highly polished navy pumps. A small dark green felt hat. Paula had always understood that these outfits for facing the world were suits of armor.

Another photograph of her mother she had put away. Like the calabash she had not looked at it in years. It had ambushed her. Long ago when her mother was already dead, Paula had been selecting pictures for a photo retrospective of the Bay Area Japanese-American community that her San Francisco Japantown collective was organizing. She had turned the photo over and frozen in her chair, staring down at her mother, when her mother was only a little older than the girl in the elaborate silver frame kneeling on the tatami mat. She wore a dark suit with a white blouse, nylons, pumps, and a small round felt hat with an oddly rakish curly feather. She sat very erect on the edge of a bench, in an anonymous room somewhere — Bay Area police station? Racetrack? Instinct with dignity, she sat erect, clasping her carefully manicured hands across a black handbag that rested on her knees. She was at an internment center, headed for the camps. A tag with a number hung from her neck. Her mother's face was expressionless, except for the tilt of her chin and her eyes that blazed with rage and something else. Irony, Paula thought, even humor. A humor honed and refined and of deepest black. Its honing and refinement marked the style of her flower arrangement that she had taught Paula; Paula thought, now, that she had taught along with it a black ironic humor. She remembered Will Cawdry's question about the flower arranging: How had he put it: 'Twas her protest?

Paula had seen that expression not long ago, that dignity, humor and rage, at an archival exhibit in Honolulu. Odd, she thought, for little physical resemblance obtained between the two women, but she had seen it in a photograph of Queen Lili'uokalani, taken at the time of the haole tribunal in 1895.

Sometimes Paula dreamed of the photograph of her mother on her way to internment. She dreamed she was listening again to the conversation she had overheard on the night of the last meeting of he Association, the night her father died. He was explaining to her mother the desertion by so many comrades in the group. Her mother's voice rose, bitter as Paula had never heard it, scornful of her father as she had never heard her mother be: *What did you expect? I told you never to get so involved with those people!*

This memory Paula never touched for it had never healed.

Her father had come to Paula's room then, before going on to his study. He had spoken to her of schism and collapse, of how despite these she must go on responsibly in the world, never forsaking the struggle.

We have to form alliances and keep on fighting. We need each other in the fight, we need every race, every group. We mustn't let them, the people who keep ordinary people down, divide us. Do you understand, Yumi? We mustn't let the rulers, the people who keep ordinary people down, divide you from your comrades, even when sometimes your comrades fail you. People are easily frightened, they are easily misled, it's a frightening dangerous world. But never forget, there's solidarity too. We come from a glorious tradition, and our privilege and duty is to build on it, carry it on. The NAACP brought the first challenge to the internment camps of any non-Japanese organization. Without the struggle, however imperfect people are, who knows how much worse things might have been for us here? We were only a few steps from Dachau. When Paula dreamed of the photograph she knew on waking that the numbers had not been tattooed on her mother's skin, only on her soul.

Paula had made a copy of the photo for herself and in the end exhibited the original. She inked the identification card carefully, herself, and in the end exhibited the picture, although she felt her mother, unlike her father, might not have wanted it displayed. But older people who had been young when her mother was young had come to the exhibit and seen the photo and wept and thanked her, and told her they had never before spoken of the internment. And young people had seen it and become angry and spoken a great deal, and gone on to do good community work in Japantown.

So perhaps in the end her mother would have agreed with her decision. Alone in her room in Honolulu, Paula raised her wineglass in a sketched formal gesture.

If not, forgive me, Mother.

11

Former Lives and Lovers

"Congratulations!" Ginnie Yamaguchi cried, and along with Paula, she and Alan Enomoto and Nani Wright raised glasses of wine, in the corner of the Italian restaurant where they were splurging on a celebration. The court had found for their side in a case involving traditional lands; beach access and fishing rights would be reserved for Native Hawaiians. "That was brilliant thinking behind those decisions. And you did most of the research and all the writing, Paula. That made the difference."

"It all made the difference," said Paula, "but thanks." Alan was a lawyer doing *pro bono* work with the Native Rights and environmental group she volunteered with. He knew the intricacies of Hawaiian law; she had argued through their ideas with them, helped them clarify them and formulate the case; then she had written it up.

"Next time," she said, "it's going to be Nani. Because she was with us all the way and ahead of us a couple of times."

The young Hawaiian paralegal intern flushed. Paula's heart clutched. She was encouraging her to go on to law school, looking into scholarships for her. The girl reminded her of herself long ago, and of Pearlie, across the Eight Seas, weaving and re-weaving her chant for all the islands.

Alan stirred restlessly, his arm draped possessively over the back of Paula's chair. Barely conscious of her movement, she shifted away.

She had dated him a few times. Ginnie had introduced them; he worked with her fiance Steve Ito in a downtown law firm. Alan seemed interested in her; she didn't quite understand why, for she felt no great compatibility. He was smart, which she appreciated, and ambitious, which made her wary. He was still embittered about his ex-wife, and their two children who lived with her on Maui now. She suspected he was heavily on the rebound. He was forty, compactly built, very smart, with thick hair and thick eyebrows and a square, strong face.

"Paula did a good job," he said. He spoke jovially, but something condescending in his tone contradicted the warmth of his arm, now across her shoulder, and she stiffened. Then she thought, in an instant's clarity, that no contradiction existed really; Alan was possessive, in the way he lived life, and tonight he was possessive of the place at the center of attention that she momentarily occupied. To his way of thinking, he would claim the attention, claim the intelligence and the success, by claiming her as a woman. For — again to his way of thinking — he possessed what a woman attached to him possessed, because he possessed her.

Three days later, in the courtyard behind Paula's studio apartment, she and Ginnie sat beneath the banyan sharing a bottle of Chardonnay and a bowl of peanuts.

On the streets nearby, tour buses roared and belched. Traffic thundered along the large boulevards all around. From just where her room jutted out at the side of the building, Paula had a view of the Koolaus. Glimpsed wonder, free but fragile. Those who decreed prices and views were building all around. She could catch sight of the swift-flowing green water of the Ala Wai Canal running to the sea. Beautiful, and behind her a few blocks she knew Kap'iolani Park was beautiful too, though the sharp side of her mind that was seldom silent observed that the canal was polluted, and kalo fields and duck ponds had been drained to create both canal and park. They had been polluted too, but they fed many ordinary people, especially the Hawaiian and Chinese communities.

Up there in the Koolaus, sun and dancing rain created a kind of beauty she'd never seen before she came to Hawai'i. Varicolored light imbued the green forest, converting the foliage itself to rainbow hues.

"How was your date with Alan?" asked Ginnie. "I think he's really interested."

"I don't. Not in me. I think he's really interested in settling down to get back at his ex-wife and I'm the best demographic fit in sight at the moment."

That was an exaggeration, she knew, and felt a twinge of guilt, but though an exaggeration her assessment was not an untruth. "He may like me okay," she amended, "or think he does, on short acquaintance and with a good many blind spots. But I'd have to change an awful lot before I'd suit what he has in mind, and I'm not about to."

"He's a nice man with a good steady income, and his politics are okay too. If I weren't with Steve, I'd snatch him."

"Well, don't let me stop you."

"Didn't you have a good time when you went out?"

"We went to a very interesting art exhibit that he told me how to evaluate. Then we went to dinner and he got mad because I said civil disobedience was an essential tool for social change and though I wouldn't use violence I could perfectly well see why others would in certain circumstances. Then we disagreed about something, I don't remember what, it was so unimportant, and I said "I think you're wrong" and left it there. But he wouldn't leave it. He kept pushing at me, bullying me to agree. He couldn't agree to disagree, you see. Any woman with him has to agree with him." She shrugged. "He pushes for anyone, man or woman, to bend and agree. I've seen him do that at meetings. But any woman he's with has to. That's my take on it, anyway."

"Well, I wouldn't slam the door, Paula. You *are* prickly, and he's not used to it. Not many men are. So tell me about the Big Island."

"There's not much to tell," she replied, hearing her own defensiveness. "I met my pilot and we flew over the Big Island and Maui, and then since I wasn't booked on a tour or anything he showed me around the island a little, and we ate at a restaurant he owns there. The hike at the volcano was great."

Paula stopped speaking, unnerved. Ginnie was leaning comfortably back in a chaise longue, with an ease that Paula herself seldom achieved even in her own home. And over the rim of her wineglass she was regarding Paula with an expression that jolted her, she recognized it so well and realized suddenly how long it had been since she had seen it directed at her: a woman, scenting news in a woman friend's life, and settling down either to receive it or dig it out but at any rate for a long sharing talk.

"What's he like?"

"Who?" Immediately she felt foolish, as if her defensiveness were exposed.

Ginnie's laugh, easy, cheerful, was a sound that had also long been absent from Paula's life.

"Where did you go? Out. What did you do? Nothing," she quoted. "Come on, tell all," and Paula was reminded of her own words to Will. "I was here and there, doing this and that," she had said to him, gently mocking his reticence as Ginnie was now mocking hers.

"How could I say what he's like?" She was annoyed. "I hardly know him."

Ginnie nodded, satisfied with the beginning she had made. "Well, tell me what you can. He owns a restaurant? And you say he's a pilot?"

"Yes. And yes. A first-rate cook too. He made us dinner. And he plays the piano. Very well."

"Is he from the Mainland?"

"Yes. But he's been here a long time."

"What's his name?"

"Will Cawdry."

"Cawdry? Is he Scottish?"

"He purports to be a good ole boy from Texas. And he probably is — among other things."

Paula stopped speaking, arrested by a sudden insight.

His accent, that was no identifiable accent, but a mosaic of many elements, from many forms and tongues, constituted aspects of personality to be brought forward or occulted according to the circumstances: bringing forth or occulting some version of himself. Will wove himself from those elements: *sui generis*, self-made man.

"So what else?" demanded Ginnie, startling Paula.

"What else? Nothing else! What do you mean, what else? I — well, if you want a comparison with Alan, Will didn't try to change me, and everything he showed me was something worth seeing. Now, let's talk about something different."

"Okay, I'll let you off the hook for now. But I'll keep checking. I still think Alan sounds like a better bet."

"I don't bet — not on men. See up there?" She pointed to the roof. "I've got rock doves nesting. One of the Waikīkī ones." They were a subgroup, feathered all in white. "And a very pretty traditional one, grey with a purple-green neck ring. I've never observed rock doves so close up. It's very interesting."

Ginnie wrinkled her nose in distaste. Even the Bird Rescue Woman, who worked for the group where Paula was helping expand a wildlife program, thought the rock doves were a nuisance. "Pick up their eggs," she had recommended promptly when Paula mentioned her housemates. But Paula had not. Two eggs: one was stillborn, no longer being brooded. That was common, she knew now from library research: twin eggs laid, one surviving to hatch. She had learned a lot.

"They are devoted parents," she said. "And very egalitarian in brooding. They're on three-hour shifts. If one of them is late, the other one looks out over the railing for him — or her — and scolds when the no-goodnik shows up." She laughed, and poured herself and Ginnie more wine.

"I like pigeons," she went on. "I admire them. Pigeons and geraniums. On the street where I grew up in Chicago some other things survived, but except for roaches and rats — and I also admire them, though I don't want to room with them — pigeons and geraniums were the only living things I saw that thrived."

She loved their rich creamy cooing, the iridescent swell of their soft-feathered throats, and exulted to see flocks rise in clouds and wheel powerfully against the sky.

"In Chicago it wasn't like it is here. I was the only yellow face in sight."

Some deep relaxation that she had never known was possible had blessed her here, in this city predominantly of ochres and browns, where no one gave her skin or eyes a second glance, where her face was not the face of the enemy forever.

"King Kalākaua invited us here," said Ginnie. "We were welcomed."

Her proprietary tone jarred Paula. Her father had used it near the end, arguing with her mother, about the Association, about the Black Star, implying she was narrow and prejudiced, as she in turn implied he was living low. The tone meant: you poor slobs on the Mainland. Ginnie had gone through most of high school and to college in Los Angeles, but that absence and the resulting partial alienation seemed to have intensified her identification with the community here.

"It didn't work out quite like Kalākaua hoped," Paula said, to be contrary. "Weren't we and the Hawaiians supposed to intermarry and form a strong group that would save Hawaiian culture in the land, and be workers who could stand against the haole settlers? Now we run politics and own hotels."

Her words annoyed Ginnie. "We don't run politics. And these hotels have nothing to do with us." "Us" meant local Japanese, "AJA"s." "And nothing ever works out quite like people hope. Still we have stood with the Hawaiian people in many ways when it counted."

What she said was true, in certain shadings at least.

"It's not just Hawaiians haoles don't love," she went on. "They don't love us, either."

That was certainly true, without shadings. Paula wondered if Ginnie was referring, obliquely, to Will.

Ginnie poured herself more wine.

"My father and my uncle," she said, "are organizing among our businessmen to put up a statue of Kalākaua. The plaque will say: 'With thanks to King Kalākaua. He invited us to the Kingdom of Hawai'i, where we have prospered, at a time when the United States people persecuted us on the Mainland and the United States government refused us with the Oriental Exclusion Act.' Something like that."

"That's good."
"Yes. It's owed."

Later, alone in her room, Paula sat on. She drank more wine and stared at the objects arranged on her brick and board shelves and thought about her past, brought to the fore by her conversation with Ginnie.

What would her life have been like if she'd grown up here, "in the community" in Honolulu? What would she be like?

Her parents had never acknowledged the battle where she almost lost an eye, never spoke of it. But she suspected they knew what had happened, for afterward, her father, ardent defender of public education, arranged for her to take an admissions test to Greenoaks Academy. He knew that to save her life she had to get out of the killing floor they called a neighborhood school.

To do that she had to buy her way with grades that won her a scholarship. Later she joked that she had been living off her wits since she was seven.

Greenoaks was private, genteel, experimental, University-affiliated and very expensive. At Greenoaks, she and Anthony Howe — a Negro, as he was called then in polite circles — were the only non-Whites except for the Negro janitors. She and Anthony had grasped at once that the terms of their being tolerated at Greenoaks were strict and absolute. They intuited that they were to behave only in ways that allayed White peoples' deepest fears. She met everyone's eyes — except Anthony's. The two of them must never seem to make alliance. They did, though, backing each other up by quick glance and brief gesture. For safety, she knew she must keep her voice pinched in a narrow range. She must display no inscrutability, no sneakiness. She must emit no *Kamikaze* cries, destabilizing to them because power-giving to her. And she acted the good Oriental.

Anthony's scalp was kept shaved so close the contours of his skull were visible. No one that denuded of menacing African hair could lead a slave rebellion. Years later, in the sixties, she enjoyed imagining Anthony out there somewhere, hair rising up in a mighty Afro.

In those sixties times, when she was living in the Haight, she had had a relationship — more than an affair — with David Harvey, a lean young man with skin like blue-black ink and a wicked sense of humor. They had gone together to the demonstration at the Oakland Naval base near San Francisco where a policeman's club fractured her skull. David had probably saved her life that day. Leaving her where she had been beaten to the ground was more dangerous than moving her, despite her skull fracture; David had lifted her from the asphalt under a rain of truncheon blows and half-carried, half-dragged her out of further peril. Looking up and beneath his 'fro, and through the streams of her own blood in her eyes, she had whispered, "Anthony."

David had been jealous but he had believed her explanation, perhaps because of her own surprise at it. She was not an open person and that explanation had brought them closer.

Soon afterward, David moved back to New York where he came from and they lost touch, but their relationship remained with her as a memory of laughter and courage; and that moment, when she whispered "Anthony," stayed with her as a revelation that the past could drive and inform current loves as well as current terrors.

When Ginnie had said that the statue of Kalākaua was owed, was she speaking of *on*? Rick Kawabata had instructed Paula that *on* was the deep and unique Japanese conception of boundless unrepayable obligation. Then she wondered if Ginnie would ever wonder that, or if she would know, in some way of knowing forever denied Paula because she had not grown up in the community but in a desolate wilderness.

Perhaps Paula thought of Rick because she was making a woman friend again in Ginnie, no doubt about it, her first since June Yasui eight years ago. And June had been the first since Caroline Anderson had become Jamilyah and removed herself from Paula's life.

And perhaps she thought of Rick because Will Cawdry had asked if he might call her and she had said yes and she didn't know if he would or if she wanted him to.

Whatever the reasons, she found herself thinking, with a vividness unequalled in years, of lovers, other friendships, other lives in earlier days, that might be scarred and silted over but went on living deep within.

June Yasui. She first came to Paula as a client, and then they became friends. Paula had spent many happy hours with her, and with her friends who congregated at the Witches' Cauldron, the woman's bookstore she ran. Unlike Caroline, June did not formally and specifically remove herself from Paula's life. But then she came out, and became partners with Jenny Haig.

Jenny did not welcome Paula. Partly it was jealousy, not sexual but the same jealousy Paula felt, each of the others' relationship with June. But Paula had been prepared to try to make the adjustments that always come with a friend's marriage, and Jenny did not seem willing to do so. Paula thought that was because the issue was not only Paula but the orientation and issues Jenny wanted to be central to the life she and June would live. Jenny was deeply involved with Lesbian issues and the city's Lesbian community.

Slowly, the circle around the Witches' Cauldron seemed increasingly to exclude Paula. June's attention turned away. The angle of her concerns leaned too far towards a world where Paula did not belong to allow Paula to participate any more.

Sometimes Paula still dreamed about the gingham chair cushions at the Witch's Cauldron, the stiff bristles of the willow broom that stood in the corner beside the gleaming copper cauldron, the tang of mulled wine and the conversation of many women's voices; and above all she dreamed of June's laugh, the only laugh she'd ever known which was truly merry, which really sounded like bells.

Perhaps Rampton Harmon Deedon III. had never been either truly friend or lover. She had thought they were friends, for the six months after they met in class at Berkeley. And she thought they had become lovers at one of the fabled week-long parties at the fabled Dana Street House. Those parties had been a feast for eighteen-year-old senses and energies: and twenty years later, her breath still caught at the memory of extravagant gorgeous music, hashish alive in the air and the blood, and beds of psychedelic cushions onto which, on that night, she and Ramp Deedon had tumbled together.

Three weeks later — weeks she had found rapturous and thought he did too — he disappeared without a word. She had not seen or heard from him for almost two decades.

Simply being a student at Cal had been Ramp's rebellion; she divined that it had been all the rebellion he could take. Someone of Paula's race and background, someplace like the Dana Street house, broke too far beyond his limits. He should have gone straight along the family's pre-ordained track, been the fourth generation to attend Yale, which was where he went when he fled '60's Berkeley, the psychedelic cushions, and Paula.

She learned later, through the lawyers' grapevine and then from media coverage of his high-profile career, that he had continued brilliantly on the course from which she and California were apparently violently-regretted detours. He married the daughter of a family with which his had been long entwined by wedlock and finances. He became a corporate lawyer and attained partnership in the predestined firm. He produced two sons and a daughter.

By the time of their night at the Dana Street House, Paula's sexual encounters had been several, varied and highly enjoyable; always at a distance from the partner. Ramp Deedon was the first partner she had known and for whom she had cared, although she did not leave that half-circle of remove she kept between her emotions and her sexual expression.

Her reaction to his abrupt and unexplained withdrawal had been a profoundly disconcerting mix of grief, humiliation, bewilderment, anger, and relief.

And a trip she had never before thought of taking, to Tule Lake.

She had been surprised to find the buildings still standing. Later in the decade she and others would ask why — what other objectionable people the government planned to send there. They were old, of concrete and rotted wood, set amidst coils of rusty barbed wire and jumbled rock, on a low hillside where a high sharp wind seemed never to stop whining. Here was no indication of the purpose the buildings had served. No plaque, no monument — then. First, collective memory had to be acknowledged, followed by collective outrage.

Paula had shivered in the bright cold sun. In which of those forbidding structures had she come, prematurely, into a threatening world? The wind lifted grit and dust and sent dancing dervishes through the air.

She advanced a few steps, aimlessly. Under which tower had her great-grandfather fallen, dead of a stressed and broken heart?

She picked up a rock, stained dark. She had studied geology; after a moment she decided the discoloration was from metal and water, not blood. She tossed the rock aside.

This is no place for an old man, she had thought, this place where I was born and my parents were held prisoner for being who they were and my grandfather was murdered — yes, murdered — for the same reason. This is no place for anyone.

She set down the bunch of wildflowers she had gathered and went away.

That night she had a dream.

In the dream she was touching an ancient map of the world, very carefully, with her fingertips. It was an old map like those drawn by European explorers in the time since Columbus — more than half-fantasy, both of nightmare and wish-fulfillment, and projection in more than a mapmaking sense. All the lands South of Italy and West of Greenland — the

Americas, the African and Asian continents, the islands of the tropical and near-tropical seas — all were distorted. Populous lands appeared as blank spaces, scrawled over with misshapen semi-human figures and improbable animals and plants. Printed in the ornate script of the era, in the middle of a vast and apparently uncharted sea, were the words, "Here be monsters."

A grave disembodied voice spoke the words in Paula's dream, and it was not the voice of those who had written them but was spoken about them.

She knew the dream concerned Ramp and their aborted relationship, and concerned Tule Lake. She did not understand it, put it aside, never forgot it.

A month later she left for Patchagoula.

She had seen Ramp one more time.

The occasion was only two years ago, and occupied a surreal space, slightly to the side of her file of regular memories. It constituted one of those places in her past and her thoughts that she did not visit.

12

Western-Mechanized Ofay Time, C.P.T., Japanese-Way

She had met Ramp Deedon in the first half of the '60's; she met Rick Kawabata at their end.

Between had been Caroline — the long desperate year of danger and difficult work they shared in Patchagoula.

And then came the loss of Caroline, who lay sleeping next to Paula when the Nightriders blew up South Regional Headquarters. Ever after, Caroline carried burn scars from her shoulders to her buttocks, and her right hand neither quite opened nor closed. But she said she rose like a phoenix from the bombing, to become Jamilyah.

Had Paula been able to follow the lead of Wendy Yoshimura, maybe she could have kept close to Caroline in spirit if not in physical terms — for Caroline declared she wanted dealings henceforth only with her people, who were Black people. But after the bomb, Paula had lost her ability to wish for violence, even revolutionary violence. That was how she thought of the change — as a disability, as one of her several lasting damages from the bombing. She still believed theoretically in social violence as a legitimate last recourse, but she was unable to wish or will it, to advocate or work for it.

She suffered the loss of Caroline, the loss of a place in the movement in the often-necessary, sometimes-absurd, sometimes tragically damaging upheaval and re-evaluation it went through in the mid-'60's. In its schism, collapse, and re-formation, lines were drawn that drew her out. The convalescence of her body and her spirit was long and difficult; neither body nor spirit had ever wholly healed. She gritted her teeth and endured law school, so she could give herself over to the grinding work and perpetual financial scraping of the Legal Assistance Co-op.

All these things, by choice or of necessity, occupied her fully. For years most of her sexual and social life lay dormant.

She met Rick Kawabata at the San Francisco jail, late in January of 1969, amidst the chaos of the largest arrest in the city's history. They were bailing out demonstrators locked up after the arrest at San Francisco State, that was meant to break the strike aimed at establishing the Ethnic Studies program at the school. We won that struggle, she would think when she grew discouraged in later years. Among the hundreds arrested were his students.

She was there because the call had gone out for Movement lawyers to take the cases *pro bono*.

The odor of confirmed enmity was everywhere at the jail.

Like a strike in a company town, where, as the months of picket duty and conflict grind on the goons and the strikers come to know each other, mark each other, the police and the strikers during San Francisco State's six-month strike were not strangers. Not by accident was the bloody boy slumped against the wall, blackened eyes swollen shut, arm broken, a prominent leader of the White Support Committee for Ethnic Studies; or the boy being dragged in now, unconscious, eyes rolled back in his head so only the whites showed, blood trickling from their outer corners, prominent in the Black students' organization.

Her affair with Rick was a matter of the man and of the moment. Theirs was one of those relationships where the first meeting was imprinted indelibly upon her recollection. When other, conventionally more intimate, memories had blurred or gone — or perhaps never been as strongly imprinted in the first place — her first view of him in the chaos of the Hall of Justice, Seventh and Bryant, that night, stayed clear and sharp.

He was only of medium height, Rick Kawabata, only of slight build, like many Japanese-American men she knew, narrow-shouldered and narrow-waisted; but that night he seemed as large as the beefy cops surrounding him, borne along by rightness, righteousness and rage. He stood beside Paula, abrasive in his denim jacket with its buttons proclaiming "Yellow Peril" and "*Kamikaze* Pilot", here where he had come to meet the Man. His shallow-set eyes were slanted spearheads, black as jet and glittering with intelligence and energy. He had a wild long shock of black hair, thick and shiny, which he tossed back from his face with impatient emphasis when he was holding forth passionately. In those days it was a bold statement even when White boys grew their hair; and for Blacks to announce themselves with naturals, for Japanese-American men to declare themselves by disarray, spoke revolutionary cultural complexities in a single gesture of laissez-faire.

When everything that could be done that night for the arrestees had been done, Rick and Paula, nerves ready to snap, left the Hall, found a hole in the wall on Market Street, ate a greasy meal, then collapsed on Rick's futon and made love. Afterwards they slept for fifteen hours. When they awoke it felt to her as if they had been together forever and that they always would be.

But they were not together forever, and when their relationship ended in the same month the '60's did it was Paula who walked out Rick Kawabata's door.

Now almost fifteen years later she rose, poured herself more wine, and walked to her window to watch the flock of chattering mynahs swoop home to the giant banyan in the courtyard. And she thought of Rick's apartment in San Francisco, of *shoji* screens and waxed and polished wooden floors in gray melancholy light, of youthful sexuality and vibrating anger at the political and social times they'd grown up in and come to, of electric intelligence, of all the intertwined strands of their tangled intimacy.

"Remember," Rick would bark at her, "we aren't on Colored Peoples' Time any more. And we aren't on Western-Mechanized Ofay Time either. What we have may look like Calvinist punctuality, but it's the meaning that counts, and our meaning isn't Western. This is Japanese-Way."

But Japanese-Way, in *on* and its other manifestations as propounded by Rick, remained elusive and ambiguous to her. It came to her always as a question, never as an answer. And Rick scorned her attempts, declaring that she was hopelessly verbal (he, a professor, she thought in Honolulu, her lips twisting with sarcasm, a man who never shut up.) Her intuition, he said, was wrecked by lawyer-training. Her mind was Western-scrambled. He refused all explanation, declaring the process intuitive or nothing.

Perhaps it was. But not until long after she broke with him did it occur to her to wonder whether he understood either, or even believed he did; to wonder if his dogmatism and frenzy were mobilized, at bottom, against his own sense of panic and cultural unrootedness.

As for her, Rick said she never got it right; she was never right.

For almost a year she bent herself to his instruction in Japanese-Way. She had known confusedly then, and she knew more clearly with the retrospective of the years, that Rick, with Ramp Deedon on one side of him and Huey Newton on the other, was struggling to create a way out of the point-counterpoint-count-me-out of imposed ideas of Asian-American masculinity — or its lack.

Later, she had come to acknowledge that she had been implicated in setting up the situation. For her, the relationship involved retribution upon Caroline who became Jamilyah and abandoned her. With Rick, she sought for herself whatever mysterious racial-cultural safe harbor Caroline as Jamilyah claimed to have found. And it represented a refuge from the emotional damage she had accumulated, in her foundered relationships with Ramp, and with Don the poet who had elegized her eyes and frozen her sexuality until she became involved with Rick. It gave her a space to explore something about femininity and self, away from gazes where she risked damage by White people through being reduced to an eroticized, objectified stereotype: geisha girl, picture bride, Dragon Lady.

Now in Honolulu, she reflected on Will's astute question about her mother's ironic stance and cultural assertiveness in her cultivation of flower arranging. She saw now that what she had always thought of as her mother's reclusiveness was also a resolute, graceful and rigid exclusiveness, a refusal of her father's centrifugality of cultural embrace. Perhaps in that relationship with Rick Paula had also been seeking some understanding of her mother's occulted stance in the world as a Japanese-American woman.

For these complex reasons she had allowed herself to play the female foil to Rick as he wrestled with his own American hurt, humiliation and anger.

Perhaps she had loved in that apartment of *shoji*-screens and melancholy light; perhaps she had been loved.

Certainly, she had learned, less importantly what Rick sought to teach her than about personality — his and hers.

He was quintessentially an instructor, Rick, of the sort that has a strong authoritarian and even sadistic streak; and when five years after she walked out the door of his apartment in San Francisco he got tenure in an Ethnic Studies program at a prestigious university and his academic career turned stellar, she perceived, oddly enough for the first time, that in that conventionality her apparently unconventional lover had found his niche. In this, she thought, he was after all not so different from Ramp, to whom she had tended to oppose him during their affair. It was she who was different; she who had chosen — or been driven by some internal compulsion — to remain in her one-room studio, continued to work in women's prisons, in Japantown tenements, based at the Legal Aid collective's cramped quarters in a grubby alley off San Francisco's Market Street, downtown.

She knew an inner obsessive aspect of Rick as instructor that later served him so well professionally, an ultimately almost sinister side that had been destructive to her. It was his personal and cultural version of the profound sexism of patriarchal nationalisms and of parts of the counterculture and the political Left, their ironic glove-fit with the dominant culture. Black Berets and Brown Berets and white-robed Karate-worshiping cultural counselors like Rick, staring down Green Berets. For her, this was a negative thread among the genuine honesty and generosity and courage of much of the political activity of her generation in their twenties and the century's sixties, that made her proud to have been part of it. And Rick's enmeshment in this negative tendency was another dimension of his unexpected conventionality.

That side of him lived for her not in visual but in kinetic memories: his hands on the shoulder damaged when South Regional headquarters blew up shot pain through her as he twisted her body because her kneeling posture was never right.

On the day their relationship ruptured her breathing was ragged from running two blocks uphill from where the bus, slow to arrive, had deposited her, and that shoulder was aching.

"You're late," he snapped in the sharp formal style he adopted for their sessions. "Go back out and start again."

So Paula, at two thirty and thirty-eight seconds — thirty-eight seconds past the appointed moment — bowed in apology, backed out into the tiny foyer before his apartment, stepped over the threshold again, assumed the kneeling posture on the mat. Felt his hands painfully — unmindfully, she had suddenly thought, and mindfulness was the foundation of the attitude he taught as Japanese-way — yes, unmindfully, on her damaged shoulder.

Without reflection, in visceral revolt, she shook him off and stood up.

"If this is J-way, fuck it."

For "J-way," he would never forgive her.

She walked out the door.

Now, in Honolulu, she drained her glass and thrust it aside with her memories, and went out past the cooing rock doves to do her shopping.

Yet, returning home, the memories came to her again in the form of a new thought.

When Will Cawdry, regarding her, intrigued and appreciative, commented on how, in a language to which she had come consciously only late in life, she recited a poem she didn't know she knew; and on her hands, which outside her awareness created patterns she had put aside and thought she had forgotten — was he talking about Japanese-Way? One kind, at least, as true as Rick's or Ginnie's?

The thought still had hold of her as she drew from her mailbox a manila envelope addressed to her in a familiar jagged hand she could not place and labeled '*Do Not Bend.*' Then she remembered it from the lettering on the menu at the Pine Tar. So Will had done the fine calligraphy, as well as the décor and the food. His writing was more legible than it seemed at first glance. He used an unusual, thick-nibbed fountain pen and jet-black ink, and wrote with assurance and ease. So he cared about his script, even casual notes. He was a pseudo-semi-literate, this self-styled good ole boy, cracker.

Carefully, she worked her finger beneath the flap and withdrew the only enclosure. She slipped the envelope in a desk drawer instead of throwing it away, setting aside the thought that she wanted to retain that connection with him, and examined the full-color glossy print.

She and Will stood, their arms full of nestling nēnē-bird. His was in profile, hers looked straight at the camera, comical and touching with its black face mask and bemused stare.

She saw her own face as she usually did, in mirror or photograph: with an alienated and alienating numbness, a dispassion or disconnectedness, that she had never analyzed. Hair that, unbound, would reveal a wave when she wore it this long. Polynesian hair, her father used to say, affectionately, at the end, when he was thinking so much about Hawai'i.

The birds' feathers ruffled slightly in the breeze, and the ends of Will's bright neck-scarf and his straw-colored hair fluttered gaily, like pennants. He had been right. She was obviously tired; shadowed places beneath her eyes made her look vulnerable, and that frightened her. What had he called it? A long-standing tiredness. It do have a certain look, he had said. Would it go away? She touched the bruised-looking places on her face.

She studied Will. He was more photogenic than she would have predicted, given his harsh exaggerated features. But they did not look that way in this representation. His upper arm lay close against hers. She did not remember that, and he did not seem aware of it. He faced directly into the camera, grinning, looking surprisingly young, unbattered or worn, surprisingly happy.

She propped the print on the brick and board shelf with her family belongings.

Lying down on the futon, she stared at it for a while in the rapidly dwindling daylight, her mind uncharacteristically blank of thought. Outside, the mynahs were shrieking, invisible in the obscure depths of the banyan, back from their day's mysterious wanderings in the city, preparing to settle down for another round of sleep.

Already the sky was almost dark. Through the accidental space that was her view and that sounded like a note of grace amongst the monstrous towers hemming her in, the lights of outlying Honolulu trailed down the lower slopes of the Koolaus, bringing to mind kukui nut torches in villages here, in bygone days.

The objects on the low board along the wall seemed to gather the darkness to them like a soft mantle. In the strange light of the brief dusk, each stood out with a unique etched line, imbued with a deep melancholy and mystery.

She was more tired than she knew, and as she drifted unintentionally into sleep, the faces in the photograph she had just placed traveled with her.

Will, unexpectedly carefree, almost radiant, with the gay neckerchief and the nestling nēnēbird.

Her own image — shadowed but smiling through shadow.

Suddenly, as palpable as if living, Euph hovered in the air before her. Complex old man, hooded eyes, gleam in them that he had bequeathed to Will, the look a passepartout beyond all barriers of biology and caste.

The telephone shrilled. She jumped. Euph vanished.

"I were thinking," Will said without preamble. Nervous? She was aware of the hundreds of miles of sea and sky that stretched between them. "I reckon you're pretty busy these days?"

"Enough to keep me out of trouble before nightfall. And I'm going to the NorthShore for a few days. I'll be back Thursday." She hesitated, and did not tell him how significant this pilgrimage was to her. "Why?"

"Oh, I were thinking" — His accent and grammar wavered under stress. "Only if you aren't busy, which you probably are being back in the big city and all, but if you weren't I was thinking there's something I could show you here, but it'd have to be this weekend coming up. It's like my music and your pool game. A lot of preparation behind it, but it's all in the moment's doing, and the moment ain't to be commanded."

"Very intriguing. I think I'll accept."

"I — you will?" He rallied from his surprise, became casual.

They made arrangements about the hotel and her arrival time. He finished with, "And, do be my guest, Yumi."

"We'll split expenses," she said firmly.

"Well, if you're sure. I try never to argue with a lawyer, lady or not."
Paula laughed.

"Did you get the photograph yet? Us and the nēnēbirds?"

"Just today. Many thanks."

"Good. Good."

They finished arrangements. She could hear his elation at his mysterious surprise for her.

"It's one of those things worth seeing," said Will.

13

North Shore, O'ahu: The Other Yumi

Paula swung the car onto Ala Wai Boulevard and drove along the canal, then crossed it at the McCully Street bridge.

This short passage across the canal from Waikīkī led out of the city through a slow-paced neighborhood of modest single-story houses sheltered behind a wealth of fertile trees, lemon and papaya, mango and breadfruit and banana, so different from Waikīkī it seemed to be in another world.

She was beginning to love this varied city — raunchy, elegant, shabby, outrageous, pocketed with unexpected treasures. Yet as she left it now she was impressed once more with how it encroached like a predator on the countryside. It colluded with the oppressive presence of the U.S. military, weighted with men, materiel, and history. Linchpin of U.S. empire, mainstay of the unending war with Asia, the prize for which the U.S. government had collaborated with U.S. settlers to bring down Lili'uokalani, and with her fifteen hundred years of Hawaiian sovereignty.

Over there, at her peripheral vision, low notch in the far mountains, through which one day planes blazing with rising suns showed against the heavens —

December 7.

Things that set her at a distance, silenced, when speaking with White political comrades: The esteemed Warren Court (but what about Internment?) The atom bomb (you're shocked, but I lost relatives in Nagasaki.) The camps (they upset you but my grandfather died there, I was born there. They didn't lock your family up.) At home, though, December 7 escalated the tension between her parents.

All through her childhood, the weeks leading up to that date thickened the air of her home to a leaden pall, and brought the daily illness of her school anxiety to a sharp pain, for although she would not be attacked there — only on the streets between school and home — the careful historical observation always forefronted in class made her yellow skin and slitted eyes burn. She became, horribly, the focus of all attention. At some point, too, she became aware that her parents argued over the day: her mother wanted to leave the radio off, her father, addicted to the news, made a point of turning it on and defiantly making comments about the fascism of imperial Japan and the imperialism of the United States, in Hawai'i and elsewhere.

Now, leaving Honolulu,

"*Kamikaze!*" she shouted, thinking of the conquistador tormentors of her childhood. She slammed her foot against the accelerator and shot away towards O'ahu's central plain, that still retained remembrance of pineapple and cane, rooted in red dirt.

She was going to Kahuku for the first time, the town near where her father's people had lived. Since her arrival in the islands she had postponed this journey; she feared what she would feel. Her conversation with Will Cawdry about her parents and her childhood had precipitated it.

Kahuku, where her great-grandfather Kajiyama had come, invited by the Hawaiian King, Kalākaua; murdered by the Americans in a concentration camp..

Kahuku, where her father had grown up.

In the last year of his life, when he began to talk story to her about his family, the stories that drove a wedge between him and her mother by breaking their pact of silence, her father told her:

My mother and father went ahead to San Francisco to start a life there. It didn't work out, my father became ill, my mother didn't send for me for years. I grew up in Kahuku, with my grandfather Kajiyama and my cousin Yumi. Yumi took care of me when my parents went away, and took me everywhere with her. You are named for her.

She always objected to the conditions we worked under on the plantation, and always explained things to me. She joined the union as soon as organizers came. They were a Hawaiian couple, Kalani and his wife Rebecca. Yumi was always a rebel. She would never behave right, according to most of the family.

Some of them said she acted so unsuitably because she'd mostly been raised by a Hawaiian neighbor family who adopted her when her parents both died young. They said she was part-Hawaiian too, and maybe she was, who knows? Something of a whispered scandal there. I never knew the details, I was too young. That would be interesting. She looked a little like you, you have the same hair. But we don't all look alike, you know.

He laughed and went on: But our old great-aunt who helped bring her up too and remembered things said Yumi acted the way she did because she was just like her mother, who was as Japanese as anybody. She had come to

Hawai'i by herself — not as a picture bride. Don't let anyone tell you picture brides were passive dolls. To come as they did meant taking great risks. But don't let people tell you all the women who came were picture brides, because it wasn't true. Some had another kind of courage.

My great-aunt said Yumi was just like her mother, when she left Japan, she went to see — for herself.

Then Cruz came to Hawai'i from Puerto Rico with his machete and set to work in the cane. Here we would call him a Negro. No one knew why he left those islands to come halfway around the world to Hawai'i. He was a very strong man, not just outside with the machete but inside too.

Cruz knew the job; Cruz knew cane. It wasn't the cane or the working in the cane that brought him trouble. It was working with the workers in the cane. Because Cruz knew men too. And he didn't just know them, he cared about them — the workers in the cane. The plantation owners tried to make him a luna, an overseer, but he didn't want that. He went on cutting cane himself, and organizing the workers with Kalani; they got to be good friends. Yumi worked with Rebecca, organizing the women. And Yumi took me with her everywhere when she did organizing work, too. After awhile she married Cruz, and those four became my heroes. They still are.

When word came that the owners were planning arrests, neighbors warned them. They went away in secret one night, no one knows where. Now I realize that they must all have been very young when they disappeared. Yumi and Rebecca were probably seventeen, and Cruz and Kalani only about twenty. But I was only nine.

And did they ever come back? Paula demanded anxiously.

No, said her father. They never came back.

Pulling up at the place she was staying in Kahuku, Paula could hear the wound from the loss in his voice as clearly as the night he first spoke the words.

I never found out what happened to them. Sometimes I'm afraid it was something bad, because I think Yumi, at least, would have tried to find me again. But I don't really know. Sometimes life takes you away even from the ones you love. One thing I know, wherever they went, they went on working for the people. But they never came back. So I went on. With life. With the work. To be like them.

In that last year of his life, when the powers that be were using threats and bribes to dislodge them, and her mother wanted them to move back to San Francisco, she overheard her father reply passionately:

I've been moved twice already when I didn't want to be. When they sent me to the camp, and when they sent me here afterward. I didn't want to come but I've made a life here, and I'm damned if I'll be moved again when it isn't my idea.

And he never had been moved, not by threat or bribe. He had died, and perhaps the powers that be had killed him. *Murder? Harakiri? Kamikaze?* But they had never defeated him. She knew that, because of how he spoke to her on the day he died. Ten years later during the struggle for Civil Rights and against the war in Vietnam, when blue waves of police and military armed with truncheons and guns swept down on her and her comrades, she would stand with interlocked arms and sing, *Just like a tree that's standing by the water, We shall not be moved.* And she thought of her father. And, before him, of Kalani and Rebecca, of Cruz and of the other Yumi.

What she had made of them and of the stories that he told gave her life shape and her heart the strength to live it.

Paula clicked shut the door of her rented cabin on NorthShore, O'ahu, not far from Kahuku, and stepped out into the night.

She walked for a long time, through dusty fields of broken wild-growing cane, along half-trails, toward the sea. The living breeze, that almost never failed, moved in her hair, stroked her skin like a gentle hand, in a caress she was coming to cherish and to trust.

At the beach she removed her sandals, dangling them lightly from her fingers. Waves lapped and laughed against the silken sand. Coconut fronds moved like long hair in blacker silhouette against a black sky. Moonbeams rippled over black water. Other black silhouettes loomed on the sand: beached outriggers and smaller craft.

She thought of her father's subversive commitment to the Beloved Community, long before it was ever called that. Joy unleashed with secrets in the stories and shouts of laughter he shared in his study with Jim Jordan late at night. In that world of the South Side of Chicago, 1950's, in the bitter struggle with the University, the Association was a fragile living thing, always threatening schism and collapse along fault lines of race and class. But her father and Jim Jordan had been able to meet along other lines of loyalty, ones that her father had come to primarily in a certain complex plantation Hawai'i. That association had held; when Paula and her mother moved to San Francisco, Jim Jordan moved to Ghana in West Africa. She received a New Year's card from him every year until he died in 1977.

From Yumi and Cruz, Kalani and Rebecca, Paula's father had learned to struggle doggedly against potentially disastrous lines of cleavage; he had learned how to forge alliance among the workers in the cane. Alliance woven of sea murmuring on sand, of the thud of poi pounders, of machete blows on canestalk, of temple bells and hula rhythms, of taiko drums and drums that called Legba, Legba come to Hawai'i from another archipelago of sugar and cane halfway around the world. Another archipelago of plantation and calabash, thought Paula now, scattered shards of the same post-Columbian disaster, invaded, colonized, suppressed, bound and uprisen. Alliance of the class-oppressed: union speeches, warnings whispered in the dark of night in plantation cabins and under palm fronds, solidarities of silence under interrogation, echoed long later on a distant Mainland binding her father and Jim Jordan as comrades: *Are you now or have you ever been. . .*

Betrayals too. Who told the authorities about Yumi and Cruz, Kalani and Rebecca? And other kinds of betrayals, as when so many of the people in the Association broke faith with her father; and he died.

Shadows and silence had disordered the harmonics of the beleaguered refugee family within the four walls of the shadowy apartment on the South Side of Chicago. Her parents had been complicitous in silences. Never to speak of the camps and the past, and little of their families. Never to speak of, or confront, the genteel silence at Greenoaks School, or the abuse shouted at them in the public streets and visited upon Paula to the extent of threatening her life.

Her mother had not wanted her father to found the Association. When the pressure upon them came from the University, she urged their return to San Francisco, as she had for as long as Paula could remember. And when her father took the case, they quarreled bitterly. In conversations overheard through her cracked-open bedroom door, late at night when she was supposed to be asleep, Paula heard her first reference to the camps. Her mother believed that for her father to make himself the spearpoint of the Association, *the lightning rod in the fight against Sam,* thought Paula on the beach near Kahuku, would bring disaster down on them again, as it had come down on them in 1942 and sent them to Tule Lake.

And, in that, her mother had been right.

There had been passion between Paula's parents. She had grown up with that knowledge and carried the capacity within her. In her childhood she knew the passion as warmth and love they held for each other and for her. But after Paula's father died, her mother shrouded herself and all passion in silence. She never spoke of the Association, or of the silences in their family, and rarely of Paula's father and then only in the most formal way.

All that passion between them was hidden terrifyingly from Paula's sight, and forbidden evocation in memory.

In those quarrels at the end, her mother punished with silence. Perhaps she sought to protect with it, too. Paula, grown, had been reflective enough to wonder if even her father, whose empowering memory she cherished, would have tried to bend and mold her, a girl-child, along conventional paths, had he lived into her adolescence; and to wonder if the insistence, the strength, that informed her mother's unbending infliction of silence had been her most powerful perceived resource in that relationship. For Paula, grown, could recognize in the recalled cadences of her father's exchanges with her mother the strain of domination that — grown — she had encountered and finally refused in her own passionate relationships with men. Her mother had been of another generation, apparently raised in a deeply traditional way. Was silence a fashion learned early in which to assert the strength of will that shone forth from her in the picture at the concentration center, and that had graced her reserve and informed the respect for another being with which she had touched Paula the child?

But the silence had cut Paula deeply; and she knew that it had cut her father deeply too. When he and her mother exchanged their last words her mother had hardly spoken for a week. Those last words Paula heard — overheard — her mother speak to him were the bitter, scornful, almost contemptuous words, an hour after the assault upon him at the last Association meeting and an hour before he died. She had said: "What did you expect, getting involved with *those people?*"

"*Those people* are our neighbors," her father had retorted.

"And you see how neighbors like that treat us!" And her mother shut herself in her sewing room, where she had never sewed, but had recourse to herself. There, she did her flower arranging. More and more in that last year she had spent hours in that room away from them.

After that bitter exchange, Paula's father came down the hall to her room and stopped in her door. There he spoke his last words to her about his understanding of life: despite betrayal not to lose faith in the struggle or in her comrades.

Paula had understood even at the time that his words to her were the response he had not made to her mother.

Silence became the weapon that slashed a chasm continuous with death.

And her father's death was the deep enigma of Paula's life with him. Natural causes, murder by betrayal and heartbreak, *Harakiri, kamikaze?*

Silence was the corresponding enigma she carried from her mother. Silence given expression in the photograph where, dressed in garb Paula could never associate with her, she knelt on a tatami mat in some unknown place, with the unknown woman she said was *her* mother.

Clues lived on in the gifts of calabash and of precision with flower and branch; clues, but not answers.

She had lost her father because her father had spoken; her mother had told her father that speech would bring disaster, and it had. After he died she told Paula that too. So Paula lived with the tacit threat that if she broke her mother's strictures enjoining silence, she would lose her mother too.

But she lost her mother anyway, into that vortex of silence.

Paula knew that her own emotional life had been narrowly channeled but deeply cut. She had been inclined to solitude by temperament, and circumstances had made her a lonely and isolated child, surrounded by menace.

After her family was destroyed and her mother grew more silent, and then died too, Paula had grown into adulthood a person of few but intense emotional commitments, deeply rooted in the past and her family. Those commitments dug deep and died hard and when they were clawed or torn from her life, they left severe wounds that remained tender beneath scarring.

She had had two passionate erotic loves — with Ramp and with Rick — and one comradeship and friendship, passionate and sensuous, maybe erotic too, with Caroline who became Jamilyah. But that line of her possible eroticism did not strike deep enough to allow her to travel into the world June Yasui had inhabited; just as other parts of her nature made it impossible for her to follow Caroline, when she became Jamilyah, into a world of emotionally stylized violence.

The experience in Patchagoula had contained all the intensity and all the truth she had garnered from her father's commitment to the Association, and from her mother's equally intense though occulted loyalties. That capacity for loyalty, for commitment, entwined with her father's beliefs, rooted Paula's social commitment in life.

The abiding treasure of Patchagoula was what she had learned and could use to nourish other communities. But it had ended in personal disaster. She and Caroline had walked the dusty country roads together for over a year. After the flame-flowering of South Regional Headquarters, when Caroline became Jamilyah, Paula still felt viscerally that Caroline's definition of 'her people' was not right. She could not find grounds to argue. Caroline's retrenchment struck an answering chord in Paula; now, after Will's question, she wondered if she had intuited it as akin to her mother's stance. Paula's mother had been right about the Association bringing disaster; increasingly, Paula felt that Caroline's position that America would never — *could* never — alter its racist society might be true.

But still, when her head ached so it blinded her and she thought she felt a shard of glass from the childhood assault by conquistadors moving through her brain along with the fragments of the bone broken by police truncheons, she still felt that the shard of glass and damaged bone were not the deepest thing. Even if because of them the last blood vessel in her brain were severed and she died, deeper than the shard or bonepoint was the feel of the silky dust between her toes and Caroline's when they sat beside the cotton fields and massaged each other's feet; and the strength they radiated to each other when they faced the death-dealing crowds.

14

North Shore, O'ahu: Plantation and Calabash

In the autumn of the last year of the Association, it became clear that the trial was set to begin and that her father would not withdraw. Paula's parents quarreled about it, quietly and bitterly at night when they thought she couldn't hear.

One evening as she sat at her desk in her bedroom doing homework, she suddenly became aware of a presence and looked up to see her father in the hall.

"When you've finished, Yumi, I've got something to show you."

On his work table in the rear sunporch of the apartment he had spread a strange cloth, deep brown, patterned with intricate angular designs in black. Awed, she ran her fingers over a fabric she had never touched before, supple, wondrously soft as a cat's short rich fur.

"Come, sit down beside me." He placed on the fabric a box of light-colored wood that yielded a faint spicy odor when he opened it. "Camphor wood and kapa, Polynesian cloth. Made from beaten fibers. This piece is Hawaiian. Both the box and the kapa are very old. So is this."

Fragment by fragment, he removed from the box irregularly shaped pieces of hard shiny material, deep brown and glowing gold, and laid them out on the kapa. "My cousin Yumi, your namesake, gave this to me, the night she and the others went away. The Hawaiian family who raised her had given it to her. She was their hanai daughter. Hanai is an old Hawaiian custom, adoption but deeper than any Western adoption. This calabash is of koa wood, very fine, unusual for a poor family to have."

He lifted the largest fragment, turning it in his blunt sensitive fingers. The surface was exquisitely decorated with patterns, some bold, some delicately filigreed in black line. "The designs are etched by burning. This was a household bowl. They were used for food, or to hold water, or sometimes for floating bouquets. The bowls are very much treasured in families, they get passed down through the generations."

"How did it get broken?" Paula was indignant.

Her father smiled. "Sooner or later they were likely to be. They were used carefully, even reverently, but they were used, for the everyday activities that kept the household going. So when they got broken, people mended them, and the mending was a highly regarded craft in itself. See here?"

He turned the fragment. An expanse of darker wood extended from the etched design, as if part of the design itself. "That's called a plug. It's a repair. So it had been broken and mended at least once before."

He traced the plug lovingly. "Fine work. We'll see if my father was right when he told me I had his carpenter's hands — he meant hands to do work like this."

It was the only time Paula could remember that he ever mentioned anything his father had said to him. He glanced at the arrangement of autumn branches she had brought him in the blue-black vase with a sheen like a blackbird's wing, and the plum blossom design in gold. "I already know you have hands like his — from your mother, if not from me." He smiled.

The smile faded.

"I haven't — directed my attention — to Hawai'i for a very long time. Then Jim and I started talking, and we founded the Association — Your mother and I — have not looked backward very much. She still doesn't want to. Respect that, Yumi. I've heard you asking her questions. Don't if she doesn't want you to. But since the Association, I've been wanting to go back, look back, bring what's back there up here. Give it to you. I've wanted to get my life back again, as something to — pass on. To you."

After that, once or twice a week, her father would look into her bedroom after supper and say, "Calabash night, Yumi?"

Her mother never objected, although Paula sensed her discomfort. In this, however, her mother respected her father's wishes, as he had instructed Paula to respect hers.

So, her homework finished, Paula would go into her father's workshop, where with fine brushes and glue and infinite care they began to fit the calabash fragments together.

Now, after the upwelling of memory stimulated by her time with Will in the Alcove Room, Paula recalled that she always took with her a seasonal flower or branch arrangement in that black lacquer vase which now stood next to her father's burial box. She would set the vase in a hanging alcove he had built in a corner of the room.

They had just recreated the calabash when her father died in the spring.

Paula had pressed José Sánchez to speak beyond the moment's endurance, and then could not speak the words that might have given him strength until he found greater endurance again. After that, and she believed in part because of that, he swung silent in the shadows and her life fell apart when his life ended.

When that happened, she had not sought the stability and security of the known and the implicitly affirming that her mother chose and Caroline chose when she became Jamilyah. Instead, she came to Hawai'i. She now knew she had come to recreate the calabash and to trace out the footsteps of the other Yumi, for whom she was named, in the place where her father had been happy.

In the Black Star Club, the neighborhood space she had found again in Euph's, the Association was born. In the meeting hall of St. Samuel's Abyssinia Baptist Church down the block, it died.

For the first time, Paula's mother had come; and for the first time, her father had not wanted her there. What had moved her? Some bitter loyalty, or something uglier — a sense of what might happen, maybe better than her father's sense, and a sense of triumph in having been right?

Shouting out against Jim Jordan's objections, Paula heard the neighbors' voices:

"Case mighta been all right, but you can't tell me he were trying. Not no-way!"

"If you so sorry, why don't you fall on your sword? Commit hari-KEERY."

When her father would not leave despite her whispered urging, Paula's mother left. She and Paula had a brief, silent tug of war as Paula gripped the edge of the pew and refused to accompany her.

Going out, later, ahead of her father, as he stayed with Jim Jordan to return his papers to his briefcase after his attempted explanation and apology to the Association members about losing the case, Paula overheard:

"Did you hear him talking in court? Voice all low and flat, like he weren't hardly interested. And what he apologizing to us for, tonight, all mealy-mouthed with that little bucktooth grin? Cain't trust these people — I know 'em from the war."

"Oh, he was interested in the case I reckon." That was Arnie Harris. He was White, from Kentucky, and worshiped at Reverend Tucker's church where they shouted the way they did here at St. Samuel's where the Negroes went. Normally he and the first speaker would not have exchanged a word, but sat apart at the meetings and looked at each other suspiciously. Tonight they came together, as the Association crumbled under Sam's assault, to huddle together and find reassurance in attacking Paula's father. "But fall on his sword? Don't count on it. No sir. He'll get something outta this, I reckon."

A second voice said, "Right. Might be papers in that fancy briefcase tonight, but sometime soon there's gonna be thick wads of green."

"Naw man, it's a job he's gonna get. Lawyer for the University. That's what I heard." A third voice.

And another voice, demurring. This one Paula recognized. Ollie Graves, who played pool with her father and Jim Jordan, and with her. "Of course you heard. The man tole us hisself, same night Jim Jordan told us he got offered a job teaching there. They was bribes, man, and they both turned 'em down. And Kajiyama always talks that way, all flat. It don't mean nothing bad, it's just the way those people talk. I think he tried. Why'd we think we could win in the ofay courts, anyway?"

"I'm with Ollie on that. I think you're wrong, man." Thomas Graves spoke. "I think Kajiyama's okay. It ain't him doing us wrong, it's this whole damn White Man's country."

A snort. "You watch. The Kajiyamas won't be on this block for long."

"Won't none of us be on this block for long. We lost the case," said Ollie.

"Yeh, but when the Ka-jee-yammas go it'll be with thick wads of green." The second man to speak was pleased with his phrase and repeated it again. "Thick wads of green."

Then the sound of Mrs. Lili'uokalani Turner arriving, slowly coming from the pews on her cane.

"You all should be ashamed of yourselves. Mr. Kajiyama's a good man. A good friend."

None chose to dispute with her. The little group broke up.

These were the people who had spoken for her father, in the meeting and out: Jim Jordan, Ollie Henderson, Thomas Graves, Reverend Tucker, Reverend Auburn of St. Samuel's, Father Hurley of St. Michael's, the local parish church, and Mrs. Lili'uokalani Turner.

Paula never forgot that roll call.

And of all the two hundred members of the Association, only they had come to her father's memorial service to eat the fine-rolled sushi laid out on translucent porcelain plates and greet Paula and her mother where they stood together at the head of the table: to do these things to honor her father.

After the meeting, at home, her mother had shut herself in the sewing room, her father had stopped at Paula's bedroom door to tell her never to abandon the struggle, then gone to his study.

Paula, alone in her room, had wept, then wiped the tears from her face. Intent, she spent half an hour finishing a seasonal arrangement, then timidly walked down the hall with the vase.

The door to her father's study was closed. She heard faint sounds, which she knew he made as he moved about, but tonight they sounded wounded and they frightened her.

She hesitated. She felt the squeeze of her fingers around the vase, and consciously relaxed her grip, fearing the fragile glass would shatter. She knocked, softly.

The door half-opened. Her father's room was filled with soft golden light, a generosity of light, blessing the corridor where she stood. Only his desk lamp provided illumination. Relief flooded her with the light. She took a step forward, black vase in her hand, with its gold plum sprig design and the delicate branches rising from its lip. Behind him she saw: desk, soft and serene in the light's benediction. Green blotter. A small round alarm clock with the burnished gold rim that matched the crescent-shaped leaves on the drapes and the gold plum sprigs on the vase. The clock was ticking quietly and steadily and read twenty-seven minutes past nine, and the second hand swept around its face in smooth contrast to the discrete ticking sound. And in the center of the blotter on the desk was the heavy thick rectangle of case documents.

For a moment she didn't look up because she didn't want to see his face seeing that document. He crossed the narrow wedge of space where she could glimpse him past the doorframe.

"Come in, Yumi," he said then; his voice sounded thick and strange. She did. He was holding the calabash carefully in his hands.

Now, she told herself. Now was the moment to speak. But what could she say, of what she had heard and overheard at St. Samuel's that night, what she had overheard in the cracked-door nights when her parents quarreled? What could she say of her bleeding nails and *Kamikaze* shouts, of the silence at Greenoaks, of everything that surrounded and infiltrated and distorted their lives? What could she say to heal his wounds? Her own? She did not know, and so, fatally, she said nothing.

She was looking directly at him but later she could never remember his face at that moment. That fact tormented her. Maybe his head was already down, hand clutching his arm, and then letting go as he crashed against the wooden floor, crushing the calabash into fragments beneath him. The earth shook when he fell.

Ever after she had been haunted by the feeling that each minute had a hole in it, a place in time where she couldn't breathe and the universe couldn't move: because her father died.

Almost twenty-five years later, Paula stood caught in that moment rising vividly around her again.

The sand whispered between her toes. Moonlight laid itself, a flat river, between her and the coconut grove ahead.

And then, a movement, and something emerged from the grove. Paula stood transfixed. She knew she could not have stirred had she wanted to, but she did not want to. The hairs on her neck rose, her entire body grew as alive as the night around her, porous and open. She thought that perhaps she should be terrified, but she was not. She simply stood, opening and opening like space, turning to space, as a moonlight figure with a face she could not see but knew as intimately as her own walked toward her, its hair continuous with the palm fronds and with the waves trailing behind her.

The other Yumi walked up to her, through her, stirring and coupling with and altering the molecules of her mind, was altered by them, walked through her, and was gone.

Behind her, when Paula turned to look for the figure, the night and the beach and coconut groves, the sand and sea, stretched beautifully and emptily away.

15

Music Over the Water

From Euph's where Will sat alone at the piano, music traveled over the dark water of Hilo Bay, flowing into the night, persuading the leaves of the banyan and banana to join their whispering with its tones.

Ben, preparing for the next day in the kitchen of the Pine Tar, recognized the intricate weaving and re-weaving: Will was making new long music.

Would the Japanese city-woman from Honolulu recognize the process too? Part of Ben didn't want to give up that unique knowledge to anyone; part of him hoped she would come to it also, if she was going to be in Will's life. He wished she wouldn't be. Why that woman, with the world full of women? But something in Will's playing told Ben this new music was about her.

He snorted and set down a dish so hard he almost chipped it.

Emma said that the woman was all right, and Ben respected her view; Emma knew a lot about many things, including a lot about people in ways that Ben didn't. But Emma did not know Will the way he did; and especially she didn't know about Will and the time before Hawai'i.

She didn't know about Will and cities. She had never known Will in the truly bad times. She didn't know how bad they could get.

Ben remembered the night, fifteen years ago now, when he and Will had glided into Hilo Bay. He remembered the sudden silence of the moment when their pilot cut the boat's engine, remembered how in the stillness he heard the waves lapping at the prow and the leap of his heart against his ribcage as they approached the last, dangerous part of their landing, where they might be intercepted, and lose the chance for a new life.

They had come to Hawai'i from an Asian city. Ben (unlike Will) knew perfectly well which one. But he was anxious never to go back. He feared being tracked down. He feared that his citizenship papers would be exposed as forged. And he feared the self-losing sickness cities caused in Will. So he never spoke its name, even when he was just thinking, as if the act of naming could draw them back under its power. Ben never explained why he had left his home, or when; he seldom explained anything. Only his sense that the Japanese woman from Honolulu was a great danger to Will had driven him to tell her that cities gave Will an illness that threatened his soul.

In the 1960's Will spent a lot of time in Asian cities; a lot of his business contacts were there. But Ben had come to know a certain look in Will's eyes — in those strange eyes without color that had taken him so long to read — when Will was especially tired, or especially under strain, or especially drunk.

Sometimes, standing at an intersection in a city, multitudes teeming around him, those eyes would go totally blank, that thin mobile mouth, that for a long time looked lipless to Ben, would suddenly, just for a moment, quiver at its edges. And for just that moment, Ben came to know, Will was all the way out of this world.

It never happened back-country, on remote islands or at sea. It never happened when he was riding or flying in the sky.

Will's self-losing sickness was connected with cities; cities stole his soul.

That was one reason Ben had felt so good when the sun came up on Hilo that first morning and he saw not a city but a quiet good-sized town. That was why he felt so happy when Will took the way he did to those rickety-rackety buildings, half tree-hidden by the lagoon, that he made into Euph's and the Pine Tar.

Even though Ben came from just a small place and first saw a city on the run, he had learned his way in cities better than Will. That was something else that even a pretty close observer would have had a hard time knowing.

On a certain afternoon of crisis, long before he met Will, when, uncharacteristically, Ben did not much care whether he survived or not, he decided to do so; and, having decided, he learned how. But he felt he had not been very smart, or he would never have ended in exile from his village, which he missed with a deep unspoken sadness. When Pearlie came to live with Ben and Emma, and there was a child in the home at last, Ben was profoundly grateful, for he took it as a confirming sign that he was not, after all, forsaken utterly by his ancestors and his gods.

He tried to spare Emma his inward sorrow. He did not want her to feel he was unhappy in their life together, and except for this old grief, he was not.

So only Will, his companion of long years, guessed the existence of that other grief in him — the loss of his village.

Before he came to Hawai'i, Ben's genius for locating the most profitable action, and for sizing up character, had gained him renown in many places across East and Southeast Asia. People sought him out in business, and spoke of him, with admiration and envy, as "like a Chinee." They were also surprised, exactly because he came from a "small place." No one knew exactly where and had the tact of those circles not to inquire, but it was rumored to be from savage regions, where people still used shells for money, and ate each other on occasion. It was true that shells had been traditional currency among Ben's people, although not since World War II. had they traded with them exclusively; no one had ever eaten anyone in the place from which he came.

Ben also never denied the rumors about his origins, and this was considered to be to his credit and taken as additional evidence of his abilities, because normally no one with any sense would have done business with a man from such a place. Those city-people who were Ben's business collaborators did not understand that, not having a written language, Ben's people cultivated a highly sophisticated abstract mental agility, and phenomenal memory; this was how they orchestrated a complicated inter-island trading system. No one knew much about them because they were few and much attached to their islands and villages. They traveled little; in this Ben was extraordinary, by inclination and by circumstance.

At the point when he and Will arrived in Hawai'i they both happened to be holding a lot of cash, although no one could have told by their appearance — that was an elementary precaution for self-preservation.

In personality, Ben possessed a fundamental balance and he drank hardly at all, which went a long way toward explaining why he was the one of them who had held on to his money steadily. Will won and lost his in wild swings of fortune. When Ben met him, he was penniless and on the brink of self-destruction — as he had been for most of his life.

Will lacked Ben's gifts for trading and finance. He hadn't the stability to assess other people, especially then when he was drinking so hard. But he had other advantages.

Some were social. He had connections at a higher level than Ben ever would, being a White man and an American and a soldier who had fought bravely in Vietnam and had the medals to prove it. He could soar with almost any machine that flew, anywhere, under any conditions. In those years, his judgment of men failed almost as consistently as his control over his behavior around them. But miraculously, neither failed him in flight. The only control he maintained regarded his flying. He had never stepped into a cockpit other than stone sober.

And then, although Will could not reliably evaluate other people, he could attract them. Sometimes, unpredictably, a possession seized him that was not of his doing, frightening and compelling him as much it did others. Ben, especially, feared this possession. He knew it was not wholly human-natural.

Will called this his silver mood, and when it lay upon him he could persuade almost anyone to anything, for they sensed him as limitless capacity, fascinating and terrifying, born of an absence of center; sensed that he could do or be anything. From nothing, anything could come.

Southeast Asia, especially at that time, offered wide scope for profit to a man with Will's abilities and absolute blankness of scruple.

But Will could hold on to nothing in life. Money, people, places, came and went like breath or dream.

Then, he met Ben, who began to exert a stabilizing influence.

In Will's state of devastation, such tattered capacity for loyalty as he could muster went to Ben.

From the moment Ben intervened to stop a particularly nasty bar brawl involving broken Scotch bottles, and got Will out into an alley where a tropical downpour drenched his raving, Will had been in Ben's life as a younger brother.

And, in a room in Hong Kong, they had undergone the deep ceremony that, among Ben's people, made them brothers, as Will said, "for true."

Once, long before he met Will, Ben had had a younger brother.

That first morning, when the sun rose over Hilo Bay and Ben and Will began to look around, Ben proposed that they start a restaurant. Among his people, all serious cooking was done by men; and he and Will shared a great gift for the preparation of food.

Ben specialized in ocean harvests. His people were above all fishers in those small clustered islands set in a wide blue sea.

Will came from inland. He was a meat man, and devoted to things that grew in soil.

Ben staked the restaurant. Will fronted it. Ben couldn't front anything, being on the run and what the authorities in this place called an illegal alien.

In the beginning, then, Euph's and the Pine Tar was in Will's name and founded with Ben's money. For the first year they bunked together in the back room, until Ben began to court Emma and moved into town.

Ben declined Will's offer to name or share in the naming. Will needed the place by the water if he were to recover from his soul-sickness; Ben did not. So Will named it, and thus in its deepest sense it was his; but it could not have come into existence without Ben.

Perhaps settling down had been more Ben's idea than Will's; certainly Will had shown no signs of settling before they took up together. But maybe Ben had known something about Will that no one else did (of course, no one else cared enough to know) — something Will didn't know about himself: that he had the urge to settle, too.

Because when Will laid eyes on that place that became Euph's and the Pine Tar, he acted almost like he'd seen it before.

He repaired the buildings and planned out how they'd look. He built the furniture, and when wind and flood undid his work, he did it all again. And as the years went by he steadied down a lot.

He stopped drinking so hard; got reliable, after awhile, even for mundane things necessary, especially at the beginning, to the difficult grind of the restaurant business.

Ben didn't know why exactly, but in those hard knockabout days before Hawai'i, being with Will steadied him. For, even though he was fairly established in a business way, until he met Will he was all alone and rootless, and he hadn't been brought up to be all alone and rootless.

Ben came from a place rich in heat and rain, so every breath of breeze was a blessing too. Each morning the people rolled up and hung from the roof-poles the mats that served instead of walls, converting the village into a single big dwelling. People called from one house to another, and the thump of pestle on mortar, children's cries, sharp and salty remarks and men's and women's laughter, often ribald, all the dappling sounds that patterned the texture of daily life, passed from hut to hut and person to person without encountering barriers.

All this he had lost.

So Will steadied Ben, too, though Will didn't know it, and Ben never said it that way to himself. But the need for companionship created by the unbarriered walls of his village was satisfied with Will; and Ben loved him.

Still, though in Hawai'i Will steadied and settled and took to the good soil, he had drives, compulsions, that Ben did not share and did not understand. What he understood was how dangerous they could be.

From the first, Will had spent a lot of time out on the Lava Wastes, which Ben felt were places best avoided by human beings. And Will had a drive toward the sun and toward the heights, the upper slopes of the island's great mountains. Fire compelled him, and power and desolation; everything about the Lady's realms. Before long he'd created Volcano Flights.

That brought extra money. Too much extra money, Ben the businessman knew perfectly well that flying for the Park, or inter-island cargo hauling, or showing tourists around, couldn't account for the bounty.

The scare came in the second year after the founding of Volcano Flights.

Ben never knew exactly what happened, but for a week Will went back to his hard bottle ways and spent most of his time lying on his cot in the room behind Euph's until Ben dug him out and made him do his drinking at the big wooden table in the kitchen of the Pine Tar. Ben wanted the company — bad as it was just then — and he wanted to keep an eye on Will. He didn't intend to let him fly on out of this world to wherever he'd been heading when Ben met him.

Along toward the end of that week, late in the evening, Will began playing the piano at Euph's. Ben would be getting ready for the next day at the restaurant — quiet, regular activities that ordered the world — and the sound of the music would come to him, haunting and mysterious over the dark water.

Of course, he'd heard Will play before, all over the places they'd racketed around together. He'd heard Will play before he heard him utter a word.

But Will had never played deep and steady till they settled in at Euph's and the Pine Tar, and never that way — the way he played in the days after the Japanese woman from Honolulu came to the place on the water — until the end of the week after the bad scare. That kind of playing, which pierced the heart, was about the closing of some profound schism, as on the last day of the annual atonement-cycle festival in Ben's village. Will's playing had the sound of the drumming on that day.

Among Ben's people, a man with a gift like Will's music, a gift that was a blessing from the gods, would have been in a Society. These were secret organizations, with ritual, where people given such gifts learned how to honor the gods and nourish the community with music and song, sculpture or dance. But Will had told him early on that where he came from they didn't have anything like Societies.

Though he knew Will didn't mean to suggest it, remembering that conversation made Ben feel a little bush, to think that even after Mission school he'd known so little about White men. But now that he did know more about them, after years of business dealings and living among them, he couldn't help feeling that they'd be better off, less crazy and uprooted, if they did have something like Societies.

The end of that bad week, in the second year of Volcano Flights, was the first time Ben heard Will make new music, a new long music, and understood through the hearing how he patterned sound.

When Will had finished with that first long music, he had come into the kitchen of the Pine Tar and got himself a bottle and sat a long time looking at Ben. Then he said,

"I reckon it's just as well not to give Sam an excuse to look too close at you. And far as I'm concerned, I'm kinda used to waking up and seeing the lagoon and the mountains, and not through iron bars neither." He took a long pull and set the bottle down and said, "This here's a pretty good place, isn't it? Euph's and the Pine Tar. The Lady."

Ben grunted noncommittally; he was preparing a sauce for ahi.

"I'm kinda used to seeing you too," said Will, making a joke. Ben remained impassive but he shivered; cold fingers touched his spine. He understood that the bad scare, whatever it was, had threatened everything they had built and both of them. Understood too that something had changed in Will, that for the first time he had really stood for a moment in relationship to the world, instead of flying through it, half in and half out; and so for the first time had understood what his actions risked, and had almost lost, for him and for someone else.

When Ben met him Will didn't care if he ever saw a place or a person again. Didn't care what happened to any place or any person he knew. Didn't really care any more than anyone else did whether he woke up and looked through bars or not. Didn't care if he never woke up at all.

Maybe that had changed when he realized Ben cared.

After the bad scare, less money came in, but it didn't matter. They had arrived with a lot, and Ben had invested it for both of them in various ways. Anyway, for two men who each, at one time or another, had been very wealthy, money meant surprisingly little to either of them. Personally they lived very simply. When he had the means, Will could be extravagant. He was fond of bright things, of color and things that glittered, and at one time, for the pleasure of handling them, he had bought and sold and smuggled jewels. But he saw color and glitter as easily in the blaze of flowers, the play of clouds and sun, in fabric and once in a cupful of strange sand and shards of metallic stone he'd found on the lava wastes and brought back to keep in a bowl in the kitchen of the Pine Tar where he and Ben spent so many hours working together.

They were not interested in money or the power that money brought, but in its making. For Ben, the satisfaction lay in engaging in and completing the architecture of complex business dealings; for Will, in devising the scheme, and taking the risk.

By the time of the bad scare, they were also doing well legitimately at Euph's and the Pine Tar. Left-handedly, unintentionally, Ben and Will had become pillars of the community.

Will had changed all right, after the bad scare. Ben still worried about losing him — he knew Will hadn't changed that much. He still had his compulsive needs — for flight, for catapulting toward flame in heaven and on earth, for risk and danger, for things Ben saw only obliquely — and Will was still driven to act on his compulsions. But Ben never again worried that Will would do something to endanger him, to draw down on him the Wrath of Sam in the form of the immigration authorities, though the worry that Sam would find him in some other way gnawed at him like disease.

This Japanese city-woman from Honolulu pointed up for Ben how he'd let himself assume things he didn't actually know about Will's life, because they'd never talked about them.

They were reticent in their closeness. There were more things they never talked about than things they did.

Some of that reticence was the habit of men who'd lived a long time shady-side of the law. Some of it was male reticence common to both their societies. Some was personal idiosyncrasy, and exactly where men weren't habitually reticent — even if not habitually truthful, either.

Before the scare Will would be gone on business flights for a week or two every few months, and for shorter times even oftener. Without ever particularly thinking about the matter, Ben assumed that on those excursions Will did whatever he needed with women. He didn't know what, and Will never volunteered, and Ben never asked.

A long time ago when they had first met, he had joked with Will about women, as men do — not about a man's particular woman, just about women — and Will had joked back. Will flirted, too, when the silver mood was on him, and Ben knew his magnetism could draw people to passion as it drew them to other risk.

But after awhile Ben stopped joking because something about Will puzzled him. They were close by then, sharing a room above a noisy restaurant in an Asian city, together long hours taking care of business. And after awhile Ben got to know what no one else would, because Will was elusive and they were on the move, so no one else had the opportunity to notice.

Will never went with any of the women he attracted so easily.

Ben went with women, and he got to know that Will knew because sometimes Will would joke him a little. But it didn't work the other way. Ben wondered for a time if for sex Will liked men not women. Such men in Ben's society married and lived as couples. He knew that White men did not, that such relationships were among the greatest tabus. Seeing several vicious beatings and a brutal murder among them over this matter had taught him to stay away from the subject completely. Their attitude was just one more thing about White men that was crazy and dangerous.

But he didn't think Will's desires flowed that way — because of how Will was with him, and with women, and with other men. And back then Ben was sure Will didn't have a steady woman tucked away somewhere, like some men did. Now he might — but back then he was too fragmentarily in the world.

One reason the Japanese woman from Honolulu had shaken Ben so deeply was that in recent years, without saying so to himself, he'd let himself come to think that somewhere, on another island, Will had found himself a steady woman, and for some reason wanted it set apart from the rest of his life. That was fine with Ben. The idea lulled him, to think that Will had steadied in that way too. His own rootlessness had been a grief of Ben's, as he and Will roamed around Asia. For Ben the world could not be truly complete without family and community. He had found Emma, and found her family, almost upon arriving in Hilo.

But he wasn't a White man, an American ex-soldier turned outlaw; his needs were not Will's. Still, Ben fantasized that Will had a woman, maybe even children, somewhere, over the sea, in a village on that other island.

Then the Japanese city-woman from Honolulu walked in to Euph's and the Pine Tar.

16

Will's House

The road from Hilo to the volcano slopes up to the Southwest with deceptive gentleness. Gradually, warm breezes that wave gold and red hibiscus blossoms as if they were kāhili give way to a cooler air, to a more austere landscape of fewer blooms, of arching fern and crowded 'ōhi'a forest, and to the somber gray and brown of rock. Lilting gracefulness, the play of bright color and water, the very presence of the sea, all these disappear. Lightness, dancing movement, yield place to the massiveness of earth.

A traveler can go far and lonely along that road.

Will had business out that way. He was building a house.

For a long time after the night when he and Ben glided into Hilo Bay in a boat guided by its taciturn owner, Will's living arrangements were pretty much what they'd always been. Bunking behind Euph's was as comfortable as he'd ever gotten. Earliest on, he'd lived in a shack in the Starvesoil, one room divided by tattered blankets. The wind whistled through weather-swollen wallboards, driving cold in winter and flinging dust in summer, always threatening explosion. Or maybe it wasn't the wind that threatened explosion but the emotions of the people inside. Three besides him, at the beginning: Grampa and Uncle Bert together against his Little Mama and him; Grampa and Uncle Bert fighting each other like devils too. Grampa and Uncle Bert against his Little Mama, how? He never went to that place in his thoughts.

Then, the situation and the feeling-patterns had changed. Grampa was gone, dead, and Will and his Little Mama moved to a smaller shack with only one tattered blanket dividing the room but otherwise just like the first one. Here — sometimes, anyway — his Little Mama barred the door against Uncle Bert, though not against other men.

Will had never known a home. He intuited that his Little Mama could never make a home around Grampa and Uncle Bert. To make one, in their one room in Chicago, he and his Little Mama, locked together, mustered everything they had and, bewildered, invented what they didn't have. Which, he reflected wryly, was the most of it. His Little Mama had had ideas of how a home ought to be. For a time they ate meals at regular hours, even put a cloth on the table; after supper he did his homework there. His Little Mama set two kitchen chairs with soft seats in the part of the room by the window, and called it the parlor, and now, he remembered suddenly, had taken him from thrift store to thrift store looking for a big dresser with a mirror like the idea of one fixed in her mind. Like the one he had himself now, in the place he bunked behind Euph's, and like the one he'd dug up for the house down Noname Lane, right after he moved in the piano.

He stopped, his hands motionless on the shovel. Funny he'd forgotten that.

He half-smiled, remembering that old dresser in Chicago, all the fuss and triumph of getting it up those narrow stairs, his Little Mama crying to the men who were carrying it, "Take care y'all, don't scratch it now!"

But in the end it didn't work out. His Little Mama had never known a home either, had too much working against her, he reckoned, from what went on in what passed for a home when she was small — that shack in the Starvesoil with her older brother Bert and Grampa. Soon enough she hurt her back, lost the waitressing job, the world skidded under them. Then came the white-powder-and-needle that she called medicine to ease the pain and worry, but that had seemed to him a sickness. It killed her in the end, after a nightmare time; mostly Will let the expanses of outer space claim those memories .

She died of that sickness when he was nine, in a room down the block, he'd heard, with the man who sold her the powder; but she'd been gone from Will in the sickness for a long time before that. Uncle Bert came to fetch him and to ride the body back down home to Hibbits; and after that it was just Will and Uncle Bert, in the shack in the Starvesoil.

Will thought it was a queer thing about Uncle Bert and Grampa, that they both could build so well, built houses and barns for folks all around. Will had been taken to help from as soon as he could carry a hammer or a bag of nails; that was how he'd learned construction. His only good memories of them were how sometimes, if they hadn't been drinking too much, they would ring his wrist with their hand and guide him to saw a board straight and true, or hit a long nail sweet on its head; and later, Bert taught him measurement. Yet they'd never built a decent place for themselves or theirs.

While he and his Little Mama were up in Chicago, Uncle Bert had gotten religion. He ranted before hysterical assemblies, whipping them to greater frenzy, menacing and exalting them with writhing rattlesnakes they passed from hand to hand, to display their cleanness in the Lord's sight when they went unbitten. Drunk, he sobbed and pleaded to Almighty God for forgiveness for his sins. Sober, his screaming impromptu sermons swelled the shack's walls from within, the wind howling from without. Drunk and sober, switch and belt buckle in hand, Will was his target, reviled as the living incarnation of his sin, of the sin of the Jezebel temptress Will's mother, Uncle Bert's sister Robbie.

Drunk and sober, advancing step by step, the cords in the back of his hands bulging with the strain of holding the enraged and terrified snake by its neck. "Admit it, boy! Admit you and your Mama's sinning together, up there in the Devil's own city! Admit it before I put you to the Lord's greatest test! You'll never pass this test, you know it! Beg forgiveness before it's too late!"

The black tongue flicked, yellow fangs surely growing larger as the great jaws gaped wider. . .

In the garden behind the house down Noname Lane Will straightened, ran his hand nervously through his hair, eyes narrowing with trouble. He struggled again to accomplish the massive mental rearrangement he'd long ago taught himself, that enabled his survival, by driving resurgent feelings out of his awareness.

He'd given up recollection informed by feeling at the age of nine, at the end of the day his Uncle Bert preached his mother's funeral sermon and buried her in the dirt, up against the rusty wire fence on the sinner's side of Hibbits's cemetery.

On the night he and Uncle Bert got back from Chicago, Will ran from his beating and spent the next three days alone in the Thornbrake.

A connection between him and Euph was forged for true, though they did not exchange a word, when on the third day Euph sat on the steps at the back of the Blue Box and talked to the boy he could not see — though Will knew he'd glimpsed him earlier — and so could not know for sure was still close enough in the razorgrass to hear him.

"I ain't gonna come after you, boy," Euph had said. "Others will. So my not doing it ain't noways noble. Cain't blame them. It's getting ugly in this town and most of the Black folks cain't get out quick as I can. But I ain't coming after you. It's up to you if you come in outta the Brake or not, or waits for the Black people to drag you in to try and save their lives. I'd rather not see you drug no more. Your uncle's doing enough of that. But you got a right to know what the results of your doings will be. They gonna come after the Black folks again; they's saying we done you some harm. They'da been here already if you was a girl or if any on 'em truly keered about you or your Little Mama, which as you know well they never have. Now, if you don't come in, 'tain't a question of it's being your fault if the mob comes after us. The people as does things bears the fault for them. 'Tis rather a question of recognizing the results of your doings, which kin give others excuses for faults. I'm telling you this because though you ain't a man yet you got a man's responsibilities laid on you today. I been watching you all your life, boy, and your Little Mama before that. She was a right spunky little lady, and you're like her. You got it in you to grow to be a manner of man worth seeing, someday."

It was then that Will Cawdry had stepped out into the yard back of the Blue Box. He was covered with blood from the razorgrass and from a boar's tusk that had caught his calf as he scrambled away up a tree, and his bare back was scored with half-healed and still-open devil's hoof-marks Uncle Bert's belt buckle made, that Uncle Bert screamed showed by their shape were a sign of Will's possession by Satan, of his lostness and damnation.

Will accepted the bucket of water and scrap of soap Euph handed him, cleaned off the blood and Starvesoil grime, and set out down the lonesome road to his Little Mama's funeral.

"You're welcome here, boy," Euph had said. "Come round when you keer to."

After that Will spent most of his time at the Blue Box, that Euph called a jookhouse and other people called by other names. From his travels here and there, doing this and that, Will knew a long list now: cathouse, whorehouse, brothel, house of ill repute. Many others. To him it had simply been Euph's place.

Euph was the only stability Will knew. But it was the cautious, furtive stability of a man whose alert eyes said that it could disappear at any moment, that he was always ready to be on the run — again. Will hadn't reckoned Euph could take a whiteboy with him if time came to move on; wasn't absolutely sure he would if he could. But he knew Euph cared for him. And even after Euph died and Will left the Blue Box, and set out in the world's wilderness alone, most of the time he had been able to function on earth in the human realm because Euph had called him in from the Thornbrake in the way he had.

For long years after Euph's death, Will's life was devoid of warm human touch. Love of other kinds sustained him on the precarious knife-edge of his chasmed soul.

He loved his music.

He loved the feel beneath his hands of each different craft that he flew, the individual way it danced and rode and cut the air.

He loved the sight of sunrise as he piloted a small plane in low, between mountain peaks, over hundreds of miles of dark green jungle canopy, over rivers broad as seas, in under the radar, or where radar had never been.

Then he met Ben, and human love entered his life again.

He loved Ben. With him, he came to the Island; and he loved the Lady.

He loved the place on the water, and the circle of people who enabled him to create its breathing life.

Within a year of their arrival in Hilo, Ben had stopped bunking behind Euph's, married Emma, and set up their home in town. But when at last Will made a change, it wasn't planned out, the way Ben had done. Will didn't plan things so.

But he began to notice in a new way the 'ōhi'a forest he roamed so often, as he roamed the desolate Lava Wastes. He began to see it as a place to live.

And sometime toward the end of the third year after he and Ben arrived on the Island, he turned off the road that led from Hilo to the volcano, and bounced the Jeep down a rutted track where the curtaining hāpu'u fronds whispered shut behind him, hiding the main road. This place was about two-thirds of the way up the slope to Kilauea, and the air was cool and dry.

He was following a map scrawled on a crumpled sheet of paper by a man named Warner, kin to Emma though she didn't approve of his low ways. Will had met him in a bar in town. Warner claimed he belonged to the high ali'i and that this land out here had been in his family for generations, bestowed by Kamehameha the Great in appreciation of superb war service.

Will had nodded, listened, and drunk. The story was okay by him, though Emma's version was different. But he himself had made deals in several bars in several Asian cities as the direct descendant of Scottish and Irish chiefs, claiming to have influence on this account. He wondered why all the people England had beaten back then sat around boasting to each other about the claymores and shillelaghs and war canoes that had done them no good against cannons. He might even have been telling the truth, come to that. His Little Mama had talked some about the Scots — Scuts, she called them — and the Irish and their lands, where her side of the family had lived before they ended up in Kintuck and then in Junebug, Arkansas where she'd been born, and before that on a wild coast called Bathsheba, on an island called Barbados, on the other side of the world from Hawai'i. She'd told how they'd risen against the British back in County Sligo and County Clare, lost the battle and lost everything, and been driven out to wander in the wilderness. That was why at one time he'd done a lot of reading about the Scots and the Irish.

But if his family was descended from Scottish chiefs or Cuchulain, he grinned to himself, he could see why the English had won. Plumb dumb, he reckoned his people'd been; dirtgrubbers, major-league losers, all the way back to the cavebears.

As for Warner, his bloodlines didn't interest Will a damn, only whether he had clear title to the land. When Will's lawyer-tax-man gave the all-clear, Will drove out to look around.

He slammed the door to the Jeep, and listened to the sound echo away into the silence. Coming here, he hadn't seen another human for over two hours.

He took a few paces down to the far end of the glade. Some old-time structure had once stood there, Hawaiian but not a heiau. When the wind blew the ʻōhiʻa foliage a certain way, the view struck him motionless: Mauna Kea, serene with its cap of icy snow.

When he looked more closely at the crumbled structure on the ragged edge of the clearing, he saw that it was a Hawaiian grave, very old and long untended. He stared at it for a while, expressionless.

He spent a long time out there on Warner's land, touching the tips of foliage, delicately, smelling plants, sniffing the wind, listening to the sounds, not human, of the ʻōhiʻa forest, feeling the resistance and give of pāhoehoe fragments crunching beneath his boots.

He stood at different points, relevant to different things: drainage slope, sun and shade, a view of Mauna Kea.

He was not consciously thinking of any of this, or of anything at all.

A kind of dreaming possessed him; the cold wind sang in his ears.

Before he left, he wrapped a stone in a large leaf and placed it on the crumbled grave.

Then he drove back to town and dug up Warner in the bar where he had met him. Over drinks, he haggled him to a little less than three-fourths of the original price asked, because he paid at once, in full and in cash, in the solemn presence of his lawyer-tax-man.

Warner and Will, both already drunk although it was not quite two in the afternoon, returned to the bar from the quick finalization of the deal. In celebration, Warner converted some of his sudden wealth to liquid form and distributed it to Will and the rest of the bar clientele.

About a week later, Warner left the island, declaring he was going someplace where people knew how to live, where big money could be made by a man like him with business know-how and riches to invest — someplace where people weren't upcountry-slow.

And Will began to spend time on the land.

For awhile, he just did what he'd done that first time. He didn't always even get out of the Jeep, just sat behind the wheel, windows wide, his head back against the leather seat, his mind occupied with that strange blank dreaming.

But the time came when he began to act.

First he cleared.

Not much, just widened the trail a little so the view of Mauna Kea came through more often, then all the time, from a certain spot.

He glanced up frequently to look at the mountain while he did the next work, clearing around the edge of the glade. He made the vegetable plot there. He planted corn, and Irish potatoes, and out along the back of the plot, in an open space, he planted oheleberries.

He was on his knees tamping down the soil around the last bush, when he caught the view of Mauna Kea, and thought: This is what I will see from the house.

That he'd bought the land from Warner was no secret; Warner'd been all over town boasting about the deal he'd made. When on the evening of the transaction Will had said to Ben in the kitchen of the Pine Tar "I bought me some land out the volcano road," he understood Ben's acknowledging grunt. Will's communication was *pro forma*, and its point was not the conveying of information, which they both knew Ben already had, but that he was learning it from Will.

But the first Will knew he was going to build a house was that moment when he glimpsed Mauna Kea.

A while later, Will took Ben out to see the place. He'd already marked out the foundation, set at an angle to get the best possible view of the mountain.

Ben went to the back of the clearing right away and checked on the crops, which were coming along well. He strolled around a bit, nodding approval. He stopped at the old structure, which Will had reclaimed by clearing a circle around the grave, marked with a stone and a leaf. Here Ben nodded approval again.

They went back to town. Will could tell Ben was glad about the land down Noname Lane. His reaction said: It's a good place for you. I would never choose it.

That was all right. Ben and Will were clear that they were different people.

And now Will had, his to love again, the feel of good soil between his fingers and the sight of growing healthy plants that he had rooted in a place.

When he wasn't busy with Euph's and the Pine Tar, or with Volcano Flights, Will worked on the house. For some of the work he got people to help. But most he did himself. The house had a big kitchen, that overlooked the garden, a bedroom, and a big front room with two armchairs by the window with the view of Mauna Kea. He called this area the parlor.

He had no plans to move to the house in Noname Lane; he went on bunking behind Euph's. But he furnished the house, after his fashion, with a grand piano, fine kitchen equipment, a large bed, a table, a sofa in the parlor. When he was away from the restaurant and still on the island, in the times he roamed the upcountry forest and the Lava Wastes, he slept and ate at the house.

Like many dwellings in this rainy country, it stood on Y-shaped stilts, and he designed the underpart and the space beneath the stairs as a shelter for marijuana plants when one of the periodic government sweeps was on and the sky buzzed with helicopters. Will's main marijuana plantings were far away and had never been located.

Behind the house, in the left corner of the clearing, by the woods, he'd put three outbuildings. He called them shacks, although they were sturdy like everything he built.

One had windows and a skylight in the roof.

The second had windows.

The third and smallest had neither, and had the only door on the place that was always kept locked.

Will was right that Ben had approved of his buying the land, and still more of the string and rock marking out the house foundations. As time went by, Ben was confirmed in this assessment. Will's trips off-island grew less frequent, and he came back less frequently now with the terrifying tremors at the corners of his mouth, sign of his city soul-sickness that Ben knew too well.

When Will met Paula, the garden had been supplying the Pine Tar for several seasons. With every axe and hammer blow, with every fork and spade of soil, Will Cawdry worked himself into the land in the 'ōhi'a forest, three-quarters of the way upslope from Hilo on the road to Kilauea.

17

Seeings and Knowings

Then he met Paula, whom he thought of only as Yumi; and it came to him that it was time to set his house in order.

In the week after their meeting, Will spent a lot of time in Noname Lane. He weeded, split wood, and harvested some vegetables to be served at the Pine Tar, breaking work at intervals to take a couple of pulls on a bottle of Johnny Black.

The nature of his presence in Noname Lane was changing again, to something that was not quite focused thought, but still was different from the blank near-dreaming that had always possessed him there.

Euph was on his mind.

He could see Euph as clear as the last time he'd seen him in life — or in death — for it was Will who had found him, gone.

Euph had died not long before. He lay on his cot in the room behind the Blue Box, eyes half closed, as if he'd fixed them on something behind Will's left shoulder but not too far away.

Will looked a long moment, then took the cardboard suitcase packed with a few belongings that he kept in the corner of the room, away from Uncle Bert's destructive rages. He pried up the floorboard that Euph had showed him and took the money Euph had said he meant for him to have when he had passed. Then Will went down the road to hitch a ride, and eventually ended up in Houston.

Only now in Noname Lane, the week after he met Yumi, did it strike him as odd that, though he talked sometimes about Uncle Bert and, less often, about his Little Mama, except for Euph's face the only visual memory of anyone from that period of his life was of the blondish bristles on the head of the man in the recruitment center in Houston in January of 1959, when he first signed up to work for Sam.

Still under fourteen and a half, Will had been big and smart, and the Service representatives were willing to arrange about his having no documentation of his age. Lots of folks beside Will had been born in shacks a long way from doctors and civil records offices. And they wanted him; he reckoned now that his being still a boy had made easier what they had in mind for him.

All the time Will knew him Euph's eyes were heavy-lidded, red-rimmed, and bloodshot, with tar likker and with age, but they had never lost the sharp sardonic gleam that lived in their depths. His face had become jowly and loose-lipped at the end, because most of his teeth were gone; but except when Euph wanted them to, which was only when he had to deal with some whiteman who thought he had business with him, neither his eyes nor his face had ever gone foolish, any more than Euph had ever gone foolish, age and tar likker notwithstanding.

Working around Noname Lane in that week after he met Yumi, Will began to wonder why he hadn't told anyone else that he'd found Euph dead; he'd just picked up and gone.

Of course, he'd known that Belle or Bertha or Major, someone from the Blue Box, would find Euph any time now; and somehow with what was between him and Euph finished in this world, his ties to the other people at the Blue Box were cut too.

Suddenly it seemed less welcoming to him than in the six years past. Maybe it never had been welcoming; maybe it had simply been the only bearable place in his world.

Others would see to burying Euph.

That part hadn't troubled Will because often enough he'd listened to Euph arguing with the people who sat for long country hours on chairs creaking against the Blue Box's plank flooring, drinking likker, chewing, spitting, swapping stories, chaffing each other. Euph was the only one who didn't want a funeral, didn't have it all planned out, have some money put aside, maybe a suit of clothes.

"Don't matter none to me," Euph would say. "Reckon the Lord can find me if He's looking, wherever the parts of me have got to. Don't want no wimmen moaning over me, no preacher whooping and hollering, telling a pack of lies." And Will could understand that and believe it, though everyone else at the Blue Box said 'tweren't noways natural. But Will's Little Mama had told him the same thing about not wanting a funeral with some man hollering; only she hadn't gotten her wish. Will admired Kamehameha V Lot so much because he'd shown his sister that respect, honored her and buried her the way she wanted, not treated her the way Uncle Bert had treated Will's Little Mama, calling her a sinner and burying her like one. Euph always finished the Blue Box conversations with, "Fact is, if it makes the fools happy, let 'em give me a funeral. I won't care none."

And he'd pour himself another shot of tar likker and go to the piano, to play for everyone the New Orleans jazzman's funeral song:

I'll be glad when you're dead, you rascal you
I'll be glad when you're dead, you rascal you
When you're lying in your grave, no more liquor will you crave,
I'll be glad when you're dead, you rascal you.

After Will went to war in Vietnam, watched so many disappear and be dismembered, be scattered to the four winds and separated, watched them die and rot in unmarked places, a feeling had grown over the years of wanting to mark the location of places and people. Could be, then, Will reflected, that what troubled him wasn't so much that he'd failed to stop a funeral, as that he hadn't honored Euph's passing formally, which was different from the preaching and hollering part.

Was it a marking for his grave that was needed? If so, it should show his whole name: Euphonious Frederick Douglass Toussaint Hiquens. Funny spelling, French, though he sounded it "Heekins."

He couldn't recall Euph asking for a marking stone. Maybe he didn't want one; maybe he didn't care. Maybe he'd got out of the habit of asking for what he wanted, or expecting it. Will could understand that too. From as far back as he could remember, in the war at home he'd been born into, he'd stopped the wanting of things that didn't seem noway likely to happen. The war abroad, the long years outside the law, had strengthened this attitude.

But then, maybe a stone wasn't the right remembrance. As he mulled it over, chopping vegetables in the kitchen of the Pine Tar, flying above blue sea and green-brown land, he began to lean more towards a prayer and a likker libation to the Ancestors, like Euph used to pour on special occasions, like Will still poured on special occasions today. Will grinned when he thought about that. He'd always figured Euph must enjoy the libation part of being an Ancestor.

Sometimes, as Will went through his days, he could see a flash of brown wide river, a crowded quarter of a city, many dark people, like Euph, like those in Chicago, music like Euph's, and — not like Chicago — high narrow buildings, graceful with intricate wrought iron balustrades and window guards. New Orleans: city by a great river, where Euph had come from, but that Will had never seen. He reckoned he'd made a picture from what Euph had told him, and later from movies, and pictures, and words in the books he'd read, voraciously.

Though Euph had been gone nearly twenty-five years, Will could see him clearly; and sometimes, like now since he'd met Yumi, he could feel him so close.

Will had a hunch Euph was around so strongly just now on account of Yumi.

Tucked into the cardboard suitcase Will had kept at Euph's was a kerchief. Now it rested in a carved 'ōhi'a-wood chest, that Will had built, himself, to house his treasures, and that he kept in the middle-sized shack, the one with the skylight, at the back of the house down Noname Lane.

Euph had given him the kerchief when he was twelve. One night, after the bar in the Blue Box was closed and just the two of them remained in the place, Euph stood up from the piano and led Will to his room.

"Here, boy," he'd said. "This is special. For a woman you'll meet someday. You're growing to be a manner of man worth being, and someday there'll be a woman to know that. She'll be a twice-seeing woman — it'll take such a woman to be with you."

It was on Will's mind now that Yumi was that woman.

There were signs that she was. For one, the way he felt around her, that he'd never felt with any woman before, so strongly drawn, almost like magic, yet somehow easy too, like it was all meant to be. And she had that gift of twice-seeing, a glance and a glance again, without the eyes moving at all. Seeing twice as far and deep, seeing twice as much, as ordinary people. Seeing things others couldn't see. He didn't even think she knew it. Will had met that expression in a very few women, Colored and White, down to Hibbits — only women had that gift. And he'd seen it now and again, since he'd left the Mainland, but always he'd seen it in old, old women. Euph did say, though, that old and young didn't mean nothing, in women who had the gift. Like Marie Laveau in New Orleans who got old and then got young again, and Mam Manotte in New Orleans who had been Euph's mambo, his kahuna. Because of Euph's relationship with Mam Manotte, Will knew that he understood about Auntie Raina Donnell, who lived up behind Honokaa on the Hamakua Coast, and had been adviser to Emma's family for generations; she'd accepted to be Will's adviser too. On the occasions when Will consulted her, it was because Euph had come to him and told him it was the right thing to do and the right time to go.

Mam Manotte had given the kerchief to Euph. It had come from Haiti, and before that from Africa, and it was older than time. Euph had laid special emphasis on how Will's Little Mama's folks had spent time in that place Barbados which Euph said was right near Haiti; both were African places. Sometimes, Will had wondered if Euph was meaning he might have had some folks way back, on the wild coast of that island, who'd come from Africa too. Will liked the idea, to connect him with Euph, and because he knew what the good people of Hibbits would have thought of that.

Will also considered how he'd seemed to know Yumi from the moment he saw her, dressed casually for the casual day's outing, pants and blouse a quiet blue cotton, faded from sun and washing, conical straw hat shading her face. For an instant the girl, the outfit, had reminded him of something deeply troubling.

Vietnam.

Then she turned those twice-looking eyes on him, and the first association tangled with the second, and sank without a trace.

The thought that remained was: It's a right long time I've been in Asia and the islands; I've been a long time here.

Her eyes reminded him of the depths he saw in the Lady's wild lands: dark and fire together. Like that song Euph had used to play: *the bright blessed day, the dark sacred night.* The thick twist of her braided hair, shiny and black, evoked fresh undulations of pāhoehoe, even to the odd hint of orange as the sun touched it. Hair like black lava, and, not visible at first sight, fire at its heart. Her hair was more islander than Japanese, but he'd sometimes seen similar, during his time in Japan.

Fleetingly he had wondered what the body beneath the blue cotton would show forth, but that thought went quickly too.

He'd known something else about her as well: that she'd been to war. Sometimes he was wrong, when he saw that in people — wrong about which war. Other wars than his, foreign and domestic, could set that same look visible, in flashes, deep in the eyes, in the way a body was held: a person hanging on, just hanging on, but how?

He had been wrong sometimes about which war, but never about a person having been to war.

Her lips were very full, and clearly defined, the ends slightly down-turned, dimpled like valleys. Vulnerable, complex, and troubling: for they stirred in him a yearning, a sharp painful hunger.

Will had never kissed a woman.

The desire to run his palm over her hair, over her brown-gold skin, escaped his consciousness. I've been a long time here: that thought marked the limits of his awareness. Beyond lay the deep troubling she stirred in him, the electricity, traveling along his palm, along the nape of his neck, setting his fine hairs erect, the submerged wondering about her body.

And he wondered something else. Signs were she was the woman Euph had meant. But what good would she see in him, who was not a man like other men? Who had not grown as Euph said he might?

Tourists seldom found their way to the bar in Lahaina called the Lantern. The regulars were local people or people passing through on business, like Will who heard about it from another cargo pilot.

The bar consisted of a dim room, about the size of Euph's, but furnished more conventionally; plain walls, some advertising signs, knocked-about tables and chairs. But no crowds, no loud music, and a bartender named Lew who talked to people only when they wanted him to.

Will took to stopping in now and then.

He met Christopher Sandoz there one night when the place was almost empty. Sandoz was Will's age, a head shorter and broader all over. Long straight black hair, caught at his nape in a leather thong, spilled down his back. He could have been Hawaiian but something in the planes of his cheeks made Will mark him as Indian. Later Lew told him Sandoz had been to war like him; but Will already knew that, from his first sight of the other man.

When Will sat down at the other end of the bar, their eyes met and they nodded.

They nodded again, an hour later, when Will left, without their having spoken.

Eventually they exchanged names. They always sat together, at the bar if they could, side by side, never facing. Sandoz drank sourmash. Bit by bit they spoke some about themselves. Dates and places of service; Sandoz's had been similar to Will's. Present occupation. Sandoz worked as a mechanic in Lahaina. He was Comanche, brought up near Albuquerque. He'd been back to the Mainland for a couple of years when the grandmother who'd raised him got sick. Returned to the islands after she died.

When they'd learned these kinds of facts about each other, they hardly spoke any more, simply sat side by side and drank.

So it went for a little over two years; and in this companionship Will found acknowledgement of a part of his life otherwise strictly unexpressed.

After the hospitals — six surgeries, the last four partially successful repairs of the botched first two — he had never gone near a vet center or anything else to do with the government and its soldiers.

He had never sought out those soldiers either, and while open enough about the fact of having served in Vietnam, he never discussed it, with vets or anyone else. And, vets or not, people soon left off trying. He discouraged them somehow, by some emanation, subtler than the smile that assured there was no trouble at Euph's, but akin.

Then one time Will went into the Lantern, hoping Sandoz would be there, because it was the third time over several months that Lew said he and Sandoz had just missed connecting, and he himself hadn't been over to Maui in a good long while.

Lew told him, with a sorrowful head-shake, that Sandoz had run his pickup off the Hana Road, at a particularly deadly curve on a road made of deadly curves, in a crash so bad the rescuers cut him out and left the vehicle behind. The body had been sent back to the Mainland somewhere. It was all over and done with going on two months now.

Will nodded and walked out. He didn't go back to the bar in Lahaina.

A year later he drove out to that particular deadly curve — he knew the one. He thought he could just see the twisted blue fender, rusting and reclaimed by vines and leaves. He stared awhile over the edge. Then he left.

So Sandoz became yet another person in Will's life smashed and scattered to the winds. And Will did not seek or find or maybe even want anymore the companionship that acknowledged that part of his life. In the ten years since Sandoz had died, Will had sealed it off, and gone about his days.

Then he met the Japanese lawyer-woman, the city-woman with the twice-seeing eyes, and she stirred that sealed-off part of his life again, and other sealed-off parts too.

18

The Stranger: Pele Dancing

Guided only by the glimpse on the drive back from Kilauea, Paula had trouble locating Noname Lane. At just nine-thirty in the morning, gloomy light filtering through the ferns and dense 'ōhi'a branches overcast the two tracks that led to Will's house.

She parked the rental car behind the cherry-red Jeep and stepped into the clearing. After the humidity at sea level, the still air felt crystal-dry. A regular chock! chock! sound that shivered the silence might have been a woodpecker, except it held no hollowness. She identified it suddenly: an axe striking a log. Reassured by such domesticity, she approached the house, just visible through thick foliage. The strength behind each axe blow vibrated through her, and the balanced weight of blade and muscle pacing the work set a compelling rhythm. Then she glimpsed him, through a lacework of giant fern fronds that dappled him with shadow.

His back was to her, bare to the waist. He wore only tattered jeans and heavy shoes. A shirt hung from a nearby branch. Some quality of absorption in his movements led her suddenly to question whether anyone else would think of driving out to his house in the fern and 'ōhi'a forest without being expected, and she halted. She watched him work, easy, capable in his strokes. Big muscles slid under sweat-slickened skin, and the sight raised the feel of them beneath her hands. She steadied herself against a wave of sexual desire that struck her like a blow. Palm pressed hard against a tree trunk, she shifted her thighs uneasily where wetness trickled.

He turned slightly. Shock rocked her as shifting light revealed surreal sculptings. A red and gold dragon-tattoo bucked and rode a deep hollow in his left side where flesh had been gouged and scarred over: along his shoulders, his ribs, his back, its triumphant wings disappeared beneath the line of his jeans, half-obscuring an eerie spidertrack webbing of whitish scars, marked at intervals by tiny triangular indentations where needle-agony art seemed to transform scar to dragon scale.

His voice soared in a melody, startling her. He had seemed too locked down for song. Strangely flat, atonal, its high, nasal quaver keened of lost things and seemed to make the leaves tremble; and his movements with the axe altered to accord with its rhythm.

> *I am a poor wayfaring stranger*
> *A-traveling through this world of woe*
> *But there's no sickness, toil or danger*
> *In that bright land to which I go.*

A pause, as if he jibbed at that point, and hummed the line, which Paula remembered: I'm going home to see my mother.

Then he resumed:

> *I'm going there, no more to roam*
> *I'm just a-going over Jordan*
> *I'm just a-going over home.*

The axe-blows went on uninterrupted, as his voice died away in the hot Hawaiian stillness.

Long ago, before her father died, Paula had begun to hear such singing from the backyards around her neighborhood, from the storefront churches frequented by White people up from the hills, near the older ones attended by Negroes.

Will's voice struck out again.

> *Amazing grace, that stoops so low*
> *To save a wretch like me*
> *I once was lost*
> *But now I'm found*
> *Was blind*
> *But now I see.*
>
> *'Twas grace that kept this soul alive*
> *And grace that set me free . . .*

She thought of his words as they stood by the heiau when he had said that he believed in sin: *Amazing grace on earth? I ain't never seen sign of that.* In an association that seemed very odd, it occurred to her that the passion in his singing sprang from yearning, that it was an appeal — a prayer. To what God, unknown, hoped for? *Could be I'm just a poor Southern Baptist boy at heart*, he had gone on to say that day.

Suddenly he stopped his blows and leaned forward on the base of the axe handle. His shoulders slumped wearily. He wiped his forearm across his face. The thick blonde hairs there were plastered flat with sweat.

He half-turned. Tears streamed from his eyes, across a frozen face. The disconnection between feeling and expression stirred disturbance in Paula: as if he's a stranger to himself, she thought.

She stepped farther back from view.

She thought that she moved silently, but through the leaves she saw him whirl so fast he was a blur. Lips pulled back in a snarl, he seemed at one with the axe blade towering above his head so that it became a weapon grown from his flesh like a tusk.

"It's me," she shouted wildly, retreating from his sight. Her heart hurled itself against her chest as if seeking to escape her body's peril. "Paula!"

Silence. Out in the 'ōhi'a forest a bird gave a single frightened call, suddenly as if knifed.

Will's voice came in an easy drawl, exaggerated, slightly mocking or self-mocking. "Yumi? Is that really you out there? C'mon in, then."

For a crazy moment she didn't want to reveal herself, wanted to run to the car and keep running. She stepped forward.

He had pulled on the light blue long-sleeved shirt, crumpled and partially buttoned, crookedly, and patching dark with sweat. His face was wet. That could have passed for sweat, but she knew it was not sweat alone. He was posed, parodically: Backwoodsman leaning on axe. Involuntarily she thought of a poster popular in Berkeley, suddenly ashamed of having found it funny: a collection of beetle-browed, rural, overall-clad, degenerate-looking men, hair tufting like straw, standing in front of a decaying shack, and the slogan "Our trained staff, eager to serve you. . ." She wondered if Will had ever seen it.

"Thought I was meeting your flight in about two hours," he said.

"I'm early," she replied, not quite relevantly to his words. "There was space on the earlier shuttle. Jeremy said he thought you were out here. At first I was going to look around town some more, but then I thought I'd save you the trip to the airport."

"But how'd you find this place?"

"You showed me where the path branched off the Volcano Road. Remember? The other night, when we were coming back from Kilauea."

For a moment in the clearing in the 'ōhi'a forest stillness held sway. Her heart gave another leap and then found a jittery beat. Will continued to lean on his axe, staring at her without expression.

Suddenly points of sunlight danced in his eyes.

"'Tis true. I did." He nodded. "And you're not early, stranger. Don't be a stranger here. Only it's just most usually best not to come on me sudden-like," he added gently. "I never did keer for it, since I were a tyke, and the time working for Sam did hone my reflexes, like. 'Tis my fault — I didn't tell you. Folks hereabouts who know me, know."

"I'll remember," she assured him grimly, and gave a shaky laugh. "I'm glad that wasn't a gun you were holding."

Will nodded. Her still-shocked gaze followed him as he propped the axe against the woodpile. "'Tis why I don't carry one," he agreed absently, looking with puzzlement at the hand he had wiped across his face. "Didn't realize I were sweating so. Sorry. Looks like I been baptised for true."

She had been right, she thought; he didn't know that he had been crying.

He came beside her, and touched his fingertips very lightly to her elbow, the way he had a week ago at the bridge over the Wailuku.

Already powerfully excited herself, the awareness that he wanted her hit her like another shock.

He didn't know that he wanted her, either.

He moved away from her towards the house. She stared after him.

Turning, he came back to her, concern alive in his eyes.

"I'm sorry I came out here without checking with you first that it was all right," she said. "That was — intrusive."

"Not early," he said. "It don't make a matter."

He led her to a bench in the shade by the house. "Sit yourself here and I'll be right back."

He was gone awhile. When he returned, his thick hair, neatly combed, was darker than usual from the shower, as before it had been darkened with sweat. He wore a fresh lime-green shirt. On the bench beside her he set a tray with a bottle of Black Label, two glasses and a pitcher of water. "This'll give you a choice, but I'm afraid it's the only choice I can offer out here, away from the Pine Tar cellars." He sat beside her.

"I'll have a weak drink."

She was a little surprised that he could make one.

He did not look at her directly. She felt his wariness of her, and his warmth. She sipped slowly, turning over the evident fact that he did not intend to take her into his house.

"That better? You ain't early. It don't make a matter. Don't be a stranger here. When you've finished, we'll start out for that which I have in mind to show you. We'll just have more time, that's all."

They had been climbing most of the day.

They crested a hillside, and Paula stopped, spellbound, staring out over mile upon mile of erect pewter-green spears of the silversword plant glowing translucent golden-red in the slanting red light of sunset.

"When I first came to the island," Will said, "there was such sights a number of places, up here in the high country. And I know from old people I've spoken to, and from books, that once these fields stretched out of view. Now there're only a few left, here and upcountry Maui. 'Tis introduced animal species of various kinds has been their downfall, and most especially humans of the haole variety and others as has taken on haole ways. Early on 'twas collectors." He shook his head. "And then, I myself have seen whole stretches where someone has dug them up and thrown them about, their roots naked to the sky, for the deep pleasure of destruction."

He spoke as if such a motive were the most common in the world. Paula cast him a sharp look, but his face was turned from her.

Away across the mountain the sun was dipping low. With the near tropical swiftness that still startled Paula, darkness dropped over the ridge.

The headlight beams cut through the blackness, along the empty road. Now they had passed the park entrance and the sign that read: HILO 29 MILES.

Without warning Will swung the Jeep to the left, throwing Paula in her seat despite the belt. Panic overwhelmed her: for a wild moment she thought he was sending the Jeep straight at the dense ʻōhiʻa forest, and braced for the shock of metal against tree. But the branches that brushed across the windshield obscured it only momentarily, then dipped and rose again, undamaged and doing no damage, closing behind and all around them. "I'm sorry," he said. "You all right? I did make a decision more sudden-like than's a good idea when driving."

The main road they had left was invisible, but in the white swath cut by the headlights she just made out the track the Jeep jounced down.

"You want to see inside my house, I reckon, since you came out to find me."

He spoke with a strange angry savagery, yet oddly she did not think it was directed at her.

He turned on a lamp. Shadows jumped and flared bizarrely across a big wooden table, an armchair and footstool, a gleaming grand piano of dark wood. A large futon-sofa stood on the right. The furnishings did not come together to pattern the room. In every direction windows would afford a panorama in the day. Now black panes reflected lamplight. Opposite the entrance a door stood open; in the wall to the left, one stood closed.

Will led her to the open door. Unlike the front room, the kitchen was complete, held a shape. Above wooden work surfaces and a large wooden working table with a single chair, gleaming pans and cooking implements hung from walls and beams. Cupboards lined the walls. Paula went to look through the window by the back door leading to the space enclosed by forest at the end of Noname Lane.

"What are the other buildings?"

"Oh," said Will, "the big one, that's the BookShack. Where I keep my books and sit to read." He paused, then said, half-defiant, half-embarrassed, "I got no formal education to speak of, not like yours, that's ordered, structured-like, still I did always like to read. I like Shakespeare; he do understand a lot about power and war and betrayal." He laughed. "Light things like that. Though he can be funny too."

"Yes. All of that. What are the other buildings?"

"Oh, the one on the right's the toolshed."

"And the other?"

He shifted uneasily, this laugh he gave was uneasy too.

"We could just call it the BackShack, I reckon. Come, let my show you the rest of my house."

They returned to the living room. Will went to the piano, and struck a random chord that vibrated, then slowly stilled itself in the night and went away. After a moment he said,

"Truth to tell, I reckon there ain't no more to show."

"What's through there?" She motioned to the closed door in the left-hand wall.

"There's too much light," he grumbled, although she could barely make out his form in the muted glow from the lamp in the living room.

"There's not enough."

"I ain't a pretty sight."

"Get undressed, Will. I don't sleep with men wearing boots."

A moment's startled silence was broken by his wheezy laugh.

"Well, I'm right glad to learn you got standards, little girl." He sat on a chair near the bed and pulled off his heavy footwear. The boots hit the floor with two thumps.

"More. I don't have anything on at all. And I'm getting cold, damn it."

"Well, you should have something on. 'Tain't no way for a nice little girl to act, sitting there buck naked." His hands worked nervously at his belt. "That Berkeley must be a 'trip' all right, like they used to say. Requirements about how your menfolks dress at such a time. . ."

She refused to rise to the bait. She stretched her arms out to him.

He was still wearing his undershirt. They tacitly compromised at that. She'd never had such trouble getting a man undressed. She thought of the dragon tattoo, its wing-scales transforming terrible scars.

"I ain't prepared, Yumi. I understand something's needed. . ."

"It's not a problem." Hadn't he ever heard of the pill, she wondered?

"But Yumi, 't'ain't tidy, 't'ain't clean, without."

"I like it better that way. I can feel it more."

"Don't talk like that. You aren't such a girl and can't make yourself one."

"I don't want to talk at all."

He felt to her, suddenly, very remote, very cold and stern.

"I ain't gonna bring you peace, little girl." He spoke almost in a whisper. "And the guilt's on me because you're too nice a little girl to know it."

The springs groaned, the mattress dropped beneath his weight. Then she heard only his breathing, ragged in the dark, as he reached for her.

Later, climbing slowly from oblivious sleep, she lay motionless. She was alone in the bed; she tried to sense whether she was alone in the house. After a moment, a movement, a breath, she could not have told what, came to her from the living room.

Her clothes lay in a tangled knot at her feet, and she shivered in the chill as she pulled them on haphazardly. The luminous dial on the bedside clock showed almost five-twenty.

She sat on the edge of the armchair, across the room from him, leaving them both space between.

"What woke you, Yumi? Not me I do hope."

"No, you didn't wake me."

Will, fully dressed, a bottle of Johnny Black in his hand, stared out the window at impenetrable dark, in the direction of Mauna Kea, and waited out the Hour of the Wolf.

"It do come on me so at times, this trouble sleeping. White nights, I have read they're called. They go with the black days." He gave his humorless grin. "Want a drink?"

She started to refuse, then said, "Yes. Thank you."

"I still just got Scotch same as earlier. Sorry."

"Scotch is fine."

She let him get the glass for her from the kitchen, not because she wanted a drink, not for the sake of having him wait on her, but hoping movement would break the curious dragging lethargy that she had not seen in him before and that she did not think was caused by alcohol. By the time he returned it had nearly vanished.

He handed her the glass, half full, neat, took a pull from the bottle, and said, "It'll be light soon."

"Yes. Things get better then."

His pale eyes were sharp as he turned his gaze on her.

"You have such nights, too?"

She nodded. He said no more for a while, just drank, then said,

"Soon's it comes light and no one will see to talk, you can go on into town and get on home. What I done to you ain't no excuse or apology for."

"One of the things I like about the Berkeley approach to life is you stop worrying whether people are talking about where you spend your nights. And a case could be made that I 'did it' to you at least as much as you did it to me."

He shook his head slightly. "You don't understand. But how could you? It'd take a man to know ain't no man alive could not want your goodness that way."

"I've known a few who managed to resist," she retorted dryly.

"I ain't man enough to say no even for your sake. You need looking after by a steady man. A lawyer, or a doctor. A professor, maybe. Someone such. . .I do see you in Honolulu, up near the University, in front of a nice house and lawn, with such a man, and two children, a little girl like you only couldn't be near as lovely, and a little boy who — whose eyes won't be afraid. You need such a man for such a life, a man from good blood who can give you good children, a house to keep regular-like, a man won't take advantage of your strong loving nature like I done tonight but who'll keep you happy enough in that way to steady you some and keep you from straying into bad company and danger. Like you done tonight. You should be married right and proper. Yumi, I ain't a man like other men. I ain't man nor mate for no woman, and least of all would I wish that on you. You're a fine girl," he said abruptly, and without any mockery. "Your views about people do tell it. Could be I doubt them, but I can feel you've been on the killing ground and you've earned the right to hold them. I'd like it if you'd go on back to Honolulu on the first plane out and find yourself a man you deserve — there ain't one good enough to deserve you — and it won't take long I reckon."

"Thanks for arranging my whole life without consulting me. I don't recall saying I wanted to marry you, or anyone, or that I wanted children, now or ever. I don't remember telling you I pined for life as a wife in corporate-professional America, and I already told you what universities have done to my life and times. I did what I wanted to do tonight and I'll take my chances. And," she said coolly, "you may be taking chances too."

For a long while he said nothing. He stood rigid as stone, his face a ghostly white with a metallic sheen in the strange light from the lamp. From his expression she could read nothing at all.

"I think," she went on, "that we could make good friends and good lovers. I don't agree with your take on it at all."

He grinned at her."Well, I couldn't expect you would, I reckon — agree with me, that is. 'Twould be right out of character. You go finish putting on your clothes like a lady — humor me and pretend for just now, okay? — and I'll make us coffee and breakfast. Still," he said harshly, "you are a nice little girl, too nice to wander the Lava Wastes with me."

"You're forgetting. I was born on the Lava Wastes."

He paused, and suddenly upended and finished the bottle with a gulp and shudder that made Paula shudder to see.

"'Tis true you were," he said, "and still I'm doing you the greatest wrong." He glanced through the window, Mauna Kea way, where darkness was thinning without yet being light. "With our talking, we've seen the White Night out."

19

The Woman In Singapore

So in the days after the Japanese woman from Honolulu came to the place on the water for a second time, and went wandering with Will in the Lady's fiery heights, Ben sharpened knives, too vigorously, in the kitchen of the Pine Tar, and waited; and the rains came.

Great gauzy curtains of water drifted the long length of Mauna Loa, shrouded the peak of Mauna Kea. They caught in the rising sulfur clouds of Pele's realm, and rose with them, tore with them in the branches of the 'ōhi'a forest, slanted away across the Lava Wastes.

Rain pounded the ground, turned the pavements of Hilo slick with crushed leaves and flower petals drummed from overhanging trees.

Geese shook their feathers in backyards along suddenly dangerous creeks. The sun had not appeared, the sky had not lightened from gray, the rain had not subsided from a torrential sheet for more than an hour in a week. Ten days. Fifteen days.

People in offices and shops and sitting in bars or coffeehouses or in front of them on the sidewalk under the metal overhangs watched the rain barrier, inexorable before their eyes. They watched first with exhilaration, then with resignation, then with an edge of irritability born of trepidation.

They lifted their eyes on high. They said to each other, "Who knows what those two mountains doing?"

The shadow of their power fell over them; they lived on the volcano, where the earth had a voice and a heartbeat, where its blood pulsed beneath their feet.

Water rushed high in the gutters, and one day people heard a strange roaring. They came to stand on the bridges over the Wailuku. They drove up and parked their cars along the street and went out to lean over the parapets.

Will heard about it out at the place on the water, and came in to town to look.

In the space of an hour the jade and turquoise stream had metamorphosed fearsomely into a wild floodtide tinted rusty blood by loads of ravaged soil borne now to the sea.

The waters hurled themselves around bends, from the island's invisible height, from Mauna Kea's heart. The obdurate shelves of rock, where in normal times fishers stood to cast their spider-lines, were now drowned from sight; still the rock distorted foaming ridges of water into cross-purposes with the river's main currents. Just beyond the Puueo Bridge, Hilo Bay swelled like a cauldron of molten lead. Its surface boiled where the river hit, and beyond the breakwater, it shattered under white assaulting waves.

As Will stood in line to buy a few items in the store around the corner from the Wailuku, he overheard the man ahead of him ask the girl at the counter if the river would endanger the town.

"No," she replied scornfully, casting an eye beyond her a block to where it roared, "You not from this side then? You from Konaside?"

Will smiled to himself, understanding that she meant, You should know that Pele has promised never to destroy Hilo. Princess Ruth had reminded her, on the outskirts of the town long ago, and stopped the tongues of fire licking near. Pele had honored her promise then. Promised not to destroy by fire, and surely not by water either, for no doubt that this weather was her doing, speaking from the depths, from the heights of the mountaintops.

The snow had prowled far down Mauna Kea's flanks this year, bringing rain, melt and flood.

In the kitchen of the Pine Tar, Ben set dishes out, chopped vegetables, told Jeremy to go away and attend to customers in the front, he wanted to be alone.

He took his mood from the Wailuku's today, because Will was gone, and had left no message on the corkboard by the stove.

Seeing the empty board, Ben realized fully for the first time how much Will's behavior had changed over the years, so that now Ben had come to expect an oblong of paper, scrawled over in Will's jagged elegant script: Back Monday, or Not Back Monday. Then Ben would assign the work at the Pine Tar accordingly. Where Will went, who he was with, where or how he was when he was gone, Ben didn't know, could only deduce from his condition when he returned. But in recent years, he had returned when he said he would. And his leaving the notes told Ben that at least when Will headed on out he was still part-way in this world, and planning on coming back, however far in outer space he traveled.

But today no paper oblong fluttered on the corkboard, and Ben thought, So, it's all going to begin again, because of that Japanese city-woman from Honolulu.

On the covered lānai beyond the screen door, Maria and Lori who worked part time in the kitchen were sorting table linen. He heard Lori's voice raised in talk-story. Something about bedsheets, about the hotel where they also worked.

"Because I tole her, take for downstairs and when you come bring for upstairs the doubles. . ."

Voices from the everyday world. The world that Will had left.

So, thought Ben, it's all going to begin again.

Out in the realm of rain and sulfur steam, Will wandered.

Water dripped from the lower leaves of dense 'ōhi'a foliage, burdened the fronds of the hāpu'u ferns, and pooled on the ground.

It slicked the gray-black expanses of the Lava Wastes, and gathered in holes and crevasses in the porous rock.

In the valley a curtain of fire flared, suddenly, above the obscuring vapors, then disappeared as if dragged back into the depths. Far beyond the smoke's black formless mass, a huge mushroom-shaped cloud, illuminated from within as if by a light that was dark at its heart, stood weirdly where the lava boiled into the sea.

One night in early December of the year that Will was eight, the Windermere Gardens blazed up. Earlier that day he had stood at the window of the rotting room he shared with his Little Mama, and watched sun glint off daggers of ice hanging from the roof, off fragile glass-like ice patches on the pitted flagstones eleven stories below.

That year as every year the firefighters' ladders did not reach above the seventh floor.

An oily black cloud of smoke billowed between his own gaze and his mother's face, that he could never see in memory nor recall on waking. Sometimes, in his sleep without remembered dreams, the acrid taste of smoke violated his nostrils again.

She must have been kneeling on the floor, holding him out the window. His nails scrabbled at the window ledge and broke to the quick so it tore, and his mother held him around the wrists as he clutched hers. For a while his bare toes caught a purchase in the brick.

Then they slipped, and he felt her body lurch and heard her groan as his weight swung into space. He kicked out and found the brick again.

He didn't know what she was going to do. He didn't know what he wanted her to do. She had been sick from her medicine and mostly gone from him for a long time by then, and maybe he was beyond wanting her to do anything, certainly beyond expecting it.

And then she let go.

He remembered the feeling at that moment, how his own hands, unsupported, slipped off her wrists. As if his body came apart; as if suddenly between his hands and his arms stretched only empty space.

Sometimes he felt that his body-parts were separated still. Sometimes he wondered if they'd come back together wrong, or if maybe he was misremembering and they had never been right, and were just made more wrong that night. He thought some of them had been lost, and that was why, times were, he couldn't find himself, or the world around him either.

All he remembered was the firefall. Not landing on the pitted icy flagstones as he had expected while clinging to the wall with bloody toes. Not landing in the fireman's net, which was what happened. When he fell, he couldn't see the net, hadn't known it was there.

People had praised his Little Mama for her presence of mind in letting him drop at the right moment.

But sometimes he wondered if she had known the net was there, either.

He didn't feel the falling, just the open spaces gaping between the parts of his body. Maybe that was the falling.

Sometimes he thought he hadn't landed yet; he was still waiting for the smash against stone, waiting for the glass-ice to shatter along with his bones.

Maybe that waiting was the falling, too.

He had felt that way sometimes since.

In the moment just after you had set weapons in motion, and before the fire from their explosion flared.

In the moment when a man was almost out the helicopter door, and the fingers clinging to the edge of the floor broke under your boot, or the nails tore, and the wind tore him away.

That night had finished his Little Mama. He didn't know why and he didn't know what made him think it. Maybe his suspicion that she hadn't seen the net when she let him fall, that that was what finished her. Maybe. He only knew that it was so.

Will slipped through the 'ōhi'a forest without making a shadow or a sound, clad in a second skin of lava mud. He waited to hear the tusks of boars rooting among the hāpu'u ferns. He crouched low, with an arrow bolt and a knife-tusk of steel.

Squeals and scurries and growls, then bolt-thuds followed by shrieks instinct with pain and rage. The rain and the sulfur garments shredded and tore, on 'ōhi'a branch, on ivory tusk, on bolt and steel tusk, that ripped and shredded flesh and muscle, that severed arteries to release erupting geysers of scarlet blood.

Once again, wetness dripped from the lower leaves of the dense 'ohi'a foliage, burdened the fronds of the hāpu'u ferns. Pooled on the ground. But this time it was not water.

Blood is thicker than water.

Blood and lava are thicker than water.

Will Cawdry had taken a woman into his bed.

He was almost forty years old and it was the first time in his life since he shared the one narrow bed with his mother, huddled against Chicago cold, that a woman had been in his bed.

He had gone to his first woman at fifteen, in Monterey, California, when he was in boot camp at Fort Ord on his way to Vietnam.

She was a whore. He pronounced the word "hoor," and Will Cawdry, who had so quick an ear for language and for foreign tongues, never heard the peculiarity of that Starvesoil pronunciation to change it even had he wanted. Like the activity associated with her, it came from a bedrock defended in him so deeply that the life around him did not touch it and so could not alter it.

She had been a scar freak, one of those women who were excited by men's pain. The record on his back of Uncle Bert's beatings had set her trembling with arousal.

He had gone to other women since the woman in Monterey — not so often as people might have thought, to hear him talk, but often enough over the years.

He had never been with a woman he hadn't paid to suffer him sexually.

He had never spent more than five minutes inside a woman.

The rest of the time was occupied transacting business.

Laying down money; because of the way he preferred to take his departure, he was willing to pass money over first, without argument. The women were always pleased by this.

Locating a place for the act.

The minimally unavoidable doing and undoing of his clothing. The women seemed to find his requirements of them rigid but not onerous.

And he never haggled. He paid what he was asked. If he wasn't asked he made an offer. If he couldn't afford what was asked or his offer was refused he moved on.

When he discussed the matter at all with his fellows, he spoke, rather formally for his milieu, of finding a woman. In his own mind the phrase was 'easing himself,' and the need came upon him powerfully, suddenly and unpredictably, at irregular intervals. Sometimes for years he was troubled only infrequently. Other times, the need seized him compulsively: he became the obsession.

He did not think much about this pattern, or about the urge; like the silver mood, it was a force from beyond, that compelled him.

His sexual activity was routinized to the point of ritual. The woman must be covered; he owned a long dress of coarse gray cotton, with elastic-rimmed sleeves that caught at the wrist so they would not ride up with movement. Now he kept this garment on a hook in the locked shack behind the house in Noname Lane. In the crotch of the dress he had cut a jagged hole, with two fierce efficient rips of his commando knife.

The woman must wear this dress. He showed her how to spread the hole so he could locate it. For preference, she would lean back, across a bed, a table, at a pinch against a wall, inside or outside a building. There must be a firm surface for him to brace his hands against, to bear the force of his big body, and for her to brace herself against, because Will Cawdry never touched his women, even through the loose gray garment, and never allowed the women he paid for to touch him, even through his long-sleeved shirt, his undershirt and jacket and fringed vest, the pants that he never removed after the night in Monterey.

Requirements explained, she must extinguish the light. Will Cawdry took his women in the dark.

Then he would push into her body, erect as he had been since he had left wherever he was staying, with the compulsive need to ease himself hard upon him.

He came almost at once, in a single long spasm like urination it seemed to him, came and came copiously and to an uncommon degree. In this as in other things, he knew that he was abnormal. He knew that he was not a man like other men.

This knowledge had been confirmed when, leaving the house where the woman in Monterey worked, he overheard her speaking of him to other women who worked there. "Like a jackass pissing," she had said. "You'd think it was the forty days' flood all over again." She had shaken her hand daintily at the wrist, her face stiff with revulsion, and then she and the other women had laughed.

After that Will Cawdry told the women he paid for not to speak, once their negotiations were completed, and otherwise not to speak at all. When he and they did not share a language (which happened often enough, since shortly after the episode with the woman in Monterey he was shipped out to Vietnam and never returned to America) he laid a large-knuckled finger across his lips and pointed at the woman's mouth.

When he was finished, he zipped up his pants while the woman removed the gray dress. He folded up the dress and tucked it into his leather carry-sack.

Then he left, still in the dark.

From listening in his childhood to the women who drank at the Blue Box and worked out of there, and from listening to his Little Mama and the other women in the bar in Chicago where she drank and later worked out of too, Will knew that women talked about the men who bought them, and often with bitter scorn. He listened to them as they dandled him on their knees, petted and humored him.

Because he had known this all his life, he blamed himself for overhearing the words on the brothel stair in Monterey; and after that, when he was looking for a woman, he sought whores on the street who looked solitary like him, and took them to rooms where he'd made an arrangement. For a long time now he'd kept a room in Honolulu this way, at the River Street end of Hotel Street, above a low-profile club named the Port of Call. Also after that he never touched them, as he had touched and been both seen and touched by the woman in Monterey.

He let himself pretend that these solitary women would not talk about him, but in any case he would never know it, never hear it, because he never went to the same woman twice and if fortune held would never see any of them again.

His one exception, his longest steady contact, had been with a woman in Singapore.

Its ending had jolted him to an awareness of the danger in that somnambulistic departure from routine, and he had never let it occur again.

It happened during eight weeks spent waiting on business associates in a complicated smuggling deal that had struck a snag somewhere along the line. The associates' part of the deal had fouled up, not his, so he was on his own even more than usual.

He had seen the whore in a splash of light from a bar one night when his need was on him and he was walking the shabbier streets that he preferred. He had already been in Asia a long time then. Besides, rural paces everywhere move somehow slower than city ones. He was not sure how he could tell, but as soon as he saw her, he thought that she was very newly in from some countryside. This was confirmed when he found she did not understand any of the languages he tried. His other thought, which he knew in his bones, was that the city had already done for her.

But if she didn't know the languages, she knew the money he held out to her under another splash of light.

She had no price; she was ready to take what anyone would give her. Will offered her what he offered all the women who set him no price: what he had paid the whore in Monterey. This one could not believe her luck.

Neither of them had a place to go; he took her in alleys for preference. Once when rain was pelting down he borrowed a car from one of the business associates. But mostly he took her in those alleys, where she bent backwards over cans and boxes full of refuse and garbage. Rats scuttered away from them. She was intelligent and quick, and understood about the dress and the silence. She seemed grateful not only for the money but that he asked so little for it. Her face was a pale oval in the night, her hair a black blur. Next to his great size her body was slight to vanishing inside the gray dress.

He went to her eight times at that corner under the splash of light, and each time she was there and alone.

Then one time he went and she was not there.

He walked through side streets, seeking her, until he lost himself in a maze of moonlight and hovels like dream.

He walked for a long time, and at last found his way back to the room where he and the business associates were staying.

He could have gone to her the next night or the next, but he didn't.

Then the associates straightened out their difficulties. The business in Singapore was finished and he went away, and by fortune holding never saw her again.

Sometimes the nights in the alleys with the whore in Singapore came back to him. When they were together there, an intensity of solitude surrounded them that was itself a kind of intimacy. Solitude of the chill before life stirs and wakens. Solitude bleak as the landscape of the moon and the Lava Wastes.

Her solitude matched his and perhaps that was what set the numb spot tingling.

The spot was somewhere beneath the scars and had been there for as long as he could remember, before friendly fire ripped him apart and Sam's surgeons butchered him. The only doctor he had ever asked about it, timidly, during a final checkup after his sixth surgery, brushed it aside as imaginary. Will put on his clothes and went away, and never went back to a doctor again.

It was during his painings that he sometimes felt he had avoided great danger, barely, with the woman in Singapore. Only once did he identify the source of the danger. He recalled almost reaching to touch the woman's hair, but his arm went numb and he could not lift it. Then, in the time afterward, he forgot the almost-reaching, and never remembered again.

"All right, y'all," Will's loud and genial voice cut through the hubbub at Euph's, "this is the moment we been waiting for, the formal debut of the newest group in East Hawai'i, the coming sensation, Sonny and Da Gang."

Laughter and applause. The band took their places and began to play, the four members looking nervous as they arranged themselves in front of the piano. They made a tentative beginning, then took off, faltered again, and suddenly found their pace. They were good, thought Paula. More laughter and applause met them as they soared. The level of conviviality rose even higher than before. Guitar music and singing voices wove themselves with the heavy rain outside.

Will stood, half in shadow, silhouetted against the light above the bar, and then he turned to sit beside her, leaning forward and smiling. She felt a rush of pleasure and warmth, and pride in him at making this place a space for Sonny and his friends, and for launching them with style. On the wave of this feeling she almost asked him the question that had been gripping her. Then she hesitated, because it wasn't, after all, any of her business, although it would not leave her.

Had she really seen him, three days before in Honolulu, in the disconcertingly swift near-tropical dusk that still threw off her perceptions, caught in silhouette as he had been just now, at the River Street end of Hotel street, against the blood-red neon sign above a bar?

She had been walking for a bus, later than she had intended, and she was uneasy, alone at night in these dubious streets. A stretch of long low buildings with overhanging roofs, housing bars and strip joints and nameless enterprises on the first floor, and on the second floor dark or dim-lit windows shut off by bamboo blinds and faded curtains. And many hotels: from deep in the previous century this raunchy strip of street near the port had its name from them. Hotels, with rooms by the week and month and night and hour.

She was walking faster toward a better-lighted intersection and the bus stop, and suddenly she thought she saw him.

She had been so sure she had almost cried out, in relief and pleased surprise, and then had caught herself and her quickened footsteps.

Why, she wondered later?

Partly for rational reasons. Why would he be in Honolulu, hundreds of miles from home? She always pictured him on Hawai'i Island.

But being in Honolulu was perfectly reasonable for a professional cargo pilot. Cora had told her that first night that he came to Honolulu. Odd, that she had forgotten that.

So it was other considerations that had immobilized her.

That if he had come to Honolulu he had not contacted her.

And something else, some strangeness in him that chilled her heart as he stood beneath the scarlet splash of light.

He moved as if he were part of the neon and of the shadows, the nameless hidden places, and yet in some way utterly alone and at their mercy.

He moved stealthily, menacingly, and at the same time seemed terrifyingly exposed: his vulnerability shocked her. In the bloody neon light, the line of his throat with the prominent Adam's apple seemed held naked to the knife.

Pushing away the irrational anxiety vibrating through her that warned her not to touch him, not to disturb him, not to interfere lest she bring down some obscure disaster, she told herself instead that she was mistaken, that it was not Will Cawdry whom she saw.

But could she really mistake him?

She did not believe it. There were not two of him.

And then he was gone from the light.

She blinked. Without seeming to move, he had vanished before her eyes like a cougar she had seen once in car headlamps late at night on a lonely Northern California road.

Almost unconsciously she hastened her steps. She passed the neon bar sign and halted again.

In the darkening and ill-lit street she was uncertain of her exact location compared to where he had stood, but even so she could find no plausible place into which he might have disappeared.

She saw only a tightly shut door below a small peeling sign that read Port of Call; and on the floor above it a row of unlit windows closed away by bamboo blinds.

After a moment she hurried on to the intersection and caught her bus and went home.

20

Wild Geese: Ports Of Call

Now in Euph's, as the pleasurable noise of conversation, music, and clinking glass rose around them, he leaned toward her with his elbows on the table and poured her a flute of champagne.

"Best in the Pine Tar cellars, Yumi."

And the best is very good indeed, she thought. She almost said,but didn't, "Were you at the River Street end of Hotel Street, three nights ago in Honolulu? I thought I saw you."

Instead she said, surprising herself, "Come see me in Honolulu, Will."

He sipped his Johnny Black.

"That's mighty kind of you, Yumi. But I don't get to the big city much. I'm a country boy at heart. Even this town is almost more than I can handle." He grinned, to show that he was joking.

But he wasn't, Paula thought.

"Ask Ben," he went on, and she remembered her brief bizarre encounter with Ben her first night at the place on the water and did not respond. Cities give Will soul-sickness, a self-losing sickness, Ben had said. She did not know what that meant.

"I know you're a city girl," Will said. "I'm most impressed with how you can manage in such places. Are you bored already here?" His tone was still light but she was convinced he spoke seriously.

"I'm not bored at all. And I thank you for your — generosity."

He made an extravagant gesture. "'Tain't generosity at all. My privilege — and pleasure." He paused. "And who knows! Might could be someday I will come to you in Honolulu after all."

Will shut the door behind Jeremy and Lori, who had finished helping him clean up, switched off the lights, and turned to Paula, still at their table before a candle and a champagne bottle. They were alone. He went to the piano and pushed back the fallboard.

Fingers quick and light: Bright blessed days, dark sacred nights. . .The song melted into the rain and the night.

He paused, and began another piece.

Music drifted like gauze, twining with the sound of the rain and the water lapping beneath the open windows at Euph's. The candle flame suddenly leaped, smokily, seeming to be a manifestation of the Lady, making the air sulfurous, translucent with fire. Paula's skin shivered, her nape hairs rose.

"That's the music you were working on the first time I came to Euph's," she said when his fingers fell still. Only three weeks ago, but something about the place on the water was timeless. "It's about the structure of the sea and the air. And you've finished it."

"I have. Just tonight. Just now." He lowered the fallboard, ceremoniously. "It's for you, Yumi."

Outside, very near, some heavy stiff tropical foliage yielded up its waterlogged weight and crashed to the ground, startlingly loud in the stillness. Will looked at Paula through half-shut eyes that like the air seemed smoky in the candlelight.

"Too far to go out to Noname Lane through all this weather. You ready to spend a night at Euph's?"

As if, she thought, his inner trouble their first time together had resolved, like the music, and he had decided on a course. She nodded slightly and smiled back at him.

In the room across the hall, behind Euph's, Will turned on the small lamp.

She slipped off her bracelet and set it amidst other items on the dresser.

He laid his watch beside her bracelet.

The lapping water sounded so close beneath the open windows that it seemed unbarriered by walls; and Will dismantled his own barriers of clothing, sardonic intelligence and drink, and they began to play.

"First, Miz Yumi, you must meet Hitch the Dragon. We have been through a lot together. I reckon he's kin in spirit to your bracelet dragon guardian you just put on the table there."

The man who in Noname Lane had undressed in the dark and refused all illumination stood before her unflinchingly, the startling remarkably detailed etching of the red and gold dragon rising and falling with his breath, seeming to glide from his left shoulder, under his armpit, down his side to the hipbone. She could not tell whether the dragon sprang from the scars or sheltered them. Astonished, she sat blinking.

He lay down on the bed on his belly.

"Show me some of that crazy liberated-woman free-love Berkeley '60's stuff I used to read about," he teased. "Massage and I don't know what all. I wait with bated breath."

"Next time I'll bring my patchouli oil."

She hesitated briefly, then her hands found their own rhythm as the massage strokes she once had known well returned to her.

"That feels right good, Yumi-kid. I've had tight muscles lately."

He shifted now, away from the massage, neck and shoulders looser. He wanted to lie with her against him, she felt, she felt the hunger and thirst in him for just that physical contact that she sensed he also avoided, as she sensed he avoided sex itself, even while losing himself utterly in it: strange lover, abrupt, hands on her as if he were just learning how to touch a person, no technique at all, she thought, but his desire and her own drove her successfully to satisfaction.

He was palpably relaxing now, talking softly and disjointedly into her hair. She allowed herself to float with the crescendos of excitement and relaxation, rising and drifting on the water and the rain that seemed to have drowned the world forever, and the still, deep night; allowed herself to be borne along by his resonant, hypnotic, semi-hypnotized voice.

"'Tisn't Starvesoil dust you smell of, Yumi, it's pāhoehoe soil, rich and promises planting, dust and rain, October rain . . . you smell of an end to thirst, like when the rains first come. Anxious, thirst is . . . like hunger . . . but you're October rain."

And he was seized by rain that drifted in great gauzy curtains, earth's breath caught in the rising sulfur clouds, the 'ōhi'a forest catching and twining the sheets of water in its thick hair, pāhoehoe ropes, earth's hair, alive with fire at its heart. Rain pounded the ground, turned rich soil slick and wet, here in hills and hollows between hills, pebbles shiny black, sudden rough brush patches there, crevasses holding all danger, Pele's hair and Pele's tears.

Water rushed high, oheleberries sacred sweet and tart, body-cast viscous spider-fishing-lines, a strange roaring, tumbling stream of jade fearsome metamorphosis into a dangerous torrent turned to rusty blood, loads of ravaged soil borne now to the sea. Hurled around bends, from deep in invisible height and heart, obdurate shelves of rocky bone, now drowned from sight, distorting foaming water ridges into body's twisting purposes. A pit of molten fire, fire-rivers boiling where they lashed the water torn in white assaulting waves beyond all breakwaters . . .

Promised not to destroy by fire, surely neither by water nor ice . . .

Snow had prowled far down Mauna Kea's flanks this year, bringing rain, melt and flood, fire and ice.

Later he said,

"You learn that in the Starvesoil; anxious thirst, and longing. Not much there: things narrowed down. The world's so wide, you know, and not much of it there. Some things sweet and good, Euph's music and teaching, the big sky, but not much. . . I never even saw a person of Japanese blood till I come to Asia. That was just one of many things we didn't have down to Hibbits, people of Japanese blood." He grinned at her, gestured at his room, at Euph's and the Pine Tar, at the night beyond. "Reckon I'm making up for all those past deprivations now."

Later he asked her:

"Does it matter? Where my people come from? Arkansas, Kintuck, before that Barbados. . .they were Irish and Scuts they say. Scots, I reckon they meant, y'know. 'Scuts,'" he repeated with scorn. "Couldn't even talk right."

"Sam decides who 'talks right.' You don't have to agree with him. No, it doesn't matter where your people came from. That they came from somewhere? Yes, I think it matters — that it's important to know that, and to know from where. And why."

"Not with those folks, Yumi."

"With all folks."

"What's there to know? The Cawdrys were Dumb Scuts. They didn't have the sense to know there was something outside the Starvesoil. And my Little Mama's folks were Dumb Irish. Ridden out of Ireland for rising against the British and losing, a long time ago. Came through Barbados, some place called Bathsheba Coast, ended up in Junebug, Arkansas, where she were born. And didn't none of 'em know what it all meant. I pieced it together from broken words and names no one outside the Starvesoil and the hills could understand. The Cawdrys and the Robinsons, they were even dumber than the Joads. At least the Joads knew which way to point when they set out for California. They didn't end up in the Starvesoil."

The Starvesoil, the Lava Wastes. These were his landscapes, she thought, the landscapes of a starved heart. She said,

"Yes those people matter. And you know, what the hill people made back there in Appalachia was amazing. For a long time they didn't have any metal, just like the Hawaiians, and they built out of wood — everything, houses, utensils, they used wooden nails in carpentry. They made beautiful things. Quilts, music, a tradition —"

"I never saw none of that."

"Yes you did. Go look at the big red and green quilt Emma made, the one hanging on the back lānai. It's an Appalachian pattern in the middle with Hawaiian changes rung. Emma will tell you all about it if you ask her. And you told me yourself your Uncle Bert learned to do carpentry from 'his Daddy.'"

"True enough he could do carpentry with wooden nails. I seen it. I learned it myself."

"You are part of that tradition. And from what you say about where your mother's family came from, and how they got there, you're descended from the wild geese."

"Wild geese?"

"The Irish who were deported from Ireland, driven out by the British after the rebellions were put down and the famines came. They were freedom fighters who lost a battle, Will, not dumb rioters. And remember, losing a battle isn't the same as losing a struggle. *A luta continua*, as they say in various circles. The people who won that battle are the ones who use words like 'rioters' and 'dumb' and tell people they can't talk a language right or the language they do talk is inferior. The wild geese got scattered to the far winds, like dust. . .Barbados, Georgia, Australia, the Appalachian Hill Country, Texas. . .and with you, the Pacific Trades got you."

"Maybe I'm not the first of them here at that. Reckon that's why Hamakua's also called the Scottish Coast." He smiled, sourly. "The Scots here, they had a right nasty reputation as the roughest lunas. But I don't recollect no one saying nothing about geese, where I come from." He pressed his face against her hair. "You're the first person come in my life speaking of geese, then there's you and me and the nēnēbirds. . .I knew I was right to get that picture took, the day we met. I knew those nēnēbirds meant something for us special. . ."

His voice was muffled. "Imagine Will Cawdry bein' a goose, wild or not." He laughed again. "I reckon I got the name for that music I just finished tonight. 'The Structure of the Sea: Nēnē: A Flight of Wild Geese.' Yeh, all that, and the main title'll be "Suite for Yumi." It's on account of you I wrote it. Ben heard that, too, he told me."

His breath lifted her hair. "Nēnē lōlō, that's what I am. That's what I'll be for you. I'll be a goose for you. What are they like, those wild geese?"

They're beautiful, thought Paula. And strong. They fly far; the Canada geese, ancestral nēnēs, flew far, until they came here to stay. They fly far, and they always come back. Unless they're shot out of the sky on their way. If one of a pair is lost, the other travels on alone: because they mate once, for life.

"Think I'm like a nēnē, Yumi?"

His arms engulfed her. His long lank hair covered her face. He pressed her to him, pressed himself into her. Talking to her, all the while.

This hungry man.

Paula took his cheeks between her palms, lightly, feeling the flat hard planes of bone beneath her fingertips. Touched his thin lips with hers. In the shadowy lamplight, she looked into his light, hungry eyes.

"Maybe some ways," she said briefly. "Not all."

Later, lamp extinguished, in the dark he whispered,

"You smell so good, Yumi. You smell so good to me. Like lava dust and rain. Yumi, you my nights and days."

The morning came in gray light and Paula sat. The breeze had grown cool in the night and she had gotten up, to her surprise not waking him, and taken one of his shirts from the clothes dowel for a nightgown. Now she reached to him, sleeping beside her. She drew a hand slowly across his chest and stopped. Her massage training and her own emotional experience told her that the hard knotted muscle between his heart and his diaphragm had been like stone for years, and would be the death of him someday, sooner more likely than later, unless something in him changed enough to relax it.

Sleepily, gently, she ran her fingertips over the place, in a circular motion.

Today would not bring that relaxation; she pulled back from the violent great strength of his sudden awakening at her touch.

He was out of the bed and across the room before she had lowered her stunned hand to the sheet. When she looked at him he was already almost dressed.

"What's the matter, Will?" she managed through stiff lips.

Some massive effort at inner organization shuddered through him. He smiled at her. He came to her and ran his palm across her hair, almost but not quite touching. Then touching, barely. Her hair, all the hairs of her body, came alive at that touch.

"Nothing, Yumi. A dream, might could be." He finished buttoning his shirt. "I'll make us a flapjack breakfast all for ourselves, here at Euph's. Does that sound good?"

She hesitated, then,

"Fine," she said.

This great violence of heart, she intuited, barely fought down, would be thrust back at them somehow, on some other day.

For now, she smiled back at him.

After the doctor told him the numb place did not exist, Will Cawdry put on his clothes and went away, and never went back to a doctor again.

He knew that he had missed great danger, barely, in Singapore. Only once did he identify it: he recalled almost reaching to touch the woman's hair, how by fortune his arm numbed and he could not lift it.

And then he forgot again, until Yumi moved her hand in widening circles across his body and stopped at the spot. The uncanny knowledge possessed by her errant yet unerring hand terrified him. For, brought to life by the soft pressure of her fingertips, his numbness began to tingle. As if he had only then, again, begun to feel not-feeling.

But that made no sense.

For a moment standing there, Yumi looking at him from the sheets where he lay to sleep, he foresaw with terrible clarity what it could mean that he had taken a woman into his bed; and what he saw must not come to pass. Devastation. Destruction. Gliding women pulled into his nightmare. Yumi and the whore in Singapore must remain as opposite sides of the moon, as different from each other as solitude and closeness. Ends to a circle reaching for each other, that must never touch, or something would explode from deep within him where the numbness lived.

He rocked with rage at them. Leaped from the bed and dressed.

He had taken a woman into his bed, his need upon him. There he had touched her and been touched by her; and when his need was eased, he had slept, in his own bed and not alone.

When the morning came, Will Cawdry woke up for the first time in his manhood, for the first time in his life, with a woman lying beside him who was not his mother.

The woman looked at him now, where he stood by the bureau as if turned to stone, staring down at her. His big hands dangled helplessly. On the dresser top lay keys, a small brown paper bag of marijuana from his own field, several books, her dragon-guardian bracelet.

The surface was cluttered, but Will Cawdry was staring at its terrifying spaces.

For he had laid no money down. She had asked no price, and he had not offered one, and still he had laid his body down beside hers; and the woman in the bed was not wearing a gray dress. She was wearing one of his own shirts, a shirt he went to whores in. Sometime in the night when he lay defenseless and lost beside her she had risen stealthily and taken it. How could he have succumbed to her so profoundly that he had not heard her go? Now he was dressed and the shirt enveloped her and fell almost to her knees, she was so much smaller than he; and still he felt that she was naked to him and he to her.

What had it mattered what he wore when he went to whores? But now he saw that it must matter since the woman in the bed wore his shirt. The woman in the bed was not wearing a gray dress and he had laid no money down. He had laid no money down and he had laid his body down.

What then would bar the way between them and stop the fall to the stony ground where the heart breaks up like shattered ice amidst the flame, and hellfire flares all around?

"Nothing's wrong, Yumi," he said again, easily. "Like I said, a dream most likely. I'll just go set the kettle for coffee, now."

The obscuring confusion and the rage moved through him, like the fog descending into the caldera. Bringing wetness dripping thickly from the 'ōhi'a leaves, thicker than water, bringing lava moving across the wastes.

Blood and lava are thicker than water.

So he turned away from the woman and the memories of women and forgot it all.

21

Kerchief and Calabash: A Man Like Other Men

"This is the place I was telling you about."

Paula followed Pearlie and stepped out of the trees on the northwest edge of Hilo, where the sidewalks turned to dirt lanes and petered out.

Away across the great central expanse of the island, a rolling grassland and forest still free of buildings or other obtrusive human presence, the eye traveled irresistibly to Mauna Kea. Today, the mountain had partially emerged from seclusion, its white peak shining pristine between favorite veils of cloud in tones of slate and blue.

They stood in a small clearing. A square tumble-down wooden house was situated at the rear, backed against the trees; a low long gallery-like building extended from its left. The house was surrounded by carefully tended patches of vegetables.

An elderly man, wrinkled and stooped, dressed in loose pants and an open shirt and sandals and wearing a pandanas hat, came around the edge of the house and greeted them, smiling.

"This is Mr. Hoopi'i. My Uncle Kimo. Uncle Kimo, this is Ms. Kajiyama, Paula."

He nodded to Paula. Pearlie said something to him in Hawaiian, and he answered. Pearlie's speech was halting next to the old man's fluency. When they stopped talking, Paula thanked him, in her own still halting Hawaiian.

"You're welcome," the old man replied, then switched to English. "Pearlie tells me you have a fine old calabash. You two work here. You can come, go, whenever you want. I gotta go now."

He went off across the paths through his vegetables and disappeared behind his little house.

"Uncle Kimo wants to see the old arts saved, so he gives me this space to work in. Uncle Kimo's waiting."

"Waiting?"

"For his land. He's on the list. The Hawaiian Homelands list," she explained formally. "He's been waiting all his life."

Pearlie went to the gallery or shed, and held the door for Paula, in a gesture that was somehow also formal in its welcome.

The shed would receive good light for much of the day. Shelves along the short ends of the rectangular building sheltered calabashes, pots of dye, tiny hammers with heads finely incised to imprint patterns on the lengths of kapa stored nearby. One shelf was laden with books and documents; the one above supported a tumble of blue satin cushions of various shapes and sizes.

Polished bamboo flutes, gourd rattles, and a fine raffia hula skirt lay lightly against the walls, suspended by coconut fiber cordage.

"This is where you can work on the calabash." Pearlie indicated a long bench. "I have to go to dance class now and then to a meeting about the demonstration Saturday, you know, about our people living in packing crates out by the airport. So I won't be back today. But if you lay out the calabash, we can start on it in the morning."

For the first time in twenty-five years, using the same measured conscious movements as when she approached the pool table, Paula drew from a camphor box a length of ancient kapa, spread it, and with vast care cast calabash pieces: inheritance, glowing present, omen of future.

In the space Pearlie and Uncle Kimo had opened to her, Paula worked into the night.

Paula learned quickly from Pearlie what she needed to know to mend the calabash. Pearlie remarked that she was not really a beginner, and it was true; the memory of her sessions with her father lived in her fingers still.

Without speaking of it, almost insensibly, Paula settled into a routine: work in Honolulu during the week, then catching the last shuttle Friday night over to Hilo; and the late-morning shuttle back on Monday.

This had been her custom for just over a year when one Thursday Will called her to be sure she was coming the next day.

"'Tis most special, this," he told her.

Full night had come as he settled her on a rocky outcropping overlooking a steep slope that went on for miles and miles down to the sea.

She waited, baffled.

"What we have come for," Will said, "I know is at hand from signs seen in the earth and skies these last days. That it's come to pass now is a sign itself, I think, about you coming to the island and to me here, because

I'm pretty sure 'tis for this very day, for this very night." His voice dropped almost to a whisper. "'Tis the Lady. 'Tis what you came for. It's what we all come for — her coming." He spoke words that she thought she had failed to hear clearly; then she realized they were Hawaiian words that she did not understand.

"'Pele dancing,'" he translated. "She's most ready, Yumi. She's dancing now, on the East Rift. We will see the Lady dance."

No moon. Indistinct movement beneath the surface, like muscles beneath skin, almost invisible. And suddenly the earth exploded with a roar and rocked beneath her feet.

Multiple violences wrenched open the flank of the slope. Heat flashed against her cheek. Flaming incandescence, orange outlined in translucent white, blew out a throbbing orifice. Will's face cut a black rapt silhouette against the lurid light. The fireriver poured down the side of the mountain. Even from where they stood, across a wide valley from the eruption, Paula heard the hiss and pop as its outrunner tongues of exploded grass and bushes turned trees to fierce blazing torches, then transformed them to blackened abstract forms weird against the weirdly illuminated sky. Other trees disappeared completely, not needing touch but succumbing to the lethal kiss of searing breath alone.

She shuddered, her knees buckling. Will caught her upper arm, and when she was steadier he let her go.

The Jeep wound down the rough track and very soon the night closed around them, empty, black and quiet.

Anxious to recoup her composure, Paula forced a conversational tone.

"How did you know the eruption would be tonight?"

"Well, I didn't know. You don't never know with the Lady. But I have been a long time here, and I have learned to feel something of her moods and get a sense of her ways. Last week coming in from a cargo run to Maui I saw it in the weather — in the texture of the clouds, you know, and the way they lay. I spent a lot of time these last days in this high part of her domain, and there were signs beneath my feet as I made my way, beneath my ear at night, and in the movements of rocks and animals, in the bending and blowing of oheleberry leaves." He looked at her, now with a triumphant smile. "I beat them at the Observatory again! Mike owes me another drink. Mind you, their equipment's right wonderful the things it can do, and sure as anything they been tracking this spot, and are on their way to it right now, but if it's like last time they didn't think it'd happen just yet. There's no substitute for respecting the fine signs, which you can only find with your feet on the earth; and for watching them most carefully, over the longest time."

He hesitated. "But Yumi, I could see 'twas a shock for you for true, and not from fear of danger tonight. I didn't mean it so. I'm sorry for it."

"Yes, a shock, but how would you know it would be?"

"'Twere about what, if you care to say?"

She told him in brief words: the Southern roads, the work, the hatred, the killing times, comradeship. Murder. The bomb.

"Patchagoula, Mississippi," he repeated. "Euph did speak of Mississippi sometimes, as of the deepest ancestral hellhole for Black people. So you was a soldier in that war." He grinned but in the new moonlight she saw only the edges of his teeth and no humor.

"Sometimes," she said, "I put down my foot and I think I'll keep falling forever."

He nodded. "It comes of being places where there's wide spaces of danger and narrow spaces of safety and no way of telling which is where."

"Sometimes, I think I've never come back from that place the explosion sent me. Sometimes I think I never will."

She had never said either of these things to anyone.

"I reckon folks don't come back. Not to where they were before."

"Thank you for bringing me tonight to see these things. It's a great honor. Truly something worth seeing, just as you promised."

"Oh," he said, with spurious off-handedness. "I've seen you move on the rocky ground. Saw how you held the nēnēbird. And you were born on the Lava Wastes. Then, mebbe too I did feel even before you spoke of it that you had that knowledge — of wide places of danger and small spaces of safety and never knowing where the which will be."

As Pearlie and Uncle Kimo had invited Paula to share the space for work, so Emma, in the home she and Ben and Pearlie made not far from Uncle Kimo's, included her in the round of family and the wider round of family and friends that spread in overlapping circles from the kitchen and the lānai onto which it opened. Paula came to allow herself the luxury of feeling, in some way at least, genuinely accepted among a group of people again.

She knew that she was not at the center of any of those overlapping circles, but she no longer expected that from life. She had lived through the time when Caroline became Jamilyah, through Rick Kawabata and June Yasui. She had lived through the political battles in San Francisco's

Japantown and the fracturing in the society of the political work of the '60's and '70's, first from violent state assault and internal inability to withstand it; and, in the '80's, from the cultural assault against everything for which she'd fought. She had lived through the repudiation of shared lives and through assertions of her own irrelevance, even by people who had been close comrades: "Don't you know the '60's are over?" At least in her time, she had come to accept, at least for her, no group, no ho'oponopono healing it, would be a single hoop with a single center.

Even among her inner circle at the place on the water, areas of overlap differed and shifted. She and Will had grown up on the American Mainland, and different as those Mainland milieux had been, that fact mattered, here in Hawai'i nei. Pearlie, too, had an experience of that Mainland, very different from either hers or Will's, and that also mattered: the three of them had lived in the Belly of the Beast. Emma had not, but, unlike Ben, she had grown up with Americans. Yet she and Ben and Pearlie all had deep roots in a kind of ancient world that Paula only glimpsed. Only Pearlie and Emma, though, were tightly woven into a net of associations tacitly acknowledging rootedness in this place, Hawai'i nei, its ways, its past, and a kind of claim to it that none of the others shared.

And Ben, Emma, Pearlie, and Will — Will through Ben, through his time and connections here, and, she had come to see, through Euph — participated in assumptions about life that were alien to Paula, that she had been raised and educated to regard as both embarrassing and frightening, signs of rank ignorance and backwardness and of realms beyond logical control. She knew that Will shared these assumptions with the others in the moment when she realized that he was serious about his consultations with Auntie Raina who lived behind Honokaa, that he accepted her wisdom as a guide in life — just as, he told her, Euph had taught him to do, long ago, by his own acceptance of the wisdom and guidance of his mambo, his kahuna, Mam Manotte.

Paula knew how these beliefs were shared by the others, and how alien they still were to her, when as blue night claimed the heiau in the clearing where Will had taken her on her first visit to the island, two women went away from making offerings, women who seemed on sight across a gulf from her in their actions and the way of life they bespoke; and then she recognized Pearlie and Emma.

Yet, even as she felt the alienation, this twilight view opened a lost memory to her.

Late one dark night, soon after she had started work at the legal co-op in San Francisco, she had left the office, alone and exhausted. Walking through familiar streets back of City Hall, she was suddenly, inexplicably, lost.

She cast about streets she should have known, and was just moving from exasperation to alarm when at a corner by a vacant lot, the world flooded suddenly with light.

Instead of a vacant lot, she was standing in front of a small white frame house, almost hidden beneath the groaning boughs of pink and white oleander that overhung it. Behind the house stood a shed and through its half-open door the pleasant stinging smell of freshly-cut pine and sawdust tickled her nostrils: it was a carpenter's shed.

On the patch of grass before the shed an old man sat on a rickety wooden chair before a card table. His face was kindly, with sagging cheeks marked with pale brown spots.

A boy of ten or so, with short-cropped hair, compact and quick in his movements, appeared from the shed and poured tea for the old man, who thanked him.

Paula understood that these were her father, as a child, and the grandfather he had cherished and who had died at Tule Lake before she was born.

She blinked, and the scene vanished. She was shivering beside a vacant lot, in a dark San Francisco night growing rapidly chillier.

She hurried on. At the corner, she recognized the intersection and went home.

Until she was walking away from her view of Emma and Pearlie, in that blue twilight on the outskirts of Hilo, she had forgotten about this experience; for it had no acceptable context in what Will called her "lawyer-life." The lawyer's world could not accommodate it; it was threatening, marked her as deviant or mentally ill. So she orphaned it.

But this world she was finding herself welcome in among the people at the place on the water, a world she comprehended only obliquely, was capacious in a way that could comprehend her alienated experience that night in San Francisco; and she was grateful to that world for returning it to her.

At the same period she recovered another half-suppressed memory of San Francisco: the last time she had seen Ramp Deedon, fifteen years after he decamped from the Berkeley scene.

A chance encounter on the sidewalk outside the expensive Fairmont Hotel, where he was staying — not a place Paula frequented. An invitation accepted for a drink in his suite before she could overcome her shock and consider. He had already had several, and as they caught up with the years that had gone by, his initial warm tone underwent a weird slide. He was doing well, he said, and certainly by Paula's understanding of his world, he seemed to be. But discontent crept in: he was not doing well enough. Others were doing better.

Perhaps it was '80's greed, perhaps it was the milieu he moved in, perhaps it was Ramp himself, the golden boy who had never been able to accept that life disappointed everyone, who took that as a personal affront. His firm was losing business overseas, mainly to Japan. *She* must be doing fine, he declared, not yet having offered her a chance to say a word about her life, being female and minority seemed to be what was required these days. And with the ugly words, a sudden ugly pass.

She was caught off balance. She would not allow herself, could not allow herself, to believe what he was saying to her, to register on the ethnic and sexual vilenesses he was spewing and slurring. She heard the words with awful clarity but she simply could not connect them with herself. At the same time she was hearing them some subterranean part of her was thinking that he was saying and doing quite the opposite, that he had come back after all to pick up their friendship, their budding romance, of twenty years before. She was completely divorced from present reality, from time, completely making it into its opposite even as she lived it. For that time, she was quite out of her mind: and, unable to accept the reality, she was unable to deal with it adequately or in time.

Once before, under a massive lilac bush in flower, *deus ex machina* had spared her. This time there was no *deus ex machina*.

Too late, she fought. She left him on his knees, retching and cursing her, gripping his kicked genitals, abusing her.

The event cracked open the foundations of her life, as if it could undo past events. Had he always felt that way? Had he never been her friend? Or had he truly changed, in the intervening years?

Stunned, Paula, feminist, never acted on the rape. Less than a year later, a scandal erupted in the papers. Ramp's wife ended up in the hospital, beaten almost to death by him after years of abuse. And three other women testified that he had raped them, too: two employees and a prostitute.

As if jarred to consciousness by these other affirming voices, Paula submitted her own testimony. Ramp went to prison.

Now, enfolded in the life at the place on the water, she allowed herself this painful memory too. She kept the vision of her father and grandfather, and was able to release the disaster with Ramp and be free of it. For both things she was grateful to the circle at Euph's and the Pine Tar. The people had become important to her, and enriched her in those areas where their spheres overlapped, although she knew that large areas of their lives' meanings were veiled to her. Why Emma should have allowed her at all into the circle of her life, Paula was unsure. Partly, she thought, because through Will who had been taken as Ben's brother, she became family too; and partly, also, from respect for those of Emma's people who in these islands long ago had raised the other Yumi, whose namesake Paula was.

Ben kept a wary eye on Will, noticing he was distracted.

Then on a Monday, the day the Pine Tar was closed, and without mentioning it to anyone, Will filled a basket with the best from the garden in Noname Lane and loaded it in the Jeep. From the 'ōhi'a-wood chest he'd carved his second year on the island, he took a small bundle wrapped in softest ancient kapa and drove up the Hamakua Coast to Honokaa to see Auntie Raina.

When he got back, he went straight to Noname Lane. He chopped wood and worked around the place for several hours. That night, he went out to the BookShack and for a long time he just sat there, in the oversize armchair where he was comfortable, in the quiet night with just the muted yellow glow from the lamp on the table beside him, and the nocturnal sounds from the 'ōhi'a forest coming through the screens.

He had noticed long ago that after he left her he had a hard time remembering what Auntie Raina had said. Once, he'd sat in the Jeep afterwards and written down everything he could recall. And what he'd come up with was that mostly she asked questions. After he answered, she would sit quiet a long time, till he got nervous and sometimes even mad, especially since the questions usually didn't seem to have much to do with what he'd come to her about. But soon after these consultations — maybe not that day or the next, but soon — a tide would seem to start deep in his mind, the kind that only folks who knew the sea could detect at first, but that before too long would put a seriously new perspective on the situation troubling him.

After noticing that, he'd stopped trying to remember what Auntie Raina asked or what his answers were, just waited. And that was what he did this time too, not even trying to remember any response to the kapa-wrapped package he'd shown her and the story that he'd told her, of how it had come to him, and why, and his dilemma about it now.

And this time the sea change arrived quickly.

"It's older than time, Yumi. It comes to me from Euph, and to him from Mam Manotte, and to her from Haiti and before that from Africa. And now Auntie Raina's held it in her hands, and told me it's for you."

In the lamplight of the Bookshack, Paula reverently spread the kapa across her knees, and across that opened out the fabric it enwrapped.

Four feet by one, too narrow for a shawl, it could have been, perhaps, an extravagant sash or a headwrapping, or adorned an item of furniture, or been draped on a wall. She had never seen anything like it, even at first glance. The material was as soft as the kapa, but gave an impression nevertheless of great tensile strength. Its shade of deep rich gold was unique and seemed, by some trick of the lamp, to be a source of light as much as to reflect it.

The intricate patterning in black was most remarkable of all. As she held it at different angles, letting the drape and fold take their own forms, she tried to follow out the design. But just when she thought she had traced it, a set of ovals would interlink in a different way, and a ziggurat would reverse and arrow off in a different direction.

"It's wonderful. If I didn't know better, I'd say it was alive. What's the material, Will?"

"Dunno. Didn't never think to ask, and Euph didn't never say. Just told me what he thought was important for me to know, I reckon. Sorry."

"I'm sure he told you what I needed to know, too," she said simply. "Thank you, Will. I will always treasure this."

Reticence had been the Kajiyama family compact, and Paula had embraced it, under the duress that all children face in the family.

She knew that she and Will mis-knew the most of each other. She knew that to each other they lay largely as dark moon-mass beyond all sight. But long years of raw battling and profound aloneness had left her parched. Drenched in Will's delight in her, encouraged by his public celebration of her, she flourished.

On the edges of her consciousness, she knew that Lilith and Emerald were receding; the black satin outfit, the extravagant multi-colored costumes, had hung a long time now untouched in the back of her closet. And she knew, at the same edges of consciousness, that this was a good thing for her.

Now, she had a set of regulars at Euph's that she played the game with, some good enough to give her a run for her money; she was becoming known for her skill, teaching some of the kids; her partners called her by a name that others knew, too.

People knew too, now, that on weekends the alcove in the Pine Tar where Euph's picture stood would be adorned with a fresh flower arrangement of Paula's.

Her nerves were steadying. The dream that was like no other dream had not raked her brain for many months. The headaches seldom gripped her now.

Much resonated between her and Will that Ginnie did not perceive: and she knew that many of these resonances were good, too.

Because of them;

Because he had never tried to change her;

Because he had never taken her to see something that wasn't worth seeing;

For his sense of play that sent them spinning and circling through the blue heaven;

For his different rhythms of life lived and work worked, that soothed the deep-bitten scars cut into her by her own life's-work discipline;

For the narrow-channeled overwhelming lovemaking that freed her from every limit of herself and yet left her inner shadowed moonscape inviolate;

For kerchief and calabash;

For the expression of self long self-rejected, found again in flower arrangements that flared beneath her fingers and became the centerpiece of Will's public centering of her in his life;

And for the sound of the name her father gave her, long unspoken, ringing out again now like a temple bell to enlighten a loved space long abandoned;

For the sake of all these things, she made the compact of silence again. By that compact, she and Will moved around the BackShack as if it were not there.

22

The Passe-Partouts: Class Order/Disorder

Will was standing behind the bar in an empty Euph's, polishing glasses, sipping at some Johnny Black, waiting for the early drinkers to show, when a shadow fell across the entrance. He looked up to see a Honolulu woman positioned there, and classed her as Japanese most likely, maybe Chinese or Korean, maybe thirty-five, and he knew right off she had to do with him in some way not so good.

He set down the cloth and the glass, and said in his best genial hotelier manner,

"Morning, Ma'am. Can I help you? I'm Will Cawdry, at your service."

He'd guessed right, he thought; he could tell from the sharpening of her glance that his name was what she'd come to hear.

"I'm looking for Paula Kajiyama. My name's Ginnie Yamada."

This was the librarian-woman who had a job up at the University, and worked with Yumi in Honolulu on the Neighborhood Association. Come to look him over, he reckoned.

"She should be along any time now, if you'd care to wait. Or I can give her a message. Can I get you something to eat or drink? On the house, of course, for a friend of hers."

"Thanks, no. I'll wait, though."

She sat down, uncomfortable, at the table nearest the door. Will went back to polishing and reflected that he'd bit back the 'Yumi' and said 'hers' instead. He didn't feel right using that name with this woman from Yumi's Honolulu life.

"Ginnie!"

The woman gave a start, and Will almost jumped too, partly from surprise — Yumi had come in behind him through the corridor — and partly from relief that she was there to cut the rising tension. Then, right away, his heart sank when he registered the alarm that was almost panic in her voice. It was gone the next instant, pressed down, so that only nervousness showed, as she went on in a way not like her, verbally out of control,

"What brings you here? You didn't tell me you were coming. Have you two met? Ginnie, this is Will, I've told you about him, Will, this is Ginnie, I've told you about her, Ginnie, don't you want anything to drink? Will, could you get her some Cabernet?"

"I already offered," he said, hearing his voice, easy, confident, stopping her in her tracks: that didn't happen often with them, either. "Cabernet, is it?" And he looked full in Ginnie Yamada's face. She flushed slightly and hesitated. He had an idea she wasn't used to drinking this time of day, but she said,

"Yes. Thank you."

"Come on, Will, sit down with us!" urged Paula, fussing, as if he wouldn't have, he thought, sounding as if she didn't think he should. Didn't want him to, maybe; maybe thought if she didn't insist, that he'd keep to his natural place serving them drinks from behind the bar?

Oddly, he felt that he was the one who was unflustered, moving in his host's manner, well-spoken in that way, distant from the two women and their furtive complex interaction. He was the one in control, setting out glasses that sparkled, uncorking the bottle with a flourish, pouring wine worth a royal ransom or a thief's ingenuity, and all of it his, in this, his place, where he didn't have to pay. He drowned them in hospitality, he served them like a king, drowning his pain too, at the living-out of what after all, he'd told himself, he took for granted — that Yumi, in her real life, her Honolulu city-life, was ashamed of him.

Just as he pushed down, scarcely felt, his jealousy of the educated men he believed she consorted with in Honolulu.

Euph had said he'd be a man worthy of her some day; but in this, he felt, as in no other thing that he knew of, Euph was wrong. For he, Will, was wrong in his flesh, had been from before his birth; he could not believe in his bones that he had grown to be that man, or that he ever could have.

And all the time, as if from outside himself, he was conscious of the sardonic thread in the voice with which he addressed Paula and Ginnie, in the extravagance that just barely touched his hospitality with mockery.

By the time they'd all sat and talked civil and correct a spell, drunk their drinks and the two of them had taken their leave of him, Yumi hustling Ginnie out and away and probably, he thought, all the way up the steps of the shuttle flight back to Honolulu, Will didn't feel a thing, didn't even know he had matters to feel things about.

"I am afraid for you," said Ginnie, and Paula knew that it was true.

"That's crazy," she retorted, her back still to her friend. They sat stiffly on the chairs beneath the banyan in the courtyard. The rock doves fussed and murmured. Honolulu evening traffic roared beyond the walls. Majestic pearlescent clouds touched with rose stood in the sky. "I don't understand why you came to Euph's, and I certainly don't understand what you mean by that. Will was perfectly – cordial – to you."

More than you were to him, she thought. Or than I was. Guilt bit her, and she swallowed a gulp of Chardonnay from the wineglass clenched in her fist.

Ginnie repeated patiently, as if to a dullard,

"I came to Euph's on the spur of the moment, when Steve and I took a weekend in Kona – on the spur of the moment. We were up as far as Waimea, and he wanted to look at cattle ranches, and I didn't, so I left him for the day and came on down. Of course I've been curious about Will, but you act like I was spying on you or something."

It was true that that was how Paula felt, and she was aware that the irrationality of it rated a close look she was not inclined to give.

"If it feels like spying," continued Ginnie, with the calmness that like her honesty sometimes annoyed Paula savagely although it was at the base of her respect and affection for the other woman, "maybe it's because you've been acting so – secretive – about him. I mean, why wouldn't you want us to meet? And yes, maybe you do have some grounds for being mad." That aggravating honesty, in play. "I wasn't spying because I wasn't secretive. But I did know that you weren't anxious for me to meet him. And that worried me as well as made me curious. And now that I have met him –" she paused, and repeated in a lower and dogged voice, "I am afraid for you."

Paula exploded, "You have no grounds for that."

"Oh yes I do. And I don't believe you don't know it."

"How can you say that?"

Ginnie couldn't resist smiling as she said gently, "From your singing while we were writing leaflets for the beach demonstration two weeks ago."

"My singing?"

"You know that Johnny Mathis song? 'A Certain Smile'?"

Paula felt her face turn hot. Around her studio, she had caught herself humming the song, and thinking of Will, but she had not been aware of doing so in the presence of others.

"'A certain smile that thrills my heart again'?"

"So?" The sound of her own belligerence threw Paula off balance.

"'Thrills.' In another verse, 'fills.' But never 'chills.'"

In the space of Paula's momentary dumbstruck silence, Ginnie went on, still gently,

"And now that I've met him — yes, he acted cordial. He's also very intelligent, very unusual, and very powerful. As powerful and as dangerous as that landscape you tell me he's so attached to. The place gives me the creeps, personally. But as a matter of fact, I don't have any trouble seeing what attracts you. And that did surprise me. But it just makes things worse. It's not a question of how he acted. It's a question of how he is. And I'm scared for you."

"But why?"

"Because he's a scary man."

One night when Paula was at the table in the front room of Hale Noname, so absorbed in the intricate nuances of a translation that she no longer knew who or where she was, Will's wheezy laugh pulled her from that place so that she heard him say, "Little Yumi, you got the deep habit of work for true."

And this became one of Will's phrases that stayed with her.

She knew it was accurate and descriptive and she did not know how she felt about it. The characterization made her feel rigid, boring, constricted: "habit" did that. Yet she sensed that partly she brought that feeling about herself to the evaluation; it didn't come from him. His words made her uneasy. She could not miss the admiration that informed his assessment; she could not dismiss her intimation of profound hostility informing it as well. And she did not want to look at her own ambivalences towards him.

On the day they met, as they stood in Euph's, she had asked him if he played piano professionally, and sensed at once that such a category was simply irrelevant in considering the way he lived in the world. Now she understood better why that was so.

He could drive a vehicle up an almost vertical wall. He could repair just about anything mechanical with whatever cannibalized or improvised parts were found to hand. He had acquired a host of other intricate and to Paula unorthodox skills, some of which she guessed at and did not want to explore with him. He knew many languages well, yet he had never studied a single one — he had learned from having to communicate with people on the ground.

As the pilot of Volcano Flights, Inc., and Chief Restaurateur at Euph's and the Pine Tar, he forced himself to live with some regularity of appearance and performance. But he chafed against it. His temperament had not been formed in a world and a way of learning involving schedules, set hours of instruction, credentials, complex, interlocking and far-reaching institutional structures. He had learned serendipitously or under extreme unanticipated pressure from people whose names and pasts he never knew and knew not to inquire about. Without certification or verification, his expertise and the adequacy of his teachers was tested often enough in situations without quarter and without redress or recourse if found wanting.

To his experience he had brought from the beginning or from very early a variety of high intelligences and abilities, and profound strengths of endurance, tenacity and certain kinds of insight. He knew a vast amount about many things. He was as intelligent and mentally complex as anyone she had ever known, in some ways more so, and this made even more disconcerting his sudden drops into abysmal ignorance with regard to things she hated to admit she thought "everyone knew" — geographical, historical, literary, grammatical. Their conversations could flow without a hitch for hours, and she could never foresee when they would suddenly hit such an air pocket. To her he seemed not only unpredictable but amorphous; "passepartout," she thought of him, he went through walls and then suddenly came up short over nothing. She was without familiar landmarks or guideposts in encountering him: that encounter made her feel like a passepartout herself. And she was ashamed to admit to herself a visceral reaction edging on scorn. She knew it for class prejudice and to admit it struck too deeply at her cherished conception of herself as a person free of such bias — her vanity, as she might have had to concede.

Yet beyond these ignorances of Will's, the character that had been formed from his experience unsettled Paula more deeply than she would admit. She intuited what Ben called his 'soul sickness'; but unlike Ben, she had no categories to class it in. She could have tried psychosis, and somewhere, sometimes, he edged on what she would name so. Yet it was both more and less than that. It was the edge of schism and collapse, and she apprehended it, accurately if not consciously, in both individual and social terms. For it was not just a question of how Will was, but how he interleaved with, how he constructed — or failed to — both his psychological and his physical sense of himself with regard to other people and to the world around him. This kind of amorphousness she had never before encountered, and did not know how to recognize. He was beyond her limits of experience.

She confused all of her reaction with the part of it that she accurately identified as "class-based." Her vanity would not allow her to go against her self-image to truly consider Ginnie's words, to sort out and set aside Ginnie's own cultural, racial, class biases and see what remained. Because she would not go against her self-image she denied herself any flexible reflection, rendered herself unable to identify and follow her intuitions about Will and explore her barely conscious awareness of that in him that was not derived from a different class order but lay beyond any order at all.

23

Memories Of Colonialism

Will's knowledge of Ben's past had a lot of gaps. Ben never spoke of that past in any detail, not because he didn't trust Will with it, but because he himself didn't want to remember. It was painful in the worst way — bitter loss, and failure that was also guilt and remorse following a rout and a defeat.

And then, he was in danger of discovery. A feeling possessed him that to speak might bring fate crashing down, a feeling similar to the one that had always kept the name of the last city where he and Will had been before coming to Hawai'i not only from his lips but from his thoughts.

But Will knew something had happened so Ben couldn't go home again, and he knew Ben was on the run, had been on the run for years. He had figured out too that whatever pursued him didn't concern the laws of Ben's people, at least not only those, because he was obviously on the run from the White man's law.

Will had slept near Ben in the time before Hawai'i. In the day, in the night, in small back-street hotel rooms above noisy restaurants and bars, or out of doors on the ground, or in boats and planes. Sometimes they traveled tense, in fear of losing their lives; sometimes, they were relatively relaxed, or at least overcome by exhaustion and not in immediate danger. Will had slept near Ben in more different situations than he ever had, or most likely ever would, with anyone else.

So he knew that Ben dreamed, and he thought often it was the same dream and a bad one.

Ben knew dreams to be, sometimes, of crucial importance in human affairs, messages from the ancestors and gods; their interpretation required consultation with wise men and women, and their advice concerning them was ignored at one's peril. Will shared Ben's reverence for dreams; Ben had encountered other White men who did, as well. This significance they accorded dreams was one of the few indications, in his view, that they had any insides at all. For a long time he visualized them as hollow.

Will was the first, and remained the only, White person he ever knew the way a person knew a human being like oneself. And Will had a stronger reverence for the land, and a stronger sense of the power of the old gods, than Ben would have thought a White man could. He suspected that this was due to Will's early tutelage by Euph, who had been father and teacher to him and who was not a White man and clearly had come from a people who knew about the old gods and respected the old powers. Ben had often stopped to commune with the photograph of Euph, which was imbued with a great power of presence, and conveyed the old man's wisdom. Paula had commented upon that wisdom once, and the comment had been the start of Ben's willingness to revise his negative opinion of her.

Euph had been father to Will, as Ben was older brother, and Euph had bestowed on Will great gifts, of teaching and of medicines, wisdom about life, a certain phial of greenish powder, a kerchief destined to a purpose about which Will had been circumspect and Ben had not inquired further; for one did not trespass inappropriately upon sacred teachings or intimate transmissions between teacher and student. When, one evening a year and a half after Paula first came to Euph's and the Pine Tar, she walked into Euph's wearing a night-black dress with the magnificent kerchief wrapped around her waist, his acceptance of her was complete; for Emma had let him know that Will had consulted Auntie Raina concerning its disposition. Paula wore it that one night, annunciatory, and never again.

Ben understood that without Euph's influence Will would not have survived to meet him. He revered the old man as a teacher and master of powers, and as protector of this younger brother of his. Further, since he and Will were brothers, Ben also stood in a relationship of son to Euph.

Ben did not know that Will's reverence for dreams actually derived from his alienation: for Will had no idea what dreams were.

Other men said they did not recall their dreams, so Will said that too, to avoid being marked and hunted as a monster. But those other men seemed to know what they spoke about, even if they couldn't recall them. Pictures in your head, as near as Will could make out: like imagining, or remembering.

Not just human beings, but dogs and other animals too, dreamed. But he did not. He took this as yet another confirmation of his unnaturalness, of the fact that he was not a man like other men.

But he had some idea of what dreams felt like, at least when they weren't good, because of the bad dream Ben had.

Will never guessed it, but this bad dream of Ben's had a profound connection with him, although Ben had been dreaming it for years before they met, which as near as Ben could calculate by the White man's reckoning was when he himself was thirty-three years old. He had therefore been twenty-three when the events of the dream occurred.

It wasn't one of those dreams you needed to consult a wise person about. Ben knew just what it was: a dream of a memory.

In the dream, he was trying to run down a mountainside, but his feet were sunk above the ankles in the clogging iron-red clay of his country's Big Rains. He pulled his feet loose and put them down again but in the dream they always came down in the same place and he never made any forward progress: a dream of how reality had seemed. Yet at the same time he felt his whole body tilting forward down the steep and slippery mountain path, and he was gripped by a great dread that he would lose his balance altogether and pitch forward or, worse, sideways into the thousand-foot ravines that lay black and invisible a few paces to the right of his bare mud-stunned feet.

And the dream ended there. Nothing more happened: except that in his sleep Ben's whole being flooded with anguish that had no referent.

For that, he had to wait until he woke, and put a waking discipline on the anguish.

This was the referent: he and three other men were carrying Ben's desperately ill younger brother Janua on a blanket-and-wooden sling down the mountain through walls of rain and sliding mud, taking him to the White man's hospital. Janua had fallen ill soon after he and Ben returned from the stint on a tramp steamer plying the neighboring islands. The herbalist in the village said the illness had come from the White man's world, and the White man's medicines must cure him.

They did not go over the cliff-edge. They made their destination, in a muddy dawn: Minuvonga Town, on the coast, the colony's capital, location of the only White man's hospital on the island.

Ben thought their exhausted and filthy appearance alone should have showed their desperation. But it seemed only to frighten the White nurses.

Ben spoke English from his three years in Mission School in Minuvonga Town. His companions, two cousins and his closest friend, had never seen these White people close up and spoke no English at all. Dealing with their discomposure and interpreting for them in addition to obtaining help for Janua unnerved him. Partly because of that and partly out of sympathy for them, he released them to meet a friend who could put them up for a while, and he stayed on alone to cope in this White man's place.

But he had failed.

The nurses ordered him to the end of the line of natives, which began behind the line of White people, who waited indoors, and was separated from them by a screen. And the end of the line was out on the muddy path, exposed to the driving downpour.

Ben objected. He spoke only the truth: that if someone did not attend to his brother at once, the boy would die.

The nurse replied sharply, refusing to come and see. Ben argued, then subsided, fearful of antagonizing her more. He squatted beside his brother, leaning over him to try and shelter him from the pelting rain.

Janua tossed and muttered, then abruptly fell ominously still. Ben steeled himself and went and spoke again to the nurse.

This time she called the doctor.

The doctor had a face that was pointed like a rat's, and he told Ben that if he persisted in his disrespectful insubordination, he and his brother would be sent again to the rear of the line of natives, a line that now stretched to the end of the street.

Ben returned to where his brother lay, wiped the boy's burning face, and tried to think what to do next.

There, they sat two hours. Suddenly, Janua gave a choked cry and died.

Ben leaned his head back against the wall of the hospital, his eyes closed. At that moment he was not aware of grief or anger, only of exhaustion and an enormous sense of futility.

Voices buzzed around him. He heard the rat-faced doctor say above him,

"Dead? Clear it away then. Was that the emergency?"

"Yes, Doctor."

"As usual, they waited too late to come. Just stupidity. Then, human life doesn't have the same value to them as to us."

That was when Ben stood up and hit him.

Minuvonga was a British colony. Ben was a native.

In those days, in such a place, someone like Ben did not hit a person like the doctor. As pandemonium succeeded shocked stillness and other White men rushed towards him, shouting at sight of the doctor's body smearing with mud in the rain, Ben ran.

In the years he had spent at Mission School and hanging around the Harbor — for which he had finally been expelled — he had received some training in Western boxing from sailors he met, and some less formal experience in bar and street fighting. Most telling of all, in his village. he had been at the top of his age-grade in the highly skilled and gruelling stick-fighting and boxing competitions that were ancient Minuvongan traditions.

So that if he hit a man in the right place hard enough to kill him, he knew it. When, an hour later, he heard in a bar down at the Harbor the excited disbelieving rumor that a Minuvongan man had struck a White man, a doctor at the hospital, and that the White man had died, Ben had no trouble crediting it — all the more because at the moment he hit the man he had wanted him to die.

Ben was already drunk, and not thinking — not about his brother, not about the dreadful ordeal descending the mountainside, not about his abandoned friend and cousins, not about his own deed. He knew the English were concerned about the independence movement; they viewed a native killing a White man as rebellion, and he knew that he would be hanged. Perhaps this knowledge motivated his next actions — certainly no conscious thought was involved.

He was drinking with a sailor he had met during his time on the tramp steamer with Janua. The sailor was having his farewell fling before getting back to his ship. He'd already told Ben they were short-handed.

The captain hadn't heard about the atrocity committed in town by the native, or didn't care, at least not as much as he did about feeding his crew. In any case, when the tramp steamer *Port Moresby* sailed a little later that day, Ben sailed too as ship's cook.

Ben had never returned to his village. He had deserted his brother's body in the White man's town, left those who had helped him to manage there alone, to search out his brother's fate at great risk to themselves, and to take the body and the terrible news back to his mother and father and village.

Somehow making his behavior worse in his own eyes was that even before Janua got sick, he had intended to leave again, and take the boy with him. His father and mother and other relatives had not wanted them to go. Only his grandmother, his mother's mother, had laughed and said she would miss them, but it would be fine to see strange sights; she envied them and they must come back someday and tell her everything.

When he originally went traveling, Ben had had no intention of leaving his village forever, of course. But having left once, he had found it confining upon his return, as he had found the Mission School confining after voyaging on the tramp steamer. Despite his parents' pressing, he wasn't ready to marry the village girl he one day of course would marry; wasn't ready to start the farming and fishing that of course he one day would start, or to start the family that the farming and fishing would one day feed.

He had thought that he and Janua might travel together on a ship like the *Port Moresby*, might see places like the ones he later saw, on his own and then with Will. Will reminded Ben of Janua; Janua too had had the gift of music, and something fiery and gay in his spirit. And Will's hair, matted dark with blood over his unconscious face in the alley in Hong Kong the first night they met, reminded Ben of his brother's mud-smeared face on the ground by the hospital wall.

Six weeks after leaving Minuvonga Town with Ben aboard, the *Port Moresby* docked in Hong Kong. Ben went ashore with the others and did not return.

He had never seen a place like Hong Kong, and it left him empty with fear. Long ago when he was a child and first came over the mountains from Minuatu Village to the Mission School, Minuvonga Town had caused the same feeling in him.

Now he remembered that, and drew comfort from remembering too that the day had come when he knew his way around Minuvonga Town, sections of it at least, as if he were at home in the village.

So he drew a deep breath and, armed with the name a shipmate had given him of a man who might provide him work as a cook — he had proved a great success aboard the *Port Moresby* — he set out through the daunting streets.

One thing he saw at once: a place like this Hong Kong was a place for a man to hide, to disappear — if it didn't sink him.

Strictly speaking he hadn't arrived there at all — for he had no papers and no name.

In the village he had a call-name, Benua, for everyday use, as well as a number of names to be uttered only by certain people under very particular and sacred circumstances, and one name that only he and a certain priest of the people knew, and which must never be uttered at all or he would die.

His call-name had been set aside at the Mission School as if it had a bad smell, and replaced by one from the Bible; they called him Hosea, and gave him the surname "Jackson," pulled out of air.

Now, he chose another name for living this new life in new places. When he presented himself at the bar restaurant, in a crowded poor street near the harbor, and mentioned the man who had sent him, the owner grunted, spat, and offered him a cook's job, one pallet among ten in a room above the place, and — as it turned out — contacts useful for a man without papers, which the owner had evidently guessed. When the owner asked for a name, he told him "Ben," which appealed to him because the sound of his Minuvongan call-name was folded into it.

He had "Miller" — pulled out of air as the White missionaries had done — ready as a second English-type name, but according to the etiquette of those circles the man did not ask for more.

The change in Ben's life was so great that he might have failed altogether. But the events precipitating the change were so correspondingly great that he was numbed, and, bent only on survival, worked effectively at what was necessary to obtain it.

He began to discover other, unsuspected talents besides cooking. Various modest business dealings, among transient folk he met in the restaurant and among people in the neighborhood, were crowned with success. Word spread; other successes followed. The hotel owner came to see that Ben was a good man to have around, for more people came to the establishment. They ate and spent the night sometimes too; and more of these people than before had a little more money to spend.

Ben was steady, shrewd, reliable, and increasingly well connected through the flow of harbor traffic.

As a signal recognition, the owner gave him a tiny room all to himself, a floor higher than the room where all the other employees slept together on pallets, barracks-style. In this new room, barroom and street noises were less and from the window a precious wedge of the sea was visible down by the harbor; and sometimes, a breeze blew.

An old piano, battered and out of tune, stood in a corner of the barroom. One night when Ben was standing by the door between barroom and kitchen, Will Cawdry came into the place.

Anyone would notice him; everyone did. They waited warily to see which way his volatile mood would swing, what he was going to do, since his eyes were preternaturally fixed from drink and had the look in them that most of the patrons had met with before, of the truly unpredictable, the truly dangerous, man.

Will looked around, and, as if the place were empty, went straight to the piano and began to play.

Later that night came the brawl and the broken bottle; Will's head laid open, his blood spilling in the alley in the rain.

But before, there was the music.

All that was a long time ago now; and Ben had tried to put the disaster in Minuvonga from him and go on.

Often enough, Ben would be absorbed in his own thoughts and not notice that while he was washing and cooking and slicing at the table in the kitchen of the Pine Tar, Will, washing and cooking and slicing too, was also watching him, noticing his distraction. Even if Will didn't know the details, he knew Ben so well that he had a pretty good idea that at moments like that Ben's past was enveloping him.

By abandoning his brother's body, deserting his friends, and removing his presence from his family and from the funeral ceremonies in the village, Ben had gravely violated his peoples' ways. He had run afoul of the laws of the powerful White man as well. His actions had cut him off, left him in the terrible situation of being isolated in the world.

Then, he met Will. They came to Hawai'i, and established the place on the water. He married Emma, came again into the circle of family, in becoming kin to her many relations.

When no children were born to him and Emma, the thought touched the edge of his mind that this was a visitation for his unatoned wrongs. But others had no children, he argued; and when Pearlie's coming blessed his household, he allowed his intimations to subside.

Apparently he had succeeded in escaping his actions. But at bottom he had always known that, unless set right, his was the sort of situation that prevented the unfolding of an undamaged future.

Then, just a day after Paula finished re-creating the calabash, and before she had shown it to anyone, Uncle Kimo died, still waiting for the land. Pearlie's unexpected, violent upsurge of feeling shattered the harmony of Ben's home and of the place on the water, along many buried rifts; and Ben knew his fate had caught up with him at last.

24

Blue Satin Cushions: Justice in the Islands

When Pearlie was a little girl Will Cawdry called her "Princess." But Pearlie wasn't a little girl any more, and after Uncle Kimo died she announced her name wasn't Pearlie, she didn't want a haole trash name, and she didn't want Will to mock her with his nickname for her either. Her name was Leilani.

But Will was having nothing of all that.

"Her name's Pearlie," he asserted dogmatically.

He and Paula sat on the screened lānai behind the house in Noname Lane. Will was half down a bottle of Johnny Black, and Paula was doing her own justice to a bottle of Chardonnay.

He continued, "That's her first given name, the name her own Mama gave her, the same way she gave her her second name of "Leilani." "Pearlie" is what we've all called her since she was a little girl. And ever since she was a little girl I've called her "Princess." You know that, I've told you that story. "'Twere my special name for her. I give her that name she don't want to hear on my lips."

He was deeply hurt. But the only way he would channel his hurt was through anger and raw ridicule, which set him at ever more furious odds with Pearlie; and none of the others around the place on the water could find a way to get either of them to lessen their fury.

Pearlie's reaction to Uncle Kimo's death, her unexpectedly inconsolable grief and sense of loss at the death of her last relative on her lost father's side of the family, was inextricably mingled for her with her grief and anger that he had died still waiting for the land. She had allied herself with the segment of her political group most exclusive of things not traditionally Hawaiian. She had thrown herself into her studies of the Hawaiian language and spoke it as much as she could. She qualified Will as a haole invader and colonialist; and, with less fervor and consistency, she described Paula as someone descended from those who took advantage of their welcome by King Kalākaua to ally themselves with enemies of Hawaiians. Ben she denounced as a retrograde who failed to understand the necessity of Pacific Islander unity, and Emma as having turned from Hawaiian ways.

"She don't know what she wants," Will exclaimed heatedly. "She's driving Ben and Emma plumb nuts, too. Objecting to folks calling her by her own name, and then what kind of sense are her running buddies talking? Near as I can make out, she's decided she can't be Hawaiian unless she calls herself Leilani, which like I say ain't the name her own Mama called her by, and unless she speaks Hawaiian, which she mostly don't and I do, which aggravates her most powerfully. And she never will speak it all that well, because she's got no turn for languages, which I don't know why it should trouble her so, with all the other gifts she's been given. The girl's got a real dramatic talent, as we all know from her private performances lately, which some might call tantrums but I will concede are most creative. But the plays she writes and puts on are first-rate, Yumi. That "Chant for All the Islands" I've seen part of — that's going to be something for the generations to remember. And you've seen her hula, not tourist stuff, real old-style, dignified for true. Then look what she can do, with the old-time crafts, d'you know anyone who does better, Yumi? Not hardly, for sure not no one as young as she is. Auntie Lydia would never have taken her on as a pupil if she hadn't showed a most special turn for them all. But she just gets mad when I say all that."

Paula drank her wine, feeling menaced and depressed. She had been at the place more than once where her intimate relations with people intersected the society around them, and the issues were still the same: power under patriarchy, land, home, culture, race. She did not want to be here, at this place where she had been before, a place of schism and collapse.

"Will, we don't really know a whole lot about how much of this is a reaction to her family situation before her parents died, and to whatever awful things happened to her on the Mainland. We do know she didn't like it there. Pearlie has her closed places, where I don't think anyone knows her well." Like all the rest of us at the place on the water, she thought but did not say. "And she's an adolescent. It's common wisdom that at least in our society kids are going to rebel. Lay off her a little and ease up. And also, you know better than I do that she's got a lot of right on her side, as far as being angry about things. You've told me often enough Hawaiians don't have any reason to love haoles, or any foreigners for that matter. Economically and culturally they've ended up on the bottom in their own country. "History never repeats itself, but it never outlasts itself either." Wilson Harris, a great novelist. The past isn't done, isn't finished, here, or Uncle Kimo wouldn't have died waiting for the land. The past doesn't get done, get outlived, until people un-do it, un-live it, in present time. That hasn't happened here yet."

"But all I just said, it's true."

"That's not the level where Pearlie's living and talking. What she says is true too."

"But I don't see what the problem is. Not among us, here at Euph's and the Pine Tar. Pearlie always was Hawaiian and nor I nor anyone else thought any different nor thought nothing of it till she and her running buddies brought the matter up so, about who was and wasn't, and that people had to do this and that and be this way and that way to be Hawaiian. And what's going to come of this all, Yumi? She's started in about pure-blood Hawaiians. Emma and me both has tried to warn her such talk is going to make more trouble than not, seeing how mixed most Hawaiians is, including the Little Princess herself, which she also gets highly riled when I point out to her. If the Queen had had children they'd've been half-American! The Queen's own niece that she chose to succeed her on the throne were hapa-haole. The Princess Ka'iulani, she were half-Scottish, just like me! All this race stuff ain't the Hawaiian way, it never was. To think of family, yes, and to pay heed to whether you were ali'i or not, which has got its own problems to my mind, but it's old-time Hawaiian, true enough. But not race. That's Sam at his worst and it hurts to see Hawaiians take it up."

"For one thing," said Paula dryly, "the Hawaiians are trying to get the land back from the U.S. government which will only — sometimes — concede it to people it legally defines as "racially Hawaiian" in terms of biology. For another — look what not caring about bloodlines has got Hawaiians. They married haoles in good faith and the haoles used the marriages to steal the land from the Hawaiian people. Look where aloha got them historically when they were dealing with haoles. Hawaiian ways worked among Hawaiians, not haoles. Maybe they figure it'll take haole tactics to survive haoles."

"I ain't arguing with the need to fight Sam, you know it, Yumi. The medals I got fighting for him I've sent to the bottom of the sea. And I ain't arguing about old Hawaiian ways, not all of them anyway. But did you hear that crazy guy over from Honolulu who gave that speech at the jail when we were bailing the Little Princess out last week? Which I noticed she took our help, though now she says she won't anymore. We'll see. Incidentally I don't care for the business with jail at all. To be in jail is to place yourself much too tightly in Sam's power for my taste. Euph and my Little Mama both taught me most particular that jail were not a safe place to be. That crazy guy were talking about rooting out every plant that didn't grow here when the haoles came. I tell you, whatever these guys like him say about it, that's no old-time Hawaiian warrior energy. I been other places, where Sam ain't laid his tainting hand like he has here, and I seen the old-time warrior energy. Ask Ben. He's seen it too, more'n me, from when he were a boy. The Princess won't listen to him when he says the same. I know that crazy guy's energy, Yumi — so do you. It's Mainland energy. Angry, aggressive, and no heart or grounding to it. It's Sam's energy. Right ugly to see.

"And that Al Murphy — 'scuse me, Kalani we're supposed to call him now, who I've had hanging around Euph's since he was yea-high. Never liked him."

Paula clearly recalled pleasant exchanges between Will and Al, and approving comments about Al, a young drummer, that Will had made. Al had hurt him too. "Did you hear him calling for Pan-Pacific solidarity at that rally last Saturday, then attacking some other group of Hawaiians that'd come to the demonstration because he said they'd brought Kaua'i pilikia to the Big Island?"

Dissension in the movement, thought Paula. The specter of schism and collapse. . .

"Every struggle has its conflicts," she said quietly. "The movement grows from them or it gets brought down. But conflicts aren't a sign that Hawaiians are feckless natives, like some of the letters and editorials I see are making out. Like I hope you aren't. That's racist."

But Will shook his head. "I'm not understanding you, Yumi. I don't know about these movements and struggles and schisms. I told you right when we met that I ain't a political person. I know you and me don't think the same about lots of things. Me, I think Hawaiian folks like everyone else is better off without Sam's bloody money, or a government like Sam's for that matter."

"'Tis for that," he went on, "I ain't never touched a penny of my veteran's benefits."

No, she thought, just money from drug-dealing and mercenary warfare and god knows what, from the days when you were here and there, doing this and that?

"All that money has too much blood on it to ever do anyone any good. Both the blood of those as were called my enemies, and sure enough was trying to kill me, given my doings then — and the blood of my buddies, as they was called at the time, and as some were, for true. And as for such-like things that you feel so deep about, and work so hard for, back-pay for Black folks for slavery times, reparations for you — all folks for the camps, to me it's of a piece with my benefits, but for you to use it for righteousness, makes it clean again."

"Not quite. I care where it comes from too. You're owed that Veterans' Benefits money, for having been gang-banged by the U.S. military and government when you were still a child, and abused by the U.S. society before that. It's reparations too."

Will shook his head. "Don't know 'bout none of that," he brushed away thinking about her words concerning him; the feelings they aroused were too threatening. "But to me, that money's tainted so cain't nothing get it clean. Mebbe it's the difference in the way we look at the world."

"I know, your particularly perverse version of Christianity. Sin without possibility of redemption. Will, you're right that I don't think money is clean or unclean per se. It's not a religious question. Reparations money is two things. For one, it's symbolic. It represents stolen things, Will. Dreams, opportunities, respect. Life. Stolen from ordinary people, and used against them. And for another, money's congealed labor. I want it back for the people who sweated for it."

"Well then, Yumi, what about us? I sweated for it, in Noname Lane and here at Euph's and the Pine Tar. And your folks sweated for it, God knows, in the cane fields, here."

"That's a reverse situation from reparations. With the reparations cases, labor and professions and property were stolen from Africans and Japanese-Americans. With Native Americans, with Hawaiians, the land was stolen, their government was stolen. Reparation for that is to relinquish the stolen land and the stolen governmental autonomy. Here, the Hawaiians were robbed, by the people you're saying sweated for the land. What Pearlie-Leilani says about the Japanese here is that even though we were invited by Kalākaua, we profited from the situation set up when the U.S. overthrew the Hawaiian government. Just as White people in the U.S. — all White people — benefit from the past oppression of Indians by living on land stolen from the Native Americans— and benefit from the oppression of Africans — who provided the unpaid forced labor that was crucial to building a prosperous nation. And later these laborers were legally excluded from enjoying the society's advantages just because they were Black, so they couldn't acquire wealth and pass it on to our generation. And they still are excluded and persecuted. I'm not saying it's easy to figure out what rights time and work, blood and tears, give people in a given place — if any. But this is what I've come to about Hawai'i, and I've thought it through over and over and talked with everyone I could find. And where I've got is that it's up to the Hawaiians to decide."

"That'll take some doing."

"That's for sure. But — somehow — it's up to them to decide what "being Hawaiian" means. The same as it's up to them to decide how traditional the society should be, and in what ways, and what governmental structure they'll have. The pivotal point is that the Hawaiian government was overthrown by U.S. settlers and the U.S. Marines. By the haoles. That was a legal and ethical crime. Not even President Cleveland denied that. And just because since the crime the robber's children and other children have been born and brought up in the stolen house, love it in their own way and want the stolen money that's appreciated after the crime, doesn't change the reality that what they have is ill-gotten gains."

"Yumi, that may be so, that last, but how about love of the land? Aloha 'āina? You can't believe that anyone has the right to damage the land, or hurt the people. How is proving your great-great-grandfather got born here gonna guarantee you love the land? How about that Ned Warner who sold me this very land we're standing on, and was dreaming about selling it to a Mainland motel chain?"

"If people are damaging the land, or other people, I'll fight Sovereign Hawai'i through Amnesty International or the U.N. or other organizations, just like I do all the other sovereign entities. And if I want to live here, I'll take out my green card or whatever and apply for citizenship and fight from inside as a Hawaiian-recognized naturalized Hawaiian. If they'll have me. But what I think and you think — that doesn't matter unless Hawaiians decide to include us. Till then I'll stay here and work the best way I can see."

"Whether they want you or not?"

She hesitated. "Yes," she said, raising her chin a little defiantly. "Maybe I'm inconsistent there, maybe not. The Japanese were invited — by the Hawaiian government, as a people. Since their government invited my great-grandfather, maybe I claim the privilege to stay until a Hawaiian government rescinds the invitation to me." And she thought too of the other Yumi, who according to one strand of her family's oral tradition had been part Hawaiian.

"So you think I should leave the place."

"No," she said at once. Then, hesitating, searching for her grounds besides her immediate desire, "You're Ben's brother and he's Emma's husband."

"Now you're talking like me. Far as I'm concerned, I took out my "citizenship" when Emma invited me to eat in her kitchen and Auntie Raina agreed to be my advisor."

"I know what I'm saying isn't perfect. But it's as consistent as I can get in my gut and my mind. I'm sure about the central point, which is that the last time the Hawaiian people were able to speak in any recognizable orderly way was when thousands of them signed a petititon to Queen Lili'uokalani. I don't count the vote for statehood in 1959. By then, the Hawaiian vote was swamped by other people. The Hawaiian people who signed Lili'uokalani's petition recognized her as their legitimate leader, and she was recognized as the head of a sovereign state and nation by many other states in the modern world — including the U.S. That petition mandated her to rewrite the Hawaiian Constitution so Hawaiians could get back the vote the haole settlers stole from them in 1887 at bayonet point. The Queen had a petition mandating her constitution that was signed by the majority of the Hawaiian population. She presented that Constitution to her Governmental Cabinet on a blue satin cushion, and Sam overthrew her for it. So starting from the position the Hawaiian people took when they signed the petition is the best I can do."

One day that week as Paula approached Uncle Kimo's shed, to pick up some supplies she had forgotten when she vacated a space no longer welcoming to her, given Pearlie Leilani's feelings, she was brought up short by an unfamiliar woman's voice coming from within.

"I, Lili'uokalani —"

Mature, confident, serene. While she was still deciding who it might be, the words came again, apparently spoken by a different person, younger and less assured.

"I, Lili'uokalani —"

Pearlie Leilani, practicing a section of the Chant for All the Islands.

"I, Lili'uokalani —"

Deeper, confident again, but commanding, almost aggressive now. Still a search, to inhabit, to bring forth, the magnificent words to which the Queen had put her name as the U.S. Marines drew up outside the Palace.

Moments passed. Silence.

Paula hesitated, then went away.

The trouble in Paradise affected everyone at the center of the place on the water.

It brought Ben face to face with his unresolved past.

It stirred in Emma long-suppressed memories of a childhood in the backwash of a disastrous epoch for Hawaiians.

It set Paula squarely at the intersection again where the people in her life were in bitter conflict, threatening her world with schism and collapse.

It drove Will increasingly towards the places in his life that he was least able to face.

And, increasingly, he responded to the pressure of now almost-continuous white nights and black days by seeking the depths of Johnny Black and the heights of the Lava Wastes.

Late one afternoon in Honolulu, Paula took a break from preparing an argument her environmental group was making against a hotel development on a Big Island beach. She wandered onto an elegant hotel veranda in Waikīkī. The hotel had commandeered the only unobstructed view on the beach of the majestic reach of Lēʻahi. Of all the beauties of this place, the clouds were the greatest unceasing pleasure and marvel to her; Paula drank Chardonnay and watched them now, huge domes far out over the Pacific. They stood immobile for hours, their outlines as cleanly cut and faceted as marble sculpture, their shadows and colors shading and shifting with the sun's glide toward the horizon. Now they were pearl-pink, now an exquisite gray-blue, here they were pale green and lavender.

A military ship had come in. A group of three uniformed White children, seventeen-year old boys with acne-ravaged cheeks and adulthood still only sketched in their features, pushed onto the veranda and, cowed, as they saw it was not the kind of place they had expected, withdrew.

She heard them, boisterous again, once clear of the precincts. Correcting a false start. Heading for the River Street end of Hotel Street? She watched them go.

They were young enough to be her sons. Two decades past, when she had stood outside induction centers, pleading with, challenging, boys like them to chance five minutes of looking at new information and exploring new ideas before taking a forward step, they had been her contemporaries.

The war was over long ago, but its legacy never ended.

The clouds were yielding to a scarlet sunset that now reminded her of blood. Out on the horizon, black and ominous against the wounded-looking sky, a warship made a steady way towards Pearl Harbor. So, once, had the U.S. ship *Boston* showed itself in the waters off this coast, slicing its inexorable way from Hilo Harbor to overthrow the Queen.

And because of that, Pearlie Leilani seeking the Queen's voice, struggling amongst discordant musical strains, voices, languages, crossed-over scripts, competing loves, among a jumble of blue satin cushions.

Sam's warship made its way evenly, silhouetted against the bleeding sun, and for a moment, Paula was gripped by the idea that it was indeed the *Boston*, caught forever in some time warp, still making its way toward shore on its fateful mission.

She shook her head against the fantasy. Yet there was a truth in it. A century apart, the ships' wakes wove a thread in the same tapestry of troubles. Today's pilikia had been woven by the crooked movements of yesterday's shuttle. New world a-comin'? Pearlie Leilani and her friends trying to straighten the tangled web they had inherited; all around the world a new world of some kind coming, adumbrated at the line of the horizon.

Paula's lifework, she saw now, in one form or another, was working to re-weave that crooked thread: on political barricades, along dusty Southern roads, in gloomy courtrooms. *A luta continua*: the struggle continues. Keep on keeping on, as we used to sing in the Blessed Community.

Staring at the wake's white line cutting the purple-blue sea, she thought how the world was closing fast now on a European-designated millennium, its last half set by the terms of European voyage, European conquest. Because of those voyages and conquests, pilikia now at Euph's.

With an uncanny clarity not experienced for years, Paula heard the voices of her father, of Jim Jordan and Thomas Graves, rising in fervent debate in the Black Star long ago.

"The problem of the twentieth century is the problem of the color line, Doctor DuBois was right about that. It's because of the White man's racism."

"No, It's because of capitalism, capitalism drives imperialism and racism."

Suddenly, tears were streaming down Paula's cheeks. She saw, also with uncanny clarity, the antique map of the world in the dream she had dreamed years before, just before she went to Tule Lake. "Here be monsters." Genocide, of dimensions never to be known. Many thousand gone. The old spiritual had it right, just an undercount if speaking of the Passage. African peoples devastated, sea-bottoms glittering with bones of uncounted dead along a deadly crossing. American peoples, Hawaiians, devastated, almost destroyed. Kealakekua Bay, the Mahele that stole the land "legally" from the Hawaiians, blue satin cushions, genocide accomplished by guns and betrayal and gold, by breaking gods and breaking hearts, words of people once trusted cutting septic wounds in hearts in darkened bars, old men penned behind barbed wire dying of heartbreak, deforming love through generations. Sovereign constitutions embodying a collective dignity trampled underfoot for military harbors that had generated the sexual suppuration of Waikīkī and Hotel Street through generation after generation of Euroamerican war with Asia. Breaking — if barely — Asia's single powerful bid for imperial equality. The voice of Thomas Graves rang in her ears again: "The Japanese beat the White man at his own game in 1905 and they damn near did it again in World War II." And though she might differ with his political conclusions, though the game was bitter and ugly, it served to point up how bitter and ugly was the world in which she had had to make her way. For she knew how much she owed him for that perspective, in sustaining her in a struggle to survive in a Euroamerican world at war with Asia, where the victors, her country-people, had made her face the face of the enemy her whole life long.

25

Kinfolk and Strangers

As the shadowy shifting in Ben's psyche continued, he slowly became aware that the questions Pearlie was raising about peoples' place here in Hawai'i nei were stirring other, related questions in him, like creatures of the deep sea. When he looked at Emma, sometimes now she seemed a stranger to him.

He had lost his past, turned his back on it. And, without shared physical extension into the past, without the ritual that confirmed it, how could there be extension into the future? Without ancestors there could be no descendants. His transgression was unrighted, and so of course he had been denied children, including, now, Pearlie Leilani, whose coming into his home he had foolishly taken as a sign that his wrong was overlooked, or — most foolishly and dishonorably of all — could be evaded. As if one could ever evade the consequences of one's deeds.

Bereft of descendants, cut off from his ancestors, was not he himself a living ghost?

So one day he gathered the best fish from the day's catch and drove North along the coast to Honokaa.

It took him several days to settle into the knowledge his consultation with Auntie Raina had given him. The idea was emotionally daunting. To go back to Minuvonga and perform the complex rites of atonement — to face any of his kinsfolk and friends who were still alive and who would speak to him — this was bad enough. And as their images rose up before him, they seemed to engulf the life he had built since — Will, his home and place with Emma, here in Hawai'i nei. And what of the perils from the White man's world? He was illegally in the United States, and he assumed he was under sentence of death in Minuvonga.

To complete his sense of being haunted and trapped, he could not talk about his dilemmas with either of the people close to him. Emma was at the root of his own conflict now. And Ben was also deeply concerned about Will, who was half mad with the stress of the situation. Ben could tell that, and though he did not know, he had a shrewd deep guess the reasons were at least partly rooted in Will's years as a soldier in Vietnam.

Inexorably, his thoughts circled in and in on the person he knew he would have to approach, have to risk trusting with his future. Will might be right in his opinion of Paula, or he might be wrong, but he was not reliable, he was too involved with her. It was Emma's favorable estimation of the other woman that finally decided Ben to take the chance.

And so, early one afternoon, as Paula stepped out of the back corridor at Euph's on her way to the kitchen of the Pine Tar, she almost bumped into Ben, giving her a flash of déjà vu: the first night she had ever come to the place on the water.

"I need to talk to you tonight. When Will's back. Just us three."

He would tell Emma after he knew where he stood.

"Yeh," said Ben, later when the place on the water was closed and Paula and Will sat with him at the proprietor's table at Euph's, under Euph's enigmatic gaze. "I killed a man. White man. A doctor. In Minuvonga, a long time ago."

His right hand clenched so hard that beneath the copper his skin turned pale.

"Why?" asked Paula, and realized from Will's glance that with her question she had once again transgressed some boundary of propriety in the milieux where they had wandered, a propriety whose terms remained obscure to her. Impatiently, she said, "If you want legal advice, you have to tell me everything a lawyer would be up against, so when I talk to an immigration lawyer I know what I'm asking someone to do. Never lie to your lawyer." She laughed. "Under the rules of my former profession, you can mislead the court later, if it's necessary and unprovable, but only after letting the lawyer know what you're doing."

Ben shrugged, almost imperceptibly. "He insulted me and my family."

Paula stared at him, long and stonily.

"I need it all, Ben, or you're better off not starting this."

And suddenly, Ben told it. "My brother was sick with a White man's sickness, and the healer said only the White man's medicines could cure him. So my friend and cousins and me brought him to the hospital in town. They wouldn't see us till they saw all the White people first. My brother died while we waited. The doctor said we were stupid. We should have come sooner, though we came as soon as we could, and then he wouldn't see us. I hit him. I killed him. Then I ran." For the first time his uninflected voice revealed the faintest tremor. "I have to go back. I left my brother's body. I left my family and age-mates. There are — things I have to do to make this right. For that I have to go back to my village."

"All right," said Paula quietly. "I'll make inquiries about what happened in Minuvonga."

Will spoke for the first time. "Don't let on about where he is, Yumi, till you get things squared away." His voice was taut with anxiety. "He didn't say but I reckon we gotta tell you now that Ben don't have his papers just quite in order to be in the U.S. of A."

"I don't have no real papers at all," said Ben flat out. "Nobody knows I'm here, who I am or where I come from. Or why."

"Actually, I'd kind of guessed that," Paula responded, her tone astringent. "I will be discreet."

"Here's the situation," she told them three weeks later, seated in the same place, at the same late hour. She opened a manila folder and read aloud. "From Minuatu Village, Minuvonga. Benua no Minuatu."

An expression crossed Ben's face as if he were seeing a ghost. Paula stopped speaking.

Ben made a quick gesture.

"Go on," he muttered. "It's just — a long time since I heard my name."

She saw how affected he was, and waited another moment before continuing. "Also known in certain quarters as Hosea Jackson. "Assaulted an English doctor, named Jonathan Taylor, at Mission Hospital, Minuvonga Town, 22 October 1955. Fled and was never apprehended." She looked into Ben's opaque dark eyes. "You didn't kill him, Ben. He didn't die. You gave him a hell of a clout; he was unconscious for days. But he recovered."

"No," said Ben. "I hit him hard. He died. I know these things."

She shook her head. "He should have died, by rights. You hit him hard enough to kill him, that's clear. But these things are chancy."

She looked back at her notes. "Dr. Jonathan Taylor went back to England seven years after that, and died as a passenger in an automobile accident in Kent in 1962. Body cremated. The statute of limitations expired long ago. It's over and done with. And given the circumstances of the offense, which were on record as you described — though you were described as at fault for making trouble about not being seen until all the Europeans had been — and given that Minuvonga was a colony and is now independent with a mildly Socialist government and no love of the colonial regime, my contacts there inform me no problem exists about your return as far as they're concerned.

You are a citizen of Minuvonga in good standing. The immigration lawyer I talked with thinks that given your years of residence, your marriage to an American citizen, and your sterling reputation as a pillar of the business community, you can obtain documents that will lead to citizenship if you want and in any case will make you legal and free to travel."

She pushed the buff folder across the table to Ben. "There are all the documents, Ben — copies for you and copies for a lawyer. I suggest you get Bill Horita to act for you — he's local, and you'll want a lawyer nearby. His office is over on Ponohawai Street, near the intersection with Kilauea — and you can trust him. I have copies of all these documents in my safekeeping in Honolulu until you make arrangements with someone over here."

Ben stared at the folder as if it were a box of bones metamorphosing into something else, he wasn't sure what. Then, brusquely, without touching it, he jumped up and walked past her and past Will and disappeared down the steps, silently, into the dark.

"Well," drawled Will at last; but she could tell he was deeply shaken.

"Did you know about the good doctor?"

He shook his head. "Not a whisper." He paused. "I ain't all that surprised, though." He grinned, slowly.

"What's funny?"

"I were thinking. 'Midst all the relief, Ben's gonna be mighty downcast that that man didn't hardly even get slowed up none when he hit him. Ben were top-ranked in boxing and stick-fighting in his village, you know, and —"

"I wouldn't exactly say Taylor wasn't 'slowed up,' " retorted Paula. "He was in a coma for the better part of a week. He probably had an unusually heavy skull. It happens. Luckily for Macho Ben. Otherwise he could have succeeded in really messing up his life."

"Almost a week, you say? That'll make Ben feel better, I reckon. I think I'll just go along after him. When he gets a grip, might could be he'd like to celebrate a little, Yumi."

"Don't hurry back. I can use a break. I don't really like the attitude to mayhem you two have."

"She's been up twice to see Auntie Raina, Emma has. She don't say it, but she's afraid he won't come back, Yumi," said Will, turning his glass around in his hands one night in the house down Noname Lane, two weeks after Ben had left for Minuvonga. Paula saw that Will was afraid of that too. "This is right heavy stuff he's dealing with."

"I know," said Paula carefully, "and I don't pretend I really understand it. Not as well as you do, certainly not as well as Emma. But I think he'll be back, Will. I always did. This is where he lives. And I'm even surer now because this afternoon Bill Horita, the lawyer he went to here in town, told me he asked him to start proceedings to become a citizen before he left. He assumed I knew."

"No!" Will banged the glass down. Relief danced across his features. "Just wait till I tell Emma!"

And Ben did come back, with gifts of cloth for Emma and Pearlie Leilani and Paula, and a magnificent carved Minuvongan fighting stick for Will, at which Paula looked askance in silence — some people never learned — and a Minuvongan carved bowl for Bill Horita. He didn't say a lot, just that the ceremonies had been completed and he could return to his village now whenever he chose. The details of the ceremonies he did not recall: they sank to the bedrock of his consciousness to sustain him, below surface memory.

But Pearlie Leilani's continued vociferousness and activities about the threat to Hawai'i nei stirred another memory for Ben.

Sitting once again in the kitchen of the Pine Tar, he remembered the recent Minuvongan afternoon when he had gone into the forest, following the new graveled road cut behind the village that had replaced the muddy track he and his age-mate friend and his cousins — friend and cousins now all dead — had taken long ago, when they set out to carry his younger brother's litter through a season of hard rains to the Mission hospital in Minuvonga Town.

A mile into the forest, behind the village, as a strange mechanical roar grew almost deafening, he had been struck motionless, appalled.

Something was tearing the mountain down.

Earth-gouging machinery had ripped away the forest and half the earth's flesh beneath it — the flesh that supported and nourished Minuatu Village. Choking on air red with dust, he stood on the side of the road like some fool from the village beyond the ridge, that Minuatu had fought with since the world began, instead of like the successful businessman that he was.

As he stared, a bulldozer's mighty horn blasted behind him. He jumped aside.

The driver pushed back his yellow hardhat and wiped sweat, smiled broadly, and called, "Ah, it's Benua, isn't it? I heard you were back! I'm

Asua, from your *tukana*." He used the Minuvongan word for the group of boys who went through their initiation to manhood together and by that were bound as brothers for life. That he had to remind Ben of their connection told him the world had changed. Once they would have lived their days out in the same village. He had gone away. The thought brought a pang of guilt.

Asua pulled the enormous machine off the road with conscious flair, and jumped down, leaving it perched precariously.

He explained that the American company wanted something deep in the mountain, not gold, but some metal like it, anyway very precious. The money they paid was very good. He was doing well. He had built a house, a real house, American-style. He had four sons and two daughters.

He broke work early for the day, and they went to greet Asua's wife and look at the new house, built American-style. Twice as large as Ben's house in Hilo, it was painted vividly in traditional Minuvongan black and red patterns that Ben knew in America would be considered bush; he hid a smile.

Then Asua took him to a little bar in the ramshackle shanty town that had sprung up around the construction site. They drank beer together. But as he consumed more, Asua became less jubilant, more confessional.

"Come."

They hurried from the bar, and Asua led Ben through the underbrush down a path. For a few fleeting moments they might have been boys again on the village trail.

They arrived at a clearing and there it stood: the house that Ben had known, the house in which Asua had grown up. The family house, and behind it the shrine house, which they now entered together.

The shrine stood in the corner. The dance masks hung from the ceiling suspended on their coconut-fiber cords.

"I brought my sons here," said Asua suddenly. "I taught them the chants, told them the stories. When they were young that meant a lot to them, but now they don't want to come. Sometimes I am very confused. It's good that there is money. It's good that there is a school. My wife is very happy with our new house because of the kitchen and because getting water is so much easier, and I am happy that she doesn't have to work so hard. We are also happy that the children can go to the school and learn. Not everyone sends the girls, but we do. It's the modern way, it's good I think, because who knows what they will need to know when they are grown? Who knows what the world will be like then, for them as much as for the boys? It won't be the way it was when their mother was young, that is certain.

"But Benua, the river is dying. The wounds to the earth are killing it too. It's full of dirt and can't breathe, and it's turned as red as blood. The fish are almost gone, the forest has been stripped, and even though the Americans say they will replace it I don't think they can, not even they with all their machines. Old Homua won't come out of his house any more. He won't talk any more. All he says if people visit is, 'I tell you, the world is dying.' Many people laugh at him. I laugh with them, sometimes, but sometimes at night I think of the river and the mountain and I think he is right. And I get confused.

"I think, 'This new thing is good, this new thing is not good.' I don't know whether there is more good that is new than bad. I wish there was a way to get the good and not the bad. But even then, everything would still be changed.

"Sometimes I wake in the night and think of the things I know that my sons will not know, how beautiful and full of power those things are, and what will be lost in the world when you and I and all of us from that time, the last ones who were fully initiated, have gone to the ancestors. And then I cry.

"And I wonder if our children can find their way there, to the land of the ancestors, if they do not know those things. I wonder if they will even want to try. And I cry then, too."

Now, sitting alone in the kitchen of the Pine Tar, Ben Miller, successful businessman, prospective U.S. citizen (taking citizenship was a good move for business and for safety) — Ben joined his tears with his age-mate's, for lost things. Asua had stayed, and yet he had lost his grip on the old ways too.

And for what he himself had abandoned —and in that way perhaps betrayed, helped to destroy — in leaving his village as he had, to wander in the wide world and not return, he was full of grief and fear.

One night, he had a dream, and this one was both a dream and a visitation. It did not speak directly of his concern about the damage to the Minuvongan earth and ways. That voice would come later, he intuited. This dream spoke to his family situation.

The face that appeared to him was his grandmother's, his mother's mother, the only family member who had not opposed his going wandering.

His parents were present, in the background, and Janua, who had died in the muddy street outside the White man's hospital in Minuvonga Town.

Then he perceived that all his kinfolk, the living and the dead, were gathered around him.

His grandmother leaned over a basket she was weaving, painfully, for as in life near the end, her hands were almost crippled with swollen joints; and as he knelt before her she looked directly into his eyes.

"Go and see," she said. She spoke in Minuvongan. "Take Janua and go and see what's beyond the next ridge and the next reef." And, as can happen in dreams, when she said 'Janua' she meant both Janua and Will. "Go that way —" she pointed with a finger so gnarled that even in the dream he flinched with the pain he remembered her feeling. "Past the village we've fought with since the world began. Leave the war behind. Go and see." And at the heart of what he would see were Will, and Emma, and Pearlie Leilani, and Paula, and his home and his place in Hawai'i nei.

Suddenly, her eyes, sunk in the wrinkled map of her face, twinkled as brightly as a young girl's. "I'd like to go and see, myself."

In the dream, a deep peace flooded Ben, suffusing his present life, his feelings for Emma, Pearlie Leilani, Will, and Paula. He bent before his grandmother more deeply, and took the old woman's hand, dry and hot and soft like powdery dust.

"Grandmother," he whispered. But the word he spoke was "Tūtū."

And she reached out her arms, which became as wide as the forest was before the Americans came, when it was healthy and strong, and like the forest when it was well she embraced them all.

Old women contained the future. Sometimes old women could be so young. . .

Tūtū. . .

After that, Emma never again looked like a ghost to him.

Paula had appeared in his dream. He thought deeply about that. And at the end of the thinking he acknowledged how much she had given to his being able to come to this place in his life where his heart was free of its long troubles, able to effect his life's reconciliation.

She was the one who had spoken his name, that night in the kitchen of the Pine Tar, and so returned him to himself again.

With this, he became able to recognize, as well, that she was good for Will.

For the first time he said to himself that, in fact, it had been a good day for them all when that Japanese woman — that lawyer-woman from Honolulu, that city-woman — had come to the place on the water.

A week later, Ben had the dream he had expected, where the ill forest and river came to him as their son.

He took an article Paula had given him from one of her environmental magazines, about deforestation and cultural destruction in Minuvonga, and went to Will.

"I want a benefit concert at Euph's," he said. "For these people here." And he tapped his nail against the name of the fledgling Minuvongan environmental defense group. He had carefully circled it in red ink.

26

Raise It From the Dust: The Beach Near Waikīkī

Emma began remembering her life while she was sorting through quilt squares, unstitching old ones she had put away to re-use.

Her tumultuous thoughts came fast these days, tumbling like a boat's wake with the strain of Ben's journey to Minuvonga and the relief of his return to Hawai'i and to health; and with the ongoing strain of Pearlie Leilani's challenge to them all. Emma felt as if her own thoughts dragged her along behind them, bruising her flesh.

Gradually, they sorted themselves into elements of a talk story she would have liked to speak aloud, but first would have to speak out in her head. In silence, she arranged it as she would speak it to Will, to Paula, not as she would to Hawaiians. Oddly, putting that half-step of distance and translation between her and her memories made remembering less painful, easier to bear, and easier to organize emotionally.

Long before the first big war, Auntie Evie and Uncle Herman Bachmann came to that valley behind Honokaa where I grew up. The Queen still reigned then. In those days many of the people in the valley were Japanese. So Auntie Evie told me when she was old and I was a little girl. Those people were not rich hotel owners like the Japanese who come here today. They were farmers – poor people, like Paula's family who came to O'ahu then. They wore straw hats and straw sandals, and sewed their clothes in patches from old rice sacks. They came to work on the plantations; they worked out their contracts, or else they got in debt and couldn't get out, either way they never went back to Japan. And by then they had children born here.

People who think the valley's far out and hard to get to today, should have known it then, when Auntie Evie and Uncle Herman came. It was the same when I was a little girl. Especially when the rains came and washed out the road, it seemed there was no place in the world but that valley, nothing in the world but rain. But the soil was very rich. That's why people came; and the place was very beautiful.

Auntie Evie's mother came from Kohala coast. She was Hawaiian and English. Her father was all Hawaiian. Uncle Herman's mother was all Hawaiian, his father was a German sailor who stayed on when his ship sailed out; he kept a rope-and-tackle shop Konaside, near Kailua.

They had eight children and four lived to grow up: Uncle Herman, Uncle Jack, Auntie Evie, and my mother. Then my mother died when I was born so Auntie

Evie took me. And Auntie Evie told me that her mother's family were the last all-Hawaiians in that part of the island.

Her father had a sister, Ellen, who married into an all-Hawaiian family near Honokaa, and they went to fish and farm on that coast. But the Americans overthrew the Queen, and an American bought all the land around there. Her sister and her husband couldn't support themselves any more against the plantations, and had to sell the land to the American; they went to work on his plantation cutting cane.

They had three children, two boys and a girl. Then came the big epidemic in the same year that Russia and Japan fought a war, the war that Japan won.

That epidemic killed many Hawaiian people, like all the ones before it, and the family died in five days. All of them — five in five days. All gone. No more all-Hawaiians in that part of the land.

But the Hawaiians are not all gone. I am still here. And so are many others.

My father's older brother Matthew married a Portuguese-and-Chinese girl from near Captain Cook, and Tom and Ned were their boys. There were two girls, too, but one died when she was a baby and the other went to Honolulu. Mary. But she came to a bad end there a long time ago.

Ned was the good-for-nothing that Will bought the land from, out along the Volcano Road.

Ned and me were cousins, though I'm in no hurry to boast about it. He drank himself to death in Honolulu, like Mary, and his brother Tom's still making mischief here and there, word comes now and then.

I have a brother, Pete, who works construction here, and two sisters, Edie and Rebecca. Edie and her husband moved to the Mainland. Rebecca married Nicholas Jenkins who was Hawaiian and English and Chinese and Ukrainian, Ukrainia's a far far place right near Russia. And Pearlie Leilani is their daughter. So I don't know where she got the idea about being all-Hawaiian blood. I'm her own mother's sister, and if I don't know her family line, who does?

And I married Ben Miller from Minuvonga, and if God had blessed us with children, wouldn't they have been Hawaiian?

Emma had her guilt too, for at first she had not wanted Pearlie to come to live with them. Emma might have welcomed a baby, although that would have wholly overturned her life by then. Still, she wouldn't have been inheriting someone else's pilikia. Pearlie was already half-grown, and not growing in such a good direction either. She'd been having trouble at school and there was a hint of a brush with the police, and Emma wasn't anxious for trouble. She worked part-time on a county clerk job and had planned to go to full-time. She liked her job and the company of the other women in the office, and the money she earned made it easier to stand her ground with Ben, who could be pig-headed and domineering, because that money she earned helped support the household too.

But Ben had been delighted at the idea of a child in the house, to an extent that puzzled her a little. Almost as if the offer of a child had been a confirmation of something — or a vindication. She understood, now, though it wasn't as if she hadn't known almost from the first that something back there, in his past, shadowed him. But having decided that he was a good man, and never having had cause to revise that opinion, she also in her way of reckoning had no reason to push him where he clearly didn't want to go.

But Emma was guilty because she feared that though she had tried to make Pearlie welcome, the child had known for most of that first year, before love developed, that Emma would rather she had not come to them; and she feared that the knowledge was partly behind Pearlie's rebelliousness and unhappiness now.

At first Emma dismissed with embarrassment the stiff attempts Pearlie Leilani and her friends were making to speak Hawaiian, a language they had to learn as if it were a foreign tongue. Why not just speak English?

But as stumbled words and phrases gained assurance, took life in the air around her, something unexpected happened.

For the first time in years, Emma remembered how she had felt the day the haole teacher reprimanded her for speaking Hawaiian, ordering her to make the most of her opportunities, show respect, stop speaking baby-talk and learn a real, grown-up language.

And then she began to remember other things.

She remembered her grandmother's story, of the one trip she and her mother had ever made off-island, when Emma's mother was nine: to Honolulu, when the Queen died.

All these years Emma had forgotten the story: of how the sound of the mourning wailing echoed off the rocky valley walls and even across the seas, from one island to another, as it had once before in her grandmother's lifetime, when the haoles drove the Queen from the throne.

She remembered the story of how it was in Honolulu when the Hawaiians came from all the islands, to bury their Queen.

She had forgotten all these years, until Pearlie Leilani began to speak.

And Emma heard her mother's voice, then her grandmother's voice, the voice of her tūtū, as they recounted the story to her that Paula had read aloud, in another idiom, quoted in a book by the woman Helena Allen, who had actually known the Queen's hanai daughter. Emma had memorized that passage. The heart of the story was the same:

As the catafalque was guided into the yard of the Mausoleum beneath the widespread branches of the monkey pod trees a curious thing happened. Perhaps the carriage lurched, perhaps it was the wind that swept down the Pali, causing the huge branches to sway, but the Hawaiian crown atop the plumed canopy was struck from its place and rolled in the dust. At this sign a shudder, a frightened whisper, swept the long line of mourners:

The Hawaiian rule is at an end. The crown is at the feet of the haole.

Tears dripped onto the quilt squares. Emma took off her glasses and wiped her eyes, glad no one was around.

So she surprised herself as much as everyone else when one night a short time after, as she and Ben and Will and Paula sat talking in the kitchen of the Pine Tar, she said,

"No."

The others all looked at her and she kept her eyes on her embroidery and cut a length of golden thread.

Her single word brought an astounded — and confounded — silence. Her voice held an urgency and an insistence that were unlike her.

"What you mean, 'No'?" Ben demanded as if he heard that her meaning went beyond the immediate conversation. His uncertainty and unease were palpable. Like all of them, thought Paula, he was seeing a new side to Emma, foreshadowed in her uncharacteristic moodiness in recent weeks; and like them he was wondering, if this, what else?

In this time of fracturing at the place on the water, every change in a person was as threatening as watching the ground open under your feet out on the Lava Wastes.

Emma looked up and straight at him then, her dark eyes lively with anger and trouble.

"I mean what I say. That man in that book Paula's talking about, that she says most people in high places get their idea of Hawai'i from, maybe he's got his numbers right, about how so many people voted for statehood except on Ni'ihau and a few other places — places where there were still more Hawaiians than others — but the way he arranges his words, it makes it seem like the feeling in those places isn't important next to all those other people. There ought to be a way to show that strong feeling is as big and important as lots of numbers, how one kind of claim to the land can be stronger than another kind, and his words don't show it. That man in the book calls it 'justice in the islands', that statehood vote, but it wasn't justice in the islands, that vote, not for Hawaiians who voted 'No' on statehood, who wanted the monarchy back. And it wasn't justice in the islands for people like me, who weren't so sure how things should be arranged, but remembered what the old people told us, and who saw what things were like around us, how Hawaiian people are at the bottom in our own land, and who didn't want to say 'yes' to the haoles, that they could keep the Crown and all it means."

She went back to her work for a moment, and without looking up concluded,

"So when I said 'No' I meant what I said. I mean I voted 'No' on statehood."

"Why you never say?" Ben floundered. "I never knew you were political so. You never voted since I know you — have you?"

"No." Her voice was very quiet now. "After 1959 I thought, 'Why should I vote? The only way to have your speaking make a change in the world is the haole way, and the haole way makes sure the Hawaiians don't get heard. That's why they overthrew the Queen, because she wrote the new Constitution so the Hawaiian people would be heard. In the haole way, the Hawaiian people count for nothing. But now, I think maybe new ways to talk are coming. Maybe there are going to be new ways to be heard, since people are beginning to remember things like I am, and the young ones are beginning to learn about them and speak out. So I thought I'd start to speak again. I've never stopped thinking," she added, "even though my thoughts weren't on top of my mind. But they come back to me full and fast now. Now I know they were always there."

She cut a length of scarlet thread and laid it beside the gold.

"So," said Will to Paula, later that night in Noname Lane, "Emma's political." He gave a humorless smile. "Ain't you-all full of surprises these days. The Little Princess, Ben with his benefit for that en-vi-ron-men-tal group you pointed out to him, now Emma. I'm just waiting for your contribution to all this brough-hah-hah."

"And yours."

He did not respond.

"What made you decide you weren't a 'political' person, as you put it the day we met?"

He had never said, as with so many other things in his life. And, as with so many other things in his life, she had never asked.

To her surprise he responded, seriously,

"I been thinking about that some lately." He turned the glass around in his hand. Light sparked off the facets. "What with this-all with the Princess. I reckon 'twere on account of what Euph taught — or how I understood him."

"How so?"

"Well — 'tweren't what he taught me." He paused a moment, organizing his ideas. "'Twere rather how what he taught seemed to apply to me. He taught that the Black Man had to become political, to undo the White Man's political wiles that had brought about the Black Man's dreadful situation in the world. He taught that the time were coming when Ethiopia would spread forth her wings. But that were for the Black Man. 'Tweren't for me. I reckon I didn't want to be like those White Men with political wiles. The same ones the Little Princess is numbering me among now." He drank. "So I just said I weren't a political person — didn't do political things."

He gave a narrow bleak smile. "Fought for Sam for years in Vietnam, telling myself I weren't a political person. But I do reckon that's the answer to your question, Yumi."

Emma snipped and stitched and arranged her quilt squares, sorted, laid out patterns, and, snipping, stitching, sorting, arranging, coming into the power of her own remembered life, considered the kind of world that she would like to see.

It would be a world that was good for the Hawaiian people, not the way it was now. A world that acknowledged their special place in the land. She thought how her heart had lifted when on television she heard one of the young people at a demonstration in Honolulu retort to a haole reporter's description of the Queen as 'the last Hawaiian monarch.' The girl had snapped: "The last Hawaiian monarch — so far." Yes, Emma would like to see a world where, at last, Hawaiian hands lifted the Hawaiian Crown from the dust. A world that made a place for other good people, not Hawaiians, who lived here now — but a Hawaiian world where Hawaiians made the place.

Some of the young people spoke about a House of the Ali'i, along with the kind of government Hawai'i had now. Emma liked that idea. She liked the idea of mana recognized somehow again in governing the land. What was the slogan Paula said she had used when she was Pearlie Leilani's age, doing political things like her? "Power to the people." Was this something like it? Power from the people. Maybe in a government with a House of the Ali'i, power could come to and from the people in a way that was both new and old.

Emma arranged and re-arranged her quilt squares, her hands trembling slightly. Yes, that idea of the young peoples' was good. But some of the things Pearlie said — refusing her name, which Rebecca had chosen so carefully, and denouncing Emma for making quilts instead of kapa!

Emma loved kapa, and admired the people who had that skill. But she didn't see how Pearlie could say quilts weren't Hawaiian. Emma knew a lot about quilts and she didn't think any people anywhere had ever made more beautiful ones than Hawaiian women, and often using Hawaiian motifs. Were Hawaiians so stupid they couldn't take something from other people and make it their own, make it beautiful in their own way? Like the ideas for a new government, wasn't that the same sort of thing, taking some things from America, some things from England where they had a House of Lords, a little like a House of the Ali'i, keeping some other things Hawaiians had worked out how to do in their own way, long before the haoles came, worked out among Hawaiians, here in Hawai'i nei?

And didn't the girl and her friends know that all the while the Queen was under arrest in the Palace, she had occupied herself making a beautiful quilt? That quilt had recorded Hawaiian history, and the Queen's own life, and Hawaiian history in her life, as a story for her people to remember themselves by.

Emma now recalled that her tūtū had told her that all during that difficult time, she had quilted too, to calm herself, and later as well, during the uprising that failed.

What a terrible time it must have been for the Queen, bearing the burdens of all her people, with haole soldiers all around. Her brother the King, killed by haoles, people knew, in San Francisco on the Mainland, far from home, and her husband dead too almost at the same time.

Emma thought the Queen must have found strength stitching her quilt, when she was a prisoner in the Palace. When the Americans forbade her newspapers, her friends smuggled them in as wrappings for bouquets. Gathering that information, considering it with other information, making her decisions about caring for her people, and saving their story to be told, drawing comfort from the firm softness of quilt squares beneath her palms, drawing ideas from arranging and rearranging them.

Sitting, quilting, Emma began to feel a new strength growing from the turmoil, born of an unexpected continuity buried deep within her that the turmoil itself had revealed. For the Hawaiian people were still here, in Hawai'i nei, and something strong and good would be built by them, out of all that was Hawaiian and strong and good that had been shattered but not destroyed at 'Iolani Palace, on the day in 1893 when under haole guns and for love of the people the Queen set her name on paper; that, shattered, remained unmended despite the night two years later, when the uprising failed and guns failed to undo guns on the beach near Waikīkī.

27

Wild Boars: Among Yumi's Things

Will rode the bus the serpentine length of Honolulu, toward Lē'ahi rising majestically in a spectacular dusk of towering clouds, gold and rose, bruise-blue, black and silver. The sight recalled to him Paula's words once about the architecture of the game of pool, its meaning to her. The words had struck so deep he'd never forgotten them: such beauty like love is a kind of wrath, like life a privilege.

The vehicle groaned to a stop at the corner where he had planned to get off; where, if he turned and then turned again, he would come to the narrow unmarked door beneath the bloody neon sign and, going down three steps, enter the smoky dream-precincts of the Port of Call.

People jostled past him toward the exits. But Will stood transfixed. He found his intention had changed. He fought the change, but his feet seemed mired in mud. The bus traveled on through the city.

Suddenly, as if emerging from a trance, he pressed through the crowd and hurried off to stand disorganized in the street.

Long ago Paula had given him directions and a key to her place, should he want to stay some night when a cargo run held him over in Honolulu. She asked him to let her know first, that was all. But he had never used the key, and she had never mentioned it again.

Tonight he figured he had no need to inform her. The overnight rush job that had brought him to Honolulu had been a last-minute commission. He would return to Hilo the next morning. Since he would be busy working, Paula, on the Big Island for a week, had elected to stay in the house in Noname Lane.

The giant banyan stood in the center of the little courtyard. His footsteps striking its flagstones rang loud in his ears.

He opened the door and switched on a lamp. In the soft golden light that spilled, the room struck him as magical in its evocation of Yumi. Disarray, life caught for a moment in passage: a T-shirt slung over the back of a chair, a gray linen skirt tossed across its seat. He never saw her wear garments like that skirt. They were part of her city world.

But there on the floor, startlingly familiar, a worn pair of sneakers lay at exactly the angle he saw so often in the house in Noname Lane, when she

235

tossed them from her toes. There, the sight annoyed him, he who aligned his boot-heels. But here, they became her presence in her absence, and he was touched by tenderness for her and deeply unsettled by the feeling.

The heavy wooden table was piled high with dictionaries and manuscripts in different languages; a copy of the *Honolulu Globe-Bulletin*; environmental magazines, a book on basic Hawaiian law, another on land law specifically, other journals. A cup with no saucer, stained with coffee. A toaster on the counter in the kitchen nook. A jar of guava jam, lid at an angle, not screwed down.

Shelves crammed with books and topped with more piled books climbed high along two walls, teetering beneath their loads. Vivid torch ginger and anthurium with wide leaves of orange and red and gold flourished among them, their pots hidden so the plants seemed to grow from the volumes. Vines sent out a profusion of shiny emerald tendrils, tumbling toward the floor.

Above the table hung one of those paintings by Escher that always troubled him deeply, unmoored him. Yumi awed him, for she ventured fearlessly into those depths and emerged unscathed. Other paintings: Van Gogh's wild untidy moon. Another painter whose work stirred deep warnings in Will. The Gauguins were less dangerous to him. Gratefully, he drank in the blue of a man and a woman together, canoes beached in the background. Gauguin had always spoken to him. He felt that the painter caught something true and deep about these islands and seas, about their people; and their balance and serenity did not threaten him.

A small television set; a radio. A phonograph, a shelf of records, several shoeboxes of tapes. Against the far wall, a dresser stood by a closet door. An armchair. A double bed on a futon frame, carelessly covered with a cotton spread, its emerald and orange pattern echoing the green of the plants and of the deep-piled rug on the scuffed wooden floor.

Photos of Hawaiian petroglyphs that she'd taken one day, below Hilina Pali; a stark black-and-white shot of the Pali against the sky, and the great sweep of lava down to the sea.

And three photographs, arranged in a triangular pattern: a small framed snapshot of two pigeons and twin naked young, on a house-beam near the banyan in her courtyard. The photograph he had sent her, the one that Tim had taken of him and Yumi on the day they met, their arms full of nēnēbird.

And — jolting him, as he remembered now that she had borrowed it — a copy of the photo he had shown her, of him, taken from the back in Euph's.

He was looking over his shoulder, lips pursed in childish mulishness that she had laughed to see. Dressed only in ragged pants that ended above his knees; his long light dirty hair fell tousled on his narrow shoulders. Shadows of scars, if you knew what they were, telling of worse to come. Uncle Bert, Grampa. The beatings began early. Skinny arms and legs, elbows pointed outward as he reached above his head to grip the edge of the bar in the Blue Box. Left knee arced as he stood on the splintered floor, bare left foot pressed against his right inner knee. What had Yumi called the way he was standing? 'Unconscious body artistry.' Said she'd title it 'Study in Triangles.' I were about six I reckon, he remembered saying to her. Bertha took that picture, just before we went on up to Chicago, my Little Mama and me.

What did Yumi want with that little-boy picture of him? The sight of it made him sad, he didn't know why, and he turned away.

And caught his first sight of the brick-and-board arrangement in the alcove, tucked to the right of the door, in line of view from the futon bed.

He stared, struck by the radical difference between the alcove and the rest of the room. Yet the alcove showed forth a side of Yumi he recognized too. That was her flower work, all right, in the old, tall black lacquer vase etched with gold plum blossoms fine as filigree.

Fascinated, he went closer and studied the framed photographs arranged on the low board shelf. Yumi's folks, must to be. And there was a snapshot of Yumi when she was almost a baby still. With her Daddy?

I didn't never know my Daddy, he had told her, as always pulling away from any thought of a father, his father: an unfathomable space where he never went.

The objects in the alcove, placed with exquisite care, emanated austerity and balanced strength, and Will, who had lived that year and more in Japan, recognized its cultural source immediately. Bemused, he remembered Paula's words, sardonic, glancing but deep-felt: I give you high marks because you never asked me about Zen, which as it happens I know nothing about. I don't know Japanese-Way.

Had she been deliberately deceiving him, to say that, when she had known how to create this space?

But then he remembered how that verse her father had taught her came up all unbidden in the Alcove Room at the Pine Tar as they ate the dinner he'd prepared, on the day they met.

She don't know she knows, thought Will, and she don't know what she knows. Just like me, that way.

He turned, took two tentative steps forward across the green carpet; stopped again. The spill of golden light seemed to enfold him.

He crossed the room to the dresser, and like a thief slid open all the drawers. They were filled with soft and shimmering garments that gave off Yumi's smell.

He lifted panties, scarves, brassieres that slipped smoothly beneath his fingertips. Color everywhere, emeralds and peacock blues and flame, and golden light. He buried his face in them, inhaling deeply, stunned by her scent, assuaging a hunger and thirst.

To sleep on that rumpled green spread that covered her bed was impossible, much less in the sheets beneath it, among the pillows rounded like a woman's contours.

Though he understood that Yumi meant him to: she had given him the key to her home.

He slept deeply the night through, on that green carpet, for the first time in almost twenty-five years. In his sleep he drew his knees to his chest, and cradled his cheek on his arm. In his sleep he sucked his thumb; and in his sleep, he wept.

"Have a seat," said Will to someone on the other side of the wall at Euph's from where Paula lay stretched out on a deck chair on the lānai, reading. "Kin I get you something to drink?"

"If you've got a nice Cab, that'd be just great."

Paula cocked an ear at the voice.

This was a surprise: Julie Danemore, Beach Bunny, California Golden Girl, who had floated in from L.A. on the tourist tide a few weeks ago, and stayed to work for a while at a curio shop on Kinoole Street. She'd dropped by Euph's the last weekend or two.

"And I just know you do. You've got the best wine cellar on the island, everybody says."

"Well, it's not bad, if I do say so myself."

Cork popping. Wine gurgling. A solid thunk — Will's shot glass striking the bar. More liquid burbling. This would be a good dose of the Usual.

"Where's your friend?"

"Who're you meaning, Julie?"

"Paula, I think her name is?"

"Paula. Yeh. Well, I think she was going swimming with Emma and some friends this afternoon."

So she had been, thought Paula. Maybe this would be an even more interesting diversion. Different, anyway.

"She's so beautiful. Such a China doll!"

"China Doll," repeated Will. "Kajiyama. Very ancient Chinese name."

"Really? How exotic! Ooh, Will, this wine is scrumptious! What is it?"

Will told her. He had picked up French in Southeast Asia and now put his knowledge to as good use as he did being sommelier at the Pine Tar.

"Scrumptious," Julie repeated. At least she was smart enough not to try to pronounce the name, thought Paula, immediately appalled at her snideness. "But you know, really, the other night in here, I was looking at her, and she looks just like those Orientals in movies, in long robes and those faces you can't tell what's going on in her head. Kind of inscrutable, I think it's called, y'know?"

"Yeh, that's Paula, I reckon." Will's drawl was getting longer and thicker with each word. "I did always say so to her, from the day we met. China Doll, Oriental and Inscrutable. Want some taro chips? It's from a batch we made up for the Pine Tar just at lunch today. C'mon, sit down, make yourself comfortable."

"She didn't even speak to you, Yumi. She didn't even know you were there."

They were fighting in the secluded fruit grove, not far from the Pine Tar, late that afternoon.

"She didn't have to speak to me! That's not the point! All those things she said — 'Oriental.' 'Inscrutable.' My God — she's a walking stereotype of a stereotyper."

"Well, I didn't say those things that upset you so, and I wouldn't. Yumi, you ought to credit me with enough sense to know Julie Danemore don't have an idea in her head worth the name, racist or any other kind. Anyhow, she and me weren't talking politics."

"Exactly what were you doing?"

He grinned, deliberately offensive.

"Polishing my moves. Look, just because a man hits on a lady a little don't mean he's endorsing her politics, if she's even got any, which in this case like I say she don't. How d'you know all this, anyway? I thought you went to the beach with Emma. Are you following me around?"

Furious, she retorted levelly, "I didn't feel well so I didn't go. And if reading on the lānai at Euph's constitutes following you around, or if I have to check in with you on my every move so I don't fall over you hitting on someone — what an aggressive hostile term! — maybe I should just stay in Honolulu!"

The fear of being left for someone like Julie Danemore had been bred into Paula from birth by her society. To return to Honolulu was to regain her own ground and reclaim her own dignity. But for Will to hear her say that struck him as threatening to abandon him for her educated city-life, and this semi-conscious fear was never far from him, as Paula's fear of abandonment was never far from her.

So, as he habitually did when he felt under any threat, he went further on the attack.

"Yumi, she's got a gorgeous body and long blonde hair and a peaches-and-cream complexion and big blue eyes. She looks like every red-blooded American boy's dream and she's sure enough more than this country boy could be expected to pass up when it comes to keeping a practice hand in."

"How can you say that to me, about how — how pretty she is, in those ways? To me? 'All-American' because she's got blonde hair and blue eyes and a 'peaches-and-cream complexion'? And a 'practice hand'? Practicing for what? And how can you insult me talking that way about women? How can you stand there and talk about a woman as if she were an assemblage of body parts, without a brain?"

"But that's what I'm telling you. That's what I acted so for, on account of her body parts. For sure it wasn't on account of her brain. And a practice hand, well, it's just like tossing a few baskets if you pass a hoop. You're too complicated for me, Yumi. Now you're defending her!"

"You're not that big an idiot, Will. You can't be."

"Lord, Yumi, have a care!'

He seized her wrist, as a branch of the mango tree split beneath her convulsive grip. His hand immobilized hers like a sprung trap.

"What's the matter with you? As smart and educated as you are and you act like you just plain ain't got sense. You can't waste good food like that, you act like you never been hungry! And see there, you hurt the tree!"

He let go of her, his fingers gently exploring the shredded ends of the limb.

"I'm sorry, Will." Guilt washed her: you act like you never been hungry. Unlike him, she never had. She was adamant about what she had said, but the guilt and the unintended damage she'd done sobered her. Then too, as he seemed to be, she was glad to leave their quarrel. "I know how much work you put into this garden."

"There's that too," he agreed, looking at the torn tree with troubled eyes. "A person's work counts for something."

She touched the branch. "Can you splint this? Will it heal?"

He nodded. He was already sorting through branches on the ground. He glanced at an enormous fruit, smashed at her feet.

"I were saving that mango. That's why I put the netting over it, to keep the birds off. I reckoned it'd be just right come Saturday to make you my Mango Delight for dessert. But don't be downhearted, Yumi." His eyes took on the gleam she had learned to recognize as humor in a deadpan face. "There's the guavas, and since the guava tree's over in the corner there, kind out of range, maybe it'll survive even if you take another fit. Reckon that's what comes of keeping company with Cawdrys. Can't say I didn't warn you, the very day we met."

He paused. "Yumi, I sure didn't mean to — to upset you so bad about Julie. I ain't saying I thought you'd be pleased, you understand — you're sure right I'm not that big an idiot — I mean, that's what I said it for, you know, to rile you, I don't rightly know why. I ain't myself, exactly, these last days. But I reckon you're right I don't understand why it should rile you so bad — all those words, blonde and blue-eyed and All-American, they're just a manner of speaking." Paula fought tears, anger gone, old grief and frustration overwhelming her.

"You just don't get it. That's what Pearlie Leilani's saying that seems so completely beyond you. White men don't have to get it. They can live life without having to get how racism structures the way the whole world runs."

"Yeah, I'm one White man who really runs the world."

"That isn't what I said. You didn't hear me."

"That's why I arranged for it to be so good to me right along," he continued, past her words. "Make me lucky and powerful."

"I never said that either."

"The world's right hard on everyone."

"And I know that too."

"But you still say I don't get it."

"You don't get it. And I'm tired of explaining. We're all tired of explaining."

They stood silent, facing each other, stymied, curled inward over their wounds. After a moment he said,

"Yumi, you don't really think I'm a racist, do you? Like the Princess is saying, these days?"

An even longer silence. Then,

"No. Not like she says. And I don't think she does either, Will, not really, because she knows you, too. But you just don't get what upsets us, or why. When you were talking to Julie today, you were moving in a world where you could go and I couldn't, because you're White and I'm not. And it's the ruler's world. Her stereotypes keep me down — 'inscrutable Oriental' versus 'All-American girl.' And even though I know you were mocking what Julie was saying, Julie didn't know that, and she insulted me, Will. She did. You know that, too, or you wouldn't have been mocking her. But you didn't call her on it. You let it stand. It's evil in the world. It sent us to the camps. It killed my father and my grandfather and destroyed my family. You're supposed to be my ally, and by not calling her on it you left me unprotected."

He shook his head. "I reckon you're right, Yumi, I don't get it. I can't seem to see it so. All I can say is I wouldn't never knowingly leave you unprotected in the world."

He paused, then said abruptly, "I paid once right and proper, to get rights in the land at last. Build up something not in the Starvesoil, not like my Little Mama's city garden where she didn't have no rights and got beat down. And I've done right by the land, and the Hawaiian people as its left to after I'm gone, and cain't no one say different and tell truth."

She understood the apparent non-sequitur; she understood that the issue of Julie Danemore was a twisted piece of the cultural fabric that was entangling them all at the place on the water. But the understanding did not lessen her own vulnerability.

Suddenly she was utterly exhausted, by the day, by the endemic contention at the place on the water, endemic contentions that marked her allotted historical time, and her, and everyone she knew.

"We must learn to live in our allotted time." Hadn't Castro said that to the Cuban people when the attack began at the Bay of Pigs? And how do I do that better, Compañero? she thought bitterly.

"Let's go in," she said. Her voice was constricted. "It's getting dark, and we've both had enough."

An incident with government choppers on a drug sweep over the island first focused Paula's growing fear that, under the stresses bearing down on their circle at Euph's and the Pine Tar, Will was unraveling.

For the look in his eyes as he followed the machines flying over the island, swaying, dipping low, clattering, was as cold and blank as she had ever seen.

She thought he was angry and concerned that they might locate his marijuana plantings. But the thin line of his lips sneered at the idea.

"Not a chance," he said calmly. "Because there ain't no one knows this island better than me. Pete, and Emma's great-uncle, mebbe knows it as well. And mebbe others too — a few. But ain't no one knows it better. For sure not them up there. Only a fool tries to know a place without putting his feet to the ground. No," he said, "'t'ain't fear of discovery troubles me. I just don't like those things above me. That's all."

He paused, and finished briefly, "I've held them above people, myself."

28

A Man On Kaua'i

Jauntily swinging his keys on their leather loop, Will walked into the kitchen at the Pine Tar one night after closing. Paula and Pearlie Leilani, leaning intently toward each other over the big scrubbed table, looked up, and their conversation died. Paula registered with dismay and a complex mingling of shame, guilt and anger, directed at herself and all of them, that now there were factions among them at the place on the water. Even though at that moment she was trying to mediate, to present Will to Pearlie Leilani as on other occasions she had tried to present Pearlie Leilani to Will, in the very nature of the situation she was nevertheless complicitous, a conspirator.

Will halted just inside the door, letting the swing of the keys die away. Paula could tell at a glance that his bravado was well assisted by Johnny Black.

"Well now, ain't this nice. Here we all are, together in Paradise." His drawl, though cheerful, trailed mockery at its edges. "But I do got a feeling there's trouble in Paradise. Pilikia for sure. And I do got a feeling what it's about. These long-standing acrimonies generate their own auras, so to speak."

"The trouble came with you," returned Pearlie Leilani curtly.

The air crackled with their mutual hostility. Suddenly Paula remembered the first time she had ever seen them together, their fingers interlacing; and her chest constricted with pain at this tragedy of estrangement.

"I know, I know, Little Princess, and you was purely descended from the Highest Ali'i. Well, I'm descended from Scottish chiefs and Cuchulain so you better not behead me for throwing my shadow across you or whatever. Irish and Scottish mana's right powerful too. My hapa-fellow-countrywoman, the Heiress Apparent, Princess Ka'iulani, must have been really humming with it. But Scottish or Hawaiian, Little Princess, you still a woman, and according to those traditional beliefs that you're always going on about, your mana ain't got nothing on a man's. Or have you and your running buddies rewritten that part of the Ancient Tradition? You could try being respectful of your elders, too, an old Hawaiian 'cul-choor-al value' as Yumi do call 'em, being as she's colleged and from Berkeley and all, and which I am yours — your elder, that is."

"You don't understand anything about mana."

"No? How about warfare? Don't give me that peaceful-world-in-the-traditional-life stuff. Does that punk Kenny you hang around with wear that picture of a Samoan Superman in a gourd hat on his T-shirt because of the Peaceful Tradition?"

"You leave Kenny out of it! How dare you insult him? Or the traditional armor? And it's Hawaiian, not Samoan!"

"One of these days Ben or me's gonna tan your britches and make sure you keep on the straight line with that guy. I don't like the way that punk looks at you. And as for his version of Hawaiian history —"

"His *version* of Hawaiian history —!"

"Yeh, Little Princess, I'm telling you that river right over yonder ran bloody enough long before the White Man came, red for days, they say, and I reckon there's not a river on any of these islands you couldn't say that about." Will was rummaging out the bottle of Johnny Black kept waiting for him in the cupboard above the sink. "Human sacrifices, cannibalism —"

"You pretend, but you don't understand anything about Hawai'i or our ways," cried Pearlie Leilani.

Paula whirled on Will. "Stop tearing at her. It's not your fault or doing that the world's in the mess it is, but she's right about the mess and she's right about how it got the way it is, and she's also right that you get some privileges from your place in it. And don't make fun of her friends. As for you, Leilani —"

Leilani didn't hear her. She was slow to express anger, but she knew how to go on with it. She snapped,

"As for human sacrifices and warfare, haoles have them worse than Hawaiians ever did. Remember Vietnam? I just bet you do."

"Will's said the same things about Vietnam you're saying," Paula raised her voice almost to a shout herself.

"I never heard that."

"Maybe he didn't say them to you. Ask him."

"Maybe she don't listen so good. " He paused. "Lemme tell you a story. Around the time I first come to this island, there was talk going round. 'Twas about a man on Kaua'i. He were a Mainlander, a haole, and had done time in Nam. He was living way upcountry with some of them Mainlander haole hippie people. Local folks didn't hold with them much. Said they went naked, and were up to all kinds of doings, which they called getting back to Nature. Anyhow, time passed, and this fella got stranger and stranger."

He pulled his bottle almost dry. Looked around at his audience. Grinned.

"He left these hippie people he was living with and moved up into Na Pali Wilderness into a cave, all by himself. He'd been a vegetarian for a long time, they all were in that hippie-commune-place. Then he cut back so he wouldn't eat animal products at all, no cheese or eggs or milk or nothing, and then in the cave got to be fewer and fewer things he'd eat. And finally, he wouldn't eat nothing at all, 'cause seemed to him he couldn't eat nothing without causing harm. And then —"

He paused dramatically, and surveyed his audience again. "And then, he starved to death. That's what happens," he said conversationally, "when you don't eat. I remember jeering, along with others, them as weren't more shocked-like, at a man being such a fool. But the story stayed with me so I guess it had something to say to me."

"Self-serving." Pearlie Leilani's voice dripped scorn.

"Mebbe. But I reckon I don't think no one's called on to commit suicide. Little Princess, Hawaiian folks just had the misfortune to live kinda cut off from other people, so when they ran into Europeans and Americans who weren't so cut off and had numbers and wealth and germs and guns to back up their way of doing things and their unholy greed, they got beat. Happened to a lot of folks these last five hundred years or so — Aztecs, Zulus, others. For that matter, some of those Marines who overthrew the Queen that shameful day in Honolulu, I reckon they was something like me. Grandsons of those as went down at Culloden Field or in County Clare, Scots and Irish beaten by the English, who ended up fleeing or transported to Kentucky and Arkansas."

"But it wasn't the same, was it?" cried Pearlie Leilani. "Those 'boys' could become 'Americans' and then come to Hawai'i and do in the Hawaiians! How many Hawaiians do you know who've made it to the Scottish Highlands and made their fortune there — at the expense of the Scottish? Been welcomed by the Scottish like we welcomed the haoles, and then ripped off the land like the haoles ripped us off?"

And that, thought Paula, is the crux of it. That is the great imbalance of this imperial epoch, and the meaning of White-skin privilege.

But Will answered for himself only, and only in part.

"'Tain't my land here, Little Princess. I never said it was and I never ripped it off. I've never called it but my place, which ain't the same thing as owning something, but means only that I got rights in it. And you know as well as I that for ten years now I ain't legally but held it in trust."

"'In trust!' Hawaiians have been on waiting lists for land for years and years!"

"Not for that piece of land they ain't. 'Twas private held and a Hawaiian who sold it to me, Little Princess, as you well know, being as he's kin of yours on your Mama's side. Reckon that even makes him kin to me, so it's all in the 'ohana, so to speak, though you won't like to hear that, 'cause he and I are kin on account of you and I are kin too, through Ben, and nor you nor I can choose about that. We're stuck with each other, Little Princess, you and me. And as for our kinsman, Ned Warner, 'tweren't his intention to hold the land for his people, nor were he keen on selling to them either. He were dreaming of selling to a motel chain, right objectionable idea and foolish in that spot even if 'tweren't objectionable. I'm the one's put the land on a list for the Hawaiian people, in perpetuity. All I claim is use for life. I wanted use for Yumi's life, too, 'tis true, but she wouldn't have that, being as she won't take nothing of money from me and so on."

"You're just another colonizer. Who gave you the right to turn Noname into a trust territory? That's just an idea you dreamed up to soothe your own conscience, such as it is, or maybe just to feed your delusions of grandeur. Like that stupid name, "No-nah-may," making fun of Hawaiian, or your fake offerings at Halem'aum'au, or your 'loving' the land. It takes thousands of years, and belonging to a people who live there and live from there, to know and love a land! What do you know about what aloha for the 'āina really means?"

"I know what it means to me. I never said I know or love the land as Hawaiians do, nor yet that I understand that knowledge and love. But I don't know as I'm too keen on other people telling me who or what to love, or how much my love's worth."

"Haoles, they think they own the world to play with! Grab Hawai'i, napalm Vietnam, fund the Contras, rape, smash, grab, destroy everything! You're arrogant. You think it's for you to forgive yourselves, I guess. Like that song I hear you playing. 'Pay back all my dues.' 'Lose this sorrow.'"

"You ain't been hearing my singing and playing no better than my words, little girl."

"You think you can forgive yourselves all the colonial wars, all the way from Columbus landing in the Caribbean to the Marines overthrowing our Queen! And Vietnam? Everyone knows what you did in Vietnam!"

"Oh no they don't, Princess. Don't nobody know that, 'cept me and God and the Devil, if they're about — and those as my doings touched in that place."

"How can you stand yourself? Do you ever think of even trying to apologize, or make reparations, as if it could be possible? How can you not die of what you did?"

"Fact is, might could be, Little Princess, I ain't got nothing to say or do could compensate. Not money, nor labor, nor life itself. Might could be. But mebbe I'm wrong, seeing how high you rate me. Mebbe I'm so valuable, being a White man and all, my hide would even things out. Still, getting to be a White man is right fine, I reckon, but it just don't seem to me like recompense enough for life's tribulations — not mine nor no-one else's. As for how I stand myself — I live with my life the same way everyone else does. You live from what you've done or you die from it. Both, in the end, I reckon."

29

Damage Drinking: The Deep Pleasure Of Destruction

On the day they met, Paula had intuited the deep schism in Will's personality.

She watched it widen now, like the chasms out on the Lava Wastes when Pele stirred in the depths.

Paula enjoyed drinking alcohol. But now as she saw what was happening to Will, her throat closed in rebellion against her Chardonnay, and she came to hate and fear the sweet smooth smell of Johnny Black.

First Will drank more, then he drank differently, and after that things got bad fast.

And bad, it seemed, especially in her presence.

Now at Euph's she saw too often a look in his eyes, as if the easiness, the wit, that seemed to bring people closer in conviviality when his silver mood was on him, were actually barriers thrown up against the pressure of other presences.

Glittering, mercurial, he slid, moment to moment, with increasing unpredictability, from that silver magnetism to a focused assaultiveness.

Or again, the high intelligent edge of his irony turned against the people close to him, to become razor-edged mockery.

"I never did tell you, did I, how I come to work for Sam?"

He had returned to the house down Noname Lane from somewhere, very late; it was later, now. Paula, curled up in a corner of the futon reading, set aside her book to look at Will facing her, in the big green armchair, Johnny Black to hand.

"No. You never did."

"Well, being as you're a Berkeley '60's radical crazy and all, I reckon you've seen that poster, shows a bridge and a young American soldier dead in a heap in the middle of it, and printed on the the poster is JOIN THE ACTION ARMY. Always reminds me of the fellow gave me the Christopher medal I keep in the plane, that you was so curious about that first day we met — yeh, I saw you looking at that, too, along with my license. I ain't been colleged, Yumi, not like you and those fancy lawyer-people you know in

Honolulu, but I wouldn't be here today if I hadn't learned to keep track of what was going on around me. Better'n that Enomoto fellow I reckon."

Paula flinched at the hostility in his voice.

"I am not," she said deliberately, suppressing the urge to retaliate by silence, "sleeping with Alan or with anyone else."

Which is more than I am sure of about you, she thought bitterly. Julie Danemore had drifted on, but others like her blew in on the Trade Winds.

"Well, no matter." He dismissed the topic elaborately. "The fellow who gave me that medal, last time I saw him he looked just like that soldier in the poster. That poster makes a right pair with the UNCLE SAM WANTS YOU one."

He drank deeply, then settled in to talk story.

"Well, Uncle Sam, he wanted me. 'Tweren't quite clear to me right off what he wanted me for, and I reckon I jumped quicker than some because I were pressed just then and to tell the truth times were getting a mite lean. This was a time ago, now. Down to Houston, which is a big little town we got in Texas, mebbe big enough you folks've heard of it up in Berkeley. Heard of it?"

"Even up in Berkeley." She tried to make her tone light, but she felt a flash of resentment so intense it bordered on hatred; he had taken to starting these conversations that made a tightrope between ostensible humor and subterranean rage, leaving her to react to one or the other and usually trigger the rage either way.

"Like I say," he went on, "'twas a time ago. March of 1959, as I recollect. 'Twas what's known as a con-cat-enation of circumstances landed me in Sam's Military.

"I were standing on a corner one afternoon, wondering how long I could get away with petty theft, being as I was kind of conspicuous, then as now, and thinking I should head on outta town, but I couldn't seem to keep enough ahead on the groceries to raise the bus fare. I didn't care for hitching, had had some bad experiences, but I was turning it over in my mind. Well, truth to tell, which is what talking story's about after all, one way or the other, 'twasn't the groceries keeping me back so much as the likker. I had done some work, yardwork and such, here and there, but seemed like times were hard and 'tweren't enough to live on. And then there was the likker. I had made my transition then, from tar likker to storebought, seeing as I'd left the Starvesoil and its tar pines — though I couldn't manage

Johnny Black yet, financially speaking. This afternoon I'm telling you about, I had a cough I couldn't seem to shake, and it had begun to rain again. 'Tis a bit like here, Houston, so warm you wouldn't think there'd come nights of rain that if you got no shelter can chill you through. And a squad car came round the corner, and though it slid on by, I didn't care for the kind of tension it induced in me.

"The tension, and the cough, was a misery for true. Even if I'd known of Travelers' Aid, should there have been one about — and I hadn't never heard of Traveler's Aid — I wouldn't have cared to go near nothing official-so.

"The bus station was out as well — they'd e-jected me the night before because I couldn't show a ticket to ride.

"So I couldn't think of but two ways out of the rain.

"One, I could put a rock through the squad car windshield, which would be a way to jail, all right, which was one dry place I could think of. But I didn't care for the sound of jail. This is as I have been trying to tell the Little Princess. I have had lots of experience with it by now, and Euph were right when he warned me off jail most particular, and my Little Mama too; later I found they sure knew whereof they spoke.

"So — with my reservations about jail, and knowing as I did the condition I'd be in when the poh-lees got through with me after throwing the rock, and fearing they might know about my living off the land so to speak, out of grocery stores, that route didn't seem like a good one to take. So that left the second way out of the rain, the San Antonio Stroll. They does the Stroll in Houston too. Mebbe even in your Bay Area?"

"Even there."

"See, the night before when I was thrown outta the bus station, this man who used to sit in his car outside and — and kinda watch for — well, I guess for boys like me, he called me over and I said No. He wrote his number down on a matchbox cover and give it to me. And the day before that a woman in a long green car had seen me near there, and pulled over to ask me to come stay at her place and cut wood." Will showed his teeth. "And light her fire as well, I reckon. Anyhow I kept their numbers so I reckon 'twere in my mind."

He took a long pull at the bottle. "You understanding what I'm talking about, Yumi?"

"Of course I understand. And it makes me more furious than I could tell you that you were treated that way."

He shook his head. "Cain't imagine what people were thinking of, letting a nice little girl like you hear about such things — and 'furious,' well, that's so nice of you, Yumi. I reckoned you'd heard about it what with all that crazy Berkeley '60's stuff."

She bit back her hurt and anger at his mockery.

"So I were standing on the corner thinking about all this. To tell the truth — which I say again is what talk-story's all about — I were trying to remember this guy's physique and whether I could beat him up and steal enough money to get outta town. The woman'd be no problem that way, I knew, but I liked having two options lined up. Well, anyway, that was what I were thinking about, making arrangements, as 'twas traditional in my family. I were a lovely youngster thinking lovely thoughts."

"In a lovely world," said Paula bitterly.

"Just the world, Yumi, the only one we got. And I looked up, and right there in front of me, just across the street, bigger'n life, I seen that poster on a storefront window. 'UNCLE SAM WANTS YOU!'

"Well, like I said, I walked on over. 'Twere two-forty-seven pee em when I pushed open the door, I remember from the clock on the wall, and seemed like by two forty-nine, I were one of Sam's fighting men."

"In March of 1959 you were fourteen years old."

"I thought you might pick up on that." He spoke with the softness of a wild cat's tread. The air crackled with strong emotions, and above all with their ambiguity: they conflicted like a tangle of power lines, rage, grief, savage humor.

Hatred too.

"I'm the same age, Will. Did the Army snafu or did they intend to enlist you underage?"

"Oh, intended I reckon. I were big and strong and twice as smart as that recruiter and I could even read and cypher. I reckon I were about the most educated boy ever to come through that little hole in the wall in that god-awful part of town. 'Twas a case of symbiotic needs. This guy needed recruits and I needed a dry bed and some grub."

"Symbiotic? The way I see it, what with Sam and the car cruisers, you were caught between two adult men and one adult woman who had power over you. And I am able to imagine a world where fourteen-year-olds don't have to choose between being child prostitutes and child cannon fodder."

"Are you now, Yumi? I always did say you were a nice little girl. Well, when that world do come to pass, you be sure and let me know. Send me a postcard or light a smoke-signal or do something to release my bated breath.

"It won't 'come to pass.' It'll have to me made. You can ridicule me all you want, but I know a good bit about how ugly the world can be — I've got the battle scars to prove it. So I also know how much better it can be. Even if we couldn't win, I'd rather fight than roll over. And, as it happens, I know from my own life that sometimes we do win."

He rose suddenly, looming over her, and upended the bottle in his mouth. "Well, it don't make no matter." He wiped his face with the back of his hand and tossed the bottle into the cardboard carton he'd taken to keeping in the corner, as if the front room of the house down Noname Lane were slowly metamorphosing into an anonymous alley somewhere. "Don't waste no grief on me. I weren't no child. I were a thief and a thug and a few other things, and ripe to be most anything else along those lines, which I were before much longer, with Sam's help and blessing and training. I weren't never a child."

"Make this the end of the talk-story." Now it was Paula's voice that was deadly. "I don't like being beat up on. Even if you're beating up worse on yourself. I don't like participating in your self-flagellation any more than in mine."

He turned from where he stood by a bookcase, wrenching open a fresh bottle he'd taken from one of the shelves.

"Oh, you didn't like that story? Okay, let's try another conversational gambit. Lemme see." He made a show of thought. "Say, Yumi, you know how Black folks died?"

Paula declined to answer.

"Black folks died along a Southern road; bled to death from being Jim Crowed."

He drank swiftly, then drank again. "Why, I made a rhyme, didn't I? Well, anyhow, that's the information Euph gave me. When I were a tyke. Whenever he got into the tar likker and was in a de-pressed mood. He'd sit there and his eyes would get red and he'd roar at me, 'They're whitetrash! Y'know how Black folks died?'"

Will threw back his head and laughed, a high, raucous laugh that was not his. Euph's laugh, Paula thought incredulously, the back of her neck prickling.

Will had always been a fine mimic, which was part of what made him such a spellbinding storyteller. But this went beyond mimicry; he was not playing the mimicry like a verbal instrument — it was possessing him. She stared at him.

"Why aren't you laughing?" he demanded.

"Because I don't think it's funny." She wondered if he could hear the jagged hostility in Euph's words and voice, resurrected by him now in the house down Noname Lane words and tone. "Not Euph yelling something like that at you. Not you laughing about it."

"'Tain't nothing to the things been done by some."

His voice had altered again .

"Things of the Devil, by Devil's spawn."

Uncle Bert's voice? She felt a chill. Abruptly she got up from the futon.

"I'm going to bed now. I wish you'd come too."

He stood, for a moment oddly lost, and she was suddenly reminded of his stance and expression the day they had gone to see Pele dance, when looking out over the field of silversword he told her of the pointless vicious damage to them he had seen, driven by what he had named "the deep pleasure of destruction."

Later, in bed, where they simply lay side by side in the dark, lightly touching, he said,

"Did you hear that bird a long time ago, Yumi?"

"You mean the one calling just now?"

"Was it just now? Seems like a long time ago ... I been having trouble finding my time and place . . ."

"Well, there was a call a few minutes ago."

"Oh yeh, that's the one. The male. Calling for his mate. 'Tis a lonesome sound. I lie here sometimes listening and remembering what Euph said, but not seeing noway how it could be so . . ."

"What did Euph say, Will?"

"That I'd find the person to give the kerchief to. That I'd find you."

"You found her, Will. You found me. Euph says so." Was it so? Had she and Will read Euph's meaning right? These days, it was so often hard to feel that she was any good to him, or he to her. Still, right then, she held him close.

But he only answered,

"Can't rightly see how it could come so for me, living as I have, being who I am." And then, "'Tis a lonesome sound, for true."

With rudeness, savage mockery, or in the case of Ben and Emma's interventions, by silence, Will rebuffed every suggestion made, every avenue of possible help, from Western traditions – therapy, AA, even, Paula thought, some godawful Starvesoil faith, if it would work (but she remembered Uncle Bert and his backsliding –) or from Auntie Raina.

When for the first time he moved to make love to her and failed, he raged, silently, deep in an internal fortress, beyond any reassurance from her.

After that, sometimes, in the intensity of loving, he began to tremble on the edge of something that led Paula to refuse him, then seek to defuse him, remove herself.

She refused to name the something violence.

In the nights after they had made love or failed at it, he talked his excoriating talk. She was never even sure he remembered the night-talkings: the bird calling for its mate, his self-lacerating denunciations of his own damnation. For a long time when he reached a certain repetitive point, Paula was able to rein him in, joking, soothing, being lightly caustic.

He accepted that, as if he trusted her judgment to know the line between where he lanced his obscure abscesses with words, and where he would sever his arteries — or someone else's. These night-talkings would never be mentioned in the morning. He woke, always early, always stone sober, easy, controlled, ready for his day's exacting work.

As the line began to slip, as he crumbled, the dark question came to Paula of whether she had encouraged those night-talkings, not only from a desperate attempt to help him but also from a self-protective need to try and control his increasingly wayward power.

With the slipping, it began to seem that the nearness of talking and loving in the night became the worst pressure on him of all. As if she had misjudged, and the contents of some severed subterranean artery pulsed darkly through him, counter to the flow of blood and warmth that drew him towards others and towards the outer world. An artery-current that drew him instead into the abyss behind his eyes, from where his Black Days and White Nights stole out to maul him.

Paula had been around alcohol, drunk alcohol, since college. Then and since, she had seen hard drinking. But the day came when she had to recognize that she had never seen what she was watching in Will: a man drinking to kill himself.

30

Trouble At Euph's

As they left Hale Noname in the clear light of morning, Will came up so short on the steps outside the back door that Paula, moving quickly right behind, cannoned into him.

He swayed, and she could tell it was not just from the impact. But he did not shift position, and his big frame blocked the doorway and her view.

"What is it?" The anxiety in her own voice alarmed her. Yet hearing her speak seemed to release him. Shaking himself, he continued slowly down the steps.

"I were just wondering what that-there is, and how it got placed so."

He stopped again, and Paula followed his gaze.

He leaned over near the steps and wrenched up an object that had been rammed into the earth.

Haft and blade were caked with dirt that crumbled off in clots.

"It's your knife, Will. I asked where it had gone, the other day, when you opened the glove compartment in the Jeep."

He raised it aloft, squinting.

The sun glanced off an expanse of blade, off the exposed tip.

Paula shuddered. Held as he held it, the knife was without camouflage, an implement to penetrate against great resistance, to withstand the shock of bone, to travel fast and far through thickness of flesh and gristle and vein. An implement superbly designed for killing and only that.

"No Yumi, I wouldn't never leave a tool outside this way, soiled so."

And it was true that such negligence would be very unlike the man she knew.

As it was unlike him — as she knew him — to leave the clots of mud on the floor that she had noticed just inside the kitchen door.

"Well, maybe you had other things on your mind," she suggested quietly. "Maybe you figured you'd wait until morning to clean up."

"What're you meaning, Yumi?"

"You must have taken it with you when you went for a walk last night."

He turned his eyes on her, blank and blue, and she imagined with shock that she saw a disorganized fathomless terror quiver within them. The edges of his long mobile lips trembled for just a second. She was distracted by the unexpected pull of her desire as she remembered their taste and feel, and then by shame at being diverted that way at such a moment.

He gave an impatient twisted grin.

"You're wrong about this, Yumi, because I didn't go out of the house last night. I wouldn't have left you unprotected so, like you said I did with Julie. This here's boar country. And this can't be my knife, because I haven't used my knife in so-long. Lately I been keeping it in the tool shed over yonder. Come to seem like the Jeep weren't a good place for it after all," he finished cryptically, with an odd vagueness, "you and me spending time there together like we do." He looked toward the shed.

Paula stared at him. "What do you mean, it's boar country? Boars can't get in the house, even if for some reason they came this close. There's no danger to me from that, you know it. And you did go out last night. I saw you. You woke me going past the bedroom window and I looked out and saw you."

He did not seem to hear her. "'Tis a right puzzle." He stared at the knife. "Must not be mine after all."

"It is yours, Will," said Paula, slowly but determinedly, angry and frightened by his lie about not leaving the house, his absurdity about wild boars, and his whole strange manner. "It's got your mark on the handle, where you burned it in."

The dragon mark was right in front of her eyes: in front of his eyes, too.

"Prowlers," Will said. "There must have been prowlers. Strangers round my house, among my things."

He strode to the tool shed and pulled open the door.

The knife sheath hung empty on its nail.

He took a clean rag from the neat pile on the tool-bench and wiped the knife carefully.

Then he restored it to its sheath.

The rag hung from his fingers, striped with obscure dark stains that Paula could see were not soil.

She shivered.

"I don't understand this at-all. It do trouble me were I so careless and forgetful-like. I do think it must have been prowlers."

He ran the tap in the sink, rinsed the rag and twisted it powerfully. She watched the water wrung from it run red.

Will did not seem to see. Carefully, he spread the rag to dry on the basin edge, and shut the shed door behind them with care.

They walked to the Jeep and headed into town.

He had his bad times and his worse times; and then, suddenly, he would steady for weeks on end.

During one such period, when he seemed, almost, possessed by gaiety, he proposed a rare trip to Paula: a helicopter outing above Na Pali on Kaua'i. For the first time in memory, he had gone two days without drinking; and Paula agreed, eager to believe in the improvement, to have their troubles ease. She thrust aside her foreboding, ignored the feverishness in his gaiety.

They took off from Honolulu. The day was sunny, the wavelets and puffy clouds as buoyant as Will's manner, and Paula dared to feel almost happy again.

They approached the great black cliffs. Even from this height the sea was formidable, crashing at the rocky base. He dropped them lower, and they skirted the edge of Na Pali Wilderness.

Then, abruptly, he turned the machine.

"Let's look at the Canyon from up here!"

As they drew near, his mood changed, as if drawing its timbre from the forbidding landscape below. Trying to pull him out of what seemed a sudden visible plunge into a vortex of depression, she asked, "Whose chopper is this?"

But his face, already stiff, went as hard as the stony ground. She suddenly wondered if she really wanted the answer.

Now they were below the canyon rim. The multi-colored ancient strata soared above them. Even in the moment of her gut-wrenching anxiety about his mood she marveled at the sure steady brilliance with which he maneuvered here, threading his way past death on the needle-spire outcroppings of stone.

"Whose chopper is it?" he shouted, over the clank and clash of metal. Call it mine Yumi. After what I done for Sam in choppers, I've bought into every one was ever built."

He jammed down his hand on the stick. The machine gave a lurch and shudder that threw Paula hard against metal, bruising her side.

"Let me show you a game I learned to play in Nam! It's called back-hoeing."

The helicopter bucked and plunged. The canyon walls streamed crazily backward, a patchwork of color and jagged shapes.

Metal and death screamed around them. Maybe Will could get them out: but no one, not even Will, could do this thing without skirting the abyss. Her body's thrust to survive told her that.

Rigid with rage, Paula stared at the blank wall of the airport corridor.

She heard his voice, genial, almost jaunty, as he spoke to the other men in the office, carrying out the routine tasks of landing. Then his steps came back, paused, and she heard the clink of money in the soft drink machine across the hall and the thunk of the can as it fell. The rip of metal as he tore the tab away. The sound of his throat muscles as he swallowed.

"Want a cola or juice, Yumi?" he asked. "This is like the day we met, flying the Sunday dinners over to Maui."

She did not answer. She could not speak. She felt him move, stand just behind her. She did not turn.

"I put my life in your hands," she said at last.

"I know you did." His tone was light. "And not the first time, either. Other times you done it, other ways. Don't ever, Yumi."

She had never hated anyone so much.

After this episode their movements and actions together were discordant, jarring, barely effective. The unlikely, ineffable harmony that they had achieved in their time together vaporized.

And they were together less, anyway. After the Kaua'i trip, Paula refused to get in a vehicle with Will. When she came to the Big Island, she rented a car. Traveling around the island, traveling between Noname Lane and Euph's and the Pine Tar, they traveled separately, and Will raged at that.

Although it took Paula and Ben a while to register the fact, and even longer to believe — and they did not even pretend to understand — Will stopped drinking altogether.

But he kept along the path his feet had started on, going down it stone sober and stone crazy.

In all the years at the place on the water, at the edge of a lagoon, beneath the coconut and banana fronds, there had never been trouble at Euph's, because Will would not permit it.

There was trouble now at Euph's because Will brought it there.

He was the trouble he brought to Euph's; his molten presence threatened cataclysm in the world.

Paula leaned against the wall by the back entrance to Euph's, arms crossed tightly against her breasts, hands gripping her shoulders. The waves clawed at the sand. The stiff palm fronds clawed at the sky. Up in the parking area, at the edge of the road, she felt the disturbance in the movements of people leaving, too early, this Saturday night at Euph's.

She was sick with the smell of blood and the sound of impacting flesh damaging flesh, and shook with the violent vibrations disrupting the air.

Around at the side of the building facing the Pine Tar, away from the departing people in front, she heard the men talking in low dissonant voices that scraped at the shadows.

Tom Tanaka, his tone level but wound tight, not his policeman's voice because he was speaking to Will, but informed by his policeman's view and duties:

"You gotta get hold of yourself, Will. I've been called out here twice this month. I'm speaking as your friend. People are stopping coming— they're afraid. They want to know what's wrong. People are concerned about you, Will, I'm concerned about you, and this gotta stop, for other peoples' sakes and for yours. This time, if it hadn't of been for me coming by on my own to keep an eye out, and Ben's help, you'da hurt that man bad."

"Then I'd just send him back to the Mainland faster." Will was cold, eerie, almost indifferent.

"If he wants to press charges, I can't stop him. And you gotta know, Will, when you fight it ain't just like anyone fighting."

"'Crazed Vietnam vet runs amok?'" Will mocked a multitude of sensationalized articles. "'His hands are lethal weapons.'"

"I'm a vet myself, Will, you know that." Tom's voice held quiet reproach. "I was there, too. But you're trained. You got more strength than most to start with and you know how to use it. That's dangerous if you don't respect it. That's just a fact."

"Why not tell that Mainland man to watch it?" His tone threatened. "A stranger at Euph's, disrespecting the lady guests!"

"Well, Will, there wasn't agreement about that. Not everyone here saw it that way."

"Disrespecting Yumi!"

Paula's astonishment at his words was interrupted by the stirring of a third presence, watchful but silent until now.

"Don't go that fool's way!"

Ben spoke with a sharpness and authority Paula had never heard him use with Will. Suddenly, she understood what Will had often said but she had never grasped before: Ben, he took on to be my elder brother . . .

"Don't make that kind of nonsense about Paula, seeing what's not there. About how other men act with her, or how she's acting. She won't stand for it. She's a woman you gotta respect truth with. You wanna lose big and fast, that's a way to go to do it."

Will fell silent. Then Paula heard him wrench away, like a limb wrenched bleeding from a tree, and heard his heavy tread away from Euph's.

The episode of the knife blade held to the light, with its dark stain and dragon mark; the episode at Waimea Canyon; and now, the trouble at Euph's, brought her to a decision violently and almost without willing.

"I'm not coming over next weekend," she told him the next morning at Hale Noname. "I have a lot of work to do the week after that. I can't keep on like this and do my job properly. It isn't fair of you to treat me this way, and I won't allow it. It isn't fair to refuse and ridicule every move I and everyone else who cares about you makes to try to help, then put on an extravagant drama of your self-destruction and maneuver us into watching. You're destroying yourself and everything you've created that's come to you so hard and cost you so much courage and work. You're destroying your relationships with Ben and Emma, and any chance of a rapprochement with Pearlie Leilani. You are destroying your place and your reputation in this community, destroying Euph's and the Pine Tar — and I know business is off at Volcano Flights, too, how could it not be?" She paused, took a deep breath, and said emphatically, enunciating each word, "You are destroying your relationship with me. You are destroying yourself — deliberately."

He did not answer. After a moment she went on, "I'll call you a week from Thursday. We can talk then about whether I come over the weekend after that. About how things — stand — with us."

Still he was silent.

Paula looked at him. He sat slouched massively in the green armchair. His face was all bleak bone and blonde stubble, hostile and bitter, mulish and unforgiving and unapproachable, utterly impervious and radiating resistance.

Love and desire immobilized her: to kiss him, to strike him, to make love to him, to hold him against her tenderly until he relaxed and softened.

But the harsh-planed set of his cheekbone warned her away: she knew no one was more vicious than the utterly vulnerable.

Her own exhaustion, from the turmoil around Will and around the place on the water, threatened to spiral her into depression. She tore herself away from the tailspin, letting her anger at Will fuel her self-protectiveness.

She hoisted her knapsack on her shoulders and went to the front door.

He spoke as her foot found the first step.

"I did warn you, Yumi. Long ago. That I wouldn't bring you no peace. Don't you remember the night we first saw Pele dance? I did speak to you then at the field of silversword of the deep pleasure of destruction."

"Well, you made sure your warning came true. Good-bye," she said briefly, stepping through the door. He did not respond.

31

Schism and Collapse (Gone)

To Will, Paula's personality seemed a finely modulated creation of mutualities and reciprocities, of obligations and order. He thought of her as music. Against that organized accomplishment of her own life, he felt he had nothing to offer, could bring nothing to bear.

Something had started in Will, as if some living thing had stirred, with Pearlie Leilani's digging into herself, into those around her, into the present and past of the land. And when Paula walked out his door, the night after the trouble at Euph's, the thing moved rapidly, awakening the blotted-out places, the shame and rage. In that deep and terrifying way, before now always closed to him, Will Cawdry began to remember.

Will Cawdry began to dream.

In his nights, memories poured through him that were more real than his waking present.

Bare toes scuffing in the Starvesoil.

He recalled awaking to noise and strangers in the room in Windermere Gardens and learning by overhearing that his Little Mama was dead. They said bad things about her and he knew that they were true, and in those first moments moving between anguish and dread, he was seized powerfully, to his own shame, by his enormous anger at her and his contempt: for her seemingly willful succumbing to helplessness that left him alone in the world, for succumbing to the men who bruised and beat her body, for abandoning him and herself as if they were garbage. He shook with the desire repressed until now to hurt and kill her for that, to hurt and crush and kill the men who hurt her.

Then all feeling fled him.

He had no recollection of what happened from that moment to the time he was in the train with Uncle Bert, hills and wheat fields and badlands whipping past outside the window, as the two of them rode his Little Mama's body back down home to bury her in a way she didn't want, in a place she didn't want to be.

He remembered her words: I don't never want to see the Starvesoil again. And when I die, I don't want no ole hypocrite leaping and praying and badmouthing me. I don't want to be lying there again and no way to fight him back.

Uncle Bert hadn't gotten religion yet, back then; but Will knew that Uncle Bert was the very last person and very last ole religious hypocrite his Little Mamma would have wanted around, and no way to fight him back.

At least she'd had one wish granted: she'd never opened her eyes again on that place she'd put behind her.

Torn by razor-grass and willow-whip, belt-buckle and boar-tusk, Will had stepped forward on the day of his Little Mama's funeral and said to Euph sitting on the back steps of the Blue Box,

"My Mama was a hoor."

Bare toes scuffing in the Starvesoil.

"Now you hush your mouth." Euph was severe. "That ain't no way to talk about your Mama."

"My Mama was a hoor," he said stubbornly, and raised his eyes to the old man's.

"It ain't no way to talk about your Mama," Euph repeated, "no matter what she was."

"My Mama was a hoor."

There was silence in the dust. Then Euph said quietly,

"Your Mama was a whore, and it takes two to make a whore. You gonna have to learn to accept her in your heart anyway. It don't mean you have to love her if you can't — love don't come to order. Though your Mama was worth loving.

"I know from time to time down here she lived by making arrangements, and I've heard here and there she fell into some sad and deadly ways, up there in Chicago. Life's right hard for everyone, but you need to know, from the beginning your Mama had more going against her than most do. I said a minute gone you'd have to come into your manhood before your time, deciding what to do about this-all evil rising in town against the Black folks. Your mama weren't but two years older than you are now when she birthed you, and none of her doing she had to. Your Mama was a whore, but she was a right smart spunky little lady. She headed on outta here with her banjo in one hand and your hand in the other, and didn't nothing bring her back here till they brought her back dead. Not every girl got you the way she got you woulda had your hand in hers when she lit out, and she'd have had a better chance if she hadn't. Now that ain't your fault — it's just a fact to weigh when weighing her. I taught you most all your music, but your gift for it and your first teaching come from her; I heard the lullabies she sang you. So don't be hard on her because she couldn't make it work out for you-all up there. Life's a powerful hard thing for anyone to make come out right. Be proud of her, that she stood up on her two feet and tried.

"And like I say, you gonna have to accept her in your heart, if you're going to grow to be a manner of man worth knowing. You have to, boy: she's your Mama. You can't get away from your Mama no more'n you can from your own face."

Now Will's nights were wracked by dreams, images and intimations of himself — the Beast: whoring and warring his way across Asia, uncaring, lustful, unclean and damned. Scattering sickness and seed to the four winds. Women and children, unidentified in his dreams, but close as his bone, abandoned and uncared for. Trading in flesh, his own for all he knew; trading in the white dust that blighted his childhood, blotted out his own mother.

With Pearlie Leilani's digging, with the overwhelming dreams, the ends of the circle had touched, as he had feared on the morning he woke to find Yumi in his bed, in a closing of the circle that spelled disaster.

You can't get away from your own face.

Will took his place at the piano at Euph's that next Saturday night, the night Paula told him she wouldn't be coming; and she hadn't come. Ben watched him with the dread and foreboding that never left him now.

The usual people were pretty much back, but Ben could tell that they were wary.

The first chords filled the place with melted gold. Then, like an airplane that soars for the sun, falters, fails and falls, the music shivered, spun out of control, and shattered.

Stillness at Euph's.

A sense of doom gripped Ben.

Will rose and stumbled through the door into the back corridor.

Ben followed.

Will went through the door at the end of the corridor; and outside, he stumbled again.

For the first time his hands had failed him on the piano keys; for the first time his feet had failed him at Euph's and the Pine Tar, on the Lady's ground.

Like the man on Kaua'i, Will Cawdry had stopped eating at last.

All his life he had loved bright things that shone, things that glowed with an inner light, bright things that glittered.

When he was a baby, his Little Mama had told him, and nothing else would quiet him, a corner of tinfoil or a copper penny rubbed shiny on her dress-hem would hold him fascinated.

And flame, bright quick and alive, had to be kept from his reach.

That was when he was very young, before fear contaminated his fascination with flame. Before the night of ice and firefall at Windermere Gardens.

In the village in Vietnam, after the girl, when noise and flame were everywhere and the cacophony and chaos of terror filled the void, and when he felt empty space at his wrists where bright nothingness separated him from himself so he lost his place and time, as in that instant when his Little Mama dropped him through hellfire and smoke to the ice of the stony ground far below — in the village, he looked through the hellfire and smoke around him, felt the quiver of air like the living female flesh that shivered in loathing against his. And then he forgot. When he was aware of any sense of his place and time he was in a hospital in Tokyo; and for fortune he had never gone back to Vietnam.

He stayed in the hospital a year while they cut and sewed and dug at sharp fragments of plastic they stumbled on, and made gestures toward putting his body back together again.

His memory was gone. Other people told him about what had happened. They said that he had been very brave, for which he received his most prestigious medal. He had rescued two of his fellows, and had been vital to holding the village until support came and he was hit by friendly fire, stepped on the thing that lived in his body still in plastic shards.

He had no other memory, only a word that glided through mind at intervals like a silvery fish in murky water — the girl. But the word conjured no images.

He had no images at all, only an awareness of flame and of space that shivered, of chaos and cacophony.

No recollection, until these recent days. When, with the other nightmares, came what might be memory. Memory, and a question.

Central Vietnam, 1960's.

Suddenly still.

The question: What manner of man?

"Because you got it in you to grow to be a manner of man worth knowing."

Euph had said that to him, in the Texas Thornbrake Starvesoil, 1950's.

But in this, as in no other thing, Will had always thought Euph had been wrong: for Will felt that from his bone before his birth he had been bent, to be a man not like other men.

What if, the thought came now to Will, Hawai'i 1980's, what if, in the midst of that chaos of movement in the village, of flickering fire and tormented breath, in the midst of that cacophony, something went suddenly still?

Someone went suddenly still?

Someone who now returned to him as a blur of blue pale cotton trousers in the night, gold-copper skin, hair black thick and long beneath your hand.

She hadn't been still, she had been fighting, and then you drove deep inside her and your arm was hard across her throat as she lay beneath you and you felt the fluttering within her throat, like a life within a life.

And then she went suddenly still.

And you knew what had happened.

And you knew that you had done it.

And you didn't stop anyway.

And you enjoyed it.

What you were doing, and then the sudden stillness while you did it.

Enjoyed what you were doing, and didn't stop doing, even though you knew what had just happened, when beneath the pulse of your own arm you felt the life within a life stop living.

What manner of man would you be?

The call came from Ben. He had never telephoned her before.

"Will? Disappeared?" said Paula blankly. "Gone?"

"Yeh."

"When?"

"Hadn't seen him for eight days. Don't know when he left. Plane's at the field at Volcano. He drove over to Kona and flew to Honolulu from there. No one recognized him, Konaside. The Jeep was parked on the street near the airport. The police contacted Hilo, when the car got reported abandoned. Hilo police got in touch with me." Ben cleared his throat.

"He'll have had papers made. He flew on out from Honolulu. Maybe sailed. Probably flew."

Once again, Will had come to Honolulu; but he had not come to her.

"I'll be over this afternoon."

"Gone," Paula said, again, hollowly, as she stood at the airfield in Volcano late that gray afternoon.

Ben, silent beside her, nodded.

Her voice sounded lost to her, and the words sounded lost too, picked up and dispersed by the wind, tuneless and toneless over the Lava Wastes.

"I'll go after him," she said. Asia and the islands of the seas stretched out before her.

"Don't." Ben's voice was uninflected but absolutely certain. "Not you. Not anyone. This is for him to do. You know a lot about him. Ways I don't. But other things, I know about him. What I will do," he said, "is go see Auntie Raina." He paused. "You can too." He paused briefly again. "This is not your blame," he told her.

Even in her shock at Will's disappearance, Paula registered astonishment at his words. Never had he spoken of such matters to her. She had never been sure he formulated them in that way to himself. And his suggestion — almost a command — that she consult Auntie Raina, his awareness that she blamed herself, and the memory of his words at Euph's, when he and Tom Tanaka had tried to reason with Will, all brought her to the realization that he respected her, and that sometime along the way of these years, he had come to accept her.

But Will was gone.

And she could not believe what Ben said — that it was not her blame. She had failed her father, then José Sánchez; and now she had failed Will because of her profound fault of silence.

I could not find the words to speak and so he died.

"No use to try and follow him anyway," Ben added with characteristic practicality. "You couldn't find him, if he don't want to be found. I couldn't find him. Can't no one find him, if he don't want to be found. And if we could find him, we couldn't touch him or reach him now."

"He's in no condition to wander," she muttered. "Wherever he is, he'll fly, and he's in no condition to fly."

"He's in no condition to live his life. Still he has always lived it so."

32

Snow Sleepers: Music Spilling

Now in the nights it seemed to Paula that she had lied to herself about her life.

She had never gone beyond the disrupted harmonics that took the stress of organizing her family's survival in the shadowed apartment of refugees on the South Side of Chicago. At every point of crisis in her life she had been immobilized by the struggle between her mother and her father. A struggle that culminated for her in the moment in her father's study just before he fell.

Obsessively, crushed with guilt and remorse, she dug herself deeper into the thoughts that had come to her as she looked out over the lonely airfield at Volcano.

She had failed to speak the words to her father just before he fell, that would have changed the course of the universe.

She had failed to speak to José Sánchez, in that last moment when he paused by her office door.

And, shatteringly, totally unforeseen even after those two failures that had gone before, she had failed to speak to Will.

The paralysis of silence had possessed her long before his disappearance. In silence, they had moved around the BackShack in Noname Glade — the building that stood at the literal center of the place they lived their lives together. And now, she had broken the lock on the door and entered, and found a gray dress, ripped, hanging on a nail.

The failure to speak had given that place its power; and she blamed herself for the silence, for silence was the deep fault of her own schismed self.

"No, Paula," said Ginnie. Paula's far-distanced attention was caught not by her words but by her grip, just below the shoulder. People who didn't know Paula usually sensed the reserve around her body; Ginnie, who knew her, knew and still had broken it. And Ginnie, equable and polite, was now almost shrill.

"You listen to me. And I mean listen. You're acting nuts."

They were in Paula's bungalow.

"What's the matter? No one's complaining about my work, are they?"

"Not about your work, no. They're concerned about you. Your work isn't the point — not yet. This is the point. This is nuts."

She jabbed her finger at the long wall facing Paula's desk. Paula had kept her life around the place on the water not only separate from her Honolulu days but, as Ginnie knew, almost secret. Now she had broken down the barriers separating areas of her life.

Her wall in Honolulu was taken over by a giant poster, featuring a blow-up of a candid snapshot Paula had taken of Will one afternoon outside Euph's, and a description based on words that Paula had penned for the guidance of Tamura and Associates, who searched for the disappeared.

Bowing to Ben's insight, she had not followed Will physically. She had even, at last, in this extremity, gone to Auntie Raina. But she could barely remember the visit, and when she tried to bring it to mind her thoughts remained thickly clouded, her heart obstructed. "You will come another time," the old woman had told her calmly as she left, and patted her hand.

Ben's approach proved too alien to her own need for knowledge, Western-style. And she hoped desperately that if Will learned from seeing her poster that she was seeking him, that he would then seek her.

She had penned a feverish description for Tamura and Associates, that they printed below his photograph.

Much Wanted In Hawaii: Name: Will Cawdry

Age:	*40*
D.O.B.:	*August 11, 1945*
Place of birth:	*Hibbits, Texas, U.S.A.*
Citizenship:	*U.S.A.*
Race:	*Caucasian. Light complexion, but suntanned and weather-beaten*
Eyes:	*pale blue.*

How to describe the things those eyes, like that smile, expressed?
Hair: Blonde, straight, thick, worn to shoulders.
Weight: 235 pounds. Build heavy-boned and lanky. Distinguishing marks and scars: Large scars from surgery for grenade wound, right torso, covered over with tattoo of dragon in red and gold.

Her pen and ink sketch of Hitch the Dragon followed, slightly modified to conform to the style of such posters.

Small, deep, pitted, crescent-shaped scars over back and shoulders to below the waist.

With the entry "Distinguishing marks and scars", Paula shuddered. She felt as if she had stripped Will naked in public.

Powerfully built, unusually large hands. Can fly just about any machine ever built. Highly intelligent, voracious reader, little formal education, very wide and deep general knowledge (but with gaps, with chasms, she thought.) Brilliant pianist, composer/improviser, especially jazz and Blues and Kī hō'alu (Hawaiian Slack Key guitar style): Favorite artists: Mozart, Keith Jarrett, Miles Davis, Gabby Pahinui, Billie Holliday. Military background (Vietnam) Martial arts and Special Forces training. Excellent carpenter. Excellent cook/chef. Specializes in meat and poultry dishes. Small farmer/businessman. Owns, runs, is chef in his own restaurant and night club (Euph's and the Pine Tar) in Hilo, Hawai'i, for the past 15 years. Very heavy drinker (Johnny Walker Black) although recently stopped cold. (How long will that last? she thought.) Excellent storyteller and mimic. Often, but not always, speaks with modified Texas/U.S. Southern accent.

Learns languages easily. Speaks Vietnamese, Chinese, Japanese, French well. Fluent in Hawaiian. Very familiar with Southeast Asia, Pacific Islands. Has not been on U.S. Mainland since early 1960's. Disappeared from Honolulu, Hawai'i. Most likely locations: Southeast Asia, Hong Kong, Taiwan, Singapore, the Pacific Islands, the Philippines; possibly Japan, New Zealand, Australia. It is unlikely that he is using an alias or has deliberately changed his appearance.

She had had a hard argument over that last point with Tamura and Associates; it went against the grain of their experience with similar cases. But she was adamant, and they conceded, still asking how she could be so sure — which she did not know.

Only in the night did she find her answer. Despite his flamboyance, she thought, Will — at bottom and especially in crisis — did not have a sufficient sense of himself, as he appeared to others in the world, to be capable of altering the way he looked or the name he was called by.

Reasons for disappearance: Personal. He was not wanted by the law when he left Hawai'i. He has no known criminal record. (A section followed, researched by one of the associates of Tamura and Associates, detailing the weaponry most likely to be familiar to Will from his time in Vietnam.) He is not known to be armed but has been routinely in the past. Favors a commando knife. He has been prone to brawling when drinking and is trained in hand-to-hand combat.

Was he dangerous? Of course, she thought, remembering, and most likely armed: Armed and Dangerous (Physically and Emotionally.) Approach with Extreme Caution.

But she could not bring herself to place him so explicitly at risk of summary execution. Anyway, she reflected grimly, rereading her own words describing him, any gambler with sense would tread with caution, given such a description.

In general he has no history of other than brief and casual involvement with women. Not a loner but private

Most likely occupations: Pilot, pianist, chef/cook, import-export

This last, she gathered from Tamura and Associates, was the understood euphemism in such descriptions for smuggling.

Likely to be involved with planes or helicopters, but not with boats.

But may be anywhere, doing anything.

And the last sentence epitomized everything she could say about Will Cawdry.

Now, standing in her office, her arms crossed over her breasts in an X, hands gripping her shoulders, in her characteristic defensive stance, she heard Ginnie repeat,

"It's nuts. And so is whatever's going on with that James Aki! People know about him, I tell you. And nowadays you don't have any attention for anything except detection and tracking techniques and Lord knows what! It's like you're being sucked into some kind of — of maelstrom!"

Paula released herself from Ginnie's grip.

"I'm sorry you feel that way," she said stiffly, with dignity, as if she were sane, "but I have to decide for myself where I put my energies."

Ginnie stared at her for a moment, angrily, then shook her head and left the room.

Paula had seen James Aki's card on a bulletin board late one afternoon, when she sat barely aware of her surroundings in a coffee house and bookshop off Merchant Street. Suddenly the rectangle of the card seemed to seize her consciousness, from the litter of other cards tacked to the bulletin board, as if it were meant for her. She rose, her coffee forgotten, pulled as if mesmerized first to the board, and then out the door and through the swiftly darkening Honolulu streets, down twists and turns to a poor building not far from the River Street end of Hotel Street where, among the seedy hotels, tarnished plaques announced the offices of marginal professionals.

A card the twin of the one she had seen guided her to the fourth floor, and there the door opened and he stood, a man her age, compactly built, and never still, bobbing and bouncing on sneakered feet, so his thick black hair fell over glittering eyes set in a face scarred by old acne, rubbing his arms through sleeves of a shirt fraying at the cuffs, and saying, "Come in! Come in!" as if he expected her.

The office was somehow off kilter, or perhaps it was the building, or perhaps it was James Aki or she herself. Crammed bookcases threatened to topple over on the two of them, papers littered the floor, buried the desk, buried everything except a computer stand and a printer spewing out paper, and a pair of globes, one of the world, and one that showed the constellations of the night sky on a black surface illuminated from within.

"I saw your card," she told him. "It said that you find the missing and the disappeared. It said that you have ways."

He had ways.

They began that very moment, when she entered his office, as he told her of his sister, Erika Emiko Aki, who had disappeared when she was seven and he was nine, but he had leads, he was on her trail. His ways were legion, as she saw, the finest in modern technology (Where did he get the money? she wondered. That was the last rational thought she ever had when she was with him. She never got an answer.) Databases and contacts too, all over the world, especially Asia and the islands, and also the globes, of the earth and the sky, which lighted up and revealed things to him, the trails others despaired of, trails of the missing and the disappeared.

Paula's life imploded. Nothing existed for her but that cramped office beneath teetering bookshelves. In the night when the globe of the heavens glowed and the computer-calculated correlations of locations darted across its surface in trails of greenish fire, Paula felt powerful in the surge of technology logically applied to a challenge. And after a time, when day came, she even, sometimes, failed to go to work. She almost stopped eating as well. She lived on coffee and doughnuts as James did, that he ordered from a shop downstairs and had left outside the door, their arrival signaled by a single loud knock. For twenty-four hours at a time they never left the office, calculating far latitudes and longitudes, and the paths of stars, speculating feverishly on where lost ones might be, and how they might be found.

She was stunned by the sacral mystery of the deep goneness of Will.

Then for a while she went back to work, and seemed to behave as before, but that was only because she hugged a secret knowledge. James Aki had revealed to her that Will Cawdry would return when the earth had made one circle around the sun.

But he did not.

The night before the foretold date of Will's return, James Aki left a message on her answering machine at home. Sputtering with excitement, he said that he was following a lead concerning Erika, he would be gone and he didn't know for how long. He didn't even mention Will. She thought, incredulous: he has completely forgotten.

When she went by his office the next day, to demand a re-reading, an explanation for Will's failure to return (the International Date Line had occurred to her as a source of confusion) the door was locked.

In the studio in Honolulu beneath the banyan in the courtyard, the air vibrated with music spilling, strange, strong music, thrilling and fine, that captivated passersby in the street, holding them in place to listen.

Her long-time neighbors were surprised. They recognized the music from passages caught on the wind in other days, but she had never played it like this. She had always lived quietly, Paula, that Japanese woman who occupied the studio. And now, music spilled into the night from golden oblongs of window, and even more surprisingly, flowed out to bless the day. And magic must truly have infused it, for she played it incessantly, and loudly, oblivious to others, yet it was so fine that people forebore to complain, as if the music were indeed a blessing and they were blessed to hear it.

Will's music spilled for a week.

Then, suddenly, it stopped.

Often now the Japanese woman was gone from the studio beneath the banyan in the courtyard.

A deliberately exoticized figure, extravagantly dressed, theatrically made up, wholly disguised, once familiar in these haunts but a long time absent, began to frequent the tourist hotels and bars of Waikīkī and, even more, of the outer islands. The single name she used changed like sulfur veils above the Lava Wastes.

Paula awoke in the nights with Will's wheezy laugh in her ears. But when she reached for him she crumpled up with pain, finding herself sleeping alone or with some other man.

Paula went back to work.

She put the tapes she had made of Will's music away in a shoebox in the back of her closet in the studio. She rolled up the poster that Tamura and Associates had sent her and placed it behind the shoebox. She took all the photographs of him off the wall and put them in an album, and put the album behind the shoebox, too.

Through circuitous routes, she heard that James Aki had landed up at his brother's home on Kaua'i, and later was committed to a mental hospital. When he got out a few months later, he had gone to work quietly at his brother's business in Lihue, as an accountant, which had been his profession once.

She further heard that he had been obsessed since the day his sister disappeared with the idea that her disappearance was his fault, although no one, not the family or the police, had ever blamed him.

33

A Fall Of Sheaves: Life's Work

When Will had been gone almost a year and a half, Paula visited Japan.

In Tokyo, she stood on a corner during the appalling rush hour, as wave after wave of people washed over her, and felt a first meaning that being here might hold for her: the Ur-meaning, so desperately important in her life from early childhood, of physical safety. Here, she would never be singled out, far less than in San Francisco with its Japanese enclave, far less even than in Honolulu.

She looked in the mirror, long and carefully, and for the first time felt that she did not have the face of the enemy, forever.

She traveled to the small fishing village where that ancestor-aunt had been born, and from where she had left on a voyage to a new home at the invitation of a King, and did not return: but became instead the mother of the first generation of her line to be Hawaiian-born: her child had been the mother of Paula's namesake, the other Yumi.

The place was very poor. Paula arrived late on a gray afternoon and from a pebbly shore watched the fishing boats return to harbor. Then she walked back to her inn through narrow streets that were almost deserted.

She rose early, and went out before dawn into a town just beginning to stir. From somewhere near she thought she heard the sound of a temple bell and a low chant like the sea moaning. She tried to greet the people she met, but her speech sounded as awkward to her as she felt she looked, tall, and with splayed American movements.

As the days passed, the Japanese words that would never ring as if she were a native speaker, her posture and gestures that would always mark her as from elsewhere, seemed increasingly to set her off as alien, all the more for the apparent similarity she bore to the people around her.

She felt that they felt that too, and showed it in their quickly averted glances — felt that they felt her more irrevocably distant than White people would have been. A White person was simply alien. She represented — what? — a renunciation, a rejection of them? A malformation of what they were?

But she was not certain of her interpretations. Perhaps the people in that first gray dawn were simply still wrapped in the night's dream. Perhaps the rebuff she thought she saw in others' eyes was in hers, or in hers first. She did not think so, but she was not certain of that either.

She had intended to stay three months in Japan, but in two weeks had changed her mind. Perhaps Caroline who had become Jamilyah would say she could not know what she felt in so short a time. But she thought that was not so. She had come, she had stood on the ancestral shore of departure. But any meaning lay elsewhere, in her experience of the people who had come from this land and left it forever.

Perhaps that was the point, and the difference between Jamilyah's reaction to Africa and Paula's reaction to this place.

The mother of the other Yumi, and Paula's other kin, had not been kidnapped and taken in chains to a foreign shore; they all had chosen to go.

Then for the first time she had another thought, astounding and heretical, stimulated perhaps by her reflections, recurring strongly now in this place, on Rick Kawabata and Japanese-Way. She had long wondered whether he had felt any surer of the meaning of *wabe* than she, despite his protestations and his flagellation of her.

Now it occurred to her that perhaps Jamilyah had never been as sure of her place in Africa as she had said she was. Or perhaps, driven by her own hunger, she had failed to see whatever might have lain in the eyes of the others, of skepticism or hostility, those who had been born on the shore to which she returned.

Someone told Alan Enomoto about Paula's trip, and he asked her out again. This time, she went.

Over an Italian dinner, he told her that he knew exactly what she felt now that she had been to Japan.

Perhaps she started seeing him regularly after that because he seemed so confident, and she had lost her confidence. Profoundly shaken by Will's disappearance, Paula had become intimidated by life and unsure of her own reactions. She was not sure what she felt about Japan; and when Alan told her, she heard him out meekly and did not contradict him.

She had, at that lost moment in her life, hoped he could give that life a shape and meaning she could not then provide for herself. Her choices of life and work were being undone. Her old comrades told her the '60's were over. Even Kaz's work on reparations bore, in its spirit, little relation to their original, communal vision of the world. And in her personal life she had swung wide and failed at every attempt: her father, José Sánchez, Will.

Since Alan was so self-assured, and because at bottom she was no longer able to care enough about much to assert herself, she did not contradict him either when at the beginning of the third month they had been seeing each other, he told her it was time to become engaged, and slipped onto the appropriate finger a very pretty jeweled gold ring.

But she knew her association with him was all wrong when he took her to see the house near the University where he wanted them to live, and everything in her rebelled under childhood memories of the University and under the memory of Will's words. "I see you in a house with a lawyer-man or a professor-man, out by the University."

Two days before the formal announcement of their engagement — Alan had insisted on that formality — Paula stood shivering in the echoing emptiness of her bungalow and clutched her elbows to make an X across her chest. The echoes of Alan's bitter steps died away on the cobbles of the courtyard.

He had wanted to be the one who was injured and abused, but she had seen the relief in his eyes and perversely it hurt her, although it also salved her guilt and confirmed her decision. I saved him the trouble, she thought, bitter herself; if I hadn't broken us up this week, he'd have done it the next.

She never even mentioned her engagement to the people at the place on the water; when she was there, it never had enough reality to make it worthwhile.

She understood, after they broke up, why she could not marry Alan: for all the reasons that she had told Ginnie, all these years, which crystallized in the seeming irrationality of what she had cried to him when he asked her for an explanation: "Because you tried to take over my life! Because you told me you knew why I had gone to Japan! You never asked me why!"

But originally, she had agreed to start seeing him again. That was her complicity, and her share of guilt. His was that she did not believe he cared for her, or even saw her, but had fixed on her long ago, angry because she went with Will, although she had decided against him first before she ever saw Will or the place on the water.

She understood that she did not want Alan's ring or what it represented. Still, standing alone in the light of the failing day, in the middle of her single room, her newly naked finger felt dangerously exposed. Life had rendered her aging, vulnerable and frail, and left her no future of ferns and lichens.

Blessed are those who know how to work.

Paula knew. After long days translating, environmental and indigenous rights cases throughout the islands benefited from the night oil she burned, burning off the pain in her life; benefited from the formidable energies and intelligence she poured into her efforts.

She began to think she should make steps to return to law — even to trial law. But, surprising herself, she could hardly bring herself to make the first moves. At last she made some inquiries.

Ginnie forgave her her break with Alan. She and Paula returned to their custom of having lunch together once a week.

Nani Wright, the young Hawaiian intern Paula had mentored, became a lawyer and went to work for a fledgling firm doing environmental and Native Rights and emphasizing employing Native Hawaiians. After a while, Paula learned that Pearlie Leilani was working with Nani part-time. Paula had introduced them; a friendship had grown.

This was a bittersweet satisfaction for Paula. She was proud of the young women and proud of her encouragement of them, and pleased at the friendship between them. But she seldom saw either of them anymore. The spheres they inhabited no longer had much overlap.

Schism and collapse. Paula had been here before.

Paula had a dream about sheaves of wheat.

The gathered golden grain stood in the air, then divided suddenly, as if dropped from loving arms, and fell gracefully into two separate lavish heaps on the ground. The very air seemed informed with light, and without words this light informed her dreaming self: It is not necessary to continue struggling to win the battle your father lost, or the ones he never lived to fight. It is enough to fight the battles following your own road in your own way. He gives you his blessing in this. And your mother forgives you your speaking and cancels her silence.

On waking she heard as if for the first time Ben's words as the two of them stood at the airfield, shocked by the vacuum of Will's sudden goneness.

This is not your blame.

And for the first time she believed it.

After a time of visiting Auntie Raina every month or so, Paula began to ponder her relationship to her work. Her reflections revolved around two things that Will had said to her: one on the day they had met: "You're your Daddy's girl. You take clients who can't pay, like he did;" and the other on the evening when, watching her, he had said in the big room in Hale Noname, "You have the deep habit of work for true."

She had always known that her work and her beliefs about it derived from her relationship with her father. Now, her father, who in her mind's eye had always been taller than she, began, not to shrink, but to reposition, and she saw suddenly that, in fact, she was the taller, by inches; and older by years than he had lived to be.

She began to wonder how her view of him as an adult would differ from her experience of him as a child. Had he truly been as free of racial prejudice as she believed? What would he have thought of David, a Black man? Of Will, White and poor-White? Of her arrests, her public combativeness?

She looked around her domain, the little bungalow in the courtyard. She was sitting in the spot that was most comfortable to her in the whole world: her own desk, surrounded by books and papers and references: by her work. With a flooding of emotion like dream, she re-inhabited her body, and realized how fulfilled and at one she was with the movements of her own mind when she did this architectural work, of the law, of linguistic interpretation. And at the same time she realized two other things: the terror she had always felt when she walked into a courtroom to put herself up for judgment before the hostile public eye, as her father had done on the last day of his life; the affliction she experienced when she had so much of another's fate riding on her ability to persuade by personality.

A tide of resentment of her father flooded her: that was your personality, not mine, she thought. The tide was followed immediately by contrition and sarcasm: it was indeed quite an accomplishment to blame her long unhappiness as a trial lawyer on her father, who had been dead ten years before she ever walked into a courtroom.

And contrition and sarcasm were followed by another jolting realization, like the one when she saw she was taller in her adulthood than he had been: in fact she did not know if he thrived on trial law or not. Probably he could have learned to, despite the cruel comments she had overheard about his courtroom manner. But if he had been able to bring to the arena of the courtroom anything of the person he was at the Black Star, he would have shone.

His bright laughter loosed in the world like a flock of birds.

But how could she know? He had tried one case and lost it and died. Still, for her, her entire life's work, and most of her deep emotional work, was locked around the events of that week: an endless repetition of the attempt to make the trial come out differently and his life not end with its ending.

What did she know of him? She knew that he had loved her, failed her in certain vital ways, overwhelmingly been her support.

Now the lock broke, as the sheaves had fallen. Paula wept, for the father she had never been able to know as an adult, for the man he had never lived to become, the work he had never lived to do. Wept, not for him as her father, but for that man, another person, with another life's work than hers.

The intellectual fulfillment she found in the law separated out and she realized she found it as fully in her work with language.

She had a new set of cards printed up for her work as a translator and editor. They carried a new design: a set of graceful sheaves of wheat, backed by a spreading heart-shaped leaf of kalo.

Paula stopped pursuing a return to the legal profession.

Will Cawdry's fate was not her blame; and her life's work was her own and not her father's.

Thinking of her father and his political times, she thought of her own times too: Cointelpro, Reagan, the rise and the fall of the Sandinistas, the struggle against apartheid, the Gulf War; in her own immediate life, the shock of Loma Prieta in California, of Iniki who tore the islands' life and disturbed her own neighborhood with invading armies of roughneck haoles, itinerant construction workers from the States, booted and harsh.

Storm and flood, quiet dawns and work; time flowed by. And she came into a quiet sense of her self-completeness in her own life, with or without Will.

Threading her way through busy noontime crowds in downtown Honolulu, the same air as in her dream spoke to her, as clearly and also without words: It is time to visit Auntie Raina.

From whom she also heard: This is not your blame.

So it broke, the lock binding her to her sense of blame and responsibility for her father's life and Will's; and another lock broke too. Bound with her sense of blame for Will's fate, she let herself become sharply aware of her guilt at the ways she had held back from speech and closeness with him because of her fear; and began to release herself not from her regret, but from her guilt.

And she faced something else too. She remembered the day Ginnie had come to Euph's, and for the first time admitted to herself that, among all her other feelings, she had been ashamed of Will. Ashamed of his not-always-deliberate erratic accent and non-standard grammar; of the startling, unpredictable gaps in what her educated circle considered basic knowledge; ashamed of his taste, considered atrocious in those same circles, so jarring next to his exquisite musical sense.

And she began to be able to face the worst of all: that she could not make any amends, that she could not try to see if he and she could come to some greater closeness and trust, and that she very likely never would be able to, because he was gone.

That part of her life's work must be to live with the gaping emptiness and unfinishedness, to hem over the wound and live with the scar and the dismemberment inflicted by the deep goneness of Will. And, paradoxically, to appreciate the central completion and completeness of her own life, that she had come to know with the fall of sheaves.

A great hungry restlessness seized her, that drove her to consult Auntie Raina about its meaning. Soon after that visit, it came to her that she had unfinished business back in the U.S.

Thankful for the flexibility and portability of her business as an editor and translator, she contacted Kaz and had him rent a small studio apartment for her. She made her necessary notifications and arrangements in Honolulu, spent a farewell weekend with Emma and Ben, sublet her bungalow, and left for San Francisco.

34

T.C.B.: San Francisco and Chicago

Flashbulbs went off. Above her the dome of the great rotunda of San Francisco City Hall revolved in her vision like the top of an observatory with the heavens circling.

The reparations group Paula had worked with so hard for so many years had just won a crucial decision. Paula, no longer formally a member of the team, had participated in their discussions, become in fact a part of their group again. She had wondered if, sitting in the courtroom, she would feel regret at not being one of those who argued the case; but she had felt only relief, and a further relief that relief brought no guilt.

A few feet away, Kaz Nakamura, who had made the summing up, was being photographed as he spoke with reporters. Dazed at the victory after so long, Paula still found it in her to feel a wry affectionate amusement at his arrogant presentation of self. He had made a brief move to resume their affair, but she had refused, and things remained on the relatively even keel they had established before she moved to Hawai'i.

A group of loyal supporters surrounded them, a few Issei but mostly Nisei. Clad in their very best, they had sat day after day in the courtroom.

Something pushed against her hands and she opened them automatically to keep the object from falling. A bouquet of crimson roses.

Mrs. Kaku, bent over now, a head shorter than Paula, leaning on a cane, smiled from a network of wrinkles.

"For you." She spoke in Japanese.

"Hello, Mrs. Kaku! I hadn't seen you in court before today!" Paula spoke Japanese too.

"I haven't been here. I was in the hospital."

"I'm sorry — "

The old woman brushed it away. "Age. Just age. I made them let me out for the decision today. I'm sorry you went away. You like Hawai'i?"

"Very much."

"I did too. I was a girl on Kaua'i." She paused a moment, looking a long way back, then focused again on Paula. "You work as a lawyer there?"

"No, I'm not a lawyer any more, though I give legal advice sometimes. I'm a translator now."

Mrs. Kaku nodded. "The same work. Making things understood. But yes, I can see that translating might be more your way, even though you were good in court."

Paula smiled. "You are generous towards both of my professions, especially the law."

The old lady laughed. "In some cases, maybe so." She indicated Kaz. "He is very good. But I liked your way of speaking in court better than his. More about what is being said, less about yourself." She twinkled. "I thank you all, though. And I am glad you are here today. You have worked hard for this day to come."

"Thank you, Mrs. Kaku."

Then Paula buried her face in the bouquet, unsure that she could speak, and tried to hide her tears, drawing strength from the deep sweetness of the flowers.

Mrs. Kaku patted her shoulder.

Another flashbulb flared red against her closed lids. She opened her eyes to find a young reporter with longish blonde hair backing the supporters up against the wall, bombarding them with questions. The depth of her rage at him, her protectiveness of the elderly supporters, surprised her, as she moved to intervene.

Mrs. Kaku didn't need her assistance in that way today. She seized Paula's wrist, more giving than getting support, and stepped forward. Her English had probably never been fluent and stress fragmented it further, but her voice was authoritative as she said, looking from the reporter to Paula,

"In our time it was not easy for us to speak out, especially about these matters. But they have been a heavy burden to us for many years, and so we are grateful to our Sansei generation."

Paula, Sansei generation, went to the cemetery where Uncle Hiro and Aunt Florence lay and stayed quietly there for a time.

Paula went to Chicago and rented a room at the downtown Y. Then she rode the Illinois Central to Hyde Park, and began to walk West. She walked along 50th Street, avoiding the University.

She didn't know why she expected the building her family had lived in to be gone. Because she did, she almost missed it, and was already turning to leave when the sight of a roofline against the sky stopped her in her tracks, catching her breath in her throat.

The building seemed smaller. Someone had painted the yellow brick white and the brown window ledges green, but she would have known that outline of her home anywhere, that view when she turned the corner into her block, walking from the school bus stop at the corner.

Two girls about eight and ten, blonde hair flying, backpacks bouncing against their shoulders, dashed from the bus-stop end of the block. Sisters, probably. They were fighting. The bigger one landed a solid punch on the smaller one's chest. They ran up the steps of the house where Paula had once lived. The younger one jammed the doorbell. An unfamiliar buzzer sounded. The door opened and they disappeared inside. The door closed.

Paula stood looking after them. Powerfully, irrationally, she thought with outrage, What are strangers doing in the home where we lived and where Father died?

She walked around the corner, to where she could see the window of her father's study.

Curtains hung there, but they were not the rough black cotton ones with the golden scimitar-shaped leaves that had framed the window in her childhood.

Her heart beat fast as she looked into the shadowy alley where long ago she had been attacked. Across it stood the huge rabbit-warren building where Jim Jordan had lived in a basement apartment, a building that in her earliest childhood had been crammed with the Poles and Lithuanians and Czechs who had been her family's nemeses, then with Southern Blacks, Whites from Appalachia, Puerto Ricans. Since Paula had gone away, the building had been engineered to affluence and good breeding. No more peeling wooden doors, no broken windows or chipped cement sills. No basement apartments at all any more, she noticed. Even the alley had been cleaned up, and the city was emptying the garbage cans these days, too; unbattered lids fitted over contents that no longer bulged with the uncollected contributions of weeks.

A big upper-middle-class apartment building in a good neighborhood.

But where had all the neighbors gone?

Suddenly ill, Paula leaned her head against sun-warmed brick. The overpowering scent of lilac and the hum of bees enveloped her, bringing back not memory but feeling, a rush of terror and rage: Die, slant-eyes! *Kamikaze!*

She pressed her fingers against the scar at her temple, against a rising threat of pain in her head. She found both hands clutching her throat.

She yielded herself to the tearing grief between her shoulder-blades; and then, to sobs she did not try to quiet and that slowed after a fierce brief time, disappearing at last, taking with them the threatened dreaded headache.

She walked to the corner, where the last building on the block had been the Black Star. In those days a small neighborhood grocery store had adjoined it; there she and her father picked up items her mother had forgotten in the weekly big shopping at the A & P, before stepping next door for a little pool and conversation. On one of those bread-and-milk runs he had told her for the first time the story of Cruz and Kalani and the other Yumi.

Here on the corner in front of the Black Star, Black men had stood about during the long months when, her father told her, the country was in recession; and often Thomas Graves would stand in his doorway and detail for the men his understanding of the reason for Black peoples' disaster, and what to do about it.

But the store and the Black Star were gone. A large brick home, finely maintained, stood in its place. Black men, first idled here, had now been banished altogether.

Where have the neighbors gone?

And Mrs. Lili'uokalani Turner. Surely her building had stood here, four doors down, where a handsome town house with a manicured lawn now reigned.

Had the meeting she was remembering occurred in 1957? One of those dreadful Chicago winter days she wondered now how she had survived, the wind off the Lake cutting her calves even through leggings as she walked beside her father along Cottage Grove. When she got home and peeled the leggings off, she knew her skin would be marked with red welts. She and her father were hurrying, yet both engrossed in their conversation: he was talking story about Hawai'i, she no longer remembered precisely about what.

A bus lumbered and belched to a halt at the corner, spewing black fumes into the air, then pulled away so fast the elderly Black woman burdened with paper shopping bags stumbled and went to her knees in a pile of dirty snow.

"Mrs. Turner!" Paula's father stepped forward and Paula recognized their neighbor from two doors down. She sat in a straight-backed chair on her stoop on summer evenings and greeted everyone who walked by.

Her father helped the woman to her feet, dusted snow off her, rescued her bags from the snow before the soaked bottoms fell out of them. Paula, cold, irritated, bored at the diversion of her father's attention, looked away, sulkily.

"Paula!"

Her father spoke sharply in a way he seldom addressed her, especially in front of people outside the family.

"Mrs. Turner has had a fall. Say "Hello" to her, then take one of her bags, and be careful, it's wet."

And they went on their way, Paula awkwardly cradling one grocery bag, her father carrying the other and his arm under Mrs. Turner's elbow. Paula sulkier now, hurt at being publicly reprimanded, and knowing, for the first time, that her father had been expressing his expectation that she would behave towards him and towards Mrs. Turner as he was behaving towards the older woman: the respect due greater age.

They slowly went up the four flights to her apartment, Mrs. Turner's breathing labored. She hesitated just a moment, then asked them in: later, in testimonial at the Association's last meeting at St. Samuel's the night the case was lost, she told how she had never spoken with a Japanese before that day, but now had come to call Mark, Mr. Kajiyama, a friend. "As many of you here know, he showed me how to say my own name."

She lived in one room and kitchen, dim like the Kajiyamas' apartment because brick walls pressed within inches of almost every window. The place was shabby but tidy and almost painfully clean, as if to make up for the poverty as much as to answer the requirements of hygiene.

The whistle of a coffee pot, cups on the worn green oilcloth covering the kitchen table, feathery homemade biscuits with honey, and conversation: somewhat stiff and shy at first. Then her father, visibly surprised, staring at a tiny fading photograph cut from a newspaper and displayed on the wall in a curlicued silvery frame. Then Mrs. Turner's surprise, her exuberance, her first name: "Though most calls me Lil," and her laugh, loud and rich, that reminded Paula of her father's in its freedom and joyousness.

"A lot of little girls in Virginia got named Lili'uokalani about the time I was." The five trips the Queen had made to Washington to try and get her country back. "You say her brother invited you folks to come there from Japan? When he was King just before she was Queen? He had the power to do that?" She told of the pride and satisfaction Black people, living deep in Jim Crow, felt about a Black Queen (for they saw at once that she was Black, and that she was every inch a Queen.) "Fact is, my full name is Queen

Lili'uokalani, though I mostly doesn't use the 'Queen'. I've been 'Lil' since I was a girl. My mother kept that picture hanging so her girls would know what a Black woman could be somewhere else in the world. Though I don't reckon she ever did get her country back from the White folks?"

"No, she didn't. But these struggles take a long time, Mrs. Turner."

"Ain't that the truth."

At Mrs. Turner's request, her father gave her a lesson in how the Queen had pronounced the name they shared.

Trying it out on her tongue: she had gotten the stop after 'Lili'. "You're a natural at languages, Mrs. Turner." Her pleased laugh. " Well, you call me by my name. 'Lili'uokalani.' Don't reckon I know anyone else who's gonna be able to get their tongue round it."

And after that he did, and she showed him off, and her name, and the story, at St. Samuel's, at the Association meetings, when they encountered each other on the street.

More about her life. Her husband, sharecropping then stevedoring in and around Charleston, the move to Chicago, laborer's work when he could get it. He had died early, "jest worked himself out, did Silas." And young Silas: a hesitation then. They had all been aware of the high school graduation portrait in another silvery frame, on top of the big radio. A smiling boy, square-faced like his mother. "He were very quick, young Silas. Specially in math. He finished high school, right here in Chicago. He died in the Pacific, 1943. His father lived to see him graduate but not to see him taken. There are mercies I'm grateful for."

The silence. The silences that slashed crevasses in Paula's life in the country where she was born. Then Lili'uokalani Turner said, "But that don't make those camps they put you folks in right. I have heard about them, and that weren't right at all."

After that, more days of tea and homemade biscuits drenched in warmed honey with her father and sometimes without, when she was walking down the street and Mrs. Turner sitting on her stoop invited her in, to talk story about her life lived in several different worlds. The details Paula no longer remembered; but the texture and cadences of those days, like the days at the Black Star, like the murmurs and laughter overheard from her father's study when he and Jim Jordan laughed and talked as she drifted into sleep, stayed with her and prepared her for friendships with David, with Caroline who became Jamilyah; prepared her to recognize them again, obliquely and unexpectedly, in Will. Prepared her for Euph's enigmatic eyes, watching from wherever he had got to.

Across the street had stood St. Samuel's Abyssinia Baptist Church, proud domain of the Reverend Cletis Auburn, who had defended her father when the Association schismed and collapsed, who had come to her father's memorial service when almost none of his congregation would, and for that been voted out as their pastor. But St. Samuel's was gone, replaced by a twin of the house that replaced the Black Star. Paula wondered where the Reverend Cletis Auburn had gone; where he was now, if he were still alive.

In the next block, she passed the great bulk of St. Anthony's Catholic Church. When she looked more closely, though, she saw that in a fundamental sense St. Anthony's had gone from the neighborhood as surely as St. Samuel's. The sign in front offered a single daily mass, not the numerous masses of her childhood; and in English only. The huge parochial school that had received the swarms of neighborhood children, Czech and Polish and later Puerto Rican, had been razed. The concrete playground area had been expanded and part of it planted as a grass lawn with picnic benches. She thought of Father Hurley, who like Mrs. Turner had never talked to a "Japanese person" before meeting her father, but had come to the Association to be a neighbor and help save the neighborhood they shared. He too had attended her father's memorial service, standing in the receiving line just behind Jim Jordan, just in front of Mrs. Lili'uokalani Turner and Reverend Auburn. How could that memory be etched so clearly before her mind's eye?

Beside the grass lawn, on the corner, the smaller two-story rectory, where Father Hurley had lived, still stood. But a discreet wooden sign planted in the grass before his front door read "University Newman Center Adjunct."

Father Hurley's front door opened and two young men and a young woman emerged onto the path. They looked like older brothers and sister to the two little girls who lived in what had been Paula's family home.

Suddenly she didn't want to be there any more. Whatever she had come for was done. She turned and walked quickly toward the lake and the train that would take her back to the Loop. She chose the route that would take her past the Windermere Gardens.

The Windermere Gardens was gone too. A row of well-tended expensive town houses stood in its place, announced by a genteel brass plaque as "University Grove."

Waiting on the IC platform, Paula's unfocused gaze traveled West along the track, then South. For a startled moment, she saw Mauna Kea etched against the sky.

Jerked back to the present by the roar of a passing train, she suddenly realized that the atmosphere was lowering, the sky had turned an unearthly greenish-black, and the hot oppressive air was completely still. Robbie Cawdry's wide blue lake had grown leaden and livid. Tornado weather.

People around her stirred and murmured. They seemed to sniff the air, toss their heads, the way horses would be doing, in danger away out there on the prairie.

The sudden falling pressure sucked the life and breath out of the world. Nature had dropped into some irreversible, bottomless depression.

An overwhelming anguish wracked Paula, doubling her over as she stood, an anguish held at bay almost all of the time since Will Cawdry headed on out without a flight plan and without sending word, since the day she turned his music off and walked out the door of her bungalow.

Oh, where is Will? she cried silently. What is going to happen? What has become of him?

A television blared in the YMCA coffee shop where Paula ate her dinner. She watched the devastation: two farms and an entire block of houses in an outer suburb had been destroyed. Three people had been killed.

On impulse she bought an inexpensive watercolor set and drawing pad in the gift shop.

Later in her room she tuned in a jazz station and sat down at the narrow desk with her ink, pen and paints. Listening to Trane and Yardbird, to Henderson, to others Will had loved and played so often, she painted a painting and remembered.

She was a very little girl, jumping up and down in front of the home she had seen today for the first time in almost thirty years. She could feel the glorious stretching in her muscles, she could feel her exaltation and exultation as she shouted to her father and mother standing near,

"When I grow up I'm going to be as tall as the sky!"

She and Will had hiked two days to reach the remote spot on the slope of Mauna Loa that had a view he wanted her to see.

He was pleased and proud like a little boy to have brought her here. He had shown her something worth seeing, for true. She had thought of the childhood chant for the first time in decades, looking at him then: "I'm the King of the Mountain!" She had remembered her own words: "When I grow up, I'm going to be as tall as the sky."

Suddenly he was anxious. She could read his moods by then. Was she pleased, was it enough? He darted a glance at her, then back to Mauna Kea, soaring in the distance.

"This is a place of great mana," he had said.

She searched for a way to let him know it was sufficient, it was all she had dreamed or could hope for, only different from her life before or imagined before because she had never known this until she came here.

She had replied simply, "I know."

But now so many years later she was gnawed by the thought that at that moment she had failed again, verbally, that he hadn't known how she felt. She was tormented by this great fault of silence in her, this insufficiency for the world.

Somewhere in her painting Snow Sleeper lay, there at the summit of the tallest mountain in the world, frozen in silence, by sleep and by snow.

Somewhere in her painting stood a Mountain King. Somewhere in her painting, in a boiling cauldron of massed black and unearthly green, outcast soldier's raiment or a tornado sky — somewhere at the heart of the pressure drop of nature into a bottomless chaotic abyss — somewhere lay a balance. Somewhere, at the heart of all radical insufficiency in the universe, something sufficed.

But that night it seemed to her that the sufficiency existed only as an affirmation she had been able to body forth in her painting. It did not reach to touch her life.

She called the painting "*Pele Dancing*."

35

T.C.B.: Southern Road

After the bombing of South Regional Headquarters, Paula had never wanted to go South again. She had lived her political life in other places.

She did not want to go to Hibbits.

On a suffocatingly hot mid-afternoon, she bounced down a rutted Texas road in a rental car, following a Black man's directions.

"Lawd, I shonuff remember Euph," he had said, and the cadences of Will Cawdry's speech echoed in her ears again. "Euph Hiquens. Why, must be near thirty years since he passed. I weren't but a boy and I weren't s'posed to hang round the Blue Box neither, but couldn't nothing keep me from his music. Ain't heard the like of it since, not since he passed and that little whiteboy he looked out for, you could tell might play as good as Euph someday, vanished from hereabouts." He made "whiteboy" one word. "Euph had a powerful teaching, that has helped me through my times. The little whiteboy?" he answered her question, "his name was Will Cawdry. If you don't mind my asking, M'a'am, how d'you come to know of all this?"

In this place her face was emphatically the face of the stranger, and for some — though not for this man, she thought — the face of the enemy too. She felt an urge to cover her tracks.

"I have met Mr. Cawdry," she said formally. "He is a successful and respected businessman. And he plays the piano the way you say Euph did — and honors Euph for it."

The man was pleased. "That skinny whiteboy? Well, don't that beat all. You see him, tell him Rufe Hollis say hello, and got hisself a gen'ral store in Andrewsville, doin' right well and glad to hear he is too. Don't that beat all," he said again, "hearin' 'bout Will Cawdry after all these years. Tell him the Blue Box is gone now. 'Tweren't never the same after Euph passed, and the county tore it down 'bout two, three years later, for a school what never got built. The Thornbrake took the land instead. The girls as worked there all went on down to Andrewsville, or further still down the road."

"Do you remember Bertha?"

"Right enough I do. Liked her likker, Bertha, and her little camera. Bertha, she passed, too, not long after Euph. But if it's the cemetery for the cullud you're after, just keep goin' straight and you'll find it right enough.

We put a good wooden cross up for Euph Hiquens, I reckon it's standing still."

So she continued on, half-blinded by clouds of dust, through the Texas Thornbrake Starvesoil, Will Cawdry's talk-stories coming to life through all her senses, somehow both surreal and surreally intense, in this blazing summer; and she arrived at what was still "the cemetery for the cullud."

She picked her way through the tough gray razorgrass whipping in the wind. Even with her care two blades drew blood across her bare calves.

She was alone. The grass, the dust, the twisted brake with its dangerous thorns beyond, and the wide sky stretched around and above her.

From the back of the car she took a small heavy rectangular plaque. She'd foreseen some of the difficulties, and brought a shovel and water, but even so had to settle for making a shallower space tamped down as securely as she could; she couldn't make any more headway in the baked earth. Still, it was on the ground, the way Will had wanted it. "I'd lay it flat," he had said, "so can't no one knock it down. It'd have his full name." When the stone reposed beside the weathered cross, she stood catching her breath and looking down at it.

The engraving read:

Euphonious "Euph" Frederick Douglass Toussaint Hiquens
Gave his music and his teaching in New Orleans
and Hibbits and other places too.
Born circa 1877 in the summer
Died December 10 1959
In Memoriam
From Will Cawdry

"I'd make the marker pink marble," Will had said, "the kind with the white veining in it. And I'd have letters carved real deep and colored gold."

Paula had shuddered, marvelling as she often did at his lapses from what to her was good taste. She felt her shame now at this, acknowledged again that he had embarrassed her in front of Ginnie, in her Honolulu life, as Will had called it at the end, with such pain and scorn. Tears pricked her eyes and she pushed them away and drew from her satchel the exquisite magical scarf that Will had given her, that Euph had given to him for her,

that had come from New Orleans and before that from Haiti and before
that from Africa, and that was older than time.

"The epitaph'd say — " he had paused, but only to organize the delivery:
she thought that he had reflected on the content often. "Oh, something
like 'Euphonious.'"

"Euphonious?" she had repeated, incredulous.

"Yeh. 'Euphonious' means 'harmony,' pretty much. His mama thought
the name were beautiful and dignified and it sure turned out to fit him too,
what with his music and all. Anyhow, since a marking stone is formal-like, it
ought to have his full name on it. 'Euphonious Frederick Douglass Toussaint
Hiquens. Gave his music and his teaching in New Orleans and Hibbits and
other places too. Born 1877' — 'course, he didn't know the year exactly, or
the date, but I remember he said it was in the summertime. And you gotta
have a date on a marking stone for the beginning as well as the end, if you're
doing it right and proper, and he always did say his timing were bad, he
come in the world the year the good laws for the cullud got repealed and the
Klan started riding, after Slavery Times. By what I've learned in my reading
that makes it the end of Ree-construction. So 1877 seems as good a year as
any. 'Born 1877, in the summer, and died December 10 1959.' And I'd lay
the stone down flat, so couldn't no one knock it down. Reckon folks'll chip
it or mar it or destroy it altogether, being as its Hibbits we're talkin' about
and being as it's got my name on it — because it's gonna have my name on
it, Euph would want it so, as much as I do. But at least it'll be laid down
flat, so can't no one knock it flat. Euph'd like that thinking: keeping one
step ahead of the opposition. And for respect I'll pour a libation for him
and the rest of the Ancestors, like he used to do, then leave a jar for him.
Johnny Walker Black — show him I made it out of the Starvesoil after all,
and could buy my likker, smooth. And for just a few minutes or hours or
however long folks let it be, it's gonna show forth in the world how much
Will Cawdry thought of Euph Hiquens."

She knelt in the dust beside the marking stone, poured the libation, set
the jar full of Johnny Black next to it, and went away.

"My Little Mama didn't want no grave."

His words returned to her with almost frightening clarity in this place
from which he'd come.

"Said she'd like to be slipped into the biggest lake in the world, just like
sailors at sea in a movie we saw one time." He'd given the smile, at once

deprecating and protective and deeply sad, that so often accompanied his tales of his mother. "She were pointing at the Pacific Ocean in my school geography book when she said that. Well, since life in its mysterious ways has worked out that I live right near the Pacific, I took care of that a long time ago." And he told her of the lei he had asked Pearlie Leilani to weave, that he had set adrift off the coast at Honokaa.

So now Paula traveled the half mile down the road in the other direction, to the White cemetery she had passed on the way to Euph's grave.

Bert's and Will's Grampa's were there, the crosses faded and askew. She found no marker for Robbie Cawdry, though she went carefully through the place, especially the untended part, the paupers' and sinners' side.

Somewhere in that expanse of dirt and razorgrass, presumably at least within the cemetery boundary of sagging wire fencing, Robbie Cawdry had long since turned to dust.

Paula stood a few minutes in the shelter from heat provided by a struggling oak of some kind, and thought about Robbie Cawdry and about Robbie Cawdry's boy. She imagined the day that Will's mother got off the Greyhound bus in Chicago with Will's hand clutched in one of hers and her banjo in the other, and headed off to see herself a lake.

But the image was too painful. She held it only a moment, then laid down on an open space a gay bright bouquet of grasses and flowers she had picked on her way to Hibbits, that reminded her of the bouquet she had left at that other, lake-named, place where she had been born.

Then she went away from this place too.

She had negotiated the dirt track and was back on the country road that would take her to the Interstate, and what felt like comparative safety, when the lawman's car pulled her over.

Paula had seen him approaching from a good distance off on this empty narrow stretch of ill-maintained tarmac, and by the time his intentions were clear her palms were sweaty.

She sat, her hands high on the steering wheel to make obvious that she had no weapon. She watched in the rear view mirror as the man got out, slammed his door, and approached; and she tried to slow her pounding heart.

He was alone, a big bulky man, ten years older than she, with a sun-creased, florid face. He wore a uniform and a wide-brimmed hat. He motioned her to roll down the window and leaned a meaty arm on its edge, deliberately impinging on her space. His nameplate read "R. Armstrong." Paula let him speak first.

"Lost?" His voice was gravelly. "Need directions?"

His intelligent water-gray eyes, sharp behind a surface laziness, told her that he knew she didn't, that he knew who she was, had been looking for her, and didn't mind her knowing.

"No," she forced her voice to be neutral. "Thank you."

"You're not from hereabouts."

"No," she agreed, still fighting down anything construable as a challenge.

"License."

She passed it over. He studied it. "Funny name," he said. "We don't git many of your kind in Hibbits. This country hereabouts is still American." He handed the license back, and continued to look at her with an impassivity that, disconcertingly, reminded her of Will, as Rufe Hollis's speech, even more than this man's, had reminded her of Will's. "Don't git many strangers at all. Quiet place. My job's to keep track of things. See it stays quiet."

She said nothing, letting him carry the interaction. Her heart had not slowed and she hoped he could not hear it.

"Ran into Rufe Hollis a piece back. One of our local niggers. Our cullud." He made the correction mockingly, assessing her. "He said you know someone from hereabouts. Will Cawdry."

She did not think that Rufe had sought the Sheriff out, nor that he would have volunteered this information unless he thought it desirable in maintaining his health and well-being, and she noted, with interest and gratitude, that even under this pressure he had not mentioned Euph.

"Yes," she allowed.

"I remember Will Cawdry," said R. Armstrong, echoing Rufe Hollis. Her sense of unreality increased. This dusty, desolate, heat-struck place, with its strange stunted foliage — the Thornbrake Starvesoil of Will Cawdry's recounting, the sky the same pale blue as his eyes — brought alive the emotions she had heard in his voice as he spoke of it to her.

And it unnerved her to hear people talk of Will Cawdry, out of the context in which she knew him, which was so different — people he had conjured by his words, conjured by his personality, by his kinship to them, at that long-ago first meeting in Volcano.

It was as if his reminiscences were being staged for her now.

Heat made the world shimmer before her eyes as she listened to R. Armstrong.

"Lighted on outta here over thirty years ago and ain't no one heard a word of him since. Till today." He continued to stare at her. "No loss. He weren't from the best of families. Weren't from no family at all, speaking proper."

"You'll be married right and proper," Will's voice sounded in her ears; and her throat constricted. "Have an 'ohana of your own."

"Yeh, I remember Will Cawdry. Robbie Cawdry's bastard. 'Twoulda been right hard to put a family name to him, I reckon. Coulda took his pick from most any man in this county. And mebbe the closer to home the closer the guess. The Cawdrys, they were known hereabouts, and some said they'd been known to breed their own stock, if you take my meaning. 'Course, I'm too young to have him laid at my door, but not too young for Robbie. Fact is, Robbie were my first woman." He leered suddenly, the veiled eyes watching for her reaction, which she fought to conceal. "Me and four friends, I were fourteen-fifteen, and the little bastard was sleeping behind a blanket hung up to divide the house — ifn you'd call that one-room shack a house. Cost the five of us a standard sack of dried peas and six cans of ee-vaporated milk. Local store didn't have the milk, so I drove all the way to Andrewsville to buy it. That were the arrangement. Robbie lived by making sich-like arrangements. Yeh, Robbie Cawdry. I shore do remember her."

He gave another leer. It vanished. "And now you're here to tell of Robbie Cawdry's boy. So you're his. Don't surprise me," he ruminated. "He went to the bad early, like his ma. Took to hanging around with niggers. After Robbie passed, up to Shee-kah-go, and Bert brought the boy back here, he practically lived with 'em, at that cathouse yonder, the Blue Box, with that ole drunk nigger piano player, Euph. One thing I'll say for Robbie, she didn't go with no niggers. Least as far as we knowed around here. Wouldn'ta put up with that. Mebbe she went that far to the bad up in Shee-kah-go. But she never carried on so around here. One thing you kin tell Will Cawdry, he kin be sure he's White. Don't look like his kids kin say the same."

"Mr. Cawdry," said Paula, through lips stiff with rage, "Mr. Will Cawdry — has made a great success. He was decorated twice for bravery in the Vietnam War." She hardly believed her own ears, what she had been reduced to by this place. "Afterwards he became a prominent businessman. He is very much respected in his own community."

The eyes narrowed. "Veet-nam," he repeated. "That explains you, I reckon. You people're moving in down along of the Gulf, I hear. Ruining the fishing. So you're one of them, huh." His eyes stripped her.

"I have a plane to catch tonight," she said, to give him pause if he had any ideas of taking his harassment further. "People are expecting me soon."

The New South. Not nearly new enough. She thought of the cemetery for the cullud, and wondered, now in 1992, as she had in 1964, where they would dump her corpse. One disappeared Veet-namese woman name of Kadjiyammer, fished out of a river, if there was one with water in it anywhere around? Or would they run her all the way to the Gulf?

R. Armstrong seemed to come to a decision, reluctantly.

"That so? Well, sounds like a right good idea. Like I say, this here's a quiet place. The likes of Will Cawdry and his friends don't fit in too good."

He stepped back and away from the car.

Paula jerked it into gear, almost stalled, willed herself to self-control, and headed down the tarmac with a screech of tires.

He followed her past the turnoff to Hibbits, and all the way to the Interstate.

"Stay," said Kaz.

The group around the court case was breaking up after their goodbye dinner for her. She would fly out tomorrow. She had vetoed offers of a ride. Of all good-byes she hated airport good-byes the most; she had too many memories of Hilo and returning to Honolulu, and of Will.

Now she shook her head.

"I'm your Hawai'i agent," she teased. "What would the group do for on-the-ground information on the Hawaiian community if I weren't there?"

"Seriously, Paula. You could get a good job here easily, you know."

"I'm flattered and touched. Instead, all of you come and visit me."

"But why? You never told me much about what holds you there."

"I live there, Kaz," she said gently. "Hawai'i is home."

She kissed him lightly on the cheek.

Walking under the dim yellow corridor light for the last time, up the three flights of stairs to her room, she thought of how she hadn't told Kaz that Auntie Raina — who came to her now, in dreams, at times — had confirmed for her that her own intuition was right, that her life's roots were in Hawai'i and that after this sojourn here on the American continent, her work in this place was done.

36

Magic Dust

For days Waikīkī and the neighboring Kap'iolani district had lain under that mist which comes down through the passes in the Koolaus and blots out expanses of the mountainside. Comes so thickly that no one who didn't know could have told that behind it lay those sharp-ribbed volcanic flanks that brace the island's spine.

At night not even the city lights trailing up their gullies like torches could penetrate that mist.

Towards twilight of the seventh day rain began to fall.

Like slipping into the sea, Paula slipped easily back into her life in Honolulu. As they had agreed, the person to whom she had sublet had cleaned and vacated her apartment the day before her return. The person using her office had cleared away his mug and released Paula's work space back to her.

But it was more than that. As her dream of Auntie Raina had confirmed, and as she had told Kaz, in returning to Hawai'i she had indeed come home.

Still she was always glad of her frequent conversations with him, and she was glad to remain a part of their group, regularly forwarding information she researched concerning the nadir years.

"I knew somebody once," she said to Kaz during one of those conversations, "who was owed government money and wouldn't touch any of it even for a good cause."

"Very noble. Nisei? We've been through all that with people. It's all right with me. I'd like to divide what we get among the rest. There won't be that much, you can bet on it, and enough of our people are old and poor. They could use it."

Paula smiled briefly, as if Kaz could see her.

"No," she said. "He wasn't Nisei." She paused. "The money had blood on it. That's why he wouldn't touch it. Even though some of the blood was his."

Paula stood in the middle of the living room at Hale Noname, and looked around, aimlessly. But what aim could she have here?

Nothing had changed that she could see. Ben maintained the place as it had been when Will disappeared. And she was afraid to ask him why, or for how long he planned to keep on.

The BookShack was the same as it had been, too: the old armchair, the fine polished wood floor, the reading chair and ottoman big enough for Will, and the little table beside it. The lamp arced just where his left shoulder would have been. Shelves stood packed tight with books. She took in again the skylight, the uncurtained window high in the rear wall. She had thought more than once that it was as if he didn't want anyone to see him reading, to know that he read. As if he, Will Cawdry, an apparition looming up from the Thornbrake Starvesoil, had no right to read.

And on the floor beneath the window, the only other object in the room, the chest of 'ōhi'a wood.

Paula sat cross-legged on the floor and lifted the lid.

Everything was still there; the leather portfolio containing copies of his few private papers — she remembered his insistence that she hold copies too, even after Bill Horita became his lawyer. Birth affidavit — sworn long after the fact; no birth certificates were issued for the lonely home deliveries in the Starvesoil — high school equivalency, military discharge, will. Title to the land in Noname Lane, title to the Caravan, papers of incorporation of Volcano Flights, of Euph's and the Pine Tar. The staples were evenly aligned, every sheet was crisp and clean. She remembered thinking, long ago, that he handled "papers" with that combination of wariness and reverence shown by the barely literate too often disempowered by them.

And here, at the bottom of the portfolio, an incomplete application to the University of Hawai'i at Mānoa, dated two years before she met him.

He had never told her of it. What had led him to initiate an application? What had made him change his mind? And why had he never spoken of it?

She recognized the length of plain white cotton Will had unwrapped to reveal the kerchief that Euph had given him for her. After her return from the Mainland, she had replaced it in the closet with his music.

The cloth bulged out as if it still protected something.

A faint recollection stirred. From that night when Will had opened the cloth, she recalled a small jar or phial. He had caught it in his big fingers as it started to roll, tucked it back inside a corner of the cotton, because it wasn't what mattered then, it wasn't the kerchief Euph had given him for her. And after that night she had forgotten it.

Now she unwrapped the cloth.

The jar was as she remembered, about four inches tall and one inch around, cylindrical, an unobtrusive brownish-gray, the color, form, texture and glazing Japanese. Hadn't Will said Euph had given him the phial too? How had Euph come by a Japanese ceramic jar, down to Hibbits?

Carefully, she rotated the cork stopper.

As she dislodged it, a tremendous thunderclap shook the 'ōhi'a forest all around, and set the BookShack trembling.

But that trembling was not just thunder — she recognized Pele's hand as well.

She jumped up, tensed to flee to open ground.

But the temblor had ceased.

Now, glancing up at the high window that gave no view of the outside but for sky, she saw that, distracted as she was, she had failed to notice how the gray day had converted itself to a lowering storm.

Like an escaping genie not yet having quite assumed its form, a little puff of dust billowed out of the phial's mouth, danced in a dull-green swarm above her left knee, then slowly settled on her jeans and on the wooden floor.

Grimacing, she replaced the stopper and shook the remaining grains of greenish powder back to the bottom of the phial. She re-wrapped it in its white cotton, replaced it in its corner of the 'ōhi'a chest, and closed the lid.

Then she brushed off her pants leg and stood up to get the whisk broom and pan that Will Cawdry, compulsive tidier, had kept behind the armchair, and that rested in its place still.

There was something strange about the powder. It seemed to resist the whisk. It clung to the floorboards, particles winking and glinting at her like silvery minerals out on the Lava Wastes.

Finally she managed to work the dust back to a corner. She thought it was cleared up until she turned off the light by the door and, looking back, saw a greenish phosphorescence, shimmering in a stormy twilit gloom.

But when she turned on the light again all trace of the dust was gone.

It's my imagination, she thought. Time to get away.

She ran to her car through the rain.

That night, as she sat reading in her bungalow in Honolulu, she suddenly remembered what Will had told her, sometime after she had glimpsed the phial. Magic Dust, he had said. Euph had given it to him. She remembered with pain that she had been sharply derisive. He had tried to explain, but after their exchange he had never mentioned it again. What had he said, trying to defend against her ridiculing of it as superstition?

"Euph told me, 'See, most folks don't understand about the dust. They think things happen 'cause they sprinkle and whoop and prance and holler and burn candles: they think they make things happen, acting that way. Just like those damn fools in Church, who think they can get a hammerlock on God with song and prayer. But the dust, it's just a sign. It shows things forth to people, about themselves, about what they're bringing on themselves, for good or bad, in time to come.'"

Glancing down, she saw that the left knee of her jeans glinted, even in the lamplight. She scrubbed at the spot for a while with her nails, but when that didn't diminish the sparkle, she let it be.

Suddenly one night Paula was awake, lying quietly in bed in the dark, staring at the grayish window pane, and Will's presence, oddly peaceful, filled the room.

She lay very still for a while, warmed by his company, then sometime she fell asleep again.

When she opened her eyes morning sunlight was flooding over her.

Will's presence had lessened, and remained at a remove during the day's activities. But after that night it never entirely left her.

What did it mean? Was he alive? Was he dead? She could not tell.

Never an enthusiastic cook, she now barely prepared meals, and often forgot to eat. When she remembered, she would buy something at a fast food stand.

She had started walking, too, at night, a strange walking that she had never done before, very fast, then almost dawdling, through the city streets. As if she were seeking another epiphany, like the one she had found that night in the streets of San Francisco, when her father's childhood home had risen before her from a vacant lot.

He followed her, as he had followed, once. . .
He stopped, shook his head to clear it.

Amazing grace, that stoops so low
To save a wretch like me
I once was lost, but now I'm found
Was blind, but now I see.

The song was always in his mind, as he followed. As once he had followed her . . . ?

But she had been much bigger, and he had been not so tall.

Tall enough, though, strong enough, to feel his strength in his arm and in the hard burning thing he carried.

And certainly he had followed her, through the dark and through the rain, down city streets with lights and traffic, stopping and starting at corners while buses and cars roared by, and the same Christmas bells had tinkled, the same decorations shone, as now.

Only then it had been not only wet but also very cold.

The knife-edged cold, a burning and killing cold.

And once she had turned, under a streetlight, and he thought she had recognized him.

If she did, he would run.

Or kill her.

Yumi didn't used to be a walker, he thought. Not like this. This walking wasn't exercise or pleasure-giving. It was the heart's necessity, born of some affliction, gnawing and unassuaged. Unassuagable?

He knew that, because she walked the way some people — he for instance, time had been — fought, and drank.

And still he followed her, as he had followed, once. . .

He stopped, shook his head to clear it. Not the first one. The time he was remembering now, he had been bigger. The second one? Something in his hand glinted in moonlight. Only hard and silvery, cold and remote as the moon or thirty coins.

Towards twilight of the seventh day rain began to fall.

Rain blotted out the Koolaus altogether now.

She didn't look well. She walked heavily, as if her body ached, even when she was moving fast.

When she stopped before a store its bright lights above her showed lines etched across her brow, beginning to cut between the corners of her nostrils and the edges of her lips. She wore glasses now, square ones with black frames.

And she wasn't eating right. That worried him. Jack in the Box. Colonel Sanders. Lots of harsh fries. He winced at the careless way the potatoes were cut, thrown in a wire basket, dipped heedlessly in spitting oil that most likely wasn't clean. Slapped on a paper plate or in a little paper bag, already staining with grease.

He yearned to prepare her a decent meal. For the first time in longer than he could remember, ideas for dishes began to come to him. Something with breadfruit, a papaya and lime sauce . . .

The lights from the stores and street lamps glinted off silver strands like metal wires running through her ebony hair.

He touched his own head: wheat marked by early frost. Touched his chin: a crater there, where a meteor had struck the moon. . .

Long ago, when the world was very young, some inconceivable wrath of the Lady's had torn part of the earth's bowels from the bed of the sea and hurled them into the sky to become that moon. . .

He went on following her through the rain, as he had followed her through the mist.

A ghost, marked by early frost, who had forfeited all claim.

If she turned and recognized him, he would run.

Night, and rain still falling. A steamy mist was beginning to pool in the uneven flagstones outside her door. The mantled twisting limbs of the banyan, ancient strangler fig, loomed thick and black against the sky.

Paula turned suddenly, the key still in the lock.

"Will," she said into the darkness beneath the dripping banyan tree.

And he did not run.

37

In Under the Radar

He stepped forward out of the shadow, and crossed the courtyard to where she stood, unsheltered, rain running down her forehead from her hairline and across the panes of her glasses.

Unexpectedly, the familiarity of the line of her skull, of her cheek and jaw, struck him forcibly. He had never realized until that moment that he knew her face and form in his nerves and muscles, like the shape of a familiar fog-line in the caldera, or a familiar shore far below the plane. The sight stirred him to a tenderness he had not known he could feel.

Impatiently, she took off the glasses, shaking water from them, then shoved them into her purse with the brusque yet tremulous gesture he had learned from his surveillance of her in recent days. She reached to his face with hands that fumbled strangely, as if she were blind and unused to her blindness. Her touch on his cheek was stunned and soft and filled him with a seemingly infinite rush of guilt and sorrow, and of desire.

"Will," she said. "Will. Are you alive? I know it's you; but are you alive?"

"Yeah, Yumi, I reckon I am."

She could not have seen him through the blurring rain, standing in the darkness at the banyan's heart.

"How'd you know I was over there?" he asked softly.

"The rain." She spoke distractedly. "It heightens everything — sounds and smells — or maybe I just knew. I don't know. You've been near," she went on, half-murmuring, "first in the dark night and after that, somewhere, all the time. Ever since I got back from the Mainland, back in September."

"No Yumi, not so long. This last week, yes, but I only been back a week mebbe. A week, I think, I dunno exactly; I lose track of the time and the days. But I know I landed on the first and for two days I couldn't find you. You're getting wet, Yumi." He pushed back the damp wings of hair from her temples, tucking them behind her ears with an old movement that his fingers remembered now. Was that movement what had taught him the shape of her cheek, her skull?

"You're wet, too." She finished working the key in the lock. The door swung open and she stepped through. "Come," she said thickly. He followed her in, and she shut the door behind him.

She turned switches, pressed buttons, until the little bungalow room was flooded with light.

Will looked away from where she stood staring at him, the skin behind his ears flaming red. His hand went to his chin. A new gesture, thought Paula. Her gaze devoured him, as if she were learning him by heart, checking him against her heart's memory.

He had changed. She was glad, spitefully, that he looked older, just as she did, more battered. She saw that he had a white scar on his chin, which was new, and the reason he held his hand the way he did, trying to hide it. But he can't hide it all the time, she thought.

"So," she asked, cool and shaky at once, "where've you been, all this time?"

He grinned suddenly. "I been here and there, doing this and that. Like I told you the day we met. I been in Southeast Asia mostly, and the islands. Hong Kong for a spell. But I been keeping low and on the move a lot of the time, till lately, and a lot of time in the back country. Hard to find and hard to turn in."

She laughed, a taut sound without mirth. She was on the very brink of losing control. She dropped into the armchair.

"Tamura and Associates will be professionally shamed. They worked hard on posters. I hired them to find you. I can't stand not to know things. Like where people are when they disappear without a word. And you're out a wad of your benefits money to their establishment."

"Yumi, you know I don't want no part of that blood money," he said crossly. "I won't miss it none. We been all over that." He spoke as if they had had the argument the night before. "But I saw one of those posters, down on King Street, a picture of me. Gave me an awful turn. What's it mean, Yumi? Am I wanted? It looked a powerful lot like a wanted poster."

"Wanted?" she repeated. "Are you wanted?" He shifted warily under her stare; the word with its multiple implications echoed between them. "The law's not looking for you, as far as I know. I was. Ben would have been interested. A few other people, too. Sometimes I can't fathom why."

Two photographs, the second half-imaginary (like all patterned arrangement?) Just a picture of what might have been, a man who by statistical projection of planes of face might have existed, given his physical notation at an earlier time — but had he? Had he ever existed as either of those men, even the first one, the only actual photograph? What manner of man was he, today, standing before her in the very flesh? His right hand cupped half-protectively, half-shamedly, over the right side of his chin?

Who could keep up with your scars? she thought. Who could predict them? But she had been right about his hair. It was faintly silver-white all over, like a powdering of snow on Mauna Kea, yet as thick as the last night they lay in bed together. Her fingers burned to tangle in it. The desire cramped them on the chair arms.

Will stood, watching her with those pale eyes, flecked like flawed ice.

The shocked nerves in her flesh sent a memory through her body even earlier than the memory of California temblors.

A memory of hurling herself to the floor of the living room in their apartment in Chicago, her toes bare, while her parents looked on. Of kicking till the floor and the very ground seemed to shake beneath her.

What had it been about? She couldn't remember. It didn't matter. She must have been very young, or neither of her parents would have tolerated such behavior.

And now she longed powerfully to scream the order at Will to get out of her life forever. She longed to beat her feet on the scuffed wooden floor of her bungalow, as she knew now she had done as a child, when life and other people proved intractable.

But she was not a child. She was a woman, nearing fifty.

And if she ordered him out of her life forever now, he would go.

But because she was not a child, but a woman nearing fifty, and because nearly half a century had left its mark not only on her flesh but in a knowledge of her life, she knew that if she acted on her impulse she would speak the truth but not the whole truth and maybe something not the truth, and knew too that she did not at this moment know what the fullest truth might be: and so she said nothing.

"If you'd pushed it far enough, I'd have declared you dead. I was already drafting the document in my mind. I don't like uncertainty." Her tone was withering.

"I'm sure you'd have done that, Yumi, and I wouldn't have blamed you none. I didn't mean none of this." He shook his head, seemingly to clear it, and his eyes squinted as if they hurt him. Another new mannerism. She wondered if he needed glasses. Bifocals, she thought sarcastically. Even on the move and keeping low, back country in the bush most of the time, traveling fast and far, hard to find and hard to turn in, the biological clock kept ticking on and down. "I didn't even mean for you to see me, tonight." He paused. "I were going to run." He shook his head quickly, as if to clear it. "Yumi, you ain't by chance got some Rose's Lime Juice, do you?"

She raised her eyebrows.

"Rose's Lime Juice?"

The shadow of a grin touched his lips. "Yeh, 'tis my drink of choice these days, a fact which is the best argument for the existence of God I've yet come across."

We'll see how long that argument lasts, she thought cynically.

"Sorry, no. I have some Realemon in a plastic squeeze bottle."

"That'll do, thank you kindly."

As she handed the glass to him, he said, again,

"If you saw me, I were going to run."

"Were you."

"Yeh. I had it planned so. . .if you saw me."

But she hadn't seen him, he thought. He was a better stalker than that. No one else would have known he was under the banyan. He was a master of how to move in under the radar, but he hadn't been able to do it with Yumi. She had sensed him, known he was there, the way he had always known when she was near.

"But you didn't run."

"No. I didn't."

"You mentioned tomorrow's date. Would that have anything to do with the timing of your return?"

For a moment the impact on him of the time he'd been gone, of aging and of change, were wiped away, and the immutability showed through: Will, a younger Will, his face gone blank and mulish, the skin behind his ears, translucent white, then flaming.

"I reckon," he allowed noncommittally. His thin lips pursed in a silent whistle. The same posture, the same expression, as in the snapshot of him at the Blue Box when he was six, that had hung so long on her bungalow wall. Irrelevantly, she thought how under pressure as in relaxation the flesh tends to take its childhood shapes forever.

The tear that ran down her cheek burned like fire.

"It was cruel." Her voice was hard, brittle. "To go away and never send word. To me. To Ben. Even if you didn't want to come back, you could have let us know you were alive. I didn't do everything right. I did a lot that was wrong and cruel too. But you could have let us know. You must have known we cared. You came back."

"That was then. This is now. And anyway, this isn't — how I meant it to be. Like I said, I wasn't going to show my face. I got no claims here and I ain't making none. I wasn't going to show my face," he repeated. "I were just going to check on you and Ben and Emma and the Princess without you-all knowing, and then be on my way again." He gave the quick head-shake, the squint of the eyes. "I didn't think it'd — be this way — I reckon I thought you'd have brushed me off your fingers long ago, Yumi. Been married right and proper. Living up to Mānoa Heights, in a big nice house with a professor-man and two chicks."

She thought of the application to the University in the folder in the 'ōhi'a-wood chest, never sent, never mentioned. She thought of Alan.

"That always was your fixed fantasy, not mine."

"I weren't going to show my face."

"But you did."

"Yeh. I did."

Abruptly, he collapsed in the armchair opposite her, as if suddenly, finally, he was exhausted too.

"Yeh, Yumi, I did do that. And just when the anniversary of my going was here again. I ain't much for dates, excepting your birthday and the New Year, and the day you come to me at the airport in Volcano, but I ain't never forgot nor the day nor the date I left. So it ain't no accident. I reckon — I reckon I didn't know right clearly what I was about, nor what I was going to do. I ain't surprised you were already drafting a paper to finish with me. You got a genius for ordering life, which is why you're better at life than I am. That paper you wrote would sign outwardly what you were doing in your heart. It's an action like the Magic Dust do tell. Freeing yourself, freeing me too since like you say it seemed to you that that was what I wanted, what with my leaving without a flight plan and staying gone so long without a word. But that were then, and I reckon I know now that I ain't never wanted that. I reckon I know now that I ain't never wanted to die in your heart, die in your life. I reckon I didn't want you to count me among your dead, after all."

38

The Wanderers

Paula walked up and down the O'ahu pathways of her life. Tapped professionally along the echoing floors of the courtrooms and administrative buildings downtown where she made her presentations on environmental issues. Moved in sandals along the streets. Clambered and balanced in hiking shoes high in the Koolaus. Padded softly in rag-sock slippered feet along the old creaking boards of her bungalow.

And the sound of her feet as she went her daily round said, Will has come back.

Tapped it out, briskly. Spoke softly on rubber soles. Sharply when rock and clumps of soil slid along the mountainside. Whispered against the wooden floors of her home.

But these words, that echoed behind all the other words she spoke and heard, failed to reach her or to move her to action or to feeling.

She was not excited, or angry, or relieved, or hurt, or disappointed. She did not feel that her life had gone on without Will and that he was part of her past. She did not feel that now he was back and she could get on with her future with him, begin living again.

She did not feel anything at all.

The night of his return he had stood and blurted suddenly, "Let me fix you a meal, Yumi." Exhausted, she had neither agreed nor refused. She sat while he rummaged through her cupboards, shaking his head, murmuring "Bricks without straw, but I'll do my best" and had produced with her meager supplies the best meal she'd eaten in months.

Then at her request he made her tea, and made himself another Realemon drink, and they sat in silence for several moments. Then, he rose and said, "I reckon it's best if I push on for tonight, Yumi." And she had nodded.

She had not asked how to contact him. Neither of them had mentioned getting in touch again. The return itself was simply too overwhelming to leave room for anything else.

The thought came to her sometimes, We must talk. But she could not think what it was that they must talk about.

Will is in Hale Noname now, she would say to herself as she stood at her own stove making dinner, which she had begun to do again, bringing order back to her life in her bungalow in Honolulu.

Or:

He is sitting in the old green armchair in the BackShack, under the brass lamp with the sharp-angled arm, reading one of a thousand unpredictable books he has collected, that, even more unpredictably, he loves.

She knew that he had returned to Hilo because three days after his appearance, for only the second time, Ben called her in Honolulu.

"So," he said, "so the man come back at last."

She could sense his strong emotion, through his phlegmatic tone.

They were silent together a moment. Then he said,

"You come over now, Paula. We all want to see you."

After she hung up, she found that she was weeping.

But she could not seem to go.

He is digging kalo in the garden, or binding up the limb of an injured mango tree. He is broiling pork in the kitchen of the Pine Tar, brooding one of his improbable magical sauces. Beyond the swinging doors, Will's fantasy is laid out in mauve and purple and white, in linens and orchids, candlelight and brass. He is playing piano at Euph's, or at the Pine Tar. He is playing piano in the big room in Hale Noname.

And the images of these scenes stood before her eyes.

His return had thrown askew the adjustment to his absence that she had made so painfully, thrown her back to where the heart of the universe had stopped, so that she could go on living. The mechanism had kept moving, but the pulse of blood, the heart itself, had stopped.

So now, tapping and whispering the minutes of her days and nights, the voice said, Will has come back. He is at Hale Noname. He is reading in the BookShack, digging in the garden, binding a damaged limb on a mango tree, conjuring a sauce, or an improvisation at the piano at Euph's.

But the heart of the universe had stopped, and had not started to move again.

So had Will gone; and so had Will come back.

He hardly knew the place, it seemed so changed.

After leaving Paula and Honolulu, where he had first returned to Hawai'i, Will had stepped out of the airport into the steamy Hilo night. He halted abruptly. The people coming behind him, encumbered with luggage, jostled him into motion.

Surely the airport was bigger, eating up ground; surely the lights were brighter.

Only the air and the shape of the two mountains against the black sky seemed the same.

He walked along the front of the terminal. A parking lot filled with ranked cars faced him, and in front of that a row of stalls: HERTZ-AVIS-BUDGET.

He didn't remember them. Had they been there when he went away?

Bemused, he moved closer to the Budget stand.

"Where'd this-all bustle come from?" he blurted to the young girl behind the desk. Under her faintly alarmed gaze something happened that was very rare for him, that he had never been able to bear before: he saw himself as he appeared to someone else.

Huge, ungainly, unshaven and scarred, ragged even if his boots though old and battered were very good quality.

A man from another world.

The girl paused, as if made uncertain by his appearance and his off-kilter question. Quickly he added,

"I been away for awhile."

She smiled shyly, and offered, "If you want to rent a car, we need a valid driver's license and a valid major credit card."

He had cash, quite a lot, as he had had once before long ago when he arrived in Hilo at night with Ben. His knife was sheathed to his ankle. But he had no credit card, and no driver's license; and he didn't want to rent a car.

"Thank you kindly, Miss," he said, touching his temple, "but 'tweren't a car on my mind at all."

He turned and walked away, at an off-angle to the directions the arrows pointed on the signs. Yet his step was sure as he vanished into the night.

In the days that followed, Ben watched him.

He wasn't confident of all he was seeing. But some he recognized.

At Euph's and the Pine Tar, greeting all the people who marveled at his return, but knew him well enough to recognize the signs that he didn't want to be questioned about where he had been and what he had done,

Will seemed to move back into his life as if he'd never gone away. But Ben would notice how his easy manner would fail, momentarily, and he would look wonderingly around, as if he couldn't believe the place was still there. He looked at Ben and Emma as if he couldn't believe that they were still there, either.

He took to wandering the town. Could it really be as different as it seemed? New buildings, new businesses, and downtown in the Keawe-Waianuenue Avenue area, two new restaurants, a French one and one run by a fake Maori who was probably a Black guy from the Mainland.

More houses stood, now, too, out the Volcano Road.

More cars and people, and more of them were tourists. Mainlanders mostly, wandering around like ghosts whose feet never really touched the earth.

They disappeared soon.

Ben watched Will walking around town, knew he was walking out on the Lava Wastes, days on end — nights too, Ben felt it in his bones. Will wasn't having enough nights spent peaceful and asleep, bunking behind Euph's or in the house in Noname Lane.

Ben felt that part of the difficulty was that not enough had changed. Will said so himself. He had thought this life of his would be gone. Now when he stood wonderingly in front of Euph's and the Pine Tar, got Volcano Flights started up again, Ben could see, though it might not have been so visible to most people, that Will wasn't quite synchronized with his actions and his words. He wasn't quite present in this life.

But the trouble went deeper than this disjunction.

Ben had seen Will's look before. In Will. In Paula.

Seen it in men who lived through wars. In women who lived through wars, too.

He'd seen it in a Mainland woman hurt and lost in the forest on Mauna Loa who didn't think she'd be found and almost wasn't; and in a man afloat at sea near a month in his fishing boat.

People got that look when life had caught up with them in a way straight out beyond their power to deal with, so that they almost died, and they knew it wasn't because of their power to deal that they didn't die.

Because of that knowledge they couldn't quite take hold of life again; didn't quite believe, anymore, that it was possible even to act as if you could.

Near the end of the third week Emma said,

"Bring him home to eat, often as you can, Ben. This is no good."

So Ben found out Emma had been watching, too, which he supposed he should have figured all along. Only, she'd thought of something to do about it.

Slowly, in the evenings at Emma's and Ben's, Will began to eat, and get a little better.

But the other situation, that kept anything else from being normal, was that Paula didn't come and Will never mentioned her.

Seven years, Will Cawdry had been away, and now once again he wandered the Lava Wastes, under the ancient moon. Prowled the 'ōhi'a forests, as his life of the past seven years moved through him.

But now, he did not go in search of scarlet, dripping thicker than water.

The long blade traveled with him but stayed in its sheath.

Now, events of those seven years gone floated past his mind's eye, like clouds passing across the face of the bone-white moon.

The events did not come in sequence and often he could not identify their place. Boiling feelings, black-and-green, threatened to overwhelm him and sometimes did.

Now, in his hallucinatory days, he went back to a land he recognized and did not recognize, merged with the places of his old life. Perhaps they were the places of his old life, revisited; and finally he had gone back to Vietnam. He knew that others had, gone before, others who thought more like Yumi did. Some vets in town had gone to help build an orphanage. Tom Tanaka was one, and sent money to help support it. But it had always seemed to Will he had had no business there to begin with, and that he had had none since, in that place where he had done such damage and been damaged so himself.

Still, once in these seven years gone he had returned to give attention to that damage. For nothing, he thought. In those days when damage was done he had lost his place and time, and when he returned he could not find the places and people again, or anyone who could remember, or who would.

That land of black and green.

So had he thought of it then, and ever since had lived with the gut-fear of green and black: camouflage cloth, jungle, night and noon-time shadow, and death everywhere.

Blank and dreaming in the clearing at the end of Noname Lane, he saw the gold of sun. He stood on embankments and watched barefoot men mud-stained to their knees, allied with water buffaloes in wrestling through the resistance of lush emerald paddies. Like the people and the land, buffaloes had suffered and died in the war. Huge beasts, seeming wise and somehow elemental, massive heads lowered, turned sideways with effort, heavy with horn. They resembled the mud of the paddy risen to work itself, in concert with human beings.

In the seven years of his goneness he had also been to other places of his old life, flying low where brown rivers broad as seas slid like great sluggish serpents through vast green expanses of rain forest.

He had skimmed in low above their impossible canopies, in wide dawns that were to him the finest hour, when night resorbed itself into day in a glorious tropical explosion of light.

He came in under the radar even if there was any, and usually, where he flew, none had ever existed. Guided by naked eye and flashlight signals, he landed on runways that were no more than narrow scratches in the dirt, petering out against impenetrable vegetation in the minimal distance necessary to avoid disaster.

There, under sketchy shelters made of sticks thrown together and tossed over with grasses for roofing, stacked crates of plastic-wrapped cargo loomed, bartered over by dangerous men. His body took beatings from torrential rains that lashed earth and flesh like blows from wet canvas; and took other beatings, in fights with other men, dangerous like him.

His hand crept to his chin.

Scarred surface of the moon and Lava Wastes.

When Paula first walked into the kitchen at the Pine Tar, Ben had been deeply disturbed. He had apprehended, at once and correctly, that she was some kind of city woman he'd never seen before. He had apprehended too that she represented a profound danger to Will, pulling in him something that held his very psychic existence together — Ben alone knew how precariously.

He had come to understand, as he came to know Paula and to see how she was with Will, that that danger had been a trial, an ordeal of the sort the old tales told: the dark subterranean passages where lightless rivers flowed and men were either destroyed by dangers and challenges with deceptive name or form, or took name and form through surviving them. For the first time then, after Paula came, Ben had begun to think about those stories. Maybe some were about women. Maybe about how, so often for men, the world — all its challenges, all its trials and ordeals —presented itself to them as a woman. And sometimes — very rarely — for a few men, who were put together in certain ways, that challenge and trial and ordeal actually came embodied for them — incarnated, as the missionaries would have said about God but not women — in a woman of flesh and blood.

Maybe Will was such a man. Paula was the woman.

But having watched life, Ben understood that the outcome of these situations the stories told about was not foreordained. The tales were warnings and guides. What happened would depend on the man's condition when he met this woman, and on what kind of woman she was. It would depend on what fate, and the gods, enemies and friends brought to him. And it would depend on the choices the man made himself.

That was why Ben had known how to withhold a final judgment about Will's disappearance and long absence; and been comforted throughout by an abiding intuition, against all evidence and logic, that Will might come through the long journey.

As Ben went about his business, he thought more and more about how what became of a man depended on the intervention of his friends as well as on his enemies and powerful forces arrayed against him.

So one day he left Jeremy in charge and drove up the Hamakua Coast.

He took with him, on ice, the carefully selected best of the morning's catch, and, in baskets, the best from his own garden. These were offerings in thanks to Auntie Raina for the help she would be giving him in this work.

As he drove, Ben turned over how he was going to describe the matter. This kind of business was grave; it shaped life, restored it and could even take it away.

On his right the broad blue sea stretched away, perhaps forever. On his left the flame-flowering tangle of deep green forest soared steeply into the mountains, riven by a myriad silver threadings of stream and waterfall.

Ben acknowledged all the strong feelings and impulses of life as he drove: killing, and forcing, and bending to the will. All the violent ways of intervening in another person's life; and, in a sense, were not all interventions, however gentle, really intrusion, even violation? Yet without it, life could not grow: it was one of the reasons people existed for each other.

He acknowledged the feelings, and rode with them all the way up towards Wai'pio, that most sacred valley; and by the time he had come to Auntie Raina's house, his thoughts were tolerably in order.

He returned from Auntie Raina's much calmed; and he and Emma worked out a plan to call Paula and urge her to come over.

But before they could act on it, malevolent fate took a hand. Jannye walked into Euph's and the Pine Tar.

39

Dragon Guardians

Rain pummeled the earth on the night Will went to Paula in Honolulu, harder than on the night he had first sought her out after his return from his wanderings. The dim yellow bulb above the door to her bungalow shone fuzzily, and, from the leaves of the banyan, water dripped against the worn stones of the courtyard.

He was not aware of knocking, but then he was blinking in an oblong of warm golden light, and Paula, after a moment's immobility, motioned him in.

She shut the door behind him and stood with a barrier of space around her, her arms making an X across her chest, her hands gripping her shoulders.

"Well, if it isn't Surabaya Johnny," she said acidly.

He hesitated. "I do know the play and the song, Yumi. Should I go, like the lady singing it wanted the fellow to go?"

"No. Not now. But if you're 'staying a spell,' take off your shoes and get dry." She nodded toward the bathroom. "Get a towel. I don't like to hear you cough like that."

Will fetched the towel and stood in the middle of the room rubbing his hair and face. Paula sat in her armchair and nodded at the futon sofa opposite.

Will sat.

"In the letter you wrote answering mine," he began. "You did say 'twas all right to get in touch."

She nodded.

"So I've come to you here." He coughed again, spasmodically, so violently that even his massive frame shook.

"If I'd known you were sick I'd have come on over."

"No Yumi, this cough ain't nothing. And 'twas time I come here to you, in Honolulu, as you did ask me to once long ago at Euph's, and as I said I might at that, one day."

His eyes went to the cupboard, in the old hungry way. Paula said,

"Is Rose's Lime still your drink of choice?" She had bought a bottle after sending him the note that it was all right to get in touch.

"Still Rose's Lime."

She got him a drink and he cradled it in his hands, setting the bottle close beside his chair. He hadn't changed, she thought; he drank his Lime the way he'd drunk his Johnny Black, and, she was certain, drunk his tar likker before that.

"Might be a few weeks ago, Ben did sit me down as he does sometimes when he feels I'm right off course. He said it ain't so strange I'm wandering in the world some now."

"Since you got back, we've both been wanderers. Dry your feet, Will."

He took off his shoes and socks and went to work thoroughly with the towel. When his feet were dry, he paused, hesitating again. This was new, his awareness that his words would affect others, his wondering how; his unsureness of being able to tell how. "I reckon you heard some talk about the girl. Jannye."

You know damn well I have, she thought. She nodded again, once.

"Yumi, the — the lawyer fellow visited you here a few weeks back, the one you knew in San Francisco. Nakamura? How's that stand, Yumi?"

"He's fine. He's back in San Francisco." What tendrils of the local grapevine had taken Kaz Nakamura's visit back to Will? Probably the same ones that had brought news of Jannye to her, she thought wryly, and then thought of Kaz calling, suggesting he take her up on her offer of a visit. Rumors of Jannye and Will in her ears, still wandering herself, thinking it might be a good time, she had told him to come along. Kaz and she, as they had been years ago. His arched arrogant nose, strong thighs, the intelligent prickly conversations, the quarreling. But more quarreling, less agreement on their views, and the sex not so good, anymore, with the years of change between, and Will yonder on the Lava Wastes, and present in her internal wilderness as well.

She and Kaz had left it as they had the last time they had tried an affair, ruefully agreeing they'd been right the first time around. The tension between them would pass; the friendship would survive.

"Will you be going over to the Mainland soon?"

"No. I'm not planning on going anywhere at all. I live here."

"And that other lawyer fellow, local boy, that you—you was set to marry once? That Enomoto fellow?"

"A long time ago. He's been practicing in Los Angeles for years. He has a family." She leaned back in her armchair. So somehow the engagement had come to Will's ears as well. No privacy in this place, people often grumbled, and how right they were. "Theirs are good lives too," she said, "Alan's and Kaz's. But they aren't mine."

Will stood and padded barefoot around the big shadowed room, glass in hand.

He opened a photo album lying on a side table. Paula tensed. She had looked at it again for the first time since putting it behind the shoebox in her closet. Will looked at the photographs. Stopped at the snapshot of the two of them and the nēnēs.

He grinned, faintly. "I do remember that day so well. Wonder how the Sunday dinners are doing. Great-great-grandparents by now. Kūpuna. Ancestors."

He studied the photograph she had taken of the summit of Mauna Kea, the view he had seen when he first realized he was going to build a house in Noname Lane.

A photograph of sunrise over Kilauea. Then, a happy party scene, mostly Asian folks, or Asian-American?

"That's in San Francisco. Our victory party, after we won an important decision in the reparations case."

A table in the Pine Tar, the orchids and candlelight on brass, napkins in origami folds like the wings of birds, and Paula's flower arrangement.

Emma, intent on her quilting. Ben, leaning over a cauldron in the kitchen of the Pine Tar. Pearlie Leilani in full dance regalia, dipping gracefully.

Pigeon nestlings above her door, the banyan in the courtyard leafy in the background. Chicks, he thought. She hadn't married that lawyer-man he'd heard over in Hilo she'd been engaged to once, hadn't moved out by the University . . .

Will, hunkering down weeding in the garden behind Hale Noname.

A photograph of him at the piano in Euph's. A photograph of him standing beside the Caravan, one palm against its skin, grinning.

"Ben put big copies of those two up at Euph's and the Pine Tar."

"Yes."

Pele Dancing, hanging on the wall.

He stared at Pele Dancing a long time.

"That's right remarkable," he said at last. "It's got the whole world in it. You got a hand for painting for true."

"Thank you. It's the only painting I've ever done."

"Painted since I went away."

"Earlier this year."

"Did it make a life for you, Yumi?" he asked, nodding at the album and the wall. "Do it add up to a life? I know that way of thinking's important to you. Life adding up."

"It made a life." She watched him, her arms still folded across her chest.

"A good life?"

"A good life."

"Most of eight years we been together, one way and another, and I never yet been here in your place to speak of. Never at all but twice."

It would take Will Cawdry, she thought, to count the years he was gone as part of the time he had been with her.

"You spent an evening here, not too long ago."

"And a night once, a long time before that, just before I went away."

She raised her eyebrows. The skin behind his ears reddened.

"I reckon I never told you about that. You'd given me the key, if you recall."

"So I had."

"That night I spent, yeh, when you weren't even here." He laughed.

"What's funny?"

"I slept on the floor. Couldn't bring myself to sleep in your bed."

"Why not? We were sleeping together everywhere else at the time."

"Maybe that was why. It seemed like — a violation, added on to all the other — violations I was doing to you. In bed. As it seemed to me. And out of bed too, by the way I were acting in general, which of the two more likely seemed to you like violations. I'm kinda crazy, ain't you noticed? Leastways I was then."

She nodded once.

"I've come to tell you, it's finished about Jannye. I think 'twere started at all because — I'd near lost my own place and time again, coming back so. Then, what with losing my time and place, I got right confused about — other things.

"When I left, I were straight out a madman. It did seem to me that you two, you and my Little Mama, was — the same. Isn't that something? The same. Like my being with her and being with you was one event instead of two, one woman instead of two, and one me instead of two, like the man-child and the man were one. Like two people, two things that happened, two different times, got collapsed in my mind. A funny thing, the mind, ain't it? Right funny, how it works. Sometimes — sometimes I even wonder, did I set it up like that for us, in my crazy mind back then — to make it the same as the first time — with my Little Mama."

He took a pull of Rose's.

"Not similar no-way," he said softly. "I were a little boy back then, not a grown man. Gawd — I were mad at my Little Mama, mad and hurting and shocked and shamed and feeling abandoned and betrayed-like. 'Twere why I spoke of her like she were a saint, most times. Reckon I was afraid once I put my mouth on her, all that bad feeling would come out. She beat me some, too, you know. Specially at the end up in Chicago. Don't think I ever mentioned that to you."

"No," said Paula, "but I had — deduced it, from some oblique things you said."

"For true? Well, you're good at — oblique things."

"Not very."

"Better'n me."

She smiled. "Maybe. You're better than me at flying planes."

He smiled too.

"True enough. But these last times, it's getting hard for me even to be mad at her. I keep seeing her in her coffin, and now I know she died little more'n a girl. I'm a grown man near fifty, Yumi, and when I saw my Little Mama in her coffin, she weren't even half my age."

Incongruously, he gave his wheezy laugh, angry and sad now too, and it was cut short by a cough that grew and grew to something that seized him from within and tossed him like a huge predator killing prey.

At last he fell back in the chair, his arms thrown out, knuckles grazing the floor, his exposed out-thrust throat with its rough reddened skin and convulsing Adam's apple reminding her forcibly of her glimpse of him that night outside the Port of Call. Its vulnerability had frightened Paula then, and it frightened her now.

"Will, that cough is bad. You had it when you first came back. It's been weeks. I'm afraid you'll get really sick and it may be damn hard to undo, what with your coming and going. As Ben puts it."

"You noticed that, too, Yumi, that I ain't been so well? 'Tisn't nothing, though, this cough," he said again. But he took the fresh bath towel she tossed him from the cupboard and rubbed his thick hair more thoroughly.

She hesitated, then said abruptly, "Jannye is very young and very beautiful, and you and she have a lot in common with your musical interests. She was right, you know. What they quoted her as saying in that article in the last issue of *Island Beat*. The one with the photo of you." Here had been a photo of Jannye too — a Julie Danemore clone, Paula had thought spitefully. "You could make a name for yourself, you know, a career — get a wide audience, respect, money on the Mainland. Las Vegas, Los Angeles, I think she was talking about. You're good, Will — you've never known how good. Never believed it. If she could make you believe it, she's done better than I ever did, and you shouldn't throw that away lightly."

He made an impatient gesture. "'Tisn't the point, Yumi. And I did always know how you valued my playing — more than Jannye did, I reckon, who sings to a different style anyway and who wants an accompanist, which I ain't. And then, I'm not a city person, Yumi, and I'm not hungry for money. Euph's and the Pine Tar weren't ever about fame and money anyway. They were about — a place. A place for people and music and such. A place for me. And for mine. Where I didn't have to pay to live and they didn't have to sell. And I already got a name," he said violently. "You oughta know my name, better'n anybody. 'Twas you insisted on it and insisted on my knowing it, every which way, Irish to Wild Geese to Starvesoil to — to my own Mama. A name to go with my face. I don't need to make me a name. I already got one."

He hesitated, then went on, "When I were with the girl, I never heard a new note of music in my head, never thought of a new dish to cook. And 'twas the same sterility for her. She sang better when she come than when she left. And she left of her own will as much as mine, to go back to this place Las Vegas, where I reckon she'll do just fine. But I wouldn't. And as for her being young, and beautiful too, well, I can see that, Yumi, I'm not blind. But you've always been young-old to me, you're twice-looking, you got the gift. Age don't make a difference with a woman such as you.

"'Twas you let me first see over the curve of my own horizon, Yumi. And as for Jannye being young, 'tis only too true. The moment it come clear to me 'twas finished between us, whatever 'twas — well, what'm I gonna do with a woman who says like Jannye did, 'Nobody thinks about the Vietnam War. It's old stuff. Nobody cares about it anymore.' What'm I gonna do? I'll always be thinking about the war — somewhere, somehow, no matter what I'm thinking about. A woman who weren't there then, who weren't even born then, she ain't gonna know or care the way one would who was. Even if she's got a sense of history like you do, with World War II and the camps f'rinstance, and got history as part of her own life-past, like you do — and Jannye ain't like that — even so, it won't be the same as if she remembers the time. How's a woman who don't care about the Vietnam War gonna care about me? How's a woman who don't remember those times gonna remember me? How kin she even see me?

"There's more though, Yumi, that brings me here tonight. I just come from another woman. I didn't have knowledge of her," he said quickly. "I — I wouldn't come into your presence after that. This woman I just come from, she's not my friend. And I'm not her friend. I were buying her valuable time. She's a working girl. 'Twas in a room above a place called the Port of Call. You wouldn't know it."

So at last, after all these years, Will Cawdry was going to talk. Instead of drinking. Or fighting. Or taking off without a flight plan and sending no word. And someday soon, she would have to talk too, instead of freezing into a snowy and somnambulistic silence in the shadows.

"I know the Port of Call," said Paula. "Near the River Street end of Hotel Street."

"Yes, 'tis the place. I am always forgetting you know about such things. You were there to see a client?"

"Yes, I was in the neighborhood to see a client. I saw you."

Will stared at her, the blood draining from his face.

"It was a long time ago," she said. "right after we met. I wasn't sure it was you. No, that's not true. I was sure."

"You never said?"

"I almost did, that night, during that same conversation at Euph's you were talking about a while ago. When instead of asking you about Hotel Street, I asked you to come and see me in Honolulu. And here you are."

"All this time, you never said?"

"We didn't have that kind of relationship," said Paula. "After all, you never said either."

"I reckon that's so."

After a moment, Paula prompted gently,

"So you were with a working woman in a room above the Port of Call."

"I sat there. I sat in a chair like the old fool she knew me for. Just sat for, oh, maybe twenty minutes. Then I began to cry. Then I come away. I forgot and left something there. Something I — I had made for me in my travels. It's a funny thing, all these years I been taking it with me when I go. Figuring I was going to them trying to find something. Now I figure maybe I was going to them trying to lose something. I don't reckon I'll go back for it, now."

Paula got up, heated a cup of water in the microwave, made herself peppermint tea. Sat down again. Will continued,

"I went tonight thinking it was the same it's been all these years. But it wasn't. Because I forgot the dress there."

"Would that have been a replacement for the gray dress you kept hanging on a nail in the BackShack?"

He stared past her at the wall, the skin beneath his ears aflame.

"Yeh, I left it here when I — headed on out. Flat out forgot. Though I must've known you'd find it. Funny thing, the way the mind works, ain't it? I — I did tell myself — you'd think 'twas a bathrobe, mebbe."

Paula raised her eyebrows skeptically.

"Go on with your story, Will."

He hesitated, then continued,

"When I came out of the woman's room tonight, I went walking. Walking and walking. I never done that before, not over here to Honolulu. I never walked so. 'Twas raining when I came out. I went walking and walking. I walked all over Aiea, all over Honolulu in the rain. And then I came here. To you. And I never done that before either in all these years, the times I come over here to the Port of Call. So it's not the same. And I shoulda knowed that, 'cause in the time I were away 'twas like that too. I'd go to wimmen like tonight and hold them against me in that dress. That's all. Then later sometimes I'd sit. Not often. Maybe four, five times, in those years I were away. Less often at the end. But tonight's the first time I ever cried. And it's the first time I forgot the dress. Which — which were for her to wear. A — a notion I took." He looked at her. "I reckon you wondered —"

"Well, I kind of figured it might be something like that. Either that or that you wore it. Something along that line. Go on."

The place beneath his ears reddened again. "Yumi —"

"Don't worry, Will. As notions go — including your notions — a dress is pretty run of the mill. Keep talking, okay?"

He paused. "Y'know, Yumi, when I left here, seven years gone, I had my rucksack and in it my passport, a roll of cash, and your dragon bracelet." He laid it on the low table between them. "My sheath knife on my ankle. And other than that the clothes on my back."

"I — I didn't know how I come to have that bracelet," he went on, as she sat holding it with wonder, as if it too had returned from the dead. "But of course I knowed 'twas yours, and I knowed 'twas a message somehow, for I remembered the day we met, when I come to fetch you at the hotel for your first sight of Euph's and the Pine Tar, your first meeting with Ben and Emma and the Princess and the other folks there, and I did remember what I said: 'So you keep a dragon guardian too.' Knowing of course that 'twas a sign, matching my own dragon as it did, which you didn't know about till later."

Paula slipped the bracelet over her wrist. "My memory about leaving this at Hale Noname is no better than yours. I've always wondered what happened to it. And I'm glad to have it back."

"Well, I have come tonight to give the bracelet back, and I wouldn't have come if I didn't believe in my heart that I've learned something for true. Thinking things over in these days since – Jannye — left. Learned there are countries of the soil, countries of the sky. Countries of the mind and heart, countries of the body. I wouldn't be here if I didn't believe in my heart for true that I'm able to behave better now in someone else's country. Before I left, I treated you right unforgivably."

"Inexcusably, maybe. Not unforgivably. If anything is unforgivable, forgiveness doesn't mean anything. Anyway, you aren't the only one who needs forgiveness. I behaved inexcusably too. I blamed you for not understanding about racial privilege, but I called myself a leftist and then when I was angry I cut you down with class privilege. Sometimes when I wasn't angry, and I didn't even see what I was doing. I didn't even think about it. I just saw the way I thought you should be as normal and reasonable."

"No Yumi, I didn't see it so."

"Come on, Will. Remember the things you called me? 'Eddicated Berkeley lawyer-politico?' 'Crazy Berkeley hippie-radical?' You said it and you were angry about what you meant by that and you were right to be angry, even if I don't think the names you called me meant what you meant."

"Well," he allowed, "mebbe." He grinned. "Anyway I forgive you, too." He laughed softly. "Ben did say to me, a while ago, 'Maybe a man can't come back all at once, from the place you been these seven years, and before that too. Maybe he comes back again and again, a little bit at a time, like the tide coming in or going out. Just watch and while you coming and going so, don't do no damnfool thing you can't undo. I reckon he meant Jannye most recently, and plenty else besides. I reckon I'm here tonight to ask did I do that — some damnfool thing I can't undo."

"No. Not if you're back the way you are tonight." She paused and then said deliberately, deliberately not creating a silence, "No more hard drinking, which probably has to mean no more drinking at all. No matter what. No more Jannye. Whatever she meant. No more gray dress and Port of Call.

And no more Surabaya Johnny, taking off without a flight plan and staying gone with no word." She paused again and then finished, "I'm not saying that all those things should be equally important or even are, and I'm not arguing about whether I'm right or not or whether right even means anything in all those contexts. I'm just telling you what I'm not willing to deal with. And if any of those things go off track, well, I'll always be on your side, but I won't be at your side. And you tell me the same about what you aren't willing to deal with in me."

"I can't rightly think of nothing, Yumi."

"Well think about it and let me know if anything comes up. I bet it will," she said dryly. Then, in a much softer voice, "I know I have a deep-seated — fault of silence. I don't know what will happen with us, Will. We — have a hard row to hoe, I think."

"Well, at least we've both had a lot of practice, one way and another."

She heard a sardonic voice - her own — say to her silently, This is not a gamble you're likely to win, this relationship with Will. And I thought you didn't bet on men.

But she decided to take it on, because he knew how to be delighted, because he had never tried to change her, and because he had never taken her to see something that wasn't worth seeing — starting and ending with himself.

"Thank you, Surabaya Johnny, for coming all the way from Surabaya, to return my dragon guardian to me." And she smiled sardonically.

His thin lips sketched a grin. "Matter of fact, I did come from there. That German writer-fella — what's his name?" Paula did not believe for a moment that Will had forgotten it. "Yeh, Brecht, that's it, he didn't get it quite right in his play, though of course it must have changed since then, but Yumi, Surabaya's a big city, near big as Honolulu I reckon, not some place at the end of the earth. I reckon, Yumi, I never yet told you how I were struck deaf and blind in Surabaya?"

"No. You never have. Talk story."

40

Struck Deaf and Blind In Surabaya

The lights were out in the bungalow in Honolulu beneath the banyan in the courtyard. Rain plopped through the leaves and onto the cobbles. Distantly, traffic sounded like the sea. They lay side by side, still clothed, talking in the dark.

"So how did you find your way back here, Surabaya Johnny? Flying as far and wild as you say, how'd you even remember there was a here to come back to?"

"Oh, I never forgot that, Yumi. I never forgot you. 'Twouldn't make no sense, would it? Since it was for you I went away. As to how I got to where I could come back – in Surabaya," he said to Paula lying near him in the night, "in Surabaya I were struck deaf and blind. In Surabaya, I died, and rose to life again. This is how it happened."

And Will began to talk story.

He had been in the street, been in the bars, he remembered in blotted-out patches, like the mist blotting out the Koolaus. In one of the bars he met the man in yellow robes, the Buddha of the BackShack.

"'Twere in a bar in Surabaya I met him. I had took to drinking again, and stopped for good after the night I am telling you about. He were a *sensei*, mebbe, looking back, though it do seem a powerful strange place to find a *sensei*, and he were drinking a powerful lot too. But he sure told me true. So a *sensei*, maybe – maybe even a Buddha. The Buddha of the Backshack. The Great Physician to treat my deepest ills – I reckon he saved my life. He said I were losing myself, told me I had to breathe and showed me how, like you did that time, first time we ever lay together at Euph's, the year the Wailuku flooded so . . .

"That's all I remember.

"Then seems I was back in my room in this low-life hotel. But I don't know for sure. Because I don't remember a thing. First the blotted-out patches, then nothing. Then I was awake."

He paused, recalling, how suddenly he was awake, suspended in nothingness, deaf and blind, with the greatest terror he could sustain and still maintain any awareness at all: he was dead.

"I can't describe it, 'tis not a place of flesh or substance, 'twasn't a dream, or if it was a dream 'twas like no other dream. 'Twas worse than the grenade I took, worse than Sam's butcheries after. 'Twas worse than — than remembering. about my Little Mama, about Vietnam. 'Tis a place without sensation, just a — a consciousness, an awareness-like, the heart of nightmare. A place with no breath, no take and give of breathing that do abolish inside and outside and keep a person from utter separation from all else.

"Yumi, I'd killed myself. The liquor were the sign and the means, but not the death. The death were deeper — in the evil sickness of my life's hurts and doing hurt.

"'Twas then I felt your hand on my chest moving in circles just the way it did long ago, that night I mentioned when the Wailuku flooded so, and the man in yellow was showing me, breath in—breath out. And I began to breathe again.

"And so I found my way to life once more."

He paused, and continued in a louder voice, still impassioned, "In the days after, I thought, 'Who am I, anyway? This man who's me? This man who breathes now like for the first time? Yet there's a thread there runs back to him, man and boy, I reckon, could I follow it so far. 'Cause sometimes — just for a minute, like, for a flash — it feels like he's the real one, the deeper one — the first-born one.

"But to claim him again requires a painwork harder than it seems like mortal man can bear, or sometimes — when I'm forgetting my sin — should have to."

He laughed, softly and sardonically. "Mebbe I got born again. Wouldn't Uncle Bert be proud? I can hear him whooping and hollering now.

"But there's more, you know. I've been a man most powerfully blessed, especially in my latter days — since coming here, to Hawai'i nei. Euph's and the Pine Tar, Ben standing by me, Volcano Flights, the Princess. Emma. Hale Noname. Then, you. Mebbe I don't want to push that luck.

"I've done lots of wickedness in my life, Yumi — lots of evil things. And when all my explaining and repenting is laid out, no matter how truly felt, the evil I have done do stay done. The Princess were right about that, long ago.

"My going were about guilt as were my behavings here that led to my going, and sometime after that night, being with the man in yellow, dying and coming to breathe again, it come to me that no man can pay back all his dues, 'tis the most monstrous arrogance to think that. 'Tis the root of *on*, perhaps, that I learned of, if I understand it rightly, during my time in Japan – the debt one's born to and can never repay; 'tis perhaps even what some Christians flail around at, I'm not too sure about that. If so, how to come to it in life did seem mightily to elude my Uncle Bert and those around him. And 'tis also, mebbe, the deep meaning and deep hope of karma, which mebbe isn't about blame or fate or predestination so much as about the muck of possibility – a raw material, like, to make life from and each second a possibility of doing better, of seeing truer.

"It come to me, Yumi, that no man can pay back all his dues, which means no man can lose his sorrow, so the only way to be is just keep acting as if he could, without worrying about ever getting to that point. So I come back home again."

Near-fatal alcohol poisoning, that's what that night in Surabaya was about, said Paula's sardonic voice; alcohol poisoning, with hallucinations.

Pearlie Leilani would say, Self-serving rationalizations.

But Paula remembered the night in San Francisco. Emma and Pearlie Leilani in a blue dusk. Remembered Magic Dust.

In Will, she thought, were Starvesoil Baptist ranters, the boy up against Sam in Texas Starvesoil and Chicago tenements and Asian jungles, the man up against himself, space shot through with delight and night and light and horror. All of this had made him, and out of the raw materials dealt him, whatever might be true, he claimed he had found a way to live and cease doing damage to himself and the rest of the world.

Will Cawdry was speaking of miracles and salvation.

That was miracle enough for her, and close enough to salvation. And it was truth enough. She had come a long way from Boalt Hall, to where she could accept that yellow-robed *senseis* – maybe Buddhas – drinking heavily in dives could body forth things unseen, and magic dust could foretell things not yet come.

Will reached his hand and drew his palm down her hair.

"Tonight," he said, "I will protect you, Yumi." He grinned; his teeth flashed white in the dark. "I reckon you would insist on that anyway. It's been a right dreadful time for diseases. You got no cause for worry, 'twas you before I left and now I'm here with you tonight, that's all, but I want you not to have questions in your mind."

"Me and me?" echoed Paula incredulously. "All that time?"

"Yumi," he said crossly, "My going weren't about going to other women."

Could what he was saying be true, she wondered? Then again, why not? Compulsive sex, violent sex she suspected, why not no sex?

She yielded the debate.

A yearning in the flesh.

"I'll take you up on your offer of protection," she said drily, and then at last she let her hands find his face again. She dropped her forehead against his chest, her lips against the tangle of salty hair.

41

A Fire In the Glade

One day a fire flared in the glade behind Hale Noname, and showed a long way off. Will had warned folks he'd be doing a burn, so no one mistook it for an eruption or a wild blaze. The fire burned fiercely for a long time; but before daybreak the flames had subsided to a glow, like Pele's lifeblood glimpsed among the leaves.

In a clear dawn, Mauna Kea's snows had gone from frozen gray-pearl to shifting shades of rose, like the movement of the blood of life, not death.

Snow Sleeper: Will's lips moved with the almost-silent words.

The BackShack was gone.

"I — I have done terrible things, Yumi."

He had said this to her, suddenly, two weeks before, as they sat one night in the big room in Hale Noname.

"I had gathered that. From the moment I met you."

"Yumi, there was violence and killing and treachery and most evil dealings in a business way. And in the war. I raped a girl. I killed her. I didn't mean to, but I didn't mind either. And I didn't stop raping her because I'd killed her, neither.

A silence fell.

"I am not surprised. Have you attended to it?"

"What you meaning, Yumi?"

She smiled sourly. "Well, in your lingo, 'gotten right with God?'"

"How do you get right about a thing like that?"

She stared at him thoughtfully, remembering a night at the Fairmont with a man she believed she had known; remembering an afternoon in an alley, a child and a gang of grown men.

"I don't know. It seems to me a good start is to want to." She hesitated, then said, "Some would say you should go to trial, to prison, lose your life. I never held with the death penalty, and the farther I go the less I hold with prison. You're less a threat to society tonight than you've ever been. So — a ceremonial apology to her? Find the people who loved her? Apology, reparations in practical terms? Counseling for them? Accepting I'd have to live with guilt for the rest of my life, and somehow accepting myself anyway? But maybe I'm unimaginative in my view of things, some ways. Or maybe different ways work for different people. I don't know. You'll have to figure it out for yourself. Have you talked to Auntie Raina about it?"

"Not ever. I — didn't remember. You reckon even she could hear a thing like that and keep me in her presence?"

"Yes. I think she could. I think Auntie Raina could hear anything and keep someone in her presence."

"I can't remember nothing about where it happened nor when — 'tweren't a registered kind of attack, you know. It was a secret operation. But I tried to find the place — I would never recognize a face. And I went to officials from that government, but they couldn't do nothing cause I hadn't nor place nor name for where it happened or for the operation. The U.S. of A. people looked at my medical record and suggested 'twere maybe my mind wasn't working so well, to say Sam's fighting men would do such things. So I left before they locked me up. I thought then mebbe 'twere right what I always held, about the reparations money, and the things Tom Tanaka does, y'know, supporting the hospital for Vietnamese children and all — it has always seemed to me that I had no business there to begin with, that it was my being there did the damage, going back and trying to fix the damage would only make it worse. But might could be I'm wrong. I will ponder on it more, mebbe even talk to Tom, in general terms like, and try to understand his thinking better. And since you say it seems right to you, I will go see Auntie Raina and lay this matter before her."

"It's a good idea, I think. And a good idea to talk to Tom Tanaka."

"Do you still want me in your presence?"

"I'd be pretty hypocritical if I didn't," she said crisply, "since I have known this all along. Not the details, but the fact."

As he had told Yumi he would, he'd laid the matter before Auntie Raina, and soon after that visit it had come to him that burning the BackShack was the first step to take.

All day, behind Hale Noname, Will chopped charred lumber and heaved rubble, heavy, harsh work, dangerous and grim. His hair was tied back and up in a blue bandanna; his face was covered with another cloth from the bridge of his nose to his throat, and his hands were encased in thick gloves. His blue eyes showed startlingly below his grime-black forehead.

By nightfall he had cleared the ground and loaded the rubble into a rented truck.

Only a deep ugly pit remained, like the socket of an abscessed tooth. An acrid pall hung over the glade.

That night, no one was around to hear the heavy rumble of the truck engine, as the vehicle left the highway and labored and teetered along precarious paths, then off paths altogether onto still more perilous ground that threatened to crumble into fire. Higher up, on other dangerous slopes, snake-tongues of flame licked against a background so black they seemed to dart out of the sky.

And no one was around to see as Will consigned the remnants of the BackShack to the lava flow, which claimed it as if consuming and cleansing an offense, resolving objects into elements: earth, fire, water, wind.

The next day strange weather prevailed over all the islands, and especially over Maui and Hawai'i, Pele's most recent homes. The radio reported that at the peak of Haleakala the wind clocked ninety miles; and, high on Hawai'i Island, over a hundred.

Yet the sky was an intense even blue, uncannily devoid of cloud. The sun blazed. The gale bent the coconut palms into graceful bows, and sent their fronds streaming out perpendicularly like hair.

The strange wind blew incessantly from dawn, and died suddenly with the day.

By contrast, the night that followed was startlingly calm. The sea and air were motionless, the sky around the moon a corona of midnight blue, and ink-black beyond.

When dawn returned, normal weather had returned too.

The Trade Winds lightly tossed the palm fronds, and complex white clouds danced gaily across the sky.

Remarkably, in Noname Glade no trace of the odor of burning remained.

Paula looked out the kitchen window of Hale Noname. She was seeing for the first time the rich soil where the BackShack had stood, now turned under ready for new planting. She thought she grasped the path in life for which Will meant that planting to stand. She wondered where, and how far, they would travel together along it, and what the journey would bring.

Later, when they were in bed, his coughing woke her. She kept still in the dark, following his progress as he rose stealthily and, without light, moved from the bedroom into the front room, seeming to breathe easier; and there, without light, disappeared into silence.

She sensed that he had gone into Wilderness Mode, when no one, nothing, could hear him.

In the front room of Hale Noname, Will sat still.

He had learned Wilderness Mode long ago, before he could remember, to save his life during his first war, the war at home. Now in the house in Noname Lane he recovered for the first time a fragment of his life that was less than memory and more than feeling.

He was crouched on rough planking. The first house: but he heard other voices, his Little Mama's and a man's. He knew somehow that it was his grandfather. No words: only the terror that emerged along with an anger that was outer, then inner, then broke up and slipped away into blackness.

Wilderness Mode: curled up now on different planking, waiting on a landing rank with urine. Out there stretched a city vast beyond imagining and cold beyond life's bearing; on the other side of a splintered door, he heard his Little Mama's voice, and a man's. The sounds of his Little Mama and the people she made arrangements with; the sounds of the arrangements. He was waiting till the arrangements were completed.

Wilderness Mode: starting bolt upright from sleep, this time with the terror and anger linked to suffocating heat, air humid as a steam bath, explosions, mutilation, and all around, death black and green.

Wilderness Mode: a kind of prayer.

In the house in Hale Noname, Will coughed.

Paula heard, and cold fear uncoiled.

It was that cough, in the night, that told her how sick he was.

Because he had coughed while he was in Wilderness Mode: that meant that he couldn't control it, couldn't stop it, couldn't keep silent even to save his life.

Huddled alone in the dark, turning all his formidable will and intelligence to self-protection and being physically unable to maintain it: that was beyond bearing.

She threw back the covers and turned on the bedside lamp, pulled on her robe. Turned on the overhead light by the door, and left the door open, and then turned the switch in the living room. Filling with light the world that Will had made.

Wrenched sideways with the coughing, Will sat at the very edge of the sofa, bent over, fully clothed down to his boots. His hands gripped the edge of the sofa frame so hard his knuckles were white. The great muscles of his back and shoulders twisted under his sweat-stained shirt like living things wrestling with the angel of death.

Paula dropped onto the sofa beside him and pressed her hands between her knees. She saw that she had folded them unconsciously, as if in prayer.

In the violence of his spasm she was afraid to touch him, afraid to speak lest he try to answer and choke, afraid to go and telephone their friend Jake, who was a doctor, lest rage make him worse, and stubbornly determined that he was not going to remain alone in the dark.

After a long time the coughing subsided, then died away.

He fell back against the cushions, throwing his forearm up to cover his face that was streaming with sweat.

At last he said indistinctly,

"It's a sight better, if you're feeling poorly for a spell, to have some light. Never thought of that before." He smiled, his arm still covering his eyes. "And some company, too."

Paula patted his knee.

Gradually, the rasping breathing calmed.

"Did I ever tell you," he asked suddenly, "that 'tweren't the piano I first played?"

"No, you didn't."

"'Twere the banjo. The banjo's an African instrument, you know. 'Banjo's' an African word. Don't know what language. But 'tweren't Euph who taught me. 'Twere my Little Mama."

He drank some water from a glass at his feet. "Don't play it no more. Not for years. Like you stopping the flower arranging all that time ago, I reckon. Might could be I'll take it up again someday, too." He was silent a moment. "Y'know what? These last days, in the midst of these coughing spells, I have remembered my Little Mama's fingers on the banjo strings. Ain't that something? Her hands were big, skin was rough — hard work she did — yet soft when she touched me, and right strong. Oval nails, pale like the moon. Skin on the back of her hands was sun-burnt like mine, but pale somehow underneath, with light brown freckles. You reckon that means she had light hair too, like mine? I can see her holding my hands in hers and showing me where to put my fingers on the strings. But that's all." He paused a moment, then smiled ruefully. "Well, I got her hands back to my memory now. You reckon I'll ever remember my own Mama's face?"

"Maybe. If you remember this, there's probably more coming along behind."

"A right terrifying thought," he said sarcastically, "plumbing my depths. You ready for bed again, Yumi? I'm a mite tired, somehow."

"You're driving too fast."

Will rammed the whole weight of his body down on the accelerator. The Jeep's lunge was his belligerent reply, and Paula's anger rose to meet his. They roared down the Volcano Road, stretching out far ahead of them, empty and overhung with hāpu'u ferns dripping rain.

Visions streamed through her: Waimea Canyon, rock spires of death, boiling hatreds and gaping absences, her radical insufficiency in seeking to attain the heart of the universe.

Will lifted his foot from the accelerator and tacitly acknowledged her words and her right and her memory. Yes, she thought, he knows how to handle anger differently now. Not easily. But he can do it. She tried to subdue her own anger.

His face was chalky.

"I said that wrong." Her words sounded stupid to her, unimaginative, radically insufficient — that was what she had said to herself when she painted *Pele Dancing*. But they were the only ones that came to her. "I'm sorry. I'm scared too, about your driving and why you drive that way, about your being sick, and I get — curt — when I'm scared."

"I were driving too fast." The explicit admission surprised her. He turned off the highway, toward Noname Lane. "But 't'ain't a question of being scared." He manhandled the Jeep up the muddy track. "'Tis a question of being mad. I don't like being in the hands of quacks. I don't trust it."

"Jake Mishima's not a quack," she said quietly. "And he's your friend."

"I know. I know. Jake's different, I reckon, but still he's talking about sending me away to strangers, to that hospital in Honolulu. I weren't counting on this talk of hospitals. For one thing, if it gets as far as documents and suchlike, I could lose my pilot's license."

"There may very well be no need for it to come to that. Jake's aware of the problem, and he'll do everything he can to avoid it. And if you get sicker, you can't fly anyway. Going to the hospital is only to get tests done that he can't do here. To keep whatever's ailing you from getting worse."

"I just don't think it's necessary, this talk of hospitals and tests and Honolulu. I don't think there's nothing that serious wrong."

You're lying, thought Paula wearily. That's exactly what you think, just like Jake and I do.

"And I can't go now," he went on, entering Noname Lane and maneuvering the Jeep to a spot near the ancient 'ōhi'a tree. The same tree Paula had stood behind, watching him chop wood and sing, the first time she came to Noname Lane. "'Tis the very worst time. It's time to start planning your birthday party, and this year's special 'cause it's the first since I'm back , and —"

"Will." She tried to force her voice to gentleness. She didn't think she succeeded very well.

He stopped the Jeep and dropped his head back against the seat.

"This is my place," he said, with helpless stubbornness, looking out across the glade. "You know that. I've been a long time getting here, and I don't want to leave. I'll never heal in Honolulu anyway, Yumi. Cities ain't no good for me. I ain't like you, Yumi. 'Tis one reason I do admire you so — that you know your way there. But I ain't got the knack. The city killed my Little Mama, and it'll kill me too. 'Tis here I belong."

"You'll come back."

They sat in a silence that Will broke.

"I ain't man enough to send you away." His voice was harsh and grating. "I ain't never been. And I weren't man enough even to do what I meant to do and stay out of your life after I got out."

"If I want you out of my life I can send you away. I don't see what it's got to do with manliness — or womanliness. I've sent men away. I damn near sent you away, when you came back from your little sojourn in Surabaya."

He heard her, she could tell — that it was true. He was still, a while. Then he began again, with difficulty.

"It's that you're loyal, Yumi, and I don't want to pressure you. I — I know our good loving has always been important to you. And things are changing now."

"It's always been important, but it's not what I stayed for. Sorry, friend, you're not that good, you couldn't hold me with that unless you had a whole lot else that's more important going for you too. And things are always changing. It seems to be the nature of the universe."

She stared at the papaya tree. Fruit clustered eagerly at its top, like a tumble of suckling puppies, like bursting breasts.

Another silence. Finally, heavily, Will climbed out of the Jeep and they went into the house.

"Will's the fourth case I've seen," Jake said at the lunch Paula had arranged for the two of them so they could discuss Will's situation. "And

I'm getting answers to my queries from other doctors about cases they may have seen. There are three from near Kailua — two brothers and a friend who served in Vietnam together. And one from Kaua'i. I have four cases from up near Honokaa — agricultural sites with heavy pesticide pollution. I've been reading up, and I'm waiting for answers from a couple of friends from med school practicing on the Mainland, who've been involved with this issue. Also, I've heard doctors in Vietnam are seeing cases like these."

Paula sat with her hands clamped around her glass of Chardonnay, staring out over Jake's shoulder at the Bayfront, the Belt Highway and the Bay beyond. Forty miles to Honokaa, the Hamakua Coast. The coconut palms beyond the Belt dipped and swayed in the Trades. A fantasy: she and Will could get in the Jeep and head North, outrun disaster and death.

"What is it? This disease? Medically, I mean? I only know what I've read as a layperson."

"I'm not sure medical persons know much more. Multiple symptoms. A syndrome, we call it, not a disease. Most of the people affected are men who were in Vietnam, or Vietnamese civilians. Others are people who work or live around heavily-sprayed agricultural sites. Dioxin's the basic culprit, I'd bet on it, and a whole lot of other physicians think so too. Getting the VA to admit all this is for the lawyers. I think the doctors have got the easier job."

"What can be done for the people who've got it? For Will?"

"I know this answer won't sit any better with you than it does with me, but the truth is, not a whole lot. I have some ideas. There've been some treatments that are often more successful than non-treatment. And every now and then, people just seem to get better on their own. But first Will needs to get some tests. I can't do them here. I do have to check him into a hospital in Honolulu."

"He'll hate it, Jake. I don't know if he'll go. He certainly won't go to a VA hospital.

"There are a lot of first-rate doctors at the VA."

"I know. Tom Tanaka and others have said so too. But Will didn't run into them, and he won't go there."

"It's going to be expensive. I told you that the other day."

"He has the money," said Paula. "For now, anyway."

The day before, after arranging to meet Jake, Paula had taken Ben aside and laid out the figures Jake had given her earlier.

"Can Will pay for it?"

"He can pay," Ben replied calmly. And Paula did not doubt that he knew.

"Then I guess something we can do is figure out how to get him in for tests . . . That should be only a little harder than cracking the medical mystery or getting the VA Administration to acknowledge the condition."

42

Glass Shattering: Lonesome Road

Paula sat on the futon in the big room of the house down Noname Lane, her arms folded across her chest, and watched Will pacing up and down like a great caged cat. Jake had sought him out at Euph's and put it to him straight about the tests. He was being pressured, Will said, cornered between Paula's moves and Jake's.

But really he listened because one night the coughing wrenched him so dreadfully he cracked a rib.

The gathering storm of his rising emotions was as palpable in the room as the clouds she could see through the wide windows behind him, massing above the mountains. Tomorrow, it would rain.

The hair along her nape was prickling. Will had paced this way before he went away.

The moment she realized this, a rage so mighty she did not recognize it as hers claimed a life of its own and possessed her, overwhelming even her concern for him and what would become of him if he took off again in this condition.

Her heart banged irregularly against her chest. Heat, then cold, swept in waves across her shivering skin.

She rose, her arms still folded, and planted herself directly in front of him as he started to stamp back across the room, his nostrils pinched and transparent with fury. When he stepped around her, she reached out and up and grabbed him by the shirt-collar.

When she spoke she did not recognize her own voice, thin and steely and humming like a guitar string stretched too far, just before it snapped.

Even through his towering self-absorption, he must have heard that hum: he stopped short when she spoke.

"You're revving up and going centrifugal. You're getting farther and farther away from yourself, and so you're getting farther and farther away from me, and from this place and everyone else here. You're heading back into outer space without a flight plan. Last time you took off and you didn't come back or send word for a long, long time. And I won't go through anything like that again. I don't want to see Ben and the others go through it again. You hear me? Not again. You know how to act differently now. You may not like it and it may be hard, but you know how. I've seen you do it.

And I expect you to do it. I'll help you all I can and you tell me how I can help, but you have to act differently than last time. You decide. I'll be back before dark. And to make it easier to hear me, watch me now."

It was totally unlike her that she did not know from one movement to the next what she would do. Yet her actions, though unplanned, were deliberate, rising like a sure swift stalk out of the heart of her anger and her determination to protect herself, and Will, and the others, and not have him be lost to all of them and to himself again.

She picked up the Minuvongan war club and brought it down across the top glass pane of the nearest bookcase. Then she broke all the other glass panes in the bookcases.

The crashes tore jaggedly through the country silence, aural representation of the craziness in glass starring out across the gleaming hardwood floor.

Silence fell.

Will stood transfixed, staring at her.

She paused, breathing hoarsely through her mouth and nose. She licked her lips, which were suddenly very dry, then dropped the club, plunged across the room and clattered down the steps, the screen door slamming behind her.

At the thump of her boots on the stairs, she thought that for all her life, since the bottles heaved at her in the streets of her childhood, the sound of shattering glass had undone her, signalled her as a target and as a victim, treacherously betrayed by her own face, the face of the enemy. Today, without premeditation, she had claimed the sound of shattering glass as her assertion in the world.

She returned in an early dusk hurried by rain clouds that were bringing night on swiftly. Trudging down the track to the glade, she noted with sudden apprehension that no lights showed in the house. Across the clearing and at the top of the lane, the earth was churned by wheels into muddy unreadable tracks, and the Jeep was not there.

She stopped short, her heart pressing against her throat, choking her breath. In the clarity of pain of that moment when she thought that Will had gone, another cruel clarity came too, slamming her with a guilt that she knew would never leave her, even though in the same moment her sardonic voice asked her how she could fail to feel what she did: relief.

And at once came a feeling as strong and swift as her feeling that morning that had guided her shattering of glass. Somehow acknowledging the guilt, but supporting her in her own feelings and actions, came a steadiness of self she had never felt before, growing out of her new relationship with shattering glass: if he is gone so be it. Her heart might break but her life was no longer breakable by others.

She went into the front room, gloomy with the approaching storm, and pressed the switch.

Light flooded the world.

At first the room looked the same as always. No traces of glass remained. Even the shards had been picked from the edges of the bookcase frames and only an eye that knew what it sought would have observed right away the empty bookcase fronts and the absence of fragile objects.

She stood a moment, utterly still. The clock on the wall behind her ticked heavily.

From the back of the house, the screen door to the kitchen banged.

The weight of dread, of exhaustion, of anger and all the complex emotions that go into the organism's bracing to suffer again great pain already known — all this drained out of her. She was left with rubbery limbs, momentarily dragged down by an overwhelming sleepiness that was an urge to oblivion.

In the kitchen she heard the familiar grunt as Will lowered a heavy box to the floor.

It would probably be kalo or yams or potatoes: roots in any case, and they would go in the pantry bin. Other garden produce went on higher shelves, and he would have set the box on the table. Or was he carrying something bought in town?

In this fashion her mind clung to familiar details, re-grounding herself in her life.

He grunted again, as he straightened up, she thought, but this time the sound was almost a groan.

And he began to cough.

Paula pressed her diaphragm against the edge of the big table, stifling her own breath, allowing herself, now when he could not see, the luxury of cringing at the sound of his tearing tissues. She thought she heard his joints creaking, separating, muscles ripped away from moorings with the awful strain.

Bones breaking.

The attack went on and on, dreadfully.

When it began to subside, he clawed for his breath in shallow, desperate draughts like sobs.

Then his feet dragged across the floor. Water ran, stopped: he had gone to the sink. Then he hawked and spit, hawked and spit.

Paula shuddered. She was not revolted; in the time since visiting Auntie Raina about her rape, she had become far more accepting of bodies, in pleasure and in pain, in illness and in health. Now she shuddered in empathy with the pain that twisted Will's body, shuddered with the memory of the traces of blood-laced spittle he hadn't been quite able to remove in the bathroom basin.

He turned on the tap. Water ran for a long time.

The sound ceased, and he came through the door, suddenly. He saw her and stopped abruptly.

"Yumi." His laugh was brief and painful. "I didn't know you were here." Almost furtively, he glanced over his shoulder at the kitchen. "That were a bit of a coughing fit there." She flinched at his attempted nonchalance. "Reckon you heard it." Beneath the deep tanning his skin was gray.

"Yes." She felt her casual acknowledgement to be as unconvincing as his insouciance; unfairly, for it had been accidental, she felt as if she'd been caught eavesdropping or engaging in voyeurism.

"Will, where's the Jeep? I thought — " She stopped, knowing she did so from foolish and dangerous pride that wanted to keep from him her desolation at the moment of thinking that he had abandoned her.

"I pulled it back around near the tool shed. It's got some kind of rattle. I were gonna check it out now, but I reckon I'll leave it till tomorrow. Why?"

If she expected him to behave differently, to be more open, she must be more open too.

"I was afraid you were gone," she whispered, and tears ran down her cheeks.

He didn't move, just looked at her; he seemed to go a little paler. She wiped her face and set her expression firmly.

"No Yumi," he said almost without expression. "I ain't gone." He grinned. "Matter of fact, I got us reservations for tonight. At Ranji's, you know the place, that new restaurant down on Keawe Street. Been meaning to check out the competition for awhile now. You should have heard his voice when I gave my name."

"What he's long feared. You're getting ready to go Māori at the Pine Tar."

"Man's no more a Māori than I am."

"And you're no more what you let your Mainland customers think you are than you're a Māori."

"That's different. I don't fake the food. And for the rest, at bottom Euph's and the Pine Tar ain't about customers, you know that. Just enough to keep the place going, so we-all can enjoy it. Oh, by the way," he said off-handedly, "one reason I thought I'd take care of checking out Ranji's tonight is I talked to Jake while I was in town, and he's booked me into that hospital-place in Honolulu this Friday coming up."

Later, when they were back from Ranji's, which had gratifyingly justified Will's scorn, he sat in the green armchair.

"Have to visit the glazier tomorrow." He grinned. "Never a dull moment around you, Yumi. Puts me in mind of that mango afternoon when you near uprooted my tree."

"This time it was different. It was intentional." And it was glass shattering. Maybe the combination was not accidental. "I'm not planning on making it a habit, but I want you to know it's in my repertoire." She herself hadn't known until that afternoon.

"'Her infinite variety.' I will remember, don't worry." He closed his eyes and rubbed his hand across the bridge of his nose, and even in the subdued lamplight Paula saw how strained and tired he looked.

"I'm an old man. What use is a man when he can't even carry a box of kalo without keeling over?"

"Not old. Your health is off, Will. You can cart fifty-pound boxes of kalo around again when you get well. So take good care of yourself. Simple."

Again, he grinned, faintly, not opening his eyes. "'Twere a hundred pounds."

"Duly noted."

The rain had begun, exploratory fingers tapping on the roof. Under the near window, the banana leaves rustled.

"You ever hear that song, Yumi?

> *When I were jest a little bitty baby*
> *My Mama would rock me in the cradle*
> *In them there ole cotton fields back home. . .*
>
> *Well, it may seem kinda funny*
> *But we didn't make very much money*
> *In them there ole cotton fields back home. . .*

And that other poem I did always like

Speaks about us all, I reckon. Aims and ambition, dreams, where they end up. . .”

His voice trailed off. She guessed that he was thinking of his Little Mama, her Lake and her hopes for him, in school, away from Hibbits. “And then, other ways too. . . ’tisn’t what the writer was meaning, I reckon, but it puts me in mind of it somehow. Like at Tule Lake, where there was nothing to see. You remember you did tell me that?”

“I remember,” said Paula quietly, and she was touched and surprised that he did. She had mentioned it only once, on the day after they had met.

“I know how that is. About how there’s nothing to see — yet there’s so much of hard life’s been lived there. I don’t reckon the Starvesoil’s changed much.”

“It didn’t look like it.”

As she spoke, she felt her stomach cramp with tension. Will fixed his pale gaze on her; he had been listening, she thought; he had understood her implication.

“You’re saying you been to Hibbits, Yumi?”

“I did. Yes, I did.”

“Did you now. And what moved you to do that?”

She had thought she knew, but now she hesitated.

“What I thought then,” she replied, “was that I wanted to put that marker on Euph’s grave that you used to talk about. And even though you set a lei afloat for her — I wanted to put some flowers on your mother’s grave too. Because — because from what you’ve told me, for all her troubles and failings, for all the hurt I think she caused you, still I think there was a lot to admire in Robbie Cawdry. I think you think so too. And — and even more than all that," she finished, "because you are Robbie Cawdry's boy. I hope that you don't think I was presumptuous to go there and do that," she said, suddenly timid, "but — but you and I have been — associated — so long."

Something stirred in Will's eyes, but she couldn't read it; and his face remained impassive. She struggled on.

"But now it also seems to me I went for another reason too. I think I already knew — had decided — I was going to write that letter — the one that declared you legally dead. And I thought I would never know a last resting place for you. So I went to the place where you began." She smiled. "Symmetry. Something like that."

"And did you talk to folks there?"

"I talked with a man named Rafe Hollis," she replied lightly. "He sends you his greetings. Her remembered how well you played the piano."

She told him the rest of what Rafe Hollis had said. Then, with trepidation, she continued, "and I had a close encounter of the negative kind with a lawman named R. Armstrong."

Now the pale eyes slitted. "That degenerate ole goat still runnin' around loose? Lawman now is he? 'Bout what I'd expect of that place." He paused. "I reckon he had a thing or two to say about me and — and my folks?"

"Indeed he had."

"What sort of thing?"

If he hadn't asked she wouldn't have said; and she would answer, narrowly, only what he asked. The truth was called for, she hoped she was right, they could not survive more silences on crucial things. If, later, he found out she had gone to Hibbits, and she had not told him first, he would not ask about it and he would always wonder. The truth, then, nothing but the truth — but in human relations — outside of court as in — not always, at every moment, the whole truth. If he wanted more detail, he could ask, now or later. She had opened the door.

And, as in court, carefully phrased.

"He spoke of abusing you and abusing your mother. Nothing I hadn't assumed from things you'd already said over the years."

"That so, Yumi? I don't rightly remember speaking of such things to you. But then, there's times I don't remember at all."

"Oh, not explicitly. I said 'assumed.' And from a long time ago. So he didn't surprise me."

The big clock ticked. A sudden spurt of rain hit the panes like pebbles and subsided as suddenly.

"Does this change things?" she asked. Wanting to cry out, angry, hurt, You left me, Will. I had to figure out how to live with that.

"Well, it do call for a readjustment in my thinking. And it do call things up for me most vividly I had put away from me long ago — I thought. But maybe not so far away at that, given my life since, what I'm feeling now. And any changes with us, they're for the best I reckon. I'm feeling like — like some barriers have fallen, like things can be — relaxed now that always were tense before. And I can't pretend your assuming surprises me. I did give you cause, I think, here and there over the years. So maybe in a way I was wanting to speak, and am just as glad to know you heard."

He paused. " And no, I don't think 'twas — what did you call it? — presumptuous of you to go. Like you say, we been together a long time. Fact is, I do thank you for going, Yumi. So that marker's laid on Euph's grave?"

"Just as you placed the order." She told him the inscription. "I took a photograph. I'll bring it over next time I come."

He grinned. "Not just quite to your taste, as I recall, my preferences for that marker-stone."

"I apologize, Will. I was being a cruel snob when I laughed at your description." She grinned, too, suddenly. "Not that I like it any better now, but that doesn't make my taste the correct taste, or any measure for yours."

"Apology accepted. 'Twas a gesture of true friendship, to arrange for that design even though I weren't around to hold you to the esthetic atrocity. And flowers for my Little Mama's grave, you say?"

"Yes. I have a photo of that too. They were just wildflowers," she added defensively.

"'Just'? Like what you took to Tule Lake, you're saying?"

"Yes," she whispered, and suddenly she was crying, because he had made the connection.

"Don't cry, Yumi. 'Twere brave and dangerous and I would have stopped you if I could've, stopped you going down to that place near where such dreadful things happened to you. I am most touched. Yeh, just like that 'Ozymandias' poem. There's nothing to see down to Hibbits — where people and pigs root in the Starvesoil. There's nothing to see at the Windermere Gardens — where my Little Mama did make her hardest choice. Between hellfire and the stony ground that do break up the heart. What an insult to name that place so. We most of us there came from the land, we knew how to make things grow and love them, the more for the coaxing we had to give them to get them to live. And they called that place of brick and rot the Gardens. But we did try to make our life there, my Little Mama and me, and others all around."

He gave her a sharp, sardonic look over the rim of his glass. "I reckon you went to Chicago in your travels, too? Looked at your old home."

"Yes. Gentrified. All dressed up, and expensive now. Exclusive, too."

"And my old home? The Windermere Gardens?"

"Urban removed. Gone. Torn down. Gentrified too. Upscale faculty housing."

"And now there's no more Gardens at all? Well, well. Praise the day. Yet in a way, God help me, I feel sad to have them gone. Long as they were standing there was something to see of all that — a sorry monument it were but to something that weren't sorry. It did count for something, those folks' work and trying and dreams, my Little Mama's work and trying and dreams. It did count for something. All gone, now. Thrown in the garbage to make room for rich folks. What did you say they've built there? Professor houses, they call 'em?"

"Faculty housing."

Her eyes had filled with tears and she was trying to blink them away. Shakily she recited the words to the old spiritual,

> So wide you can't get around it
> So high you can't get over it
> So deep you can't get under it ...

"And I don't know why I thought of that."

"It's speaking of life itself, I reckon." Will paused. "This illness is particular hard for me, " he said suddenly. "It takes me back to the hoops when I were small."

"The hoops?" repeated Paula blankly.

"Yeh — I had 'em something fierce. You know what I'm meaning," he said, noticing her puzzlement. "The hoops. It's a sickness small children is specially prone to, a most terrible coughing. I read in the paper a while back how UNICEF says it's gonna be wiped out soon in the whole world. Wiped out! Now that's something to take note of. I clipped the article and hung it up in Euph's right next to Ben's article on the smallpox being wiped out. He had that pox as a boy, you know; the signs are on his face. You'd think the whole world'd celebrate these things, wouldn't you? 'Tain't that often humanity can be right proud of itself."

"Yes, you would think so. You mean whooping cough?"

Hoors, hoops, she thought. Logical enough. But she had never heard that peculiarity of his pronunciation in any but those two words, probably because both were rooted in archaic childhood trauma.

"Yeh, that's it's full name. My Little Mama just called them the hoops, though. Oh my! She were beside herself when I were sick so. . ." His voice faded again. He looked at her suddenly, sharply, his eyes pale and expressionless. "I didn't never tell you about having the hoops?"

"Never."

He stared unseeing across the big room, out through the window and what was now a curtain of rain fast blending with a curiously obscure darkness. A gust of fresh breeze filled the space with the odors of rain and lava dust. He shrugged. "Mebbe that's so. Come to that, I don't know as I've remembered it myself till these last times. . .since this cough took hold of me. Y'know, Yumi, when I were younger I were big and strong and people took it for health. But now I reckon it's coming clear I weren't never truly healthy. This illness do bring things back. 'Twere our first winter up to Chicago I took sick with the hoops ... My Little Mama didn't think I'd come through. I did, though. I did, but I don't think she ever got over my sickness ...it were too much for her, what with the burden of me, I reckon. After that she took to the medicine." For the third time, uncharacteristically, his voice faded out.

"It wasn't your fault, Will," said Paula. "For being there. For being born. For needing things."

He turned his pale eyes on her.

"You reckon? I reckon you're right." He paused. Then,

"'Twere powerful cold," he said briefly. "Chicago were powerful cold."

On a gray afternoon lowering with rain — the day before they were to leave for Honolulu and the hospital — Paula turned right, off H11 onto Mauna Loa Road, so that she was driving across and straight at the mountain, that incomprehensible somber mass, absolute, irreducible, and beyond knowing.

The gray-brown line of narrow road cutting through the low olive-colored scrub might have seemed arrogant, she thought, but it did not because the mountain reduced it to a tenuously tolerated impudence. No sign of human life was visible, except that road.

Human presence was always timid here, faced moment to moment with obliteration, perched on the edge of oblivion. Here on the volcano there was no place to escape that knowledge and no other truth to live.

Such truth was life up against its limit, a kind of wrath, where one felt the truth that showed forth from beyond. That truth at its heart, she knew suddenly, was love. Love in all its kinds: for places, for energies, for play: climbing, thinking, flying, music, everything that affirmed: simply, being. Lava-love glowing through the fissures of the burning rock, love distorted by the schisms of the heart, recreated by its healing: what else generated power enough to make the universe?

She closed the car door quietly, walked down the trail, and, turning the corner, came upon Will, seated on a rock.

He grinned. "'Tis so great minds do work together, both of us choosing to come here just now."

"You got here first. If you want to be alone, I'll go — come back another time."

"No Yumi, don't go on my account. What do you want to do?"

"I came to be alone, like you, but now I'm glad to see you here."

"I feel the same. Sit beside me then." He patted the rock.

She sat, and they looked out across the mountain.

"You know, Yumi, yes I know you know, since 'tis you have turned me to face it, shattering glass and all, you know that I'm on a trip without a flight plan, and not by my choosing this time. Might well could be the last one, the one 'tisn't just someone crazy as me sets out on without taking any baggage." And he grinned again. Then he sobered. "If I do pass from this illness, or when I pass in any case, as 'twill come some day, I want to be cremated, not laid to rot. I want to be given to fire. My friends are to have a party at Euph's, no speeches but lots of music. And I'd like you to keep my ashes, Yumi, 'cause you're good at keeping track of things, good at keeping them close."

"All right, Will." A typical Will compliment — if compliment it was, she added to herself wryly, fending off how moved she was.

"So I don't just blow away in the wide world, lose my place and time." He grinned again. "Not right away, anyhow. And when the time for that do come, say at the end of days, I reckon I'll take the time my ashes rested with you along to wherever I go next."

She stopped distancing herself and said quietly, "I'm glad you want that, Will. I want it too, and I want the same for myself, and of course I'll do it for you. And I hope you'll do it for me. But for right now, it seems a little premature. I'm not looking away from your being sick, or from how sick you are. But there's always getting well, too."

"Y'know," he said abruptly, "most of my life I reckon I didn't care whether I lived or died. Now I'd like to live, and I don't reckon I'm going to."

"You're sick. That's all. Nobody's dead till they're dead, and you're not dead."

This time he smiled a rare smile, slow and soft.

"Well, I reckon as well that that's so. Death don't happen to schedule, and I been wrong before now, thinking to call my own hour to go. I will do my best to remember that, and act on it too."

After a moment he went on, "'Tis a lonesome way for true, this out here ahead of us. Like that old song:

> *Look down, look down that lonesome road*
> *Hang down your head and cry.*

He stopped. And Paula did not speak the words, either, that concluded the verse, aware he was as familiar with them as she was:

> *You know all friends must part sometime*
> *Then why not you and I?*

"And that other song," he continued. "Seems like the topic's been on lots of peoples' minds.

> *You got to walk that lonesome valley*
> *You got to walk it by yourself*
> *Ain't nobody else can walk it for you*
> *You got to walk it by yourself*

"A lonesome way for true," he repeated, "Still, sometimes, and here only, on the volcano, I feel — I reckon what I feel is that nobody and nothing can fall out of the universe. Folks who love don't lose each other, don't lose their love for each other. No love is ever lost. Nothing, no one, gets lost. So maybe the truth ain't lonesome at heart after all."

"I know. I feel that here too."

Slowly, they turned and went away together from the somber place of power beyond conceiving.

"Do you want something to eat?" called Paula from where she stood studying the contents of the refrigerator, foraging for a late-night snack.

"Sure." The trail ends of a pretty melody moved through the house as Will doodled at the piano; a strangely light-hearted sound, she thought, given what was happening to him. "A glass of milk would sit just right. Could you set it here by me on the bench?"

A great sleepiness overwhelmed her, a band of heaviness pressed around her skull at her temples.

Paula heard his words.

She understood what he wanted her to do.

She had not the faintest idea what motions to make, what actions to take, to accomplish it, to get herself from the refrigerator to the piano.

Then, in seconds, the seizure passed.

Back in Honolulu, her doctor told her these seizures were called temporary ischemic accidents. They were tiny strokes that resolved without any detectable damage. They were completely unpredictable. She might fall down dead with a full-blown stroke at any moment, or she might never have an incident like that again. If it did happen again, she must go at once to the emergency room.

"'Twas my stubborn wrong-headed ways brought your spell on," insisted Will, distraught.

"Or my unbridled temper."

"No Yumi, that episode with the glass shattering wasn't like you at all. I set you off. It mustn't happen again. It won't."

The terrifying seizure opened to Paula a window on the underlying organization of her brain, paradoxically gave her a view of it in its momentary disorganization that she had never had when she sought to understand it with her full powers available.

It also gave her an appalling glimpse of what life would be if the disorganization had not righted itself.

She had visited a strange country and returned. Her life and her sense of life would not be the same again.

Another intimation of mortality.

43

At the Royal Palace: A Chant For All the Islands

Harrowed, Paula crumpled against an unyielding molded plastic chair in a Honolulu hospital room. She had sat there for three days, while in the bed beside her, Will — who had come for routine tests and instead been ambushed by his body — had fought out a death battle, just now, however temporarily, won.

He had reverted to Wilderness Mode, learned in the war at home and the war abroad, in Hibbits shacks and Chicago tenements, honed in Vietnam. Writhing, cover blown. His body streaming sweat, every muscle stretching so hard and taut the waxy skin seemed at the breaking point. Wrenching the breath from his chest as if his own lungs had turned on him to become a fifth column, gone over to the enemy, in family and jungle and in his own mind long ago.

And then, as inexplicably as everything else about this affliction, in the space of hours, all of it reversed.

"Are you there, Yumi?"

She flinched. His voice rasped like a knife-edge scraping along a bloodied membrane.

"Right here."

"What the hell for?"

It seemed to her a good question.

"I guess because I want to be. More than I want to be anywhere else."

This was true but did not seem likely. She would have to file it for further consideration.

"Don't talk now, Will. It takes too much energy."

"Is it day or night?"

"Night," she replied briefly. Outside the window, palm fronds loomed blacker against the dark sky. Beyond, Honolulu city lights climbed the flanks of the Koolaus. Down there, not so far away, was her bungalow. With a sudden hunger like pain, she yearned for its familiarity, solitude and peace, for the way it supported her sense of her own self. Regardless of everything.

"I'm worried about you, Yumi. I can't have you take another spell. I don't want you here all the time, in this dreadful place."

"I haven't been here all the time. It's all right, Will. I'm taking care of myself." And it was true.

He searched her face, seemed to accept her words.

Then he began to cough.

She slipped a hand beneath the hospital gown and spread her palm firmly against his chest, her fingertips light against the thick hair, matted and wet with sweat, the skin clammy. Why was he so cold? She wondered. The damp, soiled chill seemed to seep up through some disintegrating internal lining.

But he stopped coughing at her touch. Drew a few breaths, shaky but deep. Lay still.

After a moment he managed, "That feels right good, Yumi, your hand on me so. Warms me and dries me from the inside out."

It was mysterious and she could feel that it was true. Heat began to rise from within him, began to dry the terrible soiled chill. She feared having such a tangible, undeniable impact on his physical being, feared the power of an intimacy like theirs. It had brought joy and delight and also damage. Now his intimacy with death threatened to leave her abandoned by him on earth, Along with the devastating grief and fear she would only look at sideways, she felt rage at him and shame at her exultation in the knowledge that she could survive even that.

Will dozed.

Paula waited and listened, in the unnatural hospital half-dark that never truly turned to night. She listened to the machines he was clamped to as they bubbled and clicked, their fangs driven into his flesh, their fluids forcibly mingling with his blood.

Shadowy figures moved by in the dim corridor. She listened to the distant humming hive-sounds of the hospital. People and events about which she would never know were connecting organically to her in that humming, because all of the people were gathered here bound by the same things: pain and fear, hope and humiliation and mutilation, failure and life and death.

And she waited.

At first, she didn't know that she was waiting. Then when she knew, she didn't know for what she waited. Turning the question over in her mind, she decided judiciously that it must be death. That seemed only reasonable and likely. She knew the clarity of her logic was probably hallucinatory: she was exhausted and drained by fatigue and fear.

In November of 1967 Uncle Hiro became ill with cancer of the liver. The disease was discovered very late and when Aunt Florence called Paula he was already in the hospital for the first and last time.

Her feelings for him had always been a tangle of exasperation and impatience and deep resentment for the way he patronized her. His didactic lectures, the automatic assumption that he was the head of the household, irked her beyond endurance.

The last time she had visited had been the previous spring. She had found him engrossed in one of his projects, building a teahouse in the back garden. Paula would have expected her aunt to be enthusiastic about this traditional activity, but for some reason the teahouse was a source of contention between the two of them.

Standing in an unusually balmy evening, soft light on the quiet wooden structure, her aunt and uncle bickering about the project, Uncle Hiro suddenly responded to his wife's demand of "Why are you doing this?" with unwonted geniality, almost gentle humor. "Just returning to my roots." His formal Japanese accent made the phrase hilarious. Then, to Paula's astonishment, he turned and gave her a wink.

Paula realized that this was the first positive acknowledgement he had ever made of the roil of ethnic activity around him, about which he and she argued constantly.

That was the cause of Aunt Florence's annoyance: the teahouse was, somehow, both his answer to Stokely Carmichael and his participation in the times.

In the week after she learned of his illness Paula drove to the hospital three times. The first two she never even turned into the parking lot. Her sense of grievance against him conspired each time to send her back across the Bay to Berkeley.

The third night she parked and rode the elevator to Uncle Hiro's floor, but when she got to his room the orderlies were just stripping the bed.

Over twenty-five years later Paula jerked awake in the semi-dark, on an uncomfortable molded plastic chair in a hospital in Honolulu.

Immediately, she reached to touch Will. The blood still beat in the big vein on the back of his hand, bruised and violated by the shunt. His chest still rose and fell, the raspy breath softer now. From where she sat she could see part way down the corridor.

Was someone coming? Who was she expecting?

Then she suddenly knew that she was waiting for herself.

Her scalp prickled. She felt simultaneously that she sat in the chair and that she was coming along the corridor as surely as those first two nights she had not come along the corridor to Uncle Hiro's hospital room.

And now she did hear footsteps. Her heart jolted as she saw herself approaching: step by step, walking into her own future, in a cosmic spiral where life caught up with death and death with life and one walked through the other, eternal passepartout, as everyone always came back because no one ever truly went, for no one and nothing could fall out of the universe.

But of course it was not she herself approaching. For an instant she was back on the night beach at NorthShore years ago, as the other Yumi to whom she was namesake approached her across the sand, and approached now down an echoing corridor.

"Are you okay, Paula? You look ready to faint!"

A warm hand was laid on her shoulder. Pearlie Leilani's familiar voice, vibrant now with concern, shocked Paula back to her place and time.

"Is it Will?" Pearlie Leilani asked, and turned a fearful gaze to the bed. "Is he — worse?"

Paula shook her head dizzily, then nodded, too fatigued to sort out the questions easily.

"No. He's not worse. He's better. And I'm fine. Just tired. I'm glad you came, Leilani, I was waiting for you. So was Will."

She hadn't meant to speak those last two sentences.

The girl pulled back into herself. Paula thought that she had been reassured that she had not stepped into immediate disaster, then angered that her uprush of concern had waylaid her and betrayed her into showing feelings. Feelings she wished not to show — perhaps to herself above all — or maybe even to have.

"I — I just thought I'd stop by for a second. Don't wake him up."

"He'd want me to." As she spoke, Will stirred, opened his eyes, and blinked.

"That you for true, Little Princess?" he asked groggily. Paula tensed at the nickname he had forgotten not to use, but Leilani said only,

"So Will, how you feeling?"

He was unguarded too, in his extreme state. His pleasure was almost palpable and Pearlie Leilani pulled back from that too.

"Reckon I've felt better, but mainly what's wrong is being in this place. If I could just keep the vampires here from taking my blood every ten minutes, and get on home —" He paused. "I'm right glad you've come. Right glad. Yumi, turn on a light, will you? Thanks. We got a chair around here somewhere —" He shifted massively beneath the sheets.

"I really just came to bring you this." She started to hand him a large square envelope, then seemed to jib at the fierce bristle of tubes jutting from his arms, at his pallor in the harsh narrow cone of light from the bedside lamp. She laid the envelope cautiously on the bed. "Well, I'll let you get back to sleep now." She hesitated. "Get better, Will."

And she was gone, the sound of her steps receding, then fading out down the corridor.

Cursing the entangling IV tubes, Will ran his thumbnail shakily under the envelope flap, and pulled out a stiff red and gold card and a sheet of paper. He read the sheet of paper.

"The Princess has painted an invitation for me. She writes that she is involved with planning a march on 'Iolani Palace on the Centennial Anniversary of the Overthrow. She includes a map to the Palace. In case I'd have trouble locating it, I reckon. Well now. A formal hand-delivered invitation to a salvo in a revolution. I recall hearing talk about some such march; I still got my good contacts here and there. They say that kanaka maoli will walk at the front. Reckon I'll get a fine enough view from the back, where I s'pose the haoles will be placed. I guess you-all folks can be in the middle since kanaka maoli invited you to live here. Well, I can put up with a little righteous choreographic symbolism. Yeh, it'll be a good day, at the Royal Palace."

He turned to the red and gold card, and grinned broadly.

"Announcement of the opening performance of 'A Chant for All the Islands,'" he told her. "The girl finished it after all. I'm glad. I'm right glad."

Paula thought of Ben's brief comment to her a week previously: "The girl say she finished with that long chant. I think she'll go to see Will soon. Because she couldn't finish it without fixing that." He'd hesitated, then added, "I know something about things that need to be fixed."

"And Yumi — see here!" Will exclaimed, pulling her attention back to the hospital room. "Just look at that!"

Paula leaned over and read the sentence below the title:

Nothing Pearlie Leilani could have brought, thought Paula, could equal the gift of the invitation and, above all, the dedication. Will ran his fingers over the words. Then, he moved away from the moment's emotion, continuing drolly,

"'Twas a brief visit from the Princess, but a good one, and I think maybe not the last."

He fumbled for a pen on the bedside table, drew four shaky boxes at the bottom of the leaflet announcing the performance and demonstration, labeled one "Am Attending: Performance" and the other "Am Attending: Demonstration" and two "Regrets," and made big check marks in the "Am Attending" boxes. Hesitated. Scrawled, "If the Good Lawd's willing and the crick don't rise," and handed it to Paula.

"Get this back to the Princess for me, will you, Yumi?

The exertion, and the excitement, had tired him terribly. He fell back, and his arms dropped like weights on the bedsheet.

"So," he murmured, "one day we'll be gathering at the river, so to speak, there in front of the Palace. To bear witness, and protest that shameful thing 'twere done at Honolulu to the Queen and all Hawaiians. . . . a hundred years ago. Take some steps to set it right. Mebbe our circle will be unbroken some day for true." He rested, his eyes closed. After a moment, he said, "might could be that-there's a hand-delivered invitation to a ho'oponopono of sorts. What d'you think, Yumi?"

"I think it is." She expressed her long-held idea. "And in our time, most ho'oponoponos are ho'oponoponos of sorts. Provisional, patchwork. People have too many different relationships with different people and kinds of people from different parts of their lives to have one good old-fashioned coherent ho'oponopono that clears up everything in one fell swoop."

"Kinda like your calabash. Broken, plugged, broken, plugged. A work of modern art. Post-modern?"

"Something, kinda like," Paula agreed.

He gave a sketchy grin. "Don't mock me, Yumi. This po'boy's doing the best he can."

"I'm not mocking you. I'm doing the best I can, too — to borrow some of your style."

He gave her a half-salute, his knuckles grazing his temples as if he wore his hat.

Then he slept.

She slept, too.

Now she was walking the last few feet of hospital corridor in San Francisco again, turning again into the room, in a soft dusk. But this time, Uncle Hiro still lay in the bed, sleeping under a tangle of IV tubes.

She went next to him, and heard herself speaking Japanese.

"Thank you, Uncle Hiro, for welcoming me into your home. I know it must have — disrupted your life, in many ways. I still think as I do about everything we've disagreed on, but I also think you meant only my best. Thank you for that. And I apologize for having been very rude sometimes — when we were arguing about politics."

She had thought he was asleep, maybe in a coma; she had not expected him to hear. So she was astonished when he awoke, staring at her with the same unfamiliar expression he had directed at her at his teahouse, on that unseasonably balmy evening not so long before: an expression that was gentle, humorous.

"You're very welcome," he responded in his precise accented English. "And don't worry about the arguing. I enjoyed it."

And, astonishingly, he winked at her again.

"Dreaming, Yumi?"

Sunlight flooded the room.

"I — I guess so." So vivid, the visit to Uncle Hiro had been — had it truly been just a dream? And she smiled to think of what Ben would say of such a formulation: just a dream, indeed! This time, as other times, she hoped that he was right.

She shifted in the chair, wincing at her aching joints.

"You're tired, Yumi. I feel right bad about this, what it's doing to you. You don't know how bad I feel about it."

"It's okay. I'm going hiking today with Ginnie, then out to lunch. That'll give me a lift."

"Think this place'll really spring me day after tomorrow?" She heard the yearning and the tension behind his off-hand manner.

"Jake says unless something goes wrong between now and then he'll sign you out. You've been getting better steadily for a week now."

He greeted her sleepily when she came in, late that afternoon, from her climb in the Koolaus.

"Hello, Miss American Pie. You don't look like the Miss America I met. Nor act like her neither. For both of which I am right thankful."

"What's that mean?" Paula unhooked her waist pack and dropped it on the floor, then began unlacing her boots.

"Miss America I met looked like — well, you know. We been all over that." He grinned. "I oughta be safe, though, you can't hit a man when he's down. And what're you gonna do here where there ain't no mango trees to mutilate or glass to smash? Rip out my IV tubes? Anyway, I meant it when I said I were right thankful. Something else different too," he said with mock thoughtfulness. "Oh, I got it now. She weren't wearing hiking boots."

"You're wandering again," she teased.

"I am not. You mean to say I never told you about the time I met Miss America?"

"Never. Talk story. Briefly. You're not a well man yet."

He lay silent a moment, gathering his thoughts.

'Twere in Tokyo, he remembered, but he spoke to himself. In Tokyo, in the hospital. Yeh, in the hospital. I reckon that's why I thought of it now. There we were, all of us lined up in a row on the Spinal Hopeless Ward. That were early on when they were saying I wouldn't never walk again, nor go with a woman again neither. They were wrong. For once, they were wrong in a good way about me.

And to cheer us up, us soldier boys on the Spinal Hopeless Ward, the Powers That Be sent Miss America to visit us. She come in and went from bed to bed. Squeezing our hands. I was in the first bed and I was so surprised I let her do it. One of those things I do regret.

Ain't that something? Sending Miss America to the Spinal Hopeless Ward. Not a man there over twenty-five, and I had got to know not a man there but had been told he'd never have sex again. And they sent Miss America . . . smiling and wiggling and squeezing and bending over the beds with her tits hanging out like a cross between Virgin Lady bountiful and a strip-tease queen . . . and she was thanking us for what we gave for our country.

She got two-thirds of the way down the ward before someone spit on her.

Now he wished someone had spit on the men who'd sent her, too.

Ah, he thought. So that was what Julie and Jannye were about, for me. That I could have Miss America after all.

And in the instant of recognition, all that was past and done with.

"No," he said aloud to Paula. "Let's not speak of it. 'Tain't a pretty story. We don't need it. And it don't matter no more anyhow, whereas we got enough to deal with right here that ain't so pretty. Just now I'd rather hear about you and Ginnie, what you ate at lunch and how it tasted, what it looks like up in the Koolaus today."

While Will gathered himself together and got ready to leave the hospital, Paula pulled the uncomfortable chair into the corner out of the way in the cramped room and sat still.

Now, with release from this place so imminent she could taste it, the deep, enclosed streak in her personality that wanted to be let alone, that wanted to let everyone and everything else alone, was rising up in revolt, insisting on itself after the hard care-taking.

Long ago, Ginnie had asked why Paula wanted him. Some of the hidden, more twisted, damaging reasons she had not known then. But her reply had been truthful: Because he knows how to take delight in life, because he's never taken me to see something that wasn't worth seeing, because he's never tried to change me.

And that had been strong enough, when the twisted reasons were healed, to carry them along the road to this place.

Sitting was not easy for her. It never had been; and, under stress, her drive was always to move. She hoped he could not tell how strong her urge was to get up, to interrupt him in his slowness as he did things for himself that she could do faster for him.

She had worn her waist pack to leave her hands free to carry bags, to try to support him if he were unsteady, to push a wheelchair. Now she had trouble controlling her impatient fingers. If only she had her satchel purse, or something else with which to fidget. Already she was zipping and unzipping the little pack. She looked around for something quieter, less obvious, but she'd placed herself out of reach of the bedside table with its pencil and pad of paper, its pile of newspapers. Finally she tucked her hands between her knees and squeezed them together.

Will sat on the edge of the bed while he put on his underwear, his socks, pants and shoes, but now he was standing to button the shirt, his fingers careful with awkwardness. He had asked her to bring the scarlet shirt with the flamboyant whorled designs embroidered in silver thread. She felt a surge of amusement, and was heartened that he had had the energy and the desire to think of dressing up for his departure from this place.

It took him a long time and she could see him draw breath to start the next difficult task of threading his belt through the loops of his shimmering silver pants. At last, finished, he started across to the bathroom, and she saw him sway.

He gripped the doorframe, took two steps, dropped his left hand to the edge of the basin to steady himself. But that uncertainty could just be due to the time in bed, she told herself. That alone brought on weakness. Through the open door, she watched him comb his hair, his hands trembling slightly.

He thrust the comb in his shirt pocket and looked at himself in the cruel mirror and the cruel light.

"I look like death come calling," he said.

Paula shook her head.

"No. You don't look like death come calling. Actually you look better than you have in a long time. You're pale and you look tired and you've lost weight, but your eyes are clear and the paleness is partly from being out of the sun. And the shakiness is partly from being in bed. Also you're breathing much more easily, even though you're moving around more."

"So you think the quacks are on the level about my being better? Not just clearing their bed out for a more lucrative patient?"

Patients didn't come more lucrative than Will, but that was a discussion for another day.

"You know I wouldn't let them send you away if I thought you ought to be here, and neither would Jake. You'd only be coming home today if you were better or if you were dying. And you're not dying today, Will. You know that."

He pressed his knuckles against the basin edge and stared at himself in the mirror, as if trying to see his own inner truth that his body might be concealing from him.

"No," he said. "I reckon I'm not dying. Not today."

And he grinned.

"Well." He became brisk. He turned too fast and had to catch the back of the chair. "Let's get outta this place. You know how I feel about places like this, Yumi. I want to get on home. Get some decent food. Get outta this place where they won't even let a man's woman lie down next to him and keep him warm!" He snorted. "They offered me an extra blanket when I asked could I have you stay the night! I told 'em if Gawd meant for blankets to be all a man could grab hold of, he'd have made blankets, not Eve. Reckon my religious background's useful for a debating point at least."

He hated the wheelchair, but grumbling that he'd do anything to get out faster he stopped arguing with the nurse and allowed her to guide him into it. Paula wondered if it was clear to him, as it was to her, that without it he'd never have made it down the long corridors to the elevator.

They went through the drawn-out process of arranging his discharge papers. He signed with a flourish, in his jagged script like the line of the Koolaus against the sky.

At the hospital entrance, he rose and pushed the chair away, then stood blinking, more from disconcertment than exhaustion. Terrifying, thought Paula, how rapidly institutions — jails, hospitals — got their claws into your being, isolated you, threatened to incapacitate you for any other life.

Will sank onto a bench while Paula went to bring the car around.

As she pulled to the curb, she caught an unexpected glimpse of him, as a stranger might have seen him: staring into space, his skin waxy in the floods of morning sunlight. Her throat caught at an inward frailty made more shocking by his powerful frame. His hands rested on his knees. Even now, raw and big-knuckled, they adumbrated strength and danger, conveyed tenderness and music and form.

He stood up when he saw the car, and walked very deliberately to the front passenger door she swung open for him. She could tell that for a moment he proposed to insist on driving, and she braced herself for an argument. Then he pressed his lips together and climbed in next to her.

"How much weight you reckon I've lost, Yumi?" he asked, studying the way the seatbelt fit him. "Ten pounds? Twenty?" He thrust two big fingers down his waistband, easily. "Lookit that. And the belt's already notched in three extra spaces."

"Not twenty. Maybe ten. You'll put it back on fast, when we get where Ben can feed you."

"Not too fast, though. I want to pace it with exercise. I don't want it back as flab."

"It'll work out, Will. Except it's going to take a little time. You're going to have to be patient, Will."

He gave his wheezy laugh. "We're a right pair for patience, Yumi. Comes so natural to us." He paused. "Speaking of which," he went on casually, "Yumi, don't think for a moment I don't know this sickbed duty's right hard for you. I — it's much appreciated."

She couldn't answer; didn't know how. She gave a brusque nod and pretended the traffic needed more attention than it did. Then it did need more as her tears threatened to spill.

Will turned his head so she saw it in profile, rugged as the profile of Lē'ahi behind it. He looked out at the tangle of Honolulu buildings and traffic, his gaze traveling out across the sea with a consuming hunger that startled her.

"Now let's go home," he said. "Words can't tell how much I want to be home."

But his expression told her.

44

A Kind Of Wrath

Wide pools of rainwater shimmered on the pavement when Paula and Will emerged from the Hilo airport into a gray and humid late afternoon. Paula brought the Jeep around from where she had parked it.

Will leaned his head back against the leather headrest and closed his eyes briefly. Exhaustion had carved lines like scars into his face. But by the time they were well on the road to the volcano, he was leaning forward, looking out at the lush foliage, looking toward the Lava Wastes beyond, hungering, slowly relaxing as the landscape nourished him.

Paula, slowly relaxing too, looked with him across the lowering mountain, sloping gradually to its great heights. The gray day increased the somberness of the black and gray landscape, of the rock-rubble of boulders jumbled, tumbled, strewn across an earth scarred with pocks and fissures. Apparently as barren as some moon, she thought, truly the landscape of a starved heart; yet deeply fertile, with its hidden, creative fire, its future of ferns and lichens. She felt now, as she had never ceased to feel, its immense power and mystery. To herself she repeated again, Like life, its power is a kind of wrath; like love, a mystery.

"What're you thinking about, Yumi?"

"This place."

"It's something worth seeing, ain't it? But I thought mebbe you was thinking about that lawyer fellow. The one in San Francisco. Nakamura, that his name?"

"That's his name." As you know perfectly well, she thought. "But I wasn't thinking about him."

"Do you? Think about him?"

"Yes. Quite often. He's an old friend, and we work together. That's what there is between us."

"You're not old, you know, Yumi. I reckon you may feel so now, you're feeling tired and seedy after going through all this with my illness. But I've been thinking I wouldn't want you to forget you're powerful attractive. And I don't much care for the idea of you wearing yourself out the way you been doing these hard times. I could last a long time, you know. Anything that survives the Thornbrake Starvesoil like I did is tough and hard to kill off. And when I finally go, you'll be left. My health's better, but I'm not well,

377

and seeing as the damn quacks don't even know what's wrong with me, there's just no telling —"

"There's never any telling, Will. Never."

"You ain't bound to me, Yumi. You ain't had from me what you had a right to expect."

Rain was falling again. Paula switched on the windshield wipers.

She shrugged. She thought of how part of her resented, unreasonably and savagely as if he had done it on purpose, that Will had removed himself for so long and returned to her to fall ill; and of how another part still remembered her own attack, and knew she could be felled herself at any moment, and was guilty at her resentment.

"I didn't know this was a business deal we had going here. Of course I don't know that you won't get sick again. If you do and you need it, we'll have people to help us. We have friends and we can arrange home help. And you're right, no one knows what you've got, not Jake or the other doctors in Honolulu or the ones at the Mainland research places where they're fighting over what your blood and tissue samples show. But if you dig just a little deeper, no one ever knows, not really, or knows what's going to happen when. We are not promised tomorrow. I could have been the one that got sick, and just because you got there first doesn't mean I won't claim my turn. I've had a wake-up call about my health already, you know that. The night you came back from Surabaya you said you didn't want me to count you among my dead. Well, I'm not doing that now. How could I? You're too damn aggravating to be dead. And until you are, I've got enough to think about with both of us being alive."

She banged the brakes too fast and skidded slightly, narrowly avoiding a pickup emerging suddenly from Pszyk Road.

"Which we won't be if you don't shut up for awhile now. We're going to die together in an auto accident in the prime of our fraying middle-age, before we ever get back to Noname Lane."

"'Tweren't illness I were planning for when I built these steps."

The rain was coming down harder and Paula had an umbrella over them and they each had a hand on the banister and an arm around the other one's waist as they ascended, a step and stopping, a step and stopping, not step over step or three steps at a time, the way Will traveled those stairs when he was well.

"No." She heard her tart tone that he called her oheleberry voice. "You were thinking about flooding, which was more reasonable. Sick or healthy,

you need to think about flooding in this kind of country. You were thinking
about a few other things too. Like providing a safe house under the staircase
for emergency storage of illicit agricultural products."

Will grinned. "'Tis true, in a crisis, these steps have sheltered some of
the finest mari-juana this island's seen."

He looked around at Noname Lane.

"It's so quiet," he said softly. "So peaceful."

She could tell from his voice how glad he was to be out of Honolulu, to
be home. He will get well much faster here, she thought.

She worked the key and pushed the door open.

"All your lawyer friends," he went on, "you just keep them lawyering.
We'll schedule as many benefit shows at Euph's and the Pine Tar as you
want, just keep destruction-development down, keep this place quiet and
peaceful so."

"Then quit pestering me about moving on to find true love and fortune,"
she retorted crossly. She looked around too, at the clearing, at the forest
beyond. "You built well here, Will."

She knocked the strong porch railing with her knuckles.

"Yeh, it's not a bad job," he admitted.

Paula hung their coats to dry and watched him. This was the time she
had been worrying about. He would push too far, too fast, then relapse,
rage at her if she tried to rein him in, and they would fight, in bitter ways,
and that would be no good.

And she couldn't coddle him; he wouldn't stand for it, and trying would
drive her out of her mind.

So she would have to learn to live with being afraid to see him fall.

But he seemed to recover his energy once they were inside, as if being
home healed his fatigue.

"Now you sit down, Yumi," he said bossily. "You've been doing all the
work. We're back now, and I can take over a bit."

She was surprised at how tired she was, at how grateful she felt when he
pushed her gently into the deep armchair. He pummeled one of the silk
emerald cushions between his hands and tucked it behind her shoulder-
blades. He moved the ottoman over and lifted her feet onto it.

She was deeply pained as well, understanding that his actions were also
part of the struggle to shore up his pride battered by the assault of illness
on his strength and capacity, to hold ground in his battle for a precarious
self-esteem, won so hard, so late, just in time to be assaulted by the years
and an old destiny catching him up.

"I'll get us a cool drink," he went on.

But he paused, on the way to the kitchen, there in the early near-dusk, the rain pattering on the roof harder and harder now, and looked around the big room, in obscurity because no one yet had turned on a light.

He went to the piano, massive and mysterious in the gloom, full of latency and potential. He hesitated a moment before he slid the fall-board open. He struck a few keys, experimentally. She couldn't be sure because of the dimness, but she had the impression his fingers trembled slightly. The tones they called forth, though, were sure, the sound a little experimental, a little rudderless still, like the two of them, she thought: re-entering and re-claiming a loved space long abandoned.

Then his fingers were moving, he had even lifted the hand that he had been using to support himself against the piano top. Quickly he played with both hands, forward, backward, backtracking, picking up, re-weaving. He could have sat but he never sat at the beginning of improvising a composition.

"I've never heard that before, Will. It's very striking."

"Yeah," he murmured. "It's coming. I thought there was something coming before I got sick. At first even in the hospital sometimes, I'd hear it, in the night . . . then it went away. I thought it was gone for good. Thought maybe all my music was gone for good. But it were just going down inside me, deep, to change — because I got sick, I reckon. Had to see things a new way. But it's coming."

He looked at her. "It's something new, all right, Yumi. It's in honor of you. I think I got an idea for a new dish, too, something with breadfruit, 'twill also be named in honor of you. That idea, for the breadfruit dish, it went away in the hospital too, but then no decent thought about food could do anything but wither up next to the pitiful messes they served there . . . Oh, I'm glad, Yumi, I'm so glad to know there'll be music and new dishes coming still. Well," he said briskly, sliding the fall-board shut. "I'll work more on that later. Right now, I'll get us those drinks."

He turned on the lamp beside her, at the lowest illumination. Beyond the windows dark had almost wholly come.

"Will," she said as he was going through the door to the kitchen.

He stopped, his back to her, his hands gripping either side of the doorframe as if tensed against what he feared she had to say.

"I'm still with you because I want to be. And I will be on your side always."

He didn't turn or speak, only went on into the kitchen after a moment, but his big knuckles blenched where his fingers gripped the solid wood, so she knew that he had heard.

She bathed and climbed into bed, leaning back against pillows Will had plumped up for her, the exhaustion and soreness flaring in her muscles as they relaxed. Will sat on in the front room, not eager after his hospital stay to get back into a bed again. Rain drummed hard at the ground below the black windows.

She closed her eyes and for some reason that she could not identify, perhaps the weather, she remembered the night that he had returned after being gone for so long without a word — returned to her in the rain, beneath the banyan in the courtyard of her home in Honolulu.

She had been walking. For days Waikīkī and Kap'iolani had lain under that mist which, in the autumn, comes down through the passes in the Koolaus and blots out expanses of the mountainside above the city. It comes so thickly that no one who didn't know could tell that behind it lie those sharp-ribbed volcanic flanks that make the island's spine.

At night not even Honolulu city lights trailing up their gullies like torches can penetrate that mist.

Towards twilight of the seventh day rain began to fall.

Paula burrowed deeper beneath the covers, and remembered how before he came to her, even before he had returned to the Islands, she had known that he was very near; just not known in what way.

On that night she had listened to her own rain-blurred footsteps crossing the cobblestones to her front door. She had turned the key in the lock. Then, suddenly, certain,

"Will," she had said.

And he had not run.

She closed her eyes; perhaps she fell asleep. Perhaps she dreamed; later, she was never sure.

The evening was rainy in Noname Lane, the hour late, and Will had been at the piano, working on the piece that he had begun the day they had come home from the hospital. She lay stretched out on the futon sofa across the room, reading.

After a time he stopped playing, stood, and went into the bedroom. He didn't close the fall-board. She read on awhile.

Then something — maybe the quality of the silence, maybe the fact that he had not closed the fall-board — made her set the book down.

"Will?" she called. The rain seemed louder. She raised her voice above it. "Will?"

"I'm in here, Yumi."

She found him sitting on the edge of the bed, his feet planted apart as if to steady himself, his head down, so his thick hair fell forward and she couldn't see his face. His hands clasped the edge of the bed-frame, a habit he'd fallen into since his illness, to brace himself for the effort of rising.

"Are you all right, Will?"

"I'm fine, Yumi. Had a moment there when I couldn't quite get my breath and thought I'd lie down a spell. But I'm better now. I think I'll come back out and work a while more on the piece. How's it sounding to you?"

"It's sounding good."

And she was deeply grateful that she had never been cornered into trying to lie to him about anything that mattered.

"Yeh," he said, "I think it's coming along."

"Will, should I call Jake?"

He shook his head. "I'm all right, Yumi. 'Tweren't nothing."

"Can I get you something?"

He shook his head again, then said, "Well, if 'tisn't too much trouble, a Rose's would taste right good."

She nodded, and as she went through the door, he spoke her name as she had spoken his on the night when they got home from the hospital, when, as he was going through the kitchen door, she told him she was with him because she wanted to be and would always be on his side. And as he had done then, she paused, not looking back at him nor speaking.

"Thank you, Yumi."

She was motionless a fraction of a second, hearing how much more was intended by his words than thanks for a Rose's fetched tonight.

Then she nodded once, still without turning, and went on to the kitchen.

"Ah, Will . . . you didn't even wait for me."

Standing in the doorway, a glass of Rose's in her hand, she might have spoken aloud.

Then she saw his half-smile, as he lay back on the bed where he'd fallen, his face turned towards her, eyes fixed, and when she saw how his hand opened towards her, the fingers slightly curled, relaxed and beckoning, she thought that perhaps he had waited for her after all.

She set down the glass on the coaster on the bedside table. From the drawer she drew the little phial and emptied it into the Lime's. She drank it down and turned off the light.

Then she lay beside Will, working herself against his body, beneath his arm.

He was warm and relaxed and seemed to draw her near.

A wind came up suddenly, from Mauna Loa way, and blew the rain horizontally so it rapped the black panes like pebbles.

She raised herself on one elbow and drew the blanket up over them.

"Yumi!"

He was squeezing her shoulders so they hurt, his face white with alarm. "What's the matter, Yumi? Did you take another spell?"

She was shocked at the deep fear in his eyes at the thought of her falling ill. She dragged her hands hard over his face, twisted her fingers in his thick hair, fiercely assuring herself of his living presence. Then she let her forehead fall against his chest.

"No, not a spell," she whispered. "I had a dream. That's all. Don't worry."

"You were crying out so." He drew her against him. "Aw Yumi, it's these hard days. They'll get better now. You're just plain wore out, that's what it is. I've had beautiful lady nurses waiting on me hand and foot, while you been running and fetching and hassling for me, sparring with doctors and worrying about me and fighting lawyers and Sam in all his nee-farious manifestations, multinational corporations and the VA and Sam's Army, no wonder you're having bad dreams."

He made her laugh, as he had intended

"What day is it, Will? Is it still only today?"

"It sure enough is, Yumi. Today is the only day it is."

"I mean, is it the day we came home from the hospital?"

"Yeh, it sure enough is that day. Only it's night now." He glanced at his watch. "Going on ten pee-em. If you recollect, we had a light supper and you took a bath and we decided to turn in early. Only I stayed on out there in the parlor awhile because it felt so good not to be in bed, to be wearing clothes again and sitting up in a decent chair. Then I asked if you'd like a cup of warm milk and I said I'd make it, I were feeling so lively, and you said I looked lively enough, so you guessed you'd take me up on it. 'Twere just about ten minutes ago you said that, and that's what I been doing."

He set the mug down on the coaster on the bedside table. He must have been bringing it to her when she cried out, and she thought of how good it was to watch Will prepare food, of how when he heated milk, for instance, he took time with it, nursed it, tended it.

"That must have been some dream," he said gently, "to come on you so quick and hard, and knock you plumb outta your place and time. Were Euph here, I reckon he'd say 'twas on account of your gift. Such as Mam Manotte had, or Marie Laveau, Euph'd say."

"A gift." Paula shuddered.

"Such kind of gifts," he remarked laconically, "ain't just quite the same as presents. They are more like some blades — double-edged. As you said about your feeling at the pool table, long ago now, such gifts are a kind of beauty, like life a kind of wrath, though a kind of privilege."

He reached behind her and arranged the pillows against the headboard.

"There. Now you lean back, and drink your milk. Best to get something warm on the inside after visions, which can be mighty stressful, even good ones —"

He gave his sudden wheezy laugh, that trembled on the edge of a coughing spasm. All Paula's muscles tensed. But he went on speaking normally as if he had never been so ill that the cough tore him apart inside till his bones broke and he bled.

"There's several ways to get that warm feeling on the inside, but a drink of something is one of them."

He reached across the bed, pulled open his drawer, and extracted a miniature bottle of amber fluid.

"Here. 'Tis from Auntie Raina, to help me sleep. A traditional remedy. Mighty powerful. Full of mana."

He poured it into her milk and tilted the mug several ways, gently, mingling white and amber. "I brought a Rose's along with your milk, and I'll take some of this remedy as well. And then I'll be ready to sleep too. You still needing to cry, Yumi? Then you go ahead. That'll help with sleeping also. Want to know something?"

He was undressing, pulling on his pajamas as he spoke. "I wasn't going to tell you but since this is a special night, with a vision and all, I guess I will. I cried in the night, in the hospital . . . I did! 'Twas so strange I didn't even know what was happening at first. Then it made me plumb furious. But when 'twere over I felt better. And I thought, this'd make Yumi right happy if she knew, telling me to 'express my emotions' all these years, goddamn if I'm going to let her know she's right . . . slide on over, okay, so's I can lie down. Finished with that?"

She nodded. He set the mug and little bottle on the bedside table, turned out the light, and drew her near.

He would not ask what her vision — or dream, or hallucination, she added to herself — had been about. Euph had told him, she remembered, that Mam Manotte had instructed that one did not inquire about such things.

She muttered against his chest, "I can see now, it was a good dream — or whatever it was — in a way. It told me something — told us something — we've both wanted to know."

"Then it was good," he agreed. He leaned himself on his elbow in the dark, and drew the sheet up over them and drew her close. The wind threw a spatter of water against the black windows, and he did not ask, either, what it had told, that they both wanted to know.

In the vision, had Will's hair been white with age? Had her hands been shrunken, an old woman's hands, the veins on their backs huge and black against her skin?

What might have been a memory of the event — something that would answer those questions — slipped away, disappeared like koi in a pool.

She was outside the experience now, and the answer to those questions was gone. What had Will just said? It had been a powerful dream, indeed, that had knocked time and place askew.

Will's heart beat strong against her. When she edged herself up an inch, against his chest, she felt the hair curled against her cheek, and, just below it, felt the dragon's outline.

"It told that we'll be together always," she whispered drowsily, "no matter how, or where we are. In this earthly dimension or not . . . that's what it meant."

And suddenly she fell asleep.

He sensed the sleep, and the abrupt utter relaxation of her exhausted body against his released him to his own exhaustion. A great gratitude welled up for the knowledge of what she had just revealed to him. He thought of Euph, of his Little Mama and her banjo and her work-roughened hands and oval pale nails. He thought of a city and a great river in a place he had never seen, winding down the heart of a continent to the sea. Father of Waters . . .

He thought of Mam Manotte, whom he had never known, and of Auntie Raina. Tūtū . . .

"That's a good thing all right, Yumi," he murmured into her hair. "And of course, 'tis what it meant, 'twas always meant to be, I knew it from the moment I laid eyes on you . . ." She smelled so good. Rain and lava-fire . . . oheleberries and risen 'a'ā dust. "A good knowledge to go to sleep with, Yumi."

And very soon he did.

45

An Evening At Euph's

The party for Paula's birthday and Will's home-coming was postponed two weeks because Will caught a cold. He and Paula bickered about the delay, then fought, then Paula said he could give the party but she wouldn't go if he still had the cold, and Ben said he wouldn't work to get ready for the party, and Will had to give in. So he sulked for several rainy days. Then he decided it was just as well since he still had work to do on the piano piece he was finishing in Yumi's honor, and also on her breadfruit dish. By way of revenge on her he forbade her setting foot in Euph's and the Pine Tar until the night of the party, so she couldn't hear or smell the musical and culinary creations in progress should he happen to be there working on them. Before the new date for the party he was over the cold.

Pearlie Leilani, who was busy in Honolulu getting ready for the opening of the Chant, sent a length of exquisitely figured kapa she had made. Emma and Paula spread it as an undercloth for Paula's big flower arrangement that was the centerpiece on the long trestle table laid out with food.

The party was a great success. All their friends on the island came. The festivities might have gone on all night except by pre-arrangement Jake and Paula and Ben and Emma and Tom began shepherding people out the door at midnight.

Will hated to see them go. He and Paula stood alone together at the door of Euph's, waving as the last of the guests piled into their cars.

"Just look at that moon, Yumi," said Will. "Just look at it, and the land all here-around."

She heard her father's words as they stood by the window of his study in Chicago and looked out at the city. There is no place more beautiful than Hawai'i, he had said. I know that, because no place could be more beautiful. And he had laughed at his own reasoning.

Will put his arm around her waist. She relaxed against the strong firm beat of his heart.

"It was a good evening, wasn't it?" he said. "Good people."

"It was a very good evening. And very good people."

"This is a pretty good place." She knew he meant the island, the place on the water, their friends and family.

"Yes." She paused. "You can be proud. Euph's and the Pine Tar is a good place you've made for yourself. And for other people."

"I didn't make it alone. And most especially I didn't keep it alone. Couldn't have made or kept it without Ben first and later you too."

The breeze, moist and perfumed with plumeria, came to them off the lagoon.

Through his body close against hers, Paula thought she felt a cough rising from his depths, the way he said you could feel the deep tremors on Kilauea if you pressed your ear to the earth. She tensed.

And then it passed. Or maybe she had imagined it. Not even a cough — maybe a quick caught breath, as if a finger were trailing lightly across his ribs, his chest, his heart.

She stepped away, making an X of her arms across her breasts.

"Maybe we'd better go in. It's a little cool."

They went back through the door. Voices were calling from the road. "Good night! Good night! Best party ever at Euph's, Will! Welcome home! Happy birthday, Paula!"

"Thanks to you-all for coming!" he called back. "The best ain't happened yet! Yumi's and my meeting-anniversary's coming up pretty soon now! Then you'll see a party!"

"We'll be there!"

Will closed the door: they were alone. He watched Paula where she had moved away from him to stand beneath the embrasure and the photograph of Euph. Tonight he had placed a candle in front of the photograph, along with a small flower arrangement she had made. The candle was still burning with a bright clear flame. He watched how her arms were crossed so tightly.

"Don't go away from me that way, Yumi," he said softly. "Stay by me, Yumi, and I'll stay by you the best I know and can." He grinned. "And like I just told those folks, you can cheer up, the best ain't happened yet!"

She smiled. Slowly she opened her arms, yielding up her fear of pain, and he went to her and drew her face against his chest.

Later, in Hale Noname, Will stared out through the black panes, out Mauna Kea way. The lamplight was behind him and he could see nothing — except himself, reflected in the glass: a big man, no longer young, all crags and prominent joints and planes of bone, a shock of straw-and-silver hair, big-knuckled hands gripping the window frames. He thought he was thinking of nothing, and perhaps he was.

Paula entered the room: the sight of him struck her still. He stood only a few feet from her as he stared out the window, but he seemed as isolated and remote as the far side of the moon, the air around him chill, his inturned smile a knife-blade. In that moment she felt as she had felt on the day he had met her at Volcano with his plane, and had smiled that appalling smile and she knew that in that moment nothing could touch him, nothing at all.

She felt now, as she had felt then, his profound latent discontinuity, his chasms and fissures. She felt the violence in him, a fire down below, and equally felt the profound chill of zero: blankness of reference point, potential for explosion and for creativity, for schism and collapse. He could be anywhere, she had written when he disappeared to stay gone for so long without a word: doing anything.

Then, she saw him change. His stance loosened, he relaxed: he was back in the present.

Behind him, Will heard the creak and soft glide of Paula's sock-feet on the polished boards, as she closed out the day and readied herself for bed. And now it came to him, for the first time with clarity, that once, in the war at home and in the war abroad, he had followed women.

The war was over long ago, he thought; the damage it did ain't never ended.

After he had been in Vietnam, and been wounded and sent to the hospital and then to other hospitals, he was finally released, forever mistrustful of hospitals, nurses and doctors. More than a year passed, he thought, maybe two, after the night in the village, before he had a recollection of which he was fairly sure. He had lost his time somewhere along the way. And he could not have told how many months went by after his release before he felt again the need to ease himself with women, for he had lost most of himself, too, somewhere along the way.

He could hardly have told, because he hardly knew, until this night on the volcano after the evening at Euph's, that he had followed women through starry black nights where they swam and sank like fish in a black starry sea.

Sometimes, in those times, bright noons would bring sudden disconnected flashes.

Images of blackness and dim figures of women swimming ahead of him. Images of remembered knife-edged wind, and steel that burned and excited his fingers as he caressed it.

Then the images would vanish.

It would be day again, in some crowded Asian city, and he would be sitting on a hotel patio clutching a drink and arranging details of an operation in a low voice with other shadowy low-voiced men.

Then he met Ben.

He would never have been able to tell in which of those cities it was, except that Ben, who was on the run but had not lost either his time or himself, knew and had finally told him that it had been Hong Kong.

Now, in Hale Noname, as he heard Yumi gliding behind him, that time before he met Ben came back powerfully.

He felt himself, once again, in a city he could not name, in the dark in a narrow street, stalking another woman gliding ahead unaware.

Some inner warning pulled him back sharply to his present. He looked at the window to see his place and time: it was there, for sure, the black night and his own face, reflected in the panes; and Mauna Kea, he knew, out there beyond.

Rage engulfed him, rocking him physically as he stood, lava-rage welling up from some era long before. From the time in that first city where he had followed the first woman in his life down streets shattered by the war at home, as she made her arrangements to survive.

The streets were ankle-deep in snow, and he was very small.

But he knew there was amazing grace on earth, because he had been able to encounter Ben when he met him, and begin to follow other streets, to leave those unnameable cities, unrecognizable to him then, with the swimming women and he himself stalking them through his nightmare, trembling on the edge of dragging them into his hell and making it theirs as well.

Terror gripped him, at the knife-edge of emotional precariousness he had known, at the unpredictability of human self-control.

Yet, he had been able to come to this island and bring forth the place on the water and the house down Noname Lane. Been able to stop at the brink and save himself and the gliding women from destruction; been able to come at last to a place within and without himself where he could not only meet, but at last even know, Yumi: to whom he now turned.

About the Author

Sandra E. Drake was born in Chicago, Illinois, and spent most of her childhood there and in Ghana, West Africa. She studied in the MFA-Creative Writing Program at San Francisco State, and taught in the Creative Writing Program at Stanford University, where she was a tenured member of the faculty in the Department of English and in the Program in African and African-American Studies. In recent years she has lived in California and in Hawai'i. She currently resides with her husband and three dogs in Menlo Park, California, near San Francisco, where she is at work on her next novel.

Photograph by Linda A. Kamas